Betsy and the Great World
and
Betsy's Wedding

The Betsy-Tacy Books

Book 1: *Betsy-Tacy*

Book 2: *Betsy-Tacy and Tib*

Book 3: *Betsy and Tacy Go Over the Big Hill*

Book 4: *Betsy and Tacy Go Downtown*

Book 5: *Heaven to Betsy*

Book 6: *Betsy in Spite of Herself*

Book 7: *Betsy Was a Junior*

Book 8: *Betsy and Joe*

Book 9: *Betsy and the Great World*

Book 10: *Betsy's Wedding*

The Deep Valley Books

Winona's Pony Cart

Carney's House Party

Emily of Deep Valley

Betsy and the Great World and Betsy's Wedding

Maud Hart Lovelace

Illustrated by Vera Neville

HARPER**PERENNIAL** MODERN**CLASSICS**

NEW YORK • LONDON • TORONTO • SYDNEY • NEW DELHI • AUCKLAND

HarperCollins books may be purchased for educational, business, or sales
promotional use. For information, please e-mail the Special Markets Department at SPsales@harpercollins.com.

Betsy and the Great World was first published in 1952 by Thomas Y. Crowell
Company. First Harper Trophy edition published 1996.

Betsy's Wedding was first published in 1955 by Thomas Y. Crowell Company.
First Harper Trophy edition published 1996.

FIRST HARPER PERENNIAL MODERN CLASSICS EDITION PUBLISHED 2009.

Library of Congress Cataloging-in-Publication Data is available upon request.

ISBN 978-0-06-179513-8

HB 03.05.2024

Foreword

ments and earns and succeeds in what she wants capabilities, and heart — not their physiology. And that honoring individuals because of their humanity, not their physiology.
And that is why my theme today is: Betsy Ray, Feminist

When I was first asked to speak about Maud Hart Lovelace
I had to reread all ten of my Betsy-Tacy books. I would
like to make this sound like a hardship, but most of you
know better. There are three authors whose body of work
I have reread more than once over my adult life: Charles
Dickens, Jane Austen, and Maud Hart Lovelace. It was, as
always, a pleasure and delight.

And the truth is that I have been preparing for this
speech, in a variety of ways, for thirty years, and especially for the last ten. That was the decade in which I
began to examine most closely what it meant to be a
feminist in America, as I am, and why I felt so strongly
that the women's movement and what I believe it stands
for has changed my life.

Many of those issues have been explored in my column
in *The New York Times*, and over and over again I have tried
to reinforce a simple message that I believe has been dis-
torted, muddled, misunderstood, and just plain lied about
in recent years by those who want women to go, not forward, but backward.

And that is that feminism is about choices. It is about
women choosing for themselves which life roles they
wish to pursue. It is about deciding who does and gets and

merits and earns and succeeds in what by smarts, capabilities, and heart—not by gender. It is about honoring individuals because of their humanity, not their physiology.

And that is why my theme today is: Betsy Ray, Feminist Icon.

Could there be better books, and could there be a better girl, adolescent, young woman, to teach us all those things about choices than the Betsy-Tacy books and Betsy herself, along with her widely disparate circle of Tacy and Tib, Julia and Margaret, Mrs. Ray and Anna the hired girl, Mrs. Poppy and Miss Mix, Carney and Winona, Miss Bangeter and Miss Clarke? All these different women, who go so many different ways, with false starts and stops, with disappointments and limitations, and yet a sense that they can find a place for themselves in the world.

Do you realize that not once, in any book, does any individual, male or female, suggest to Betsy that she cannot, as she so hopes to do, become a writer? Can anyone possibly appreciate the impact that made on a child like me, wanting it too but seeing all around me on the bookshelves the names of men and seeing all around me in my house the domesticated ways of women?

In the early books, of course, this is not what we see. We see prototypes, really, as surely as Snow White and Rose Red, or Cinderella and her stepsisters. We see three little girls who begin as types: the shy and earnest one; the no-nonsense and literal one; and the ringleader, the storyteller, the adventurer, the center—Elizabeth Warrington Ray. Then the adventures and, more important, the traditions begin—the picnics on the Big Hill, the forays to little Syria, the shopping trips at Christmastime, and Betsy's sheets of foolscap piling up in her Uncle Keith's old trunk.

The books are simply stories of small town life and enduring friendship among little girls, and so it is easy to overlook their importance as teaching tools. But consider the alternatives to children in the early grades. The images of girls tend, overwhelmingly, to be of fairy princesses spinning straw into gold or sleeping until they are awakened by a prince.

Even the best ones usually show us caricatures instead of characters. Recently, for example, I wrote an introduction for a fiftieth anniversary edition of *Madeline* (Viking, 1989). It is one of my favorite picture books for children, has been since I myself was a child, mostly because of one line which sums up the rest of it: "To the tiger in the zoo Madeline just said 'Pooh, pooh.'"

Madeline, unlike the straw-spinning princesses, has attitude. She is nobody's fool.

But attitude, truth to tell, is a surface, two-dimensional characteristic, attractive as it may be. The stories of Betsy, Tacy, and Tib transcend attitude just as the simplistic drawings of the early books give way to the more realistic (albeit, to my mind, slightly oversweet) pictures. They are ultimately books about character, and especially about the character of one girl whose greatest sin, throughout the books, is to undervalue herself.

For those are the mistakes Betsy finds she cannot forgive, when she sells herself short, when she is not all she can be. As opposed to the shy, retiring, and respectful girl who became so valued in girl's fiction, Betsy does best when she serves herself, when she is true to herself. In this she most resembles two other fictional heroines who, not surprisingly, also long to be writers and take their work very seriously indeed. One is Anne Shirley of the *Anne of Green Gables* books, and the other is Jo March of *Little Women*.

But the key difference, I think, is a critical one. Both Anne and Jo are implicitly made to pay in those books for the fact that they do not conform to feminine norms. Anne begins life as an orphan and never is permitted to forget that she must work for a living—in fact, you might call her the Joe Willard of girls, although she is far less prickly and far more easy to like than Joe Willard. Jo March of *Little Women* habitually reminds herself how unattractive she is and settles down, in one of the most unconvincing matches in fiction, with the older, most unromantic Professor Bhaer. It is her beautiful sister Amy who gets the real guy, the rich and romantic Laurie.

❧ x ❧

* * *

Betsy, by contrast, never had to pay for the sin of being herself; in fact, she only finds herself under a cloud when she is less than herself. At base, she is a charmed soul from beginning to end because she can laugh at herself and take herself seriously at the same time, because she is serious but never a prig, and interested in boys but never a flirt. Can anyone forget the moment when, returning from the sophomore dance at Schiller Hall with that absolute poop Phil Brandish trying to worm his fist into her pocket, she turns to him with desperation and blurts out, "You might as well know. I don't hold hands."

In fact it's probably in that book, *Betsy in Spite of Herself*, that we see Betsy most the way I think we were always meant to see her, as a girl who will do what is right for her, not necessarily what the world wants her to do. But first, like most of us, she has to do what is wrong for her to find out what is right. She decides to nab Phil just for the fun of it, and to that end she adds the letter E to the end of her perfectly good name, sprays herself with Jockey Club perfume, and uses green stationery to write notes instead of her poetry or stories. It's inevitable— when the real Betsy sneaks out, in the form of a song parody she and Tacy invented before the Phil/Betsy affair began, they break up. But instead of a sore heart, Betsy is left with Shakespeare: "This above all: to thine own self be true."

Betsy already knows, as do we, that that self varies widely from girl to girl, that there is no little box that will fit them all. In *Heaven to Betsy*, she says, in the passage that made the future so clear and yet so mysterious for me:

> She had been almost appalled, when she started going around with Carney and Bonnie, to discover how fixed and definite their ideas of marriage were. They both had cedar hope chests and took pleasure in embroidering their initials on towels to lay away. Each one had picked out a silver pattern and they were planning to give each other spoons in these patterns for Christmases and birthdays. When Betsy and Tacy and Tib talked about their future they planned to be writers, dancers, circus acrobats.

Betsy never looks down on those aspirations of Carney and Bonnie's. But she never looks away from her own aspirations. She follows a sensible progression from writing, to dreaming of being a writer, to actually saying she is going to be one, to sending her stories (when she is a mere senior in high school) to various women's magazines. She makes the mistake so many of us make—like Jo in *Little Women*, she learns early on that writing about debutantes in Park Avenue penthouses is doomed to failure if you've neither debuted nor visited Park Avenue—but her gumption carries her through.

And there are, interestingly, no naysayers among her

family members. While the Rays have three daughters, early on two of them are already committed to having careers outside the home, Julia as an opera singer, Betsy as a writer. Betsy's parents are totally committed to this idea for them both, sending Julia to the Twin Cities and even to Europe to further her training as a singer, and arguing vociferously that Betsy's work is as good as any that appears in popular magazines.

The idea of something that is yours to do became narrower and narrower as my mother grew up. As Betty Friedan wrote in *The Feminine Mystique* (Dell, 1963), by the time my mother was ready to enter what Julia always called The Great World, it had narrowed to one role and one role alone, that of wife and mother.

I don't know when exactly I knew that that was never going to be enough for me. But I know where I got the idea that more was possible. It wasn't from career women or role models—when I was a girl, there really weren't any.

I learned it from books, and none more than from the stories about Betsy, Tacy, and Tib. Because the most important thing about Betsy Ray is that she has a profound sense of confidence and her own worth.

Of course, if this had been wrapped in a sanctimonious, plaster saint package, Betsy would have been—perish the thought—Elsie Dinsmore, the perfect, boring little girl of popular fiction who Betsy herself once mocks. And, if there had been no boys in the books, I, for one, wouldn't have read them.

But we did read them, many of us, for so many reasons: because Maud Hart Lovelace had a real gift for adapting the prose to the appropriate age level, and the themes, too; because we fell in love, not only with Betsy but with Tacy and Tib and all the others, and wanted to know from year to year what was happening to them; because of Magic Wavers and Sunday night sandwiches and smoky coffee brewed out of doors and all the other little ordinary things that, in some fashion, became our ordinary things.

And because they were just like us.

But we know there are many us's, with many different goals and aspirations. For many years those goals and aspirations were truncated by one simple fact: our sex. Everything around us reflected that, from who sat on the Supreme Court, to who listened to our chests when we were sick, to who oversaw services when we went to church on Sunday.

But from time to time we encountered a teacher, or a parent, or even a book that told us that we should let our ambitions fly, that we should believe in ourselves, that the only limits we should put on what we tried for were the limits of our desires and our talents. When I told people I was going to give this speech, most had never heard of Betsy-Tacy, and I had to describe them as a series of books for girls. But they were so much more than that to one little girl who grew up to be a woman writer and who, perhaps, learned that she *could* by the example given inside these books.

—ANNA QUINDLEN
(Adapted from a speech given to the Twin Cities Chapter of the Betsy-Tacy Society on June 12, 1993)

Betsy and the Great World

For
ELIZABETH LESLIE

Contents

1

Traveling Alone

*"Down to Gehenna or up to the Throne,
He travels the fastest who travels alone."*

BETSY WAS CHANTING IT under her breath to give herself courage as, laden with camera, handbag, umbrella, and *Complete Pocket Guide to Europe*, she started up the gangplank to the deck of the *S.S. Columbic.*

Behind her was a barnlike structure, crowded with carriages, automobiles, baggage carts, and milling distracted passengers. Before her loomed the great bulk of the liner. Thirteen thousand tons of it, according to the advertisements over which she had pored—far, far back in Minnesota. It had layers of decks, a smokestack in the center, and tall masts flying flags. She could smell the waters of Boston Harbor—cold, salty, fishy—into which she would presently be sailing.

"'Down to Gehenna or up to the Throne . . .'" Her teeth were almost chattering. Not from cold, for she wore furs over her long tight coat and carried a muff. Fur trimmed, too, was her hat. She shivered because she was shaky inside, fearful and bewildered.

"'He travels the fastest who travels alone . . .'" She wasn't alone, exactly. A porter had seized her suit cases, and he strode beside her shoulder. But he was a stranger, like the throngs of people all around her. And they all seemed to be in groups—sociable, laughing, chattering groups.

Of course, Betsy, too, would be with someone else shortly. Her father and mother had seen to that. A bachelor professor and his unmarried sister, friends of Betsy's father's brother, had agreed to keep an eye on her during the voyage. But at her first meeting with them, this morning at the Parker House, she had managed to convey the impression that their chaperonage was extremely nominal. And when they had suggested that she join them for some travel later, she had been purposefully vague. It wasn't her idea to go through Europe with the Wilsons, kind as they were, and homesick as she already was.

"Tacy ought to be here," she thought forlornly.

She and Tacy had planned trips through all the long years of their friendship. They had planned to go around the world together, to see the Taj Mahal by moonlight, to go to the top of the Himalayas and up the Amazon, and above all to live in Paris . . . with ladies' maids.

Celeste and Hortense, they had christened their maids . . . imaginary ones, of course.

"Thank goodness I have Celeste, at least," Betsy muttered. For Tacy had faithlessly married. Julia was married too. Betsy had been her older sister's maid of honor in December.

It was January now, 1914.

"Julia settling down!" Betsy scoffed.

Julia wasn't, of course, settling down. A singer, she had married a flutist, and they planned to pursue their careers together. But Betsy was in no mood to be fair. The confusion on deck was more subtly terrifying even than the tumult below. The well-dressed men, the women with corsage bouquets blooming on their shoulders, seemed so assured, so gaily sufficient to themselves and one another, so completely indifferent to the great adventure of one Betsy Ray, aged twenty-one, from Minneapolis, Minnesota.

The porter turned her over to a uniformed steward. She was taken below decks, along labyrinthine corridors, carpeted, smelling of the sea, to her stateroom, Number 52.

Number 52! They had selected it back in Minneapolis. She remembered the chart on the travel agent's desk and her family rejoicing because this stateroom had a porthole giving on the ocean.

There it was, the porthole! And the room was a small white affair with a washstand and two bunks, one above the other. Miss Wilson would have the lower one. Betsy's steamer trunk had already been placed in a corner. The steward put her bags on it, and she tipped him, trying to act casual.

Back on deck, she secured a steamer chair—Julia had told her that was the first thing to do. But what about her ticket? Shouldn't she give that to someone? She found the office of the purser.

He was very busy, besieged from all sides, but when she said with anxious dignity, "I'm Miss Elizabeth Ray," he turned quickly.

"And it's Miss Betsy Ray herself," he remarked surprisingly.

He spoke with an Irish inflection and he looked the

Irishman, too . . . smooth black hair with a touch of gray at the temples, blue eyes with a light in them, a dimple in his chin.

Betsy felt her color rising. How maddening to blush before his gay assurance!

"I beg your pardon?" she said and remembered to sink into her debutante slouch.

This fashionable pose became her, for she was very slender. (Some girls had to wear special corsets to get the debutante slouch.) She was glad her fur boa was tossed lightly over her shoulder.

Mr. O'Farrell—that was the name above his window—continued to look at her.

"Faith, and I'm inter-r-r-ested to meet you!" He rolled his *r*'s in a fascinating way. "Letters to Miss Betsy Ray take up half that mountain of mail in the library yonder."

"Really?" Betsy forgot her pose. Her smile was a burst of sunshine.

A small space between her teeth in front gave her a look of candor. She had a friendly merry face with brown hair pushed over her cheeks in the soft disarray affected that season, and hazel eyes that glowed now into Mr. O'Farrell's.

Letters from home! Letters from that paradise lost, lying three long days behind her!

"Oh, how wonderful!" she cried.

"Telegrams, too," said Mr. O'Farrell teasingly. "And boxes! I believe there are even some blossoms. Are you traveling alone?"

"Yes . . . practically."

"Well, I'm going to give you a special place at table so you won't get lonely. You pick it up after we sail."

"But what about my ticket?"

"The steward will collect it in your cabin," he said.

Betsy pushed her way eagerly through crowded corridors to the paneled library, but the mail was not yet sorted.

"The flowers are though, Mum," a steward said. All the stewards sounded as English as Mr. O'Farrell did Irish. He looked over a line of green boxes and selected one for her.

Betsy opened it with joyful fingers. Bob Barhydt's card lay on top. Inside was a corsage bouquet of pink roses and lilies of the valley.

"Oh, how sweet of Bob!" she cried.

She pinned on the flowers at the nearest mirror, lifted her chin, and went out on deck less afraid of the surging indifferent people.

"That was really sweet of Bob," she thought again, and felt guilty because he and the University of Minnesota campus seemed suddenly so remote.

It was a bleak afternoon. The sky was overcast and the air had a damp bite. She found the Wilsons engaged with the deck steward.

Dr. Wilson was a thin erect little man with white mustaches and a pointed white beard. His complexion was as pretty as Betsy's. That came, perhaps, from his theories on diet which he had explained to her at breakfast. He scorned coffee and meat. Carrots, lettuce, apples, and whole-grain breads were his delight.

His sister, like himself, was white-haired, slender, and erect, but she liked a slice of pound cake now and then, she had admitted to Betsy with a twinkle.

Having greeted them, Betsy went to the rail and looked down on the chaos below.

Now long lines of Italians were filing into the steerage. Some were wrapped in red blankets. They carried tin dishes and piles of canned goods. Little dark-eyed children danced along in front, or crowded close to their parents, frightened and crying. Betsy wondered why they were going back to Italy.

A gong clanged commandingly.

"That means good-by," said a woman in a large noisy group at Betsy's left. And suddenly all around her people were kissing and embracing. A line began to push down the gangplank.

Soon the windows of the building below were of faces . . . people crying and laughing, waving handkerchiefs and blowing kisses. The passengers leaning over the rail were likewise crying and laughing, waving handkerchieves and blowing kisses. The air was full of ejaculations. "Oh, *there* he is! Oh, *there* she is!"

"Don't forget you're married!" called the man who had left the group beside her.

Betsy noticed a sobbing Italian woman, gazing at the steerage passengers who were bound for her native land. At times she would forget to cry. She would catch her breath, like a child distracted by a toy; then she would remember, and start to sob again.

Somewhere, someone was strumming a guitar. "*O sole mio . . .*" A lump swelled in Betsy's throat.

"I'd better get out of here," she thought.

Suddenly she couldn't imagine why she had wanted to go traveling. Her thoughts reached back yearningly to her family. How could she have left them!

Her darling father who worked so hard for them all, and was always so cheerful about it! Her pretty red-haired mother who had shopped so tirelessly buying these new clothes! Margaret, now sixteen, so sweet, and beginning to have beaux. And Julia, such a wonderful big sister, even though married!

Betsy sniffed.

She could see them all, and the gray stucco cottage out in Minneapolis with snow clinging to the bare vines and lying on the evergreens around the glassed-in porch. Inside, there would be a fire in the fireplace. They always had Sunday night lunch around that fire. Her father made the sandwiches.

Tears flooded Betsy's eyes.

Someone beside her called to someone else. "Did you know we had an author on board?"

An author? Betsy dashed away her tears. For a wild moment she thought they meant her, for she planned to be an author. That was one reason she was going abroad.

"Yes," came the answer, shrilling above her head. "Some reporters were talking to her down in the library. They're taking pictures now, over there by the gangplank."

Betsy turned eagerly to look.

She saw a small stout woman with bright auburn hair under a purple veil and hat. Her purple coat was laden with flowers. Flashbulbs popped.

"Maybe they'll be doing that for me someday," thought Betsy.

Then the photographers shouldered their cameras and ran down the gangplank with reporters following—the last ones to leave the ship.

Betsy looked over the railing quickly. There was something familiar about one of the reporters. There was a swing to his shoulders . . . He had taken off his hat, and she saw that his hair was blond. Before she realized what she was doing Betsy leaned still farther and called out frantically, "Joe!"

But her voice was lost in the hubbub, for now the gangplanks were being pulled up and the engines began to tug and strain. Deep-throated horns were blowing. Screams and shouts of farewell rose in a frenzied babel.

Betsy's eyes searched the windows of the building below. And sure enough a blond head appeared. She recognized the pompadour haircut. But this young man had a mustache—a close-cropped blond mustache! Nevertheless he was, he was. Joe Willard!

He was scanning the rail, frowning. He didn't see her. At least, she didn't think he did, and she didn't call again. She was glad he hadn't heard. He would never forgive her—probably he was never going to anyway—but he certainly never would if he knew she had come through Boston without letting him know.

Now he was frowning down at a paper of some kind.

The passenger list? Betsy had one in her pocket; she had seen her own name. He looked up sharply.

But the S.S. *Columbic* was moving. Slowly, inexorably, the horn still blowing, it edged out of the pier. A line of churned white foam appeared, and the space of cold green water widened. The barnlike building faded, and the shoreline came into view.

Betsy couldn't see it, for her tears were back again.

It wasn't surprising, she thought, as the steamer picked its way past a fringe of ships at anchor, and along a busy channel, it wasn't at all surprising that Joe was at the ship. She knew he worked part-time on the *Boston Transcript*.

"I wish I hadn't seen him," she thought. It would be harder to forget him now, and that was another reason she was going abroad . . . to forget Joe Willard. She wiped her eyes with grim determination.

"'Haply I may remember and haply may forget,'" she quoted flippantly.

The woman standing next to her looked around, startled.

Then Betsy turned her back on the Hub of the Universe, which was rising along the horizon. She'd write a letter or two to go back with the pilot, she decided abruptly.

In the library she found a desk and scribbled a note to her family. She tried to sound ecstatic, and didn't mention Joe, although she longed to share the news of his mustache. She thanked Bob Barhydt for the flowers. Returning to her stateroom, she replaced her hat with a scarf, got out her steamer rug, and went above, hoping that good-bys were over. But the pilot was just leaving, waving, followed by cheers. His boat bobbed off into gathering fog.

The *Columbic* now had left all traffic far behind. They were in the open ocean. Betsy leaned against the rail and the wind tore at her unkindly. Looking out at the leaden waves, the joyless, circling gulls, she felt unutterably lonely. Seeing Joe had made her hurt inside. She didn't even want to read her mail.

The water grew rougher. Her body could feel the new movement, the climb up, the drop down. A poem she had learned one time began to toll in her head:

"Up and down! Up and down!
From the base of the wave, to the billow's crown . . ."

But suddenly there was too much up and down. Walking unsteadily, she found her deck chair and the steward tucked her in. He offered her tea, but she didn't want tea. Burrowing miserably into her rug, she watched the vessel rise and fall.

People were walking around the deck with incomprehensible zest. Presently she saw Dr. Wilson, walking briskly, smiling. He recognized her and paused.

"Would you care to walk, Miss Betsy?"

She shook her head. "I don't feel so good."

"Seasickness," he said, "can be controlled by diet." But he looked sympathetic. "My sister hasn't learned how either, and she believes in going to bed. She always goes to her bunk and stays there until she's accustomed to the motion."

"I think that's what I'll do," Betsy replied, struggling to her feet. He helped her to the passageway.

Miss Wilson was in bed and greeted her faintly. Betsy undressed too, although, above decks, the bugle was blowing merrily for dinner. Pinned to her innermost garments was a chamois bag containing money, some extra American Express checks, and a check signed in blank by her father—for emergencies. Betsy transferred this treasure to the bosom of her flannel nightgown. Then, without even stopping to wind her hair on curlers, she climbed to the upper bunk, pulled up the blankets, and lay flat.

She could see a patch of sea and sky through the porthole, but down here, too, it appeared and disappeared in menacing rhythm. She closed her eyes.

After a time the stewardess came in. She was a dainty little Englishwoman with an encouraging manner. She asked Miss Wilson and Betsy whether they wanted dinner. They both declined.

"I'd like to see my mail though," Betsy said feebly. Her letters, telegrams, and boxes had been sent to the cabin and made a tantalizing pile, far below on her trunk.

The stewardess handed them up, and although Betsy didn't feel able to read them, it was comforting to have them near. She found a fat letter from home. It would be a round robin—the Ray family was always writing round robins—and put it under her cheek.

An orchestra was playing now. For dinner, probably. It had said in the folder that there was music for dinner. People dressed up for it and it had sounded such fun.

"It's a long way to Tipperary,
It's a long way to go . . ."

Betsy had danced to that tune and she had always liked it, but it sounded dreary now. Tears dripped into the round robin.

She wasn't sick, exactly . . . not like Miss Wilson was. Miss Wilson occasionally jumped out of bed and was very sick indeed. But Betsy felt frightened and lonesome and forlorn.

She wondered just what she was doing here. Why should she be in the bowels of a ship ploughing through sullen, turbulent waters, going to a foreign continent alone? Why? Why?

She turned her thoughts backward and tried to pull all the reasons together.

2

"Haply I May Remember"

SHE HADN'T, BETSY CONFIDED to her pillow, done
what she wanted to in college.

She had gotten off to a bad start because her
freshman year was interrupted by appendicitis, and
afterward she had gone to California for a long con-
valescence in her grandmother's home. She had loved
California. It seemed unbelievable to find rioting

flowers and oranges on shiny green trees and warm fragrant air in the middle of winter. She had loved the peace of her grandmother's home. An actor uncle who grew grapes near San Diego had given her a typewriter, and she had sold her first story.

"I found myself out there," Betsy had declared more than once.

Yes, but back at the University she had lost herself again. Was life always like that? she wondered. A game of hide and seek in which you only occasionally found the person you wanted to be?

It had been discouraging, next fall, to be a year behind her old high school class. Everyone else was a sophomore while she was still a freshman. And it had seemed unjust to find Advanced Botany and Higher Algebra still lying in wait. Betsy loved English and French but she had always hated mathematics and science. Feeling herself almost a professional writer now (because she sometimes sold a story for ten or twelve dollars), she resented these unpleasant subjects even more.

Plunging zealously into activities, she became Woman's Editor of the college paper. (A tall well-dressed young man named Bob Barhydt was also on the staff.) She wrote stories which were accepted by the college magazine. One was better than the others. It was really good and Betsy didn't quite know why, for it was just a simple story laid in her Uncle Keith's vineyard. But the famous professor, Dr. Maria Sanford, had praised it. She had written Betsy a letter about it. This success made science and mathematics all the more arduous, and Betsy's grades had slipped.

Joe Willard, on the other hand, to whom she was almost—but not quite—engaged, had done very well at the U, although he was a part-time copy reader on the *Minneapolis Tribune*. Because of his outstanding work he was offered a scholarship to Harvard and went east at the beginning of his junior year.

Betsy was happy for him, and very proud, and he planned to come back the following summer, which made parting easier. Yet his going had hurt her, too. After he left she gave up all scholastic strivings. Her friends were juniors; she was only a humble sophomore.

"I'll be a success socially, at least," she decided flippantly and joined a sorority although she had never liked them.

It wasn't a good thing to do. She soon grew tired of pretending that her deepest interests were social. She made a few close friends in the group, but not many, and the exclusive Greek letter club separated her from congenial girls on the *Daily* and the *Mag*.

But after she became a sorority girl Bob Barhydt started to rush her. He was very much the fraternity man. (Joe had never joined a fraternity. He had no time or money or inclination for them.) Because of Bob, Betsy's sophomore year went in a gay whirl of parties.

She wasn't happy, though, in spite of her social success, her achievements on the *Daily* and the *Mag,* and her name on committees and the membership lists of many organizations. Betsy felt that she had failed herself. She hadn't meant to be sucked into the social current. She hadn't meant to flirt with Bob, or to settle down to any one man while Joe was away. She had meant to get an education. And she wasn't doing it.

It wasn't, she knew, the fault of the University. People all around her were getting excellent educations there. It wasn't even the fault of the sorority. Many of the outstanding girls on the campus belonged to these groups.

Betsy admitted to the night and the deep Atlantic that the fault had lain strictly with herself.

As spring came on she became more and more frivolous. The gossip column in the *Daily* was full of jokes about her and Bob. (A corner of the Oak Tree, the campus ice cream parlor, was called the B and B.) The Year Book showed kodak pictures of them riverbanking—the University phrase for strolling along the Mississippi.

Joe subscribed to the *Minnesota Daily* and he bought a copy of the Year Book. Suddenly his letters became as cold as ice.

Betsy was looking forward longingly to his promised visit. Her dissatisfaction with herself, her wasted year, the flirtation with Bob, couldn't be explained in letters. If she and Joe could talk, she could make him understand. But he didn't come back. He wrote that he had a good summer job on the *Boston Transcript*. He mentioned his roommate's pretty sister. Their letters grew farther and farther apart.

"I believe I like Bob better anyway," Betsy told Tacy, who knew that wasn't true. For something in Betsy had always reached out to Joe Willard—blond and stalwart with a proud swing in his shoulders, a deep contagious laugh, and a look of clear goodness in his eyes.

He was an orphan. He had earned his own way since his early teens, gallantly ignoring shabby clothes and lack of money. He had been her ideal since her freshman year in high school. And Betsy was tenacious in her affections.

Tacy, too, was tenacious in her affections, and when she completed her course in public school music that June, she had married Harry Kerr.

He was an aggressive young salesman whom she had met at the Rays' four years before. They had planned a festive wedding with her sister Katie as maid of honor and Betsy and Tib as bridesmaids. But early that spring Tacy's father died. Everyone agreed Tacy's marriage should not be postponed, but it was celebrated quietly with only Katie and Harry's brother present.

Before starting off for Niagara Falls on their honeymoon, Tacy and her husband had come for a few days to the Ray house. The Rays moved out for them. Mr. Ray took Mrs. Ray on a business trip. Betsy and Margaret moved over to Betsy's sorority house.

They couldn't have helped Tacy more. The Ray house for many years had been a second home to her; and in Minneapolis as in Deep Valley it was always the same—a fire in the grate in winter, flowers in summer, the smell of good cooking in Anna's cheerful kitchen, and above all an atmosphere of happiness, of harmony, of love.

That atmosphere and her husband's tenderness helped to assuage Tacy's grief. It was a help, too, after she and Harry moved into their Minneapolis apartment, to have Betsy near. And Tacy's need of her helped Betsy.

That summer, Betsy made her bedroom into an office. She was still going on dates with Bob. They went dancing on the Radisson Roof, and canoeing on the Minneapolis lakes. They went to band concerts and the movies, and he came to Sunday night supper. But Betsy's really happy hours were spent at her desk.

She worked faithfully every morning on short stories and at last settled down to one she liked, trying to make it as good as the one Dr. Sanford had praised. Meanwhile, as she had done since she was in high school, she kept all her old stories on the go. Neatly typed, with return postage enclosed, they went from magazine to magazine.

Betsy had long ago worked out a system. When she finished a story she made a list of magazines to which she thought it might sell. As soon as it came back from one it was sent to the next. Many of her manuscripts had made twenty and thirty trips, and the record of their journeyings was kept in a small notebook which was now in Margaret's keeping. She had promised to send out the stories while Betsy was abroad.

September brought the beginning of the senior year for Joe. Betsy would be a disconsolate junior. More than once the pages of her story . . . underlined, crossed out, written in the margins . . . were damp with tears shed, not at the woes of her heroine, but at the prospect of beginning so miserable a year.

At last, in a desperate moment, she went to her father. She broached the idea that perhaps—for a girl who wished to be a writer—two years of college were enough.

He listened thoughtfully, sitting in his armchair with his legs crossed and his thumbs hooked in his vest. He looked at her with his kind, wise hazel eyes.

"I don't think so, Betsy," he said. "I have an idea that the more education a writer has, the better. It's a mistake, too, in this life, to start things and not finish them."

Betsy bent her head dejectedly. She had been sure that was what he would say.

Mr. Ray took a cigar out of his pocket. He clipped off the end and lighted it and began to puff slowly.

"Of course," he went on, "we all make mistakes. If you've made a mistake in getting so little out of college, why, you have . . . that's all. And it would be a pretty poor world if we couldn't sweep up our mistakes, now and then, and go ahead.

"You might make yourself finish college. But you certainly wouldn't have much heart in it. And it seems too bad to throw away two years of your life just as a matter of discipline."

Betsy looked up quickly. This was encouraging. And the aromatic smell of his cigar, beginning to drift through the room, had something comforting about it. He always smoked when he was advising his children.

"Don't think," Mr. Ray continued, "that Mamma and I haven't seen which way the wind was blowing. You haven't been happy, Betsy, and we've known it."

Betsy didn't speak.

"You're going to be a writer," he proceeded thoughtfully. "No doubt about that! You've been writing all your life. And you've worked harder this summer at that story you're writing than you've worked for all your professors put together. What's the name of it, anyway?"

"'Emma Middleton Cuts Cross Country,'" Betsy replied. "It's about a little dressmaker, like the one who made my Junior Ball dress. She gets disgusted with everything and walks out and makes a new start."

"Sounds good," said Mr. Ray, nodding sagely, although he never read stories, except Betsy's. "You certainly write like a whiz. Do you remember the letter Dr. Sanford wrote you about your story in the college magazine?"

Betsy nodded, moist-eyed.

"I was very proud of that letter," Mr. Ray said, which made her tears spill over for it seemed to her that she had given him very little reason to be proud of her lately. He put down his cigar.

"You're going to be a writer," he repeated, "and you need more education. That's plain. But college isn't the only place to get an education. I have a 'snoggestion.'" That was what Mr. Ray always called a particularly good suggestion. "I've sounded Mamma out and she approves. How would you like a year abroad?"

"But, Papa!" Betsy had thrown her arms around him, frankly crying now. "What a glo-glo-glorious snoggestion! I've always planned to go. But I never thought of you sending me. I thought I'd earn the money for myself someday."

"Oh, I don't think it would cost so much more than a year at the U!" said Mr. Ray. "You'd have to go in a modest way, of course. But Julia had two trips abroad. You're entitled to one, too. Maybe when Margaret goes, Mamma and I will go along."

"Would I . . . would I go to school over there?"

"You don't seem to be getting what you need out of a school. But judging by our experience with Julia, you learn a lot just from traveling in Europe . . . seeing the art galleries, learning the languages, and all that stuff. You could go on a guided tour, like Julia did."

"No, Papa!" Betsy knelt beside him, her hands on his knee. "Guided tours are all right for some people, but not for a writer. I ought to stay in just two or three places. Really live in them, learn them. Then if I want to mention London, for example, in a story, I would know the names of the streets and how they run and the buildings and the atmosphere of the city. I could move a character around in London just as though it were Minneapolis. I don't want to hurry from place to place with a party the way Julia did."

Her father looked perplexed.

"But it doesn't seem safe, Betsy. You're only twenty-one. You know how much confidence Mamma and I have in you, but we wouldn't want you living in those big foreign cities all alone."

"Maybe we could pick out cities where I know someone . . . or you do, or Julia."

"Maybe. I'll talk it over with your mother."

So Betsy dashed off to Tacy's apartment and they talked, talked about the wonderful trip.

"I'm just going to travel around like Paragot," Betsy said, referring to a character in William J. Locke's novel, *The Beloved Vagabond,* a favorite with both of them.

She wrote Tib, still in college in Milwaukee. And Carney, who was now Mrs. Sam Hutchinson and lived at Murmuring Lake. She took a yellow streetcar over the Mississippi to the University and told her sorority sisters. It sounded so glamorous, "studying abroad."

She went downtown and collected travel folders. She bought a paper-bound *Italian Self-Taught* and dug out her German grammar. She had studied German for a year in high school. She was thankful for her college French.

"French is really all I need. French is the universal language," she told Tacy grandly.

"Of course, you'll see Joe while you're in the East," Tacy said. Red-haired Tacy was so happy in her own marriage that she was anxious for Betsy to get married, too.

Betsy shook her head. "Joe and I don't even correspond anymore."

As Tacy was silent Betsy burst out indignantly, "You know, Tacy, I don't usually quarrel with people. You and I have been friends since my fifth birthday party. I'm still friends with the high-school gang and the people I knew in college. Joe is just too touchy."

"You don't quarrel when you're together," Tacy answered. "He's so perfect for you, Betsy." She looked at Betsy with pleading tender eyes. "Maybe you'll just let him know about the trip."

But Betsy was stubborn. She didn't write her great news to Joe. And presently her attention was distracted by greater news. Julia, the coquette, had fallen in love, and this time, she wrote, it was for keeps!

She had met Paige in New York, where she was singing in the opera. Like Julia, he came from the Middle West, from Indiana, where he had attended the University before studying the flute in the East. Now he played with one of the orchestras there. He was, Betsy discovered later, a very attractive young man, tall, light haired, and ethereal looking.

Julia wanted to be married at Christmastime. Bettina must be maid of honor; Margaret must string ribbons.

"That's all I care about. You plan the rest of it," Julia wrote her mother.

And because of all this excitement Betsy didn't miss college at all. At Thanksgiving Julia came briefly to introduce her fiancé, and at Christmas they were married.

It wasn't a large wedding, but it was candlelit and flower scented. Margaret, straight and slender, her dark hair in coronet braids, carried ribbons down the aisle of the Episcopal Church. Betsy, wearing green chiffon over pink, was maid of honor.

Julia, in trailing bridal white, looked gravely lovely as she looked when she sang. An Indiana friend of Paige's came to be best man, and afterward there was a merry supper at the Ray house.

But through it all Betsy had felt an aching loneliness. What joy was there in a beautiful green dress, long and draped to the front, and an armful of pink roses, if Joe wasn't there to see?

Julia had insisted upon sending Joe an invitation.

"He's my friend as well as yours, Betsy."

"All right," Betsy had conceded grudgingly, and for a few days she had felt a fluttering in her heart. If Joe was looking for a chance to make up, here it was! Maybe he would come!

But he didn't. He sent a silver serving spoon with a rhyme he had composed himself.

"Could Betsy do as well as this?" he scrawled across the bottom.

"Maybe he thinks I'll use that as an excuse for writing him. Well, I won't!" Betsy said.

While Mrs. Ray and Betsy were busy with the wedding, Mr. Ray had occupied himself with Betsy's trip. He had written his younger brother, a professor at the University of Chicago. Perhaps Steve knew some Europe-bound traveler who wouldn't mind keeping an eye on Betsy?

Steve did know just the person. Dr. Wilson and his sister, both on sabbatical leave, were sailing in January on the S.S. *Columbic* from Boston.

Boston! Betsy wouldn't have chosen that port. It was too near Harvard University. But she was far too proud to raise this objection. And the plan dovetailed beautifully with another which had already been worked out.

Julia had a friend studying singing in Munich. Miss Surprise wouldn't mind, she wrote, helping Betsy get settled there. Betsy had never thought of going to Munich. But it would do as a starting point. So her tickets were bought for the S.S. *Columbic,* which would take her to Genoa, where she could board a train for Munich.

A crowd of friends saw her off at the Minneapolis station one January night. The green baize curtains of her berth drawn tightly, she had looked out at a dark, ghostly world rushing past. She had changed trains at Chicago, sending back a shower of excited postcards, and for two days had journeyed eastward, leaving the lakes and the flat familiar Middle West behind, climbing snowy mountains and pausing at towns full of staid green-shuttered houses.

In Boston, she had made a patriotic pilgrimage . . . Faneuil Hall, the Cradle of Liberty, the State House, and the Old South Church.

"If I lived in Boston I'd wear red, white, and blue costumes and eagle headdresses," she wrote her family.

She went through the Public Library and inspected the Art Museum. She marveled at the narrow twisting streets and walked elatedly across The Common. But she didn't go out to Harvard. She did look up the telephone number of Joe's college house and stood for a long time with her hand on the receiver. But she took her hand down at last, and walked away.

Although lonely, the day had been exciting. It was

fun to sleep in a hotel, and she had met the Wilsons at breakfast. Everything had gone according to plan.

It had seemed like a wonderful plan. But it didn't now, as she lay lonesomely in the upper berth of stateroom 52 listening to the dinner music being played above.

3
"And Haply May Forget"

BETSY WASN'T SEASICK any more. Observing with sympathy and alarm the depths of Miss Wilson's anguish, she suspected next morning that her own miseries had sprung more from homesickness than from mal de mer.

Although Miss Wilson refused even coffee with a groan, Betsy ate breakfast in her bunk, charmed with the discovery that there was no salt in the butter and that hot milk was offered instead of cream. How continental! She lay down with the snowy blankets pulled up to her chin and her head on two fat pillows and reflected with astonishment on last night's despair. Travel was delightful. How could she ever have thought otherwise?

Later, she began on her steamer letters. Bob had sent one for each day of the voyage. So had Tacy. Tib, Carney, Cab, and Effie, her favorite sorority sister, had marked their letters "to be read when homesick" or "to be read when seasick" or "to be read when you need advice." Betsy didn't open many.

But she did open Tib's. (Tib Muller, next to Tacy, was her oldest friend.) And the letter was hilarious. She and Tacy had teased Betsy about picking up an American millionaire abroad, and Tib enclosed a sketch of Betsy strolling on deck in the moonlight with a man who was obviously a millionaire. He was dressed in a golfing suit, used a cigarette holder, and wore the dollar sign like a flower in his buttonhole.

Julia and Paige had sent a box with a small gift for each day. The first one was a leather-bound book titled in gold lettering, "My Trip Abroad." From other friends and relatives came a fountain pen, a lacy handkerchief, a collar and cuff set, a traveling clock, books. It was like Christmas morning in Betsy's upper bunk.

Presently the bath steward rapped. "Your bath is ready, Mum." And Betsy descended softly past the stricken Miss Wilson. She put on her cherry-red bathrobe, boudoir cap, and slippers, collected tooth-brush, soap, and towels, and tiptoed down the sway-ing corridor.

The salt bath was exhilarating, and after she was dressed she regretted that she had not put her hair up on curlers last night. To offset its lamentable straight-ness, she tried to tie her scarf artfully.

"I wish Julia . . . or Tib . . . was here," she thought. They were good at coquetries like scarves. She squinted critically into a hand mirror. "Oh, well," she said, "Celeste does her best."

Miss Wilson was still sleeping. Donning coat and furs, Betsy picked up a pencil and one of the small notebooks she always liked to carry to catch random thoughts "that might work into a story." Her letters home were to be her diary.

But when she was settled in her steamer chair, wrapped in the rug, her head back and her feet up, she had no wish to write or read or even think. The waves rose and fell and broke into foam as far as her eye could see and she gazed in dreamy fascination.

She roused when two large ladies, rigidly corseted beneath their flopping coats and with elaborately waved coiffures under hats tied down by veils, settled into the chairs at her left. Two younger women helped them and ran errands patiently. At first Betsy thought these were merely devoted friends. Then she realized that one was called Taylor and the other Rosa (in kind but patronizing tones), and it dawned on her that they were ladies' maids.

Ladies' maids! She was always putting them in stories. What luck to see some in the flesh!

"I must write to Tacy," she thought gleefully. "I'll tell her that Celeste finds them most congenial."

She got out the passenger list and, sure enough, there they were! "Mrs. Sims and Maid. Mrs. Cheney and Maid." But it was too bad, Betsy thought, to say just "Maid" as though these pleasant women had no names! She resolved to study them a bit.

"And I want to get acquainted with that authoress. Maybe she can give me some hints . . ."

But Betsy caught herself short. The authoress might, she just might, comment on Joe. And he was already too painfully clear in Betsy's memory. She didn't want him brought further to life by a vivid phrase or anecdote.

She stretched back in her chair and watched the promenaders. There weren't many, for the water was increasingly rough. Dr. Wilson was out, and Betsy noticed a pretty girl making the rounds. Her clothes were sensible and dowdy and her heels flat but she had a handsome aquiline nose and long fair hair blowing like a veil behind. When she came to rest at last it was in a deck chair but one removed from Betsy's. Betsy smiled but she didn't respond.

Mrs. Sims and Mrs. Cheney, however, were extremely affable. Betsy chatted with them over the mid-morning bouillon. They were sisters, Bostonians, and well accustomed to travel.

They went to the dining saloon for their lunch. (Saloon was what they called it, which seemed surprising to Betsy. A saloon, she had always thought, was a disreputable place where whisky was sold.) Betsy let the steward give her a tray on deck and she ate with appetite in the gray windy cold, watching the unremitting waves.

The afternoon went like the morning. No reading, no writing, just lazily watching the water. Betsy bestirred herself only to visit Miss Wilson, who waved her away with feeble moans.

At four o'clock the steward brought tea with fascinating little scones and cakes.

"And they do this every day! What bliss!" Betsy cried to Mrs. Sims and Mrs. Cheney, who smiled indulgently. "I love eating out of doors."

Over their trays she told them about the picnics she and Tacy had had since they were five. She told them about the Ray family picnics. Betsy was always a talker, but her loquacity today was partly the fault of her companions. They sustained it with questions—politely indirect, at first; then amused; then frankly startled. Was she going abroad . . . alone?

"Practically," Betsy answered as she had answered Mr. O'Farrell. "I want to be a writer, and my father thinks I ought to see the world. A writer has to *live*, you know," she explained, feeling dashing. She glanced toward the second chair at her right, but the pretty girl was engrossed in a magazine.

"*Comme elle est charmante!*" said Mrs. Sims.

"*Et excessivement naïve,*" replied her sister.

Betsy was annoyed to be thought naive but delighted to be found charming. She wondered whether honor compelled her to say that she understood French and decided that it didn't.

Returning from one of her fruitless calls on Miss Wilson, Betsy found it hard to keep her footing. Luckily she encountered Mr. O'Farrell, who removed his stiff cap, guided her safely back to her chair, folded her into her rug with solicitous care. When she thanked him he said, "It's a pleasur-r-re to me!" and smiled into her eyes.

"He's a charmer!" Betsy thought. Looking after the trim erect figure in nautical blue, she decided to go down for a nap and put her hair in curlers.

"Do we dress for dinner, Mrs. Sims?"

"Not formally, except for the Captain's Ball and the *Diner d'Adieu*. A dark silk will do."

Betsy was pleased that she had a dark silk. It was maroon, piped with old gold and trimmed with gold buttons. The skirt was long and fashionably tight. The sleeves, too, were long and tight with frills at the wrists. Betsy liked the frills for she knew her hands were pretty.

She knew all her good points—or thought she did. (She never included her smile, unaware that it was quick and very bright.) She valued highly her slender figure, pink and white skin, and red lips.

She was even more conscious of her defects—straight hair, irregular features, the space between her teeth in front. But she did not brood upon them as she had in her teens.

Like most girls she had worked out a technique for fascination. With Betsy it was thoroughly curled hair, perfume, bracelets, the color green, immaculate daintiness, and a languid enigmatic pose. This last was less successful than she realized. People were likely to think of her as full of fun, friendly, and responsive. And her friends knew that she was doggedly persistent—anything but languid.

Betsy was strong in her faith, however. Out in the corridor, after a cheerful good-by to Miss Wilson, she paused to assume the debutante slouch. Then she sauntered, with the swaying gait required by a hobble skirt, up to the dining saloon.

"The Hungarian Rhapsody" came out to greet her.

Cheeks flaming, she stood in the doorway and a steward beckoned to her. She found out then where Mr. O'Farrell had placed her. It was at his right.

"I thought since you were all, all alone, I'd have you where I could look after you," he said.

He looked very worldly in his dress uniform, with its debonair short jacket. Betsy wondered how old he was. Pretty old. Thirty-five or so.

"But I like older men. I wouldn't mind marrying an older man," she thought, wishing Joe could know what she was thinking. He and his mustache!

Dr. Wilson was at the same table, asking for raw carrots, and an English lady, and a pallid young Bostonian named Mr. Glenn. Betsy was confused by all the strange accents. The missing r's and the long soft a's. Even Dr. Wilson was a New Englander, although he taught in Chicago.

No one seemed to know much about the Middle West. The English lady had never even heard of Minneapolis. Mr. Glenn asked what state it was in, and Mr. O'Farrell questioned her about the Indians out there. But he, of course, was joking. He seemed to know everything.

"He's the most cosmopolitan person I ever met in my life," Betsy thought.

Speaking rapidly, his Irish brogue becoming more apparent as he warmed to the subject, he steered the conversation with easy skill so that everyone entered in.

"Maybe some night you'll tell us about those Indians," he teased, lighting a cigarette. Having secured the ladies' permission to smoke, he smoked continually.

"I could tell you about Minnehaha Falls."

To her surprise everyone looked up with interest.

"Really?" (It sounded like "rilly.") The English lady leaned forward. "Have you actually seen the Minnehaha Falls?"

"Of course. They're in Minneapolis."

"How extr'ordinary!" A faraway smile lighted her plain face. "Do you know, we used to study it in school.

"Where the Falls of Minnehaha
Flash and gleam among the oak-trees . . ."

Mr. Glenn's face glowed. "That isn't the part I remember. It's . . .

"By the shores of Gitche Gumee,
By the shining Big-Sea-Water . . ."

"I remember something else entirely," Mr. O'Farrell said, his eyes laughing.

*"In the land of the Dacotahs
Lives the Arrow-maker's daughter
Minnehaha, Laughing Water
Handsomest of all the women . . ."*

"Let's call Miss Ray, Minnehaha."

Betsy blushed.

The dinner was in a multitude of courses, and the orchestra played alluringly through it all. For dessert they had little steamed puddings with a sweet hot sauce. Afterward there was coffee in tiny cups, nuts and raisins, biscuits with cheese. Mr. O'Farrell asked (in French) for a special kind of cheese. He had a genial but masterly way with the waiter.

Betsy went down to her stateroom fairly dancing.

"What luck to meet such a fascinating man! And won't Tacy be pleased because he's Irish?"

She prepared for bed softly, not to disturb Miss Wilson, but she put her hair up on curlers tonight, tucking them carefully under her boudoir cap. Settled in her bunk, she wrote her letter home, telling her family about Mrs. Sims and Mrs. Cheney, about Taylor and Rosa and the girl with the long hair who wouldn't speak. Lady Vere de Vere, Betsy dubbed her.

"And now . . . 'Hearts and Flowers,' please . . . our purser, Mr. O'Farrell, who looks like Chauncey Olcott."

Finishing her letter, she got out her Bible and Prayer Book. And finishing her prayers, she snuggled beneath the warm blankets. She looked at the port-hole. It seemed cozy and not alarming tonight to think of the vast heaving blackness outside. She was so happy she could even think about Joe. Or rather, she could even *not* think about Joe.

"'And haply may forget,'" she murmured, flouncing beneath the blankets.

For a day or two the sea was so rough that the decks were shut in by canvas. Betsy and Lady Vere de Vere were the only members of their sex at divine service on Sunday, and the weather made especially solemn the prayer For Persons Going to Sea.

"O Eternal God, who alone spreadest out the heavens, and rulest the raging of the sea . . ." Betsy resolved to read that to herself every night during the voyage.

Deck chairs were deserted, and dishes were clamped to the tables, but Betsy ate straight through the menu at every meal.

"Say you were ill and just came to keep me from being bored," Mr. O'Farrell implored her when she first appeared at breakfast.

"Why, I'm not a bit ill!" Betsy began but he interrupted, his eyes dancing.

"Oh, keep me in me fool's paradise!"

"I really must write Tacy about Mr. O'Farrell," Betsy often chuckled to herself.

She was thinking about him as she made her way

to the bow on the fourth day out. The *Columbic* was still tossing, although buckets of sunshine seemed to have been thrown over the water, and the waves were merely frolicsome, not alarming, any more. She had paced the deck every day but had never gone this far front . . .

"Front!" she checked herself scornfully. "I mean forward, on the starboard side!"

Shocked by her inland ignorance, Mr. O'Farrell had been instructing her in nautical terms—bow and stern, port and starboard, forward, midships, aft. He had explained ship's bells and the changing time.

"The sun rises in the east and so, since we are going eastward, we gain time. Every noon the ship's clocks are set correctly and you should set your watch correctly."

"I'll remember, teacher."

"No frivolity, Miss! There's a difference of five hours between New York and London."

"And I have to add two hours for Minneapolis!" Betsy grumbled. "I can't even think what my family is doing without solving a problem in arithmetic first."

Mr. O'Farrell shook his handsome head. "You leave your family behind when you start out to travel," he told her.

Betsy was very happy. It was amazing, she thought, inching forward, how quickly one fell into this lazy routine: deck chairs, bouillon, promenading, luncheon, promenading, dressing for dinner, DINNER.

"I feel as though I'd been born on this old ship!" she thought, reaching the bow at last.

She clung to the railing in scared exhilaration and watched the *Columbic* plough its white furrow, until the spray drove her back. Presently the long-haired girl came up. Ignoring Betsy, she, too, looked out at the waves' wild see-saw. But one exuberant wave leaped the railing. It spilled over Lady Vere de Vere, and Betsy could not help laughing.

"I'm sorry," she apologized as the blonde girl ruefully stood on one sopping foot to shake the other. "But that was funny."

And Lady Vere de Vere laughed back, all her aloofness washed away.

"You'd better go right down and change," Betsy advised.

"Oh, there's no danger from saltwater drenchings!" This was a new accent. Canadian, Betsy suspected. English, Irish, Bostonian, and Canadian, so far!

"Then won't you sit down and dry off? My name's Betsy Ray."

"I'm Maida Bartlett from Toronto."

"You're a good sailor. You must have crossed before."

"Many times, to England."

They began eagerly to talk.

"I'm going to Europe to study," Betsy said.

"Alone? How frightfully jolly! Mother and I are going to Madeira for her health," Maida replied.

A junior officer came hurrying up. Mr. Chandler was good-looking, big-shouldered, with thick hair set in glistening waves and large white teeth. He showed his teeth in a wide smile now as he said chidingly, "You young ladies aren't supposed to be up here. The Captain sent me to fetch you."

He took them back, one on each arm, to their deck chairs, and sat down between them.

Betsy didn't care much for him, but Maida seemed to like him, and he certainly liked Maida. He waved her hair in his fingers to dry it. He called her a Christmas angel.

"Maybe you two will come to tea in my cabin. I've been saving my Christmas cake, and now I know why."

"How frightfully jolly!" Maida cried. Over his head, to Betsy's surprise, she winked.

After he left they sat talking about him with bursts of laughter. Betsy confided her admiration for the purser. They had tea, still talking, while Mrs. Sims and Mrs. Cheney looked on benevolently. The waves were growing calmer. And Miss Wilson, when Betsy went down to dress for dinner, was sitting up with her dinner tray on her knees.

Her plain bed jacket was impeccably neat. Her white hair was smoothly arranged and her eyeglasses perched on a straight, well-formed nose. She watched with interest as Betsy twisted her hair in intricate loops, and put on a peg-top skirt and her best lace blouse which had frills around both neck and wrists. Betsy added bracelets and sprayed perfume on her hair. She directed a spray at Miss Wilson's bed jacket.

"Mercy!" Miss Wilson cried, but she looked pleased.

"Tomorrow night you'll be coming up. And you're going to love our table. Mr. O'Farrell is perfectly fascinating. Last night we talked about South Africa. He served there with *distinction*, and he told about his adventures with an absolute flood of eloquence."

"Really?"

"He and I sat arguing afterward for ages. I sympathize with the Boers, you see. So does my father."

"Did he mind?" asked Miss Wilson. "The purser, I mean?"

"No. He likes to argue. But when we stopped, he said, 'Faith! Think of discussing such subjects with a woman!'" Betsy tried to imitate the Irish inflection and Miss Wilson laughed.

He had a way of looking at her, Betsy remembered, his head bent, a cigarette between his fingers, his eyes intent or gaily quizzical. She didn't try to imitate that.

Books came up for discussion that night. The

rough sea of the day before caused Mr. O'Farrell to mention the storm in Joseph Conrad's *The Nigger of the Narcissus*. Betsy had never read it, but Joe Willard had.

"A friend of mine has told me about that description."

The English lady was reading *Jean Christophe*.

"My sister considers it simply magnificent," Betsy contributed.

Joe had read Ibsen and Julia had read Shaw. Betsy was increasingly grateful for these two inquiring minds. Betsy, too, was a reader, but she read Dickens, Thackeray, and Scott. She read Shakespeare and the poets. Shouldn't an author know the classics?

But people at dinner tables, she discovered, didn't talk about the classics much.

Fortunately she had one dear love among books that was not a classic. And Mr. O'Farrell mentioned it.

"*The Beloved Vagabond*? Why, I've read that over and over!" Betsy cried.

"I've read it more than once myself," said Mr. O'Farrell. "Every seaman has something of the vagabond in him, I suspect. And Paragot was partly Irish."

"Do you remember when he decided to go to Budapest, and just went, all of a sudden? That's the way I like to do things," Betsy declared.

The English lady knew Paragot, too. "But I wished

he'd cut his nails," she remarked. "And I didn't like it when he put his hairbrush in the butter."

"Pooh!" said Betsy, smiling so she wouldn't sound rude, and Mr. O'Farrell proclaimed, "Your attitude, Madame, seems to us effete. But I'm afraid Mr. Glenn agrees with you."

"I haven't read it," said Mr. Glenn seriously, "I don't like hairbrushes in butter, though." Which sent them all into laughter.

Their table was gayer even than the Captain's table, although Betsy knew that was supposed to be the smartest. It was really stuffy, according to Maida, who sat there. The lady author, whose name, Betsy had learned, was Mrs. Main-Whittaker, sat next to the Captain. She always dressed for dinner, complete with jewels and feathers. She was smoking. Betsy had never seen a woman smoke before except on a stage.

"I hope it isn't necessary to smoke in order to write. Papa and Mamma would never let me," she thought.

The evening air was almost balmy. For the first time the decks were more attractive, after dinner, than the lounge. Maida and Betsy stayed out in their chairs and were joined by Mr. Chandler, Mr. Glenn, and a Mr. Burton, middle-aged, with mustaches that drooped to his shoulders.

That night Betsy changed to a thin night gown—pink silk, trimmed with lace.

"Well! I look more like it now!" she remarked as

she tucked her curlers under a lacy cap before the mirror.

"More like what?" asked the mystified Miss Wilson.

"A young lady on a *romantic* Mediterranean cruise."

In the morning she put on her red blazer and a red and green cap. The cap was reversible—red on one side and green on the other and could be poked into jaunty shapes. When she emerged onto the scrubbed glistening deck, she was greeted by golden sunshine, and there was something in the air . . .

"It's summer! It's the tropics! It's glorious!" Betsy cried, running to the railing.

The ocean was sparkling and dancing as though it had never in all its existence caused a ship to lurch and roll. It was like her own prairie on a summer morning, Betsy thought. She could almost smell flowers.

"Oh, I'm so happy!" she confided to Taylor who was passing. "Honestly, I could tango down the deck!"

"Yes, Miss, I'm sure you could," Taylor answered politely. She was thin and rather stiff. Rosa was short, chunky, and cozy. Both of them were nice, but not so glamorous as Celeste.

Mr. O'Farrell immediately noticed the cap.

"You look like one of the little people of Ireland," he said. "All you need is a harp in your hair."

This was something else for Tacy! But Tacy not being available, Betsy sought out Maida.

"Can you imagine your Mr. Chandler saying a thing like that?"

"He might."

"Well, he wouldn't have a thrilling Irish voice to say it in!"

Quite as a matter of course today Betsy and Maida joined forces. They roamed over the ship with Betsy's square box camera. They tried their skill at shuffleboard. Together they called on Miss Wilson who lay in her deck chair, pale and apprehensive, but smiling.

"She teaches higher algebra," Betsy told Maida. "But you'd never guess it. She's a perfect peach."

Maida introduced Betsy to her mother who was playing bridge in the lounge. She was a slender, stately lady, very stiff at first, but Betsy was beginning to understand Canadians. Their characteristics had gone into her notebook along with Mrs. Main-Whittaker, Taylor, and Rosa.

Betsy told Maida about Celeste and Hortense. Maida cried that *she* wanted a maid, so they created Gabrielle. Betsy revealed that Maida had been Lady Vere de Vere. Exchanging these hilarious confidences, Betsy felt as though she were back in high school.

She was enchanted when Maida said "frocks" for "dresses," "boots" for "shoes." Maida, on the other hand, teased Betsy about "I guess," "cute," and "cunning."

"And you call everyone a peach. Why a peach? Why not a pear, or an apple, or a fig?"

"You're a perfect fig," Betsy said experimentally.

This chaffing was interrupted by visitors—Mr. Glenn, of course, and Mr. Burton. And Mr. Chandler was not the only officer to come to rest in their vicinity.

"My sister asked me," Dr. Wilson said at lunch, "whether you and Miss Bartlett held a fire drill down by your chairs. It was a joke," he explained, "because there are always so many uniforms there."

Mr. O'Farrell looked at Betsy. "Ah, she didn't miss me at all! The flirt!"

"I did, as a matter of fact," Betsy replied.

But although the "fire drill" was held again after lunch, Mr. O'Farrell didn't put in an appearance. A purser, Betsy had discovered, was a very busy person.

"Why, oh, why," she wailed to Maida, "did I have to fall in love with a purser?"

They went to tea in Mr. Chandler's cabin; Maida's mother had given permission. He had a canary with which they made friends. He showed them photographs of his mother and sisters.

"I wish Mr. O'Farrell would ask us to tea," Betsy thought. "I'd like to know what *his* family is like."

Maida poured the tea and Betsy cut the Christmas

cake—fruit cake and almond cake in layers, over-spread with white icing and ornamented with candles, ribbons, and toy robins. They had a very good time, but Betsy remained loyal to Mr. O'Farrell.

That night he and Betsy lingered again at the table. They were talking about Betsy's writing. She told him about the small sales she had made, and how she kept her stories going out to the magazines and how they kept coming back.

"One story has brought in sixty-one rejection slips!"

"The deuce it has!" He was looking at her with attention. "I'd never be able to take it."

"Oh, I don't mind!" Betsy replied. "I think how foolish all those editors will feel when I'm famous."

Mr. O'Farrell burst into laughter. "We have an author . . . pardon me . . . another author on board. Did you know? A Mrs. Main-Whittaker. Would you like to meet her?"

"Well, I would normally, but in this case . . ." She didn't want to, because Mrs. Main-Whittaker knew Joe. It was idiotic. But Betsy's face turned scarlet.

Mr. O'Farrell changed the subject deftly. He was very tactful, Betsy realized—sensitive, too.

"That's why I like him," she thought later, on the upper deck. "It's not just that he's so handsome and flings compliments around."

There were groups and couples on the upper deck looking at the stars. Betsy was with a group but Maida was with Mr. Chandler. "Fussing," Betsy accused her later down in Maida's cabin.

Maida's mother was playing bridge as usual and they had the small room to themselves. They had put on bathrobes and caps, rung for lemon squash and sandwiches. Again Betsy had the feeling that she had turned back the clock.

Maida was a little younger than herself, but it wasn't that. For Maida didn't usually seem younger. Mrs. Sims and Mrs. Cheney would never, Betsy realized, call Maida naïve. But she had gone to a private school and she had not, like Betsy, had boys around all her life—in the classroom, in the schoolyard, in and out of her home. She didn't understand boys as well as Betsy did.

"What's 'fussing'?"

"Flirting."

"I don't believe he's flirting, actually."

"That's it!" Betsy thought. "I'm only joking about having a crush on Mr. O'Farrell, but I'm afraid Maida is really falling for Mr. Chandler."

4

Enchanted Island

"SEVEN O'CLOCK and land in sight!"

These words of high romance were accompanied by a rattling of the stateroom door.

"Miss Wilson!" Betsy cried. "Do you hear that?"

"Yes, yes!" Miss Wilson was groping into a dressing gown. Betsy scrambled down the ladder and joined her at the porthole.

There romance was written along the horizon in a wavy line. It looked no more substantial than the airy cloud-built islands they had often seen at sunset. But this was a real island; it was one of the Azores.

"St. Michael's, probably," Miss Wilson said. She and her brother had stopped here before.

Excitement beat like wings over the breakfast table.

"Imagine," Betsy babbled, "finding islands out here in the middle of the ocean! Of course, I've always known they *were* here. But I never realized before how big the Atlantic was, and how brave it was of a little island to push right up in the middle of it."

"It didn't push," said Mr. O'Farrell. "It was flung up by a volcano. Eat your porridge, child."

"Porridge!" said Betsy scornfully. "I'm too uplifted to eat." But she poured the thick cream with a generous hand.

There were nine islands in the Azores Archipelago, Mr. O'Farrell said—all volcanic, mountainous, and rising steeply from the sea. They were farther from Europe and nearer to America than any other group of islands. Portugal had discovered them.

"Portugal!" The English lady didn't seem to believe it.

"Yes, Madame. It was in those adventur-r-rous days when Prince Henry, the Navigator, was pushing out the world's boundaries. And the islands had no human inhabitants when the Portuguese arrived."

"When were they discovered?"

"Corvo, the last one, around 1452. After that, men kept on searching. They felt sure there was more land farther on, for some rocks on Corvo"—Mr. O'Farrell's voice warmed to the drama—"are shaped like a horseman pointing west."

Betsy felt shivers down her spine. "Did Columbus ever see that?"

"He may have."

"How simply, absolutely fascinating!"

Out on deck passengers gathered in the sunshine. Now the distant wavy line had resolved itself into mountains. They were the vivid green of grass after rain, divided off like a checkerboard by darker green hedges. And where the mountains swept down to the bay lay Ponta Delgada.

At first the little city was a splash of dazzling white. But nearer, it took on color. Many of the houses, all small and of similar shape, were tinted in pastel hues.

"It looks like a toy village! I want to sit right down on the floor and play with it!" cried Betsy.

"It's like a stage setting," said Maida.

Shortly they missed the throb of the engines. The *Columbic* had stopped and small boats were racing toward it. Betsy ran down to the stateroom for her jacket, cap, and camera.

"And some stout shoes!" Mrs. Sims warned her. "The cobblestones are fiendish."

"And your purse!" added Mrs. Cheney. "The embroideries are divine . . . and so cheap!"

Maida, too, sped below and returned with a flat sailor hat perched above her flowing hair.

The crew had let down a stairway from the lower deck, and the passengers descended to rowboats, manned by dark, barefooted boatmen. Their gibble-gabble was Portuguese, Dr. Wilson said. The boat tipped and joggled as though sharing the general excitement, and the little toy city came nearer all the time.

Landing at a rock platform, the visitors climbed stairs to the street and were at once surrounded by smiling, clamorous natives. Men and women alike were barefooted. The women wore bright shawls, and many carried black-eyed babies. Some attempted English. Little boys held out their hands with captivating grins, calling, "Mawney, mawney!" "I 'peak English. Give me mawney!"

Flowers were offered. Betsy bought a bouquet of violets and their wet fragrance intoxicated her. She looked around eagerly at the tiny streets—the little colored houses.

"Oh, this darling place! This dear, sweet, cunning, adorable place!"

Carriage drivers, with gestures, urged everyone to ride. But Betsy wanted to walk. She wanted to be on her own feet, able to stop and look about as often and as long as she chose. Fortunately, Dr. Wilson believed in exercise as much as he believed in raw vegetables. He and his sister would be walking, he said, and Betsy and Maida could go with them. Maida's mother took a carriage with Mrs. Sims and Mrs. Cheney, and the girls agreed to meet them at Brown's Hotel for lunch.

The cobblestones were rough, as Mrs. Sims had warned, but Betsy was walking on air. And the steep streets were very narrow—many didn't even have sidewalks—but that only brought the travelers closer to the enchanting little houses.

These were built of dried lava, Dr. Wilson said; then plastered and tinted to suit the owner's fancy. They were pale green, blue, pink, lavender, and orange. They were striped, checkered, tiled like a bathroom floor. They looked like little frosted cakes or bricks of Neopolitan ice cream. They had second-story balconies with green wrought-iron railings that hung above the cobblestones.

"I love them! I adore them!" Betsy kept saying. "I'm going to come back and stay at least a month.

Celeste and I are going to live in a pale green house with a balcony."

Maida laughed. "Just wait till you see Madeira!"

"But it can't, it *can't* be as nice as this!"

"Madeira is supposed to be the most beautiful spot on earth. It was probably the Garden of Eden."

Dark-eyed women smiled from the balconies where they sat working on the embroidery for which the Azores, as well as Madeira, were famous. Children, irresistibly pretty, peeped over the railings and crowded about the visitors in the street.

Betsy was taking snapshots madly. She snapped the children. She snapped a Portuguese soldier, in gray and red, with a jaunty beret. She snapped an old man with a tassel cap, sitting on top of a load of brush that was sitting on top of a donkey.

There were donkeys everywhere, flanked with bulging panniers or patiently pulling two-wheeled carts. There were oxen, too, but very few horses.

Suddenly Maida stopped abruptly. "My word!"

Betsy turned her head. "Golly!" she breathed.

From among the brightly shawled women one had emerged wearing an unbelievable costume. It was like a nun's habit, blown out to a grotesque size. The cloak was as large as a tent, and the huge hood, shaped like a sunbonnet, was so contrived that the face could be completely concealed.

"That is the *capote e capelo*," Dr. Wilson said, "the traditional costume of the island. We are lucky to see one, for they are going out. The younger women object to them, I hear," he added regretfully.

"I should think they jolly well would!" Maida cried.

"But it's a perfect disguise! It might be convenient . . ." Betsy was already putting one into a dark romance.

"I think," Miss Wilson said, "the costume was devised on account of the showers." It was true that showers and little bursts of sunshine alternated every few minutes. "On our other visit I counted eleven showers and nine rainbows in the time we were ashore."

No one minded the rain. It was like a bright mist through which struck quite plainly the little doll houses with their dainty balconies. After every shower there was a smell of heavenly sweetness.

"It must be freesias . . . or roses!" Betsy sniffed rapturously. "This place reminds me of California," she added.

The palm trees were indeed familiar, and she recognized the giant geraniums, red and pink, which had astonished her long ago in her grandmother's garden. In California, too, she had first seen bougainvillaea, which was pouring cascades of purple, red, and blue over these walls.

More and more houses had gardens now. The owners attempted to conceal them with high walls, but great masses of fragrant flowers surged up and over, to greet the passers-by.

"There seem to be so few people around these bigger houses," Maida observed.

"The upper-class women," Dr. Wilson replied, "lead lives of great seclusion. Men servants do their shopping for them. And when they go out . . . to church or to pay calls . . . they go in carriages."

"I don't blame them for staying in their gardens," Betsy said, pausing at a white wall where a white cat with yellow eyes sat in a torrent of yellow bloom.

Dr. Wilson wanted them to see some "sights," so they visited a public garden. Here were grotesque lava formations—caves and grottos and little hills—and more lavish vegetation. Orange trees with shiny green leaves, white blossoms, and golden fruit. Huge camellia trees, covered with red and white flowers. Magnolia trees, banana trees, figs, peaches, apricots. Mountains of cactus, forests of ferns, and oceans of flowers.

"It isn't hard to make things grow in these islands," Miss Wilson remarked. "The trouble is to keep them from growing too much. It looks untidy, doesn't it?"

But Betsy thought it was a garden out of a dream.

They went to the Old Jesuit Church. The portals were guarded by beggars; Betsy had never seen a beggar before. The church was almost three hundred years old, Dr. Wilson said, and she looked around with awe. The altar was astonishing. It was an enormous mass of cedar, carved with a multitude of little fat cherubs. Cherubs were as thick as leaves on a tree.

When they left the church, Betsy and Maida were too hungry, they told Dr. Wilson, to imbibe further education. He had brought his lunch in his pocket—a carrot and a slice of whole-grain bread—and his sister had a sandwich. They were going on to the Matriz Church.

"One of the doors is a very interesting example of the Manueline," he told them earnestly.

"But what *is* the Manueline, Dr. Wilson?"

"The Manueline style? It's like the Plateresque."

"Heavens! How much I have to learn!" Betsy said to Maida as they climbed to Brown's Hotel.

This modest white plaster building was situated on a hill with terraces overlooking the city and bay. The showers had stopped and the air was very warm.

"Just think," Betsy said, "at home it's winter! The roofs and lawns are covered with snow, and Papa is out shoveling walks."

They were hot and tired. It was pleasant, when

they went inside, to find the hotel deliciously cool. The Browns were English people, but their hostelry seemed very foreign, with high ceilings, bare, white-washed walls, and cement floors.

The room to which the girls were escorted to rest was high, bare, and cool like the others, with long white curtains at the window, an iron bed, a wardrobe, a dresser, a washstand with a china bowl and pitcher.

"Not much like a room at the Radisson," Betsy said. "But then, the Radisson doesn't look out on a garden."

"What is the Radisson?" Maida asked, dropping down on the bed.

"It's a hotel in Minneapolis. That's near the Minnehaha Falls, in case you don't remember."

Betsy was as tired as Maida, but she couldn't leave the window. It was thrilling to stand in a strange room and look out into a flaming garden.

"I'm in a foreign land," she thought. "No wonder people love traveling!"

"Betsy," Maida said suddenly. "I want to talk something over with you. Why don't you get off at Madeira with us? You could go on to the continent later."

Betsy was too astonished to reply.

"You like the Azores so well," Maida continued.

"And Madeira is even more beautiful."

"But would your mother want me?"

"Oh, yes! I asked her last night. She'd love to have you visit us."

"Why, why . . . that's the nicest thing I ever heard of! It's wonderful of you and your mother. But I don't know what to say."

"It would be ever so jolly to have you," Maida urged.

Betsy stretched out on the bed beside her, trying to imagine what it would be like to stay in Madeira—if Madeira were as beautiful as this. It would be like living in another world. But would it be sensible? What would her parents think? She'd have to write Miss Surprise.

Maida began to whisper confidences. "Mr. Chandler is really in love with me, Betsy. It isn't just a shipboard flirtation."

"Really?" Betsy was sympathetic. She couldn't help feeling secretly doubtful, though.

"He feels terrible that I have to get off at Madeira. Betsy, do you suppose Mamma would mind if I married a ship's officer?"

Presently they took turns at the washbowl and went out to the dining room where Mrs. Bartlett and others from the *Columbic* were waiting. Mrs. Main-Whittaker wasn't there. She had gone to the

Portuguese hotel, someone said.

"Looking for atmosphere," thought Betsy.

All the guests ate at one table and they were served by two Portuguese women—one old, with a white turban on her head, the other, young and pretty with a pink skirt and a blue and white striped waist.

Conversation was in French and Portuguese as well as in English. Betsy rejoiced when she occasionally understood a *merci* or a *s'il vous plait*. She was almost rested after the fatiguing morning, and the cool, dim, lofty room refreshed her.

Moreover, the luncheon was delicious. They had first a thick soup, then a slice of beef with salad, then an omelet, with apricots and fresh pineapple for dessert. The Azores shipped pineapples everywhere, Mrs. Bartlett said.

No wonder! Betsy thought. She had never eaten one so sweet and full of juice.

After lunch she and the Bartletts went out to the terrace and Mrs. Bartlett repeated Maida's invitation.

"We have a villa rented . . . and servants arranged for. We'd love to have you."

"You're so sweet to ask me!" Betsy cried. "And it would be wonderful. But I don't know whether I ought to."

"The Wilsons are your chaperones, aren't they? They could speak for your parents?"

"Yes," answered Betsy. "I could do anything the Wilsons approved."

"The purser could arrange it very easily. This line permits stopovers. Another ship could pick you up and carry you on to Genoa in a month or two . . . say, in early spring."

"Then I wouldn't go to Munich at all." Betsy's head was whirling, but the plan tempted her greatly. Back at the quay she told the Wilsons about the invitation.

Dr. Wilson was dazed and dubious. He and his sister were charmed with the Bartletts, he said.

"But Munich is a great metropolis, a famous center for music and art. I really can't advise you to give it up merely for a picturesque island."

His sister agreed, and Betsy had an uncomfortable feeling that her parents would, too. And Julia wouldn't like her missing all that music.

"But it would be something," she insisted, "to spend six weeks in a perfect earthly paradise."

"Yes, of course! And if you want to do it, I can assure your parents that it would be quite proper." His reluctance was obvious, however.

They were all exhausted when they got back to the *Columbic,* laden with big bunches of flowers, pineapples, postcards, and embroideries. It was like coming home, Betsy thought, to return to the little stateroom.

The stewardess scurried about making them comfortable.

While Betsy was taking a hot salt bath, she felt the engine begin to throb again.

She thought of the little island—such a tiny scrap of land—melting from sight as the steamer moved away.

"Maybe it goes back into the ocean and rises up again when another steamer comes along. It's lovely enough to be enchanted."

If Madeira was really nicer than St. Michael's, she ought to accept Maida's invitation.

"I almost believe I will." She sprang out of the tub and rubbed herself until she tingled. "I'll ask Mr. O'Farrell to arrange it."

At dinner the orchestra was playing Strauss waltzes, and everyone was bursting with the day's adventures. The English lady, like the Wilsons, was talking of Manueline doors. Mr. Glenn had visited a pineapple farm. Betsy was delirious and knew it.

"It's the most entrancing little place I ever saw. Celeste and I are going to go back someday and live in a pale green house with a balcony."

"Celeste is your sister?" the English lady asked politely.

"Oh, she's my maid! I mean . . . she's my imaginary maid. I mean . . . aren't those balconies adorable?"

Mr. O'Farrell rescued her adroitly. "They're very important. The boy courts the girl there . . . from the street. He doesn't come into the house until they are engaged, and he doesn't see her alone until they are married."

"What kind of marriage would that be!" Betsy would have been glad to expand the subject of marriage. She had often wondered why anyone so charming as Mr. O'Farrell had stayed so long a bachelor. But he kept the talk on island customs.

"Just wait," he said to Betsy, as everyone had, "until you see Madeira!"

Dinner was breaking up. They were standing by their chairs.

"I'm not only going to see Madeira," Betsy replied saucily. "I'm going to get off and stay there."

"I beg your pardon?" He was genuinely startled.

"With the Bartletts. They have invited me."

"Isn't this rather unexpected?" he asked slowly.

"I like to do things unexpectedly. Like Paragot going to Budapest, you know."

But although he admired Paragot so much, Mr. O'Farrell didn't seem pleased.

"Sit down," he said abruptly, pulling out her chair again, "and tell me all about it."

While she explained he sat looking at her, frowning. His eyes left her face and she felt them on her hands, clasped on the table under their lace frills.

"Have you made up your mind?" he asked without looking up.

"Not entirely. But it seems like a wonderful plan."

"I could arrange it, of course." Then his blue eyes lifted. They looked hurt, almost tragic. (And he was so very handsome with his shining black hair, touched with gray.)

Surprisingly he said, "Faith, and it's sad for me it will be if you leave at Madeira!"

He didn't seem to be joking . . . but he must be! Betsy felt her face flush.

Sometimes after dinner Mr. O'Farrell took her out to her chair although he never stayed there. But tonight she went out alone. She looked around for Maida, but Maida was with Mr. Chandler, leaning over the rail. Betsy, too, went to the rail. The moon was coming out, spreading a tremulous silver light over the water.

Madeira would be beautiful, of course, thought Betsy. But beauty wasn't everything. She pursed her lips judicially.

"I believe," she decided, "that it would be a mistake to miss a great metropolis like Munich for the sake of a picturesque island."

5
The Deluge

MADEIRA WAS BEAUTIFUL, as reported. It was bewitching. It was idyllic. Yet Betsy didn't regret her decision to go on with the *Columbic*.

She regretted parting from Maida. Shipboard life had wrought its usual miracle, and the friendship of hardly more than a week seemed like the friendship of a lifetime. But Maida and her mother had affectionately extended their invitation to some time in Toronto.

"Why, of course! Toronto and Minneapolis aren't far apart. We'll see lots of each other," Betsy planned enthusiastically. She had seen very little of Maida, however, during the run to Madeira.

Maida had spent every available moment with Mr. Chandler. She and Betsy had not even had a stateroom spread on the last night, although Betsy waited up to a very late hour. The farewells must have been harrowing, Betsy thought. Mr. Chandler seemed to be in earnest after all.

Her own parting from Maida had been unsatisfactory. The *Columbic* was anchored off Funchal, and the passengers stood waiting for a tender to take them ashore, enjoying an exquisite view. The mountains were higher here than at St. Michael's. Against the verdant lower slopes the city shone radiantly white.

Betsy kept looking about for Maida but when she arrived on deck it was with her mother, and a boy carrying bags. Embracing Betsy, she whispered, "The parting was terrible! He's so in love! And I think I am, too. Don't answer! I haven't dared breathe a word to Mamma."

What a difference in mothers! Betsy thought. *Her* mother would have wanted to hear every word.

Mrs. Bartlett kissed Betsy. "Remember, you're coming to visit us sometime!"

"I'll remember. I'd love to, and thank you again. I'll be writing," Betsy added to Maida. "And Celeste asked me to say good-by to Gabrielle."

Maida's laugh rippled. "Gabrielle is desolated!" she replied, and she was gone, her long light hair floating behind her.

Watching her depart, Betsy mused on how the course of her own life might have been changed by staying on in Madeira. "I might have married an Englishman."

Madeira, she had been told, had a large colony of British and other foreigners, some attracted by the climate, others owning vineyards or sugar cane plantations. This was by far the largest and most populous of the Madeira Islands.

The Madeira Islands! Suddenly, without wishing to, Betsy remembered a visit she had made to Beidwinkles' farm back in Minnesota. She and Joe Willard had looked through a stereopticon set at "Views of Europe with Side Trips to Egypt, Algiers, and the Madeira Islands."

The memory brought a vision of Joe visiting a foreign place like this. She could see him walking about with his quick step. He would be asking all sorts of questions. Joe didn't just enjoy things in a dreamy way as she did, he always wanted to find out everything about them.

It took an angry effort to exorcise this vision. But she did it. She reminded herself—it was a dulcet thought—that Mr. O'Farrell had not wanted her to stop at Madeira.

She had told him casually, "I decided it would be foolish to give up a metropolis like Munich for a little island like Madeira."

"You were very wise, Miss Ray." There wasn't a hint in his suave reply of the feeling he had shown before.

She and the Wilsons had a wonderful day in Funchal. First, they rode in an ox-drawn sledge. Even Dr. Wilson was willing to forego the benefits of walking to test this curious vehicle. Wicker seats, set on runners, faced each other under a square red canopy from which white curtains fluttered down.

The Wilsons and Betsy wanted the curtains open so they could enjoy the quaint streets. The Portuguese driver, for a reason he could not communicate, wanted them shut. He would carefully tie those on the right, but as soon as he crossed to tie those on the left, Dr. Wilson would untie the ones on the right.

The driver jabbered and gesticulated. He was a small dark man with a worried face, wearing a short jacket over a yellow shirt. Dr. Wilson jabbered and gesticulated back until his white beard quivered. The tying and untying continued until Betsy, putting her head on Miss Wilson's shoulder, collapsed in laughter. Miss Wilson began to laugh, too, and the driver joined in, showing his white teeth. He rolled his eyes at the little professor, shrugged, and slapped the nearest ox.

"You have to be firm with these guides," Dr. Wilson said in a satisfied tone.

Certainly it was desirable to have the curtains open. In Madeira, too, the houses were tinted in rainbow hues. There was a sprinkling of English people on the street, and other Europeans in conventional dress, but as in the Azores there were comely natives, distressing beggars, and crowds of ragged adorable children.

Betsy took picture after picture of the children while she waited for a tram to carry them up the mountain. Each child had a rose or a camellia or a handful of violets, and wanted a penny in trade. One little olive-skinned fellow with a smile like Madeiran sunshine kept climbing up a post to throw roses at Betsy. He would cry with an ingratiating inflection, "Only one penny!" When her pennies were gone and she showed her empty hands, he kept on throwing.

The tram started its climb. Tinted houses draped with flowering vines stood one above the other.

Wedged in, here and there, were native shacks. Fields of sugar cane began, and vineyards, and orchards. Mounting steadily, the tram reached the home of pines, and tangles of wild luxuriant growth broken only by streams and waterfalls.

"Oh, what a beautiful ride!" Betsy exclaimed for the dozenth time as they lunched in the lofty Monte Palace Hotel. The dining room commanded a view of mountainside, city, and sea.

"But wait for the ride down!" Miss Wilson's face shone with pleasure at Betsy's delight.

"I know. Maida told me. We go on a toboggan."

It wasn't, she discovered, a toboggan in the Minnesota sense. It was like a broad settee on runners, cushioned, and extremely comfortable. Barefooted natives stood on either side, holding the contraption by ropes, and at a signal they began to run.

They ran like the wind down the steep precipitous slope. There was no track; they used the narrow cobble-paved street, and Betsy couldn't see how they missed the dogs, and children, and women with jars of water on their heads.

Plastered, flower-covered walls sloped down on either side. Above them the rainbow-hued houses flashed past, and arbors, and gardens. Leaning over the walls and out the windows were lovely laughing girls who pelted the tourists with flowers as they rocketed downward.

Back in Deep Valley, Betsy thought breathlessly, boys and girls were coasting down the Big Hill. They were rushing down an icy road between towering drifts of snow. And here she was sliding down a blooming mountainside under an avalanche of flowers!

"I never did anything so strange, so unusual, so fantastic in my life!" she chattered, climbing out at the foot of the mountain.

"I knew you'd like it," Miss Wilson answered, beaming.

"Very novel, very novel!" Dr. Wilson agreed.

They went shopping, of course. Shopping, Betsy had already discovered, was one of the amusements of traveling. You were supposed to bargain with the merchants, and their prices slid down like the toboggans. With treasures of embroidery and wickerwork for gifts and a string of pink beads for herself, she went triumphantly back to the *Columbic*.

Mr. O'Farrell was nowhere to be seen. He was always busy in port, she had discovered.

"Celeste and I are coming back here, too," Betsy promised herself, and went below to leave her packages.

When she returned to the deck the weather had changed. It was beginning to rain, and the sea was misty and rough. Mr. Chandler joined her. He must be feeling terrible, Betsy thought sympathetically, but he showed no sign of anguish.

He took her arm gaily. "How about a spot of tea, Miss Ray?" And entering the cheerful lounge, where the orchestra was playing and stewards were moving about with appetizing little trays, he murmured, "If only that fellow Glenn will leave us alone!"

Betsy glanced at him sharply. "Of course he won't leave us alone. Why should he?" she asked. She was disgusted with Mr. Chandler. Here Maida was barely out of sight and he was already mooning around her! As soon as she finished tea, Betsy went below to be rid of him.

She couldn't forget Maida as Mr. Chandler apparently had. But even without her, she felt completely happy. Luxuriating again in a hot salt bath, her hair in curlers in preparation for dinner, Betsy reflected on it in perplexity.

She was always happy these days. She seemed to have shed all her bewilderments and perplexities. She wasn't homesick anymore, although she poured out her heart to her family each night in voluminous letters. Bob Barhydt had faded and even the stalwart figure of Joe was growing dim.

She liked shipboard life. She liked everything about it. But best of all—she couldn't deny it—she liked the dinner table!

She was increasingly aware that she looked forward eagerly to dinner. Not because it was the social climax of the day. Not because of the music or because everyone looked festive. It was because of the talk—and Mr. O'Farrell.

Sometimes, she admitted, she felt beyond her depth. The other people were so much older than she, so much more cultured, so much better educated.

Led lightly by Mr. O'Farrell, they talked of music, perhaps. Fortunately Betsy knew a good bit about opera because of Julia. And Julia had made her listen to modern music—Debussy and Ravel and Stravinsky.

But modern art! Betsy hadn't known anyone took that seriously. Talk of an International Art Exhibition in New York had reached Minneapolis, certainly. But Betsy remembered only one echo. "The Nude Descending the Staircase," at which everyone laughed.

And although she seldom missed a change at the local stock company and always saw stars, like Maude Adams and Otis Skinner, when they came to Minneapolis, she couldn't keep up with these people who went to the theatre in New York and London and Paris.

She got on better with history. That had always been a favorite subject in school, and she had read Dumas, Hugo, and Scott. It was fun to sit and argue about Napoleon, or the Crusades, or Mary, Queen of Scots. She did well enough, too, when they discussed

Irish home rule, international peace, President Wilson's policy in Mexico. Her father talked a lot about such things.

Betsy would get excited and flushed and turn her bracelets around and around as she defended her opinions. When Mr. O'Farrell talked, it was like a flame leaping.

"I never knew anyone who could talk like Mr. O'Farrell," Betsy thought. His wit was so nimble; his choice of words, so exact and colorful.

Their conversations weren't always profound. Sometimes, after the table emptied, Betsy told him about the Rays—her father's sandwiches, her red-haired mother's love of fun, Julia's singing, and Margaret's surprising turn of interest from cats and dogs to boys and girls. Mr. O'Farrell liked to hear about them.

He never talked about his own home.

"I wish I knew his story," Betsy thought. "He must have had some sad love affair. Maybe the girl died."

She took more and more pains dressing for dinner.

"How could I ever have thought I was in love with Joe?" she wondered, arranging her hair in three little heart-breaker curls on her neck. "I really prefer a man of the world."

That night the dinner conversation turned to women's suffrage. In the United States the campaign for votes for women had progressed without much violence. In Great Britain, too, at first, the women had merely paraded and made speeches. But then they had started picketing the House of Commons and breaking windows. They actually tried to be sent to jail in order to call attention to their cause by hunger strikes.

"Women," Mr. O'Farrell remarked, "are certainly ingenious at making themselves annoying. One window smasher up for trial kept her back to the judge and sang the 'Marseillaise' all the time he was talking to her."

"Good!" Betsy cried.

The English lady was startled, but not so much so as Mr. O'Farrell.

"You're not a suffragette!" he exclaimed.

"I certainly am."

"I don't believe it."

"Why, of course I am!" She was astonished that anyone could doubt it. "We're having a suffrage parade in Minneapolis this spring. I'd be marching if I were there."

"But you're not a militant?"

Betsy wasn't sure she was a militant, but she wouldn't back down. "I would be if I had to be."

Mr. O'Farrell's gaze turned mocking. "You, a militant!" he said. "You'd get your brick all poised to throw and then ask the nearest man, 'Oh, *should* I, or *shouldn't* I?'"

Betsy flushed crimson. "I would not!"

"You don't need to be ashamed of being feminine."

"I don't think I'm especially feminine. I can barely thread a needle."

"You're feminine! You're pure Victorian! You don't belong to the twentieth century at all, at all."

"Well, I can do the modern dances!" Betsy said indignantly, which made everyone laugh.

"Will you put me down for a Hesitation at the Captain's Ball?" Mr. Glenn asked. Mr. Chandler, who had stopped by her chair, spoke for a tango.

"Alas, all I can do is waltz!" said Mr. O'Farrell. He didn't ask her to save a waltz and Betsy didn't offer one. But she recalled with gratification that she was supposed to waltz exceptionally well.

She was exhilarated by the discussion and went out on deck smiling. A rain-filled wind was blowing now, but she had brought a cape. Wrapping it about her, she stood by the rail and went over in her mind everything Mr. O'Farrell had said to her and she had said to him.

"I wonder why he thinks I'm Victorian. But he said it as though he liked me."

She was annoyed when Mr. Chandler came out, taking her arm in that possessive way he had.

"We're in for a bit of a blow."

"So it seems."

"You're a ripping good sailor, though." He showed his big white teeth in an admiring smile.

"Not like Maida," Betsy answered pointedly.

He brushed that aside.

"How about a walk?"

"No, thank you. I have some post cards I must address."

Disengaging herself, she went into the lounge. But Mr. Glenn and Mr. Burton came up; she didn't write post cards after all. They played three-handed bridge with diverting lack of skill, and Mr. Burton ordered ginger ale, and the two stayed beside her all evening. It served Mr. Chandler right, she thought.

Her spirits were still high when she went below at eleven.

"I'll write my family a wonderful description of that suffrage fracas," she planned.

Miss Wilson, in a dressing gown, was standing at the porthole against which water was swishing heavily.

"This doesn't seem to be fastened properly," she said. "I'm fixing it, though."

"It's a cold night," responded Betsy, hanging up her dress. It would be cozy writing in her little upper bunk. "I'm going to go back to my warm nightie," she added, and pulled the ballooning blue and white flannel over her head.

She washed, brushed her teeth, wound her hair on curlers, and climbed to her lofty perch. Ready to begin her letter, she realized that she had forgotten her cap. Miss Wilson was still at the porthole; she would hand it up, Betsy thought, and leaned out to make the request.

The ship was really pitching now. A suit case had toppled over; the towels on the washstand were swaying; and the boudoir cap, which usually hung on a hook with her bathrobe, had fallen to the floor.

"Miss Wilson," Betsy began, but stopped with a gasp. The porthole had swung open, and a roaring gray torrent rushed in, drenching Miss Wilson and flooding the stateroom with water to a depth of a foot or more.

Miss Wilson ran shouting out into the alleyway, and Betsy stared down in astonishment. Suit cases and bags were afloat. Her boudoir cap was sailing along, trailing its pale pink ribbons, as though on a gay adventure.

"Oh! Oh! And my best brown shoes!" Betsy began to wring her hands.

She heard excited male voices in the corridor. The door burst open, and in came a trail of agitated stewards.

Oh, dear! Betsy thought in panic. No boudoir cap,

and the awful flannel night gown! But, of course, stewards were used to seeing ladies in queer outfits . . .

An angry, all-too-familiar Irish voice froze her in horror! Mr. O'Farrell strode in, so handsome in his dress uniform with its swagger short jacket that Betsy could hardly bear it. She looked at him aghast.

Mr. O'Farrell's face twitched. "Miss Wilson has gone down to Number 87 to sleep. You must go, too," he said.

"I'll stay right here," said Betsy.

"You can't do that."

She tried for a crushing dignity. "My bunk is perfectly dry."

"It is impossible for you to stay. The men will be working here till morning."

"But I don't know where to find my bathrobe or slippers!" Tears rose and almost spilled over. She pointed an outraged finger. "*There's* my cap!"

"Get a wrap and go!" said Mr. O'Farrell, and he motioned the stewards to leave and went out himself, very quickly, shutting the door.

Betsy climbed down, sniffing back tears. She caught the boudoir cap, but it was too wet to wear. Her slippers swam beyond her reach. The bathrobe, still on its hook, was soaked around the bottom, but she put it on anyway and clutched both bathrobe and night gown up to her knees.

The water was icy around her bare feet, but she

couldn't resist stopping to look in the mirror.

"Oh, oh!" she moaned, recoiling. Wading to the door, she fled down the crowded corridor to Number 87 and Miss Wilson's arms.

"Why, why did I have to be wearing this hideous flannel night gown?" she wept.

"It was very sensible, dear, on such a cold night!"

"But why couldn't I have been wearing a pink silk night gown? Why couldn't I have had my cap on? Oh, these ghastly curlers!" Betsy was laughing now through her tears. "I'm *not* going to see Mr. O'Farrell again! Not ever! Not even if I have to jump off the boat!"

"Don't talk such nonsense!" said Miss Wilson, and hugged her warmly, and kissed her. "The stewardess has gone for hot tea, for both of us, and all our clothes will be sent to the tailor for pressing. Everything will be shipshape by morning, she says . . ."

"Morning!" Betsy shuddered, and they both shook with laughter. "I won't go to breakfast! I absolutely won't!"

But she did, and Mr. O'Farrell strode in, smiling broadly.

"Do you know," he said, as he unfolded his napkin, "last night proved to me the truth of a French proverb. 'Even in the misfortunes of our friends we find a certain pleasure.'"

"What do you mean by that?" asked Betsy.

He poured his tea zestfully. "That stateroom was the drollest sight of my whole life! You were staring over the bunk, looking as though you'd seen a banshee, and down below, shoes and stockings and bags were floating around, and a little cap sailing like a lacy frigate . . ." Mr. O'Farrell choked with laughter.

"I don't see what's so funny," Betsy said, trying not to laugh herself, "about poor Miss Wilson being soaked, and both of us being hustled down cold halls . . ."

"Come on with the militancy!" Mr. O'Farrell cried.

The table was uproariously merry. Such wild tales were abroad that Betsy almost came to believe she had floated through the porthole onto an angry sea and been rescued from direst peril by the Captain, no less.

Mr. O'Farrell said that the Minneapolis papers would probably run extras with her picture.

"'Minnesota belle in flood! Minded loss of cap more than salt water.'"

Catching Miss Wilson's eye, Betsy laughed and blushed.

6

The Captain's Ball

MR. O'FARRELL HAD SEEN her with her hair in curlers and he still liked her, Betsy thought joyfully, coming out from breakfast. The sea was smiling today. Rosettes of foam, scattered all over its surface, twinkled in the sunshine.

It was Sunday, and she attended Divine Service again. She enjoyed it, although the clergyman always prayed for King George and Queen Mary, King Victor Emmanuel and Queen Elena, before he got around to the President of the United States!

Mr. Chandler continued to dog her footsteps. No snubbing deterred him, and Betsy was furious. Why, Maida had really liked him! She had wondered if her mother would mind if they got married! And now he was showing his big white teeth and tossing his wavy head, trying to charm her, Betsy.

He was always slamming Mr. O'Farrell.

"A deuced charming chap! Of course, he isn't an officer of the line."

"What do you mean by that?"

"Why, a purser just keeps the accounts, attends to freight and tickets! Sort of like a clerk."

"He wasn't much like a clerk in South Africa!" Betsy thought indignantly, but she didn't say it aloud. She wasn't going to discuss Mr. O'Farrell with Mr. Chandler!

She was delighted when his duties called him away, and she had a leisurely, lovely afternoon. She opened some of her steamer letters—she was three behind on Bob's daily epistles—and read cozily while Mrs. Sims chuckled over *Daddy-Long-Legs* and Mrs. Cheney perused *The Inside of the Cup*.

Part of the time she lay back in her chair and watched the water. Twenty-one from thirty-seven made sixteen! Was sixteen years' difference in age too much? she wondered dreamily. She didn't think so. Husbands were proud of young wives.

"Faith, you're hardly more than a child!" she heard Mr. O'Farrell saying tenderly.

His word would be her law. She would listen while he talked with her eyes raised to his in adoration—almost.

"What a sweet ending!" Mrs. Sims remarked, closing *Daddy-Long-Legs* with a long, romantic sigh. Now *that* heroine, Betsy remembered, had married an older man!

After tea she went to the upper deck to watch the sunset. The western clouds were golden as the sun sank, but afterward they changed to copper-color and then to raspberry pink. She rested her arms on the railing and gazed.

Mr. O'Farrell came up behind her. "And do you see Proteus rising from the sea?" he asked.

Betsy turned a glowing face; she loved the Wordsworth sonnet. "The world *is* too much with us. I don't see half enough sunsets and sunrises, and I adore them both."

"I'm starting a little list of things Miss Ray adores: islands, balconies, sunrises. What else now?"

"Waltzing," said Betsy artfully, for it had been announced that the Captain's Ball would be held tomorrow night after they left Gibraltar. Mr. O'Farrell had once told her that he waltzed. But Mr. Chandler bounded up inopportunely, and Mr. O'Farrell strolled away.

That evening a crowd was singing on the upper deck—Mr. Chandler next to Betsy of course. The stars were brighter than she had ever seen them, although they were familiar stars. She saw the Pleiades, in a dainty sisterly group.

Betsy loved to sing, and relaxed happily as they went from "Annie Laurie" and "Tavern in the Town," through "Down by the Old Mill Stream" and "Shine on Harvest Moon," to the newer song hits, "Peg o' My Heart," "Trail of the Lonesome Pine," and "Giannina Mia."

Surprisingly, Mr. O'Farrell joined them.

"And why not some Irish melodies, if I may be so bold?" he asked, resting lightly against a tier of lifeboats. Moonlight outlined his nautical cap, his slim uniformed figure.

They gave him "Kathleen Mavourneen," in parts.

"Would you be knowing 'The Harp That Once Through Tara's Halls'?" He rolled the *r* in "harp" and "Tara."

No one knew it except Betsy, who had sung it with Tacy long ago. But Betsy didn't mind singing it alone, although she wasn't a real singer, like Julia.

❦ 95 ❧

> *"The harp that once through Tara's halls*
> *The soul of music shed,*
> *Now hangs as mute on Tara's walls*
> *As if that soul were fled . . ."*

When the last note died away, Mr. O'Farrell touched her lightly on the shoulder. "It's a pretty good Irishman you are," he said, departing.

Gibraltar was overshadowed by the Captain's Ball. Britain's Rock was high, it was mighty, but it couldn't compare—for Betsy and the other young people who had slipped into Maida's place—with the only real ball of the voyage, scheduled for that evening.

There had been casual waltzing, fox trotting, and Castle Walking, but this was to be a real ball, with programs and everyone in formal dress. And next day part of the company would leave the ship at Algiers.

Of course, it was exciting to see Gibraltar. The *Columbic* was in the Strait when Betsy came rushing up, camera in hand. Mr. Chandler, lying in wait as usual, took her forward. The huge familiar Rock loomed against the horizon. Back of it curved the coast of Spain, and opposite ran the misty shoreline of Tangier. Europe and Africa, making a pathway to the Mediterranean Sea!

"Oh! Oh!" Betsy stared. The Rock looked just like the pictures, but something was missing.

Mr. Chandler chuckled. "I suppose you expect to see that dashed advertisement there."

That was it, Betsy admitted to herself. But she gave him a crushing look. "I was thinking," she answered with dignity, "about the Pillars of Hercules."

They had discussed them last night. Mr. O'Farrell had remarked that the great Rock and its companion on the opposite side of the Strait were said to have been tossed up by Hercules.

"He was looking for the oxen of Geryon!" Betsy had cried. (There was some advantage, after all, in knowing the classics.) "It was during one of the Twelve Labors!"

The table had tried then to remember the Twelve. With much merriment, they had managed to name eight.

Mr. Chandler brought her back to Gibraltar. It was a British fortress and Crown colony, he explained; captured from the Spanish in 1704. They could see the city now, glittering white against the Rock.

Presently the *Columbic* passengers were on their way, in a big launch that was half fancy-work shop. Shawls, embroideries, drawn work, and hand-made lace were laid out for sale by importunate vendors.

"But don't buy a thing until you get ashore!" Mrs. Sims warned. "Shopping in Gibraltar is an occupation for the Gods!"

Ships from every corner of the world brought treasures to this crossroads port.

Barely off the launch, they were caught in a babel of beseeching tongues. Arabs held up wicker bags of tangerines and strawberries. Dusky children lifted flat baskets of roses, pansies, daffodils. And swarthy merchants, in open-fronted shops, flung out dazzling wares—shawls and silks, precious stones and Oriental scents, carved ivory and cedar.

The ladies from the *Columbic* were bargaining furiously. Taylor and Rosa, who had been permitted by their mistresses to come ashore, snatched at Malta lace collars. Betsy bought gifts with reckless abandon, and for herself a pair of jade and silver bracelets.

"They're probably not real jade; they only cost sixty cents. But aren't they ducky, Miss Wilson?"

She would wear them tonight, she planned, with her maid-of-honor dress, at the Captain's Ball.

Because of the ball she did not regret that they had only two hours ashore. She and the Wilsons had time to drive, in a shabby little carriage with a fringed top, through the city and up to the fortifications.

Betsy looked eagerly around the crowded streets. There were Englishmen, Spaniards, Portuguese, Japanese, Chinese.

"Othello!" she whispered, squeezing Miss Wilson's

arm, at her first sight of a Moor in a robe and turban.

In spite of the polyglot population and the semi-tropical vegetation, the place seemed very English. Statues of Wellington and Queen Victoria. Burly policemen. Rosy nursemaids. Tall, well-built soldiers pacing before the sentry boxes or lounging around the barracks that grew more frequent as they climbed the hill. An Anglo-Saxon air of propriety hung about the houses. These were of the Spanish type, but they looked English just the same.

Betsy remarked on the absence of beggars.

"They are allowed only on Friday and Saturday," Dr. Wilson explained.

"That shows the British influence, probably," Miss Wilson observed. "But this horse certainly doesn't."

Their horse was so pitifully thin and the road so nearly vertical that the Wilsons and Betsy got out and walked.

At the fortifications, Betsy surrendered her camera and they acquired a guide.

The Rock was tunneled out and the openings bristled with cannon. The British could certainly command the Strait in case of war, Betsy thought. But there was never going to be another war, so why all this fuss? She went back to the carriage where it was pleasant sitting in the sunshine, thinking about the ball.

The ball, when they were afloat again, triumphed over the Mediterranean, although this was blue, as reported. It was cornflower blue, and so was the sky, with boats spreading snowy wings against the brilliance. But Betsy was longing for the evening.

"I want to get those curlers out of Mr. O'Farrell's mind," Betsy confided to Miss Wilson when, at last, she was dressing for dinner. Miss Wilson was assisting. It was almost like having Julia to help her, Betsy said. She looked around.

"Where are Margaret, and the cat?"

And Miss Wilson laughed, for she knew the Ray family now. She knew how Margaret, pussy in arms, used to watch her older sisters get ready for a dance.

Betsy's hair was dressed, hiding her forehead and ears under soft shining loops. She shook pink powder on a chamois skin and rubbed it over her face while Miss Wilson watched with interest. Miss Wilson never used powder, pink or white.

Under a frothy petticoat, Betsy's legs shone elegantly. (A pair of silk stockings had been in Julia's package today.) She slipped into green satin slippers, and Miss Wilson lifted the maid-of-honor dress carefully over her head.

It was a beautiful dress—filmy green chiffon over pink, with roses sewn into the bodice. The sleeves were short, ideal for her new bracelets. She wore them both on one arm, and they matched her jade and silver ring and the jade and silver pendant Julia had given her for a maid-of-honor gift.

After spraying perfume on her hair as usual, Betsy looked into the mirror and was glad—since only actresses used rouge—that her cheeks always flushed for a party. Assuming a blasé expression, she sank into the debutante slouch and revolved languidly.

"Don't I have an indefinable Paris air?"

Miss Wilson chuckled. "You look very nice."

Everyone looked nice! The English lady had bared her scrawny shoulders in a jet-trimmed gown. Miss Wilson was winning in prim black silk with a cameo in a nest of soft lace at her throat. Dr. Wilson and Mr. Glenn were wearing evening clothes, and Mr. O'Farrell was resplendent. Above the swagger dress uniform, his hair shone like satin.

Talk was all of the ball. Mr. Glenn reminded Betsy of their Hesitation. Mr. Chandler came up to hang over her chair and ask how many dances he could have. As many as possible, he pleaded, and one of them must be a waltz. Mr. O'Farrell said nothing. Leaning his head on one hand, a cigarette in the other, he smiled musingly.

Leaving the table, Betsy managed a gay hint. "My waltzes are going fast."

It didn't work.

"I'll not be spoiling your evening with my old-fashioned dancing," he replied. She smiled back (like a Cheshire cat, she told herself) to cover her disappointment.

The deck was hung with the flags of all nations. Red and green electric lights glimmered. The floor was waxed. There were cozy corners for fussers, and chairs at one end for lookers-on. The Mesdames Sims and Cheney, and Miss Wilson, sat there, self-appointed chaperones for Betsy.

The musicians started tuning up. They plunged with hearty jollity into "Over the Waves." Betsy danced with Dr. Wilson, who was as light as a puppet on strings—a puppet of a little professor with mustaches and a trembling spike of beard.

Dr. Wilson yielded her to Mr. Glenn, to Mr. Chandler, to Mr. Burton, and others. The sea was like glass, and moonlight poured over the world. In spite of Mr. O'Farrell Betsy couldn't be unhappy. She floated effortlessly, the skirt of the maid-of-honor dress caught lightly in her hand.

She loved the new dances: the graceful Boston Dip, the demure Hesitation, the rollicking Turkey Trot, and the absurd stiff-legged Castle Walk. Mr. Glenn, pale and slender though he was, proved to be marvelously adept. Mr. Chandler, too, was excellent, although he held her too tightly.

"'Peg of my heart, I love you . . .'" he sang meaningfully.

She was taught the new Marjory Step by a New Yorker who said he knew the Castles. He studied Betsy through half-closed lids as they danced, and told her that she was a fascinating type.

"A tropical beauty!"

A tropical beauty from Minneapolis! Betsy thought, wishing Mr. O'Farrell could hear.

Mr. O'Farrell, she noticed, was being charming to the chaperones. She glanced at him now and then during the intermission, when sandwiches, lemonade, and chocolate ice cream were served. He was talking with Mrs. Main-Whittaker, who had doubled her feathers in honor of the ball. She wore a low-cut gown of raspberry pink.

Dancing began again, and now Betsy saw him watching her. Perhaps, she thought later, he noticed that she was a good dancer. Perhaps he noticed that she hadn't smiled or waved at him as usual. At any rate when the orchestra began the rolling opening phrases of "The Beautiful Blue Danube," he made his way to where she stood with Mr. Chandler to whom she was engaged for the dance.

Mr. O'Farrell offered his arm.

"Isn't this my waltz, Miss Ray?"

Betsy's face broke into joy. "Why, yes! I believe it is!"

Mr. Chandler was very angry. "Dash it all!" he cried. "What do you mean . . ." But his furious voice died away.

Betsy, in Mr. O'Farrell's arms, was dancing to the Blue Danube.

They didn't talk. Betsy didn't want to talk. His dancing *was* a little old-fashioned, but that didn't matter. He was dancing with *her*!

Over his shoulder, as the music wove its rhythmical enchantment, she looked at the golden moon. She looked down the quivering golden avenue it made across the water, and it almost seemed as though they were dancing on that avenue, circling and swaying to the cadence of the waltz.

But the music ended. As it died away, Mr. O'Farrell said, "Thank you, Miss Ray! Faith, for a few minutes there, I thought I was young again!"

He kissed her hand. Betsy had never had her hand kissed before, and she was transfixed into silence.

Mr. O'Farrell bowed and left, and the wrathful bulk of Mr. Chandler immediately filled his place. Betsy dreamily gave him the next dance, although it had been promised to Mr. Glenn. It didn't matter. Nothing in the evening mattered now.

"I believe, I believe, I'm in love with Mr. O'Farrell," she thought.

"What the deuce did you do that for?" Mr. Chandler

demanded, backing Betsy around in the long-legged Castle Walk.

"Do what?" asked Betsy, gazing at the moon.

"Give my dance to that fellow O'Farrell."

"Was that your dance?" Betsy was still circling and swaying on that trembling golden path along the sea.

"You know deuced well it was my dance! See here! Will you listen to me for a moment?"

She shook herself out of a vision in which she was pouring coffee from a silver pot at Mr. O'Farrell's glittering table. She was definitely Mrs. O'Farrell, and the table wasn't in the dining saloon of the *Columbic*. It was in London, or Paris . . . or Dublin, maybe.

"Certainly," she said, and led the way to the railing. She was glad to be able to stop dancing. It was a . . . a desecration, almost . . . to dance any more tonight.

Mr. Chandler objected. "Why, we can dance! I don't have anything *that* important to tell you."

"Oh," said Betsy irritatingly. "I thought you did! I thought you had some great and important statement to make."

"Like what? A proposal, I suppose."

"Why not? Don't you propose to every girl you rush?"

Her teasing was light. She was too happy to be cruel, even for Maida's sake. But it seemed to impress

Mr. Chandler profoundly.

He turned and looked at her. He riveted his eyes on her with grimness and power.

"I see," he said. "I see it all!"

"But what is all?" asked Betsy, laughing.

"Why you've been treating me so. You think I've been fickle."

His expression softening, he drew her tenderly from the railing toward one of the dark corners arranged for fussers. "A man wouldn't be fickle to a girl like you. I know what you're thinking, though, and that explains a lot. I wondered how you could cut a dance with me for an old married man with five children."

"Why, I didn't . . ." Betsy started to say, but she stopped.

Mr. Chandler was curious. "You knew, didn't you, that O'Farrell is married?"

Betsy's world was whirling, but instinctively she hung on to her pride. She heard a voice, still teasing, coming out of the cozy corner in which they were now seated.

"Of course! We girls always assume that you men are married. How many children do *you* have?"

"I'm single. And I want you to get it out of your head that there was anything serious about that little flirtation with your friend."

"You did call her a Christmas angel though!" Betsy heard a tone of sweet reproach. She heard herself say next, "Listen to that tango! Let's try it! If your tango is as good as your Boston . . ."

"Did you really like my Boston?" He stood up exultantly. She was dancing again, but only on the S.S. *Columbic,* not on an avenue of moonlight any more.

"You leave your family behind when you start out to travel," Mr. O'Farrell had told her.

7
The Diner d'Adieu

ALGIERS WAS THE FIRST PLACE they visited to which Betsy did not wish to return. It was beautiful enough at first sight, spread out on a half moon of hills in the blazing sunshine . . . white, flat-roofed houses, the dome of a mosque hinting of the mysterious Orient, palm trees in green rows. And the modern section was a perfect little Paris, Mrs. Cheney told her as they went ashore. But Algiers frightened Betsy; it made her long for Minnesota.

In fairness it should be stated that she was in very low spirits. She was chagrined, furious with herself. Getting a crush on the first attractive man she met! Married at that! Five children!

Girls were always getting crushes, of course. People were amused by such affairs, but they weren't funny, really. They hurt.

"I feel as though I were coming down with the grippe," Betsy thought. But she wasn't, she knew, coming down with anything. She was getting over something.

In their stateroom after the dance she had told Miss Wilson merrily about Mr. O'Farrell's marital state. And up in her bunk she had confided the same news to her family. She worked rather hard over that letter.

"I guess my letters so far have had a decidedly O'Farrellish flavor. Don't worry! I haven't lost my young heart, but my wits have certainly been sharpened.

"He's thirty-seven years old and terribly attractive. (That fatal Irish charm, tell Tacy!) He's witty and full of blarney, with a dimple in his chin. He's traveled everywhere, was decorated in South Africa, speaks French, wears evening clothes just right, and knows how to manage waiters. Absolutely cosmopolitan!

"And the first little lesson I've learned on my travels, I've learned from him. Hold your breaths now. He's never told me he's married!!! He doesn't know I know it, but Mr. Chandler mentioned it tonight.

"The lesson? Not all married men are middle-aged and fatherly."

That had a fine light touch, she thought.

And sailing to Algiers next day over a sea that seemed spread with cloth of gold, she had covered her misery with gaiety. She had roamed the ship in carefree company, trying out new dance steps on the promenade deck, flirting with Mr. Chandler. Especially at luncheon, she had been all vivacity and sprightliness.

Mr. O'Farrell told of meeting ex-President Theodore Roosevelt, and that started the table talking of famous people. The English lady had seen Lillie Langtry. Mr. Glenn had glimpsed the aged Longfellow. Miss Wilson, as a little girl, had presented a bouquet to Patti, and her brother had viewed President Lincoln in his casket.

"Well, I've seen Carrie Nation," Betsy said. And the famous termagant who invaded saloons with a hatchet made more of a sensation even than the Jersey Lily.

"Where?"

"Oh, she was out in Minnesota smashing up a few saloons!"

"What did she look like?"

"She wore a funny little bonnet and a shawl and spectacles. My friends, Tacy and Tib, and I were walking along the street when we heard mirrors cracking and bottles and glasses crashing, and out she came!"

"Did she have her hatchet?" Mr. Glenn asked eagerly.

"She shook it at us."

"Now, now!" Mr. O'Farrell admonished.

"I admit," said Betsy, "she was shaking it at everyone, but she looked so fierce I was sure she had us in mind."

"What happened next?"

"Our fathers found us," Betsy answered sadly. "We were only seven." And Mr. O'Farrell shook his head at her, laughing.

"Oh, Miss Ray! I derive such exhilar-r-ration from your company!"

Betsy gave him an enigmatic smile.

For Algiers she wore her suit. The red and green outfit admired by Mr. O'Farrell wasn't citified enough for a French colonial capital, she decided. Besides, it made her look too artless, too much like a girl who didn't know a married man when she saw one.

The blue suit with its cutaway coat and draped skirt rustling over taffeta seemed much more sophisticated, especially when she added a blue hat with a tall green "stick-up" on it, and her best kid gloves.

At first the city seemed very French. It showed a formal square, wide tree-lined avenues full of carriages and automobiles, and on the sidewalks, under awnings, little tables where people sat drinking wine or coffee. She saw Frenchwomen, chic on high heels; Frenchmen with tiny mustaches; French officers in ravishing uniforms of soft horizon blue.

"Why, it *is* a little Paris!" Betsy exclaimed, looking around.

But she soon became aware that it was the Orient, too.

She saw robed men in turbans. There had been a scattering of them in Gibraltar, but here they were everywhere. She saw her first veiled women!

Waiting for a tram (as streetcars seemed to be called) that would take them up to the old Moorish fortress, Betsy saw Moors, Arabs, Spaniards, Biblical-looking Jews in robes—but the veiled women were most fascinating of all.

They wore long, loose white bloomers, short jackets, and veils covering all their faces but their eyes. Even girl children were shrouded like that.

"The poor little things!" Betsy cried.

Some of the women were tattooed between their eyebrows. Betsy thought it was a pathetic attempt at adornment, but Miss Wilson said it was a mark of caste. Some of them stained their fingernails bright red.

"That's rather pretty," Betsy remarked.

At the Fort, they joined a group from the *Columbic* and secured an English-speaking guide for the trip through the Arab quarter. This was quite unsafe for tourists alone, they were told. Mrs. Main-Whittaker was in the party and Betsy met her for the first time.

The author was wearing a red suit. She loved bright colors, and was undeterred by the fact that she was short and stout. Her red plumes were even higher than Betsy's "stick-up." She was loaded with jewelry and moved in a cloud of perfume.

She talked all the time. Had Joe liked her? Betsy wondered, trying to see her with his eyes as the party descended into the native quarter. Soon the squalor, the misery, the eeriness of the Kasbah reduced even Mrs. Main-Whittaker to silence.

The tourists were on foot, for the passage was too narrow for a carriage. There were a few starved-looking donkeys around, and a good many starved-looking people. Sometimes the narrow street was only a flight of steps, lined by ancient houses which all but met overhead. It had a twilight dimness although the time was early afternoon.

The people lived in what seemed to be little dens scooped out of the walls. Some were quite open, so that you could look in. Others had doors bearing tiny iron hands on them—for luck, the guide said.

"Luck!" ejaculated Betsy, for it was almost incomprehensible that human beings should live in these unlighted, evil-smelling, filthy caverns and still hope for luck.

"Yes," said the guide. "And if they can't afford the iron hands, they paint some on the door."

Most of the people were so ragged, dirty, and emaciated that it was painful to look at them. The children, especially, almost broke Betsy's heart. They were pitiful, little, dirty, tangled creatures, some bearing still smaller children on their backs.

Men wearing flat round hats with tassels were smoking Turkish water pipes, or sat in circles drinking small cups of black coffee. A public letter writer was ensconced in a doorway surrounded with maps and papers. For a franc he would write a letter for you, the guide said. There were bakeshops where circular loaves were piled in the dust, fly-haunted meat and fruit shops.

"I don't think I can ever eat again!" Mrs. Sims whispered.

What made the awful place still worse was that

everybody seemed to hate them. These people gave the visitors no sunny smiles or pleasant greetings such as had been general in the Azores and Madeira. The veiled women flashed hatred from their dark eyes, and the unveiled women motioned the visitors furiously not to look their way. All except the beggars drew away with sullen looks and mutterings.

"Why do they hate us so?" asked Betsy, almost trembling.

"We're aliens and infidels," Mrs. Main-Whittaker replied.

And perhaps, thought Betsy, holding the skirt of her suit above the refuse as she picked her way downstairs, they didn't like well-fed, well-dressed, comfortable-looking travelers coming to stare. But if such people didn't come—how would anyone find out that the misery existed?

The beggars were crowding about them now. Betsy had seen them first on the wharves among the clamorous guides and vendors. They had been bad enough there, but they were frightful now as they pressed close, screeching, whining, and holding out their hands.

Betsy held fast to Miss Wilson's valiant arm. She tried to think about Minnesota, about Deep Valley where she had grown up, the river, and the peaceful sunny hills. And at last they came out of the Kasbah!

No, Betsy didn't want to return to Algiers. She told Mr. O'Farrell so at dinner, where she was quieter than usual, thinking of the beggars and those unsmiling children carrying smaller children on their backs.

A few of the *Columbic*'s passengers had left and some new people had come aboard. One was a friend of the English lady, a Mr. Brown, but he sat at the Captain's table and Betsy did not meet him. He was a tweedy, undistinguished-looking young man, very thin and partly bald. Later she saw him circling the deck and she liked his swinging easy gait. He carried a cane which he swung in rhythm. He wasn't unattractive, but Betsy wasn't sorry they had not been introduced.

"Men!" she thought.

The first lesson she had learned on her travels had left her feeling cynical.

Dressing for the *Diner d'Adieu* was no such pleasure as dressing for the Captain's Ball had been. She didn't even begin until the bugle sounded. Then she jerked out a yellow satin formal. It was old, but it had made a hit at plenty of college parties.

As dinner began she had only that false sprightliness that had been with her since Gibraltar. But the atmosphere of the dining saloon was irresistibly convivial. The musicians played with spirit: Waldteufel

waltzes, the *Pink Lady* music, the "Pizzicato Polka" . . .
And the nine-course dinner was elegantly described,
with a sprinkling of French, on a souvenir menu.
What fun to send it home!

She would underline her own choices: *hors d'oeuvres
variés; consommé aux pain grillé; turbotin au cham-
bertin*; calves' head *en tortue*; forequarter of lamb,
mint sauce; roast guinea chicken *anglaise*; dressed
salad; and the dessert—it was her favorite, *pouding à
la St. Cloud*! Then would come coffee and cheese, of
course. Betsy's spirits began to rise in spite of her.

People went skylarking from table to table. The
Captain proposed toasts, and so did Mr. O'Farrell.
And each table had its own nonsensical toasts:

"To Miss Wilson, heroine of The Flood!"

"To our Militant Suffragette!"

"To Carrie Nation!"

They drank them in *punch à la Romaine*.

Mr. O'Farrell looked at Betsy now and then with a
slightly puzzled expression. He probably noticed that
she seemed different, she thought. Or perhaps he was
surprised that she was having so much fun?

"Probably he's used to girls who find out he's married, and are heartbroken about it. Well, he can see
that I don't care!" And Betsy grew gayer and more
audacious all the time.

He was chaffing her about saying something

unkind to him after the flood.

"It isn't true. I never said anything unkind to you or about you either . . . oh, yes, I did once!"

"You did?" He was almost startled into seriousness.

"It was in a letter home," said Betsy.

"By all the saints I'll know what it was!"

"By all the saints you won't!"

She could see that he was really curious, and it was a satisfaction to be provoking.

"Miss Ray," he pleaded. "I asked the chef for this *pouding à la St. Cloud* just for you. I've noticed that it was your favorite sweet. Shouldn't such devotion be rewarded?"

"Oh, well!" said Betsy. "In that case . . . may I borrow your pencil?"

She turned over her menu card and wrote:

"And the first little lesson I've learned on my travels, I've learned from him. Not all married men are middle-aged and fatherly."

While he read it she looked at the ceiling and her color rose until even her ears were red. She didn't look down until his laugh burst out. It was a tremendous shout, and all of a sudden, Betsy felt elated and triumphant. He kept on laughing while the table smiled in bewildered sympathy, but at last he wiped his eyes.

"Ladies," he said, "and gentlemen, too, of course!

Won't you do me the honor of coming to me cabin? I'd like to brew you some of me own coffee, which is superb, if you will par-r-don me saying so. And I wish to show Miss Ray a picture of the future King of Ireland."

"The future King of Ireland?" Miss Wilson asked, startled.

"Dennis Leo O'Farrell, aged four, and said to be the image of his father."

He was, too, Betsy discovered when the group was gathered merrily in Mr. O'Farrell's cabin watching his ritual of coffee-making. He was an enchanting little boy. Chubby, of course, but he had that laughing light in his eyes.

"Faith, and he's a spalpeen!" Mr. O'Farrell frowned at the radiant Betsy. "And so are you!" he added.

Mr. O'Farrell, Betsy decided, was a dear. After the party was over, she paused on deck to think about him. The S.S. *Columbic* was churning softly through the mild dark.

He had taught her a lesson, all right. She would watch out for married men.

"But he did more than teach me . . . that skim milk masquerades as cream."

He had awakened her interest in so many things—faraway places and strange languages, folklore and legends, pictures and books she might never have heard of, beauties of every sort. She would never forget him, although she wasn't in love with him any more—at all, at all.

It was strange, Betsy thought, how your estimates of people changed. Bob Barhydt seemed like a callow adolescent since she had known Mr. O'Farrell. Joe Willard stood up, though. No one could make Joe seem callow although he was young and had never traveled beyond Boston.

She wished she hadn't lost Joe.

"That was the most foolish thing I ever did," Betsy said in a small whisper to the rain and flying spray. "I wonder . . . . if I wrote him . . ."

But she knew she wouldn't. She was too stubborn.

8
Travel Is Broadening

IN THE BAY OF NAPLES a hateful sensation which Betsy had almost forgotten began to creep back into her body. It was that feeling of forlornness, of not belonging, of "What am I doing here anyhow?" that she had felt when the *Columbic* set sail.

At first she laid it to the weather, for a dreary drizzle had begun. It was hard, too, to part with so many friends. What made it harder was their overflowing kindness. They all gave her calling cards, and Betsy offered her own in return. She seldom used them at home, but she had found out that they were important when traveling.

Mrs. Sims and Mrs. Cheney wrote down their Boston addresses and asked her to come and visit them sometime. Taylor and Rosa shook her hand, and Rosa had a little gift for her—a silk handkerchief with the Rock of Gibraltar on it.

Betsy promised them post cards of Minnehaha Falls. And Mr. Glenn asked for one, and so did the English lady. She invited Betsy to have tea with her in London. Betsy felt ashamed, for she had barely been aware of the lady's name. It was Mrs. Trevelyan.

Hardest of all was parting with the Wilsons, who were touring Italy and Greece before starting northward. She had grown fond of the humorless, kind, little professor. And as for Miss Wilson . . .

"Why, I love her!" Betsy realized in surprise.

They suggested again that she join them for some travel, and Betsy felt very different about the proposal than she had felt in Boston. She was even tempted to telegraph Miss Surprise that she was staying in Italy now. But she refused to yield to this unvalorous impulse.

"I'll write you from Munich, though. I'll write to

you at the *Casa delle Rose d'Oro*." That was the Wilsons' first mailing address, the House of the Yellow Roses in Venice.

She promised them, and half a dozen others, to report her arrival in Munich. She was given instructions about changing money and getting through customs. Dr. Wilson was wiring a Thomas Cook agent to meet her in Genoa.

"And Mr. Brown can help her," Mrs. Trevelyan said, referring to the thin young man who had come aboard at Algiers. "He's going on to Genoa. Where is Mr. Brown?"

Everyone looked around for him, but he had already gone ashore.

Most of those who were continuing to Genoa fared forth with mackintoshes and umbrellas to see Naples.

"See Naples and die!" they reminded Betsy brightly, but she felt as though, in her case, that would be all too true.

"We could go to the movies," Mr. Burton urged, but she shook her head.

The deserted ship was uninviting; it was taking on coal. Betsy undressed, piled into bed under warm blankets, and rang for a pot of hot tea. She remembered that she had some steamer letters left and started to read them, but they made her want to cry. She opened Julia's present for the day, and that did make her cry. It was a small silk American flag! Just as twilight fell, she saw a great steamer, blazing with lights and flying those same dear Stars and Stripes, move majestically out of the harbor, bound for home. Home!

"Life is just too short," wept Betsy, "to spend a year away from home!"

But she felt different the next day.

The rain had stopped, and sunshine was pouring golden warmth over the world. On the upper deck, she got wind-blown and freckled, gazing at the Bay of Naples.

It looked startlingly familiar. The sky and water were as brightly blue, the amphitheatre of hills as richly green, the city as white and shining, as in all the pictures. And there was Vesuvius, its summit wreathed in smoke!

"Oh, I wish I had time to see Pompeii! But I'll be coming to Europe often." She saw herself this morning as a woman of the world who would travel and write for many years before she married—if she married at all.

Mrs. Trevelyan's Mr. Brown strolled past, swinging his cane. He was almost good-looking, in spite of being bald. His tweed suit, although rumpled, sat jauntily on his bony shoulders. He gave Betsy a friendly look, but she didn't respond with her usual ready smile.

"Married, no doubt!" she thought tartly.

Mr. Chandler and Mr. Burton encamped on either side of her. As the *Columbic* sailed out of the famous bay, they pointed out the shore where St. Paul had landed in Italy, the hillside where Virgil was buried, the island on which Cicero had visited Brutus after the murder of Caesar.

The great names brought back hushed churches, dusty classrooms, a red morocco set of *Stoddard's Travel Lectures* in the bookcase at home. But here, today, the water rippled and gleamed; gulls were swooping; sails were bellying in the wind. It was alive! . . . and it had been like this for Cicero and Virgil and St. Paul. They had been alive! Betsy felt as though she had made a great discovery.

The olive-green islands showed shining towns, or melancholy ruins. The loveliest one bore only a castlelike building set in thick-clustering trees. She told Mr. O'Farrell about that one at luncheon where they had the table to themselves.

"Celeste and I are going to come back and stay there some time," she informed him.

"I hardly think you'd enjoy it," he answered. "The residents are all life convicts . . . . the murderers of Italy."

"Oh, dear!" said Betsy with a laugh.

Mr. O'Farrell didn't laugh. "Miss Ray," he said gloomily, "you don't know enough about the world to be traveling around all alone."

"Why, Mr. O'Farrell!" She was disappointed in him. "I'm twenty-one years old."

"You're very young for twenty-one. Besides, you're too trustful."

Betsy glanced at him quickly. Was this a joke? She decided that it wasn't, for he looked really troubled, brooding over a cigarette.

"I don't see what could happen to me," she answered patiently. "I won't speak to strangers, or do anything I shouldn't. I intend to behave in Munich just as I did in Minneapolis. But if it will make you feel any better, I am going to a friend of my sister's. She's promised to look after me until I'm settled."

"Faith, and I'm glad to hear that!"

"The only bad thing about traveling alone," Betsy confided, "is getting homesick."

Mr. O'Farrell looked up. "Do you get homesick?"

"Terribly."

"What do you do about it?"

"Just put up with it until it goes away."

He shook his head. "She's a naive intrepid spirit," he remarked as though to someone else.

"I wish to goodness," Betsy said with irritation, "that people would stop calling me naive!"

Then Mr. O'Farrell's face crinkled into its charming smile. "Miss Betsy," he said, "you're a very winsome girl!"

The rest of the day had a hurried unsettled feeling. She said good-by to everyone she met. She thanked the stewards and stewardesses, and gave her modest tips, and Mr. O'Farrell asked her to come to his office, to exchange some American money for Italian *lire* and *centesimi*. When this was done, he smiled delightedly.

"I have a gift for you," he said, and spread a map of Europe across his desk. In one corner was a picture of the newest steamship of the line, a monster of forty-six thousand tons. Across the top was printed in red letters, "Six days from Munich to New York."

Betsy marveled. "Could I really get home in six days?"

"You could that!" He folded up the map and handed it to her. "Now keep this handy for when you get homesick!"

"Oh, I will! Thank you!"

But she did not forget the great lesson. It was brought home to her at dinner, for he ate hastily and seemed abstracted. Asking her pardon, he rose before dessert, and to her astonishment began to speak farewells.

"Why, why . . . I!" Confused, Betsy got to her feet. "I'll see you in the morning, surely."

"Alas, I'm afraid not! It's a madhouse here at the

end of a voyage. But the Thomas Cook man will look after you like a father." He took both her hands with hurried gallantry. "I bless the saints that led me to put you beside me at table." He smiled and was gone.

Betsy sat down slowly. She understood! His wife would be coming on board!

"But I wouldn't have minded. I'd have liked meeting her." An unpleasant thought dawned. Maybe *she'd* have minded?

Mrs. Trevelyan's Mr. Brown smiled at her from the Captain's table. Betsy looked straight through him in a snub. Mr. Chandler dropped by her chair. He hinted pensively that it was beautiful on deck, but Betsy said she had to pack. Taking a leaf from Mr. O'Farrell's book, she put out her hand. She'd be busy in the morning, she informed him, smiling. His despair was flattering but she knew he was already wondering how many pretty girls would make the return voyage.

"Travel is broadening," thought Betsy.

Next morning she had to say good-by to the *Columbic*. She hated to do it, for she had loved it all, down to the merry bugle that called them to meals. But a cruise had to end. Like a dance! Like a dream! Soon the deserted ship would be scrubbed and polished in preparation for another voyage—another escape from life, thought Betsy, for still another group of people.

She stood waiting with her suit cases piled at her feet, holding her handbag, camera, umbrella, and *Complete Pocket Guide.* Her heavy coat hung over her arm for she was traveling back into the winter.

"Yes, I'm Miss Elizabeth Ray," she said to the man from Cook's.

Mr. Feeney saw her ably through the customs. He guided her to the railway station, bought her tickets, and supervised the weighing of her trunk. With his help she sent a telegram to Miss Surprise, announcing her arrival the following morning. It seemed good to think that someone awaited her in Munich! And she was surprisingly glad to see dull Mr. Burton, who appeared with some chocolates for her.

He and Mr. Feeney put her into a first-class compartment which she occupied in solitary glory. She had planned to travel second class; first class was only for royalty and rich Americans, she had been told. But she was feeling too timid to protest any arrangements.

The little room opened into a corridor, and on the opposite side a window let down like a streetcar window for the admission of luggage. Mr. Feeney pointed out the dining car—the restaurant car, he called it. He reminded her that she changed trains at Zurich; she could get a sleeping car there. Then a bell rang. He jumped off, and the train began to move.

"Down to Gehenna or up to the Throne,
He travels the fastest who travels alone . . ."

She was alone again, all right, thought Betsy.

She went to the restaurant car in some trepidation, wondering whether she ought to be trying to remember German or French. "They couldn't expect me to know Italian!" She was both relieved and disappointed when the waiter greeted her in English.

"I work in Chee-ca-go. A ver' fine ceetee," he said.

"How do you suppose he knew I was an American?" Betsy thought, and looked studiously out the window as Mr. Brown came in.

While she was eating they went through Milan, and she saw the snowy dome of the great cathedral. Milan, she thought, was another place she must come back to. But she was feeling less and less like that adventurous woman of the world. Returning to her compartment, she plastered her nose against the pane.

There were mountains on the horizon, hazy as cloud mountains at first, but the train climbed past hillside pastures and sloping vineyards. Soon pine-clad mountains were rising all around her. Now and then a stream or waterfall caused Betsy to squeal with delight.

But the lakes choked her with their beauty.

"A lake at the base of a mountain is the loveliest sight in the world. It must be!" she thought.

Sometimes the water was a tranquil mirror reflecting its giant companion. Sometimes both mountains and lakes were veiled in blue-gray shadows. She leafed through her guidebook eagerly. Were these lakes Como, Lugano, Maggiore? The towns adjoining them seemed to be made up of glittering hotels.

She knew when they entered Switzerland because Swiss customs officials came in to examine her bags. They could understand her French, it seemed, but she couldn't understand theirs. Her questions brought forth a babbling torrent of words which seemed to bear no resemblance to anything she had heard in her French class.

"And I was an A student!" she thought disgustedly.

After they left, her door opened again, and Mr. Brown looked in.

"I don't believe we've met," he said, "but I was on the *Columbic*. My name is Brown." He had brown eyes, Betsy noticed, very alert and bright.

"How do you do?" she replied.

"I'm a friend of Mrs. Trevelyan," he added hopefully.

"And how many children do you have?" Betsy asked mentally. Aloud she responded in an icy tone, "Yes?"

He looked embarrassed. "I just wanted to say that if you need help with French or German, I'll be glad to interpret."

"Thank you," answered Betsy. "I've studied French and German." This sounded so childish that she flushed.

"Well, I'm in the next compartment if you need me," said Mr. Brown, and left her.

Betsy tossed her head. She went back to the window and told herself that these were the *Alps*. They were so high that she could scarcely see their summits. When she did crane her neck to view the rounded blue-white peaks, she saw more peaks rising behind them, and more, and more.

The cataracts leaped now from dizzying heights. Toylike chalets perched in terrifying niches, and down in the valleys were red-roofed villages. It was so *Switzeresque*! she thought.

"Oh, I need Tacy, or Tib, or Julia!" She needed some one to share it all with, to exclaim to. She was almost tempted to summon Mr. Brown. But she resisted even when daylight faded, and the lights came on, and she could no longer divert herself with views.

Her excitement subsided, and she began to feel increasingly forlorn. The beautiful *Columbic*, she thought, had been only an oasis in the desert of this awful trip. Here she was, alone in Europe, while her family sat heartlessly around the fire at home. . . .

The lights in the compartment blurred.

"I'm hungry; that's what ails me," she decided and walked down the corridor looking for the restaurant car, but it wasn't there any more. She opened Mr. Burton's chocolates.

After a while the conductor came in and said something in German. It must have been German for she caught the word *Fräulein*, but the rest was as baffling as the French had been. Of course, she hadn't studied it since high school.

"What could he have wanted?" she thought when he went out. "Well, I should worry!"

She sat still and awaited developments, but nothing happened—especially nothing in the dinner line. They rattled along through the dark, and she grew hungrier and more wretched.

Presently Mr. Brown came in again, a checked cap in his hand.

"Please excuse me for intruding all the time!" His tanned face was so thin that his teeth looked large when he smiled, but the smile was very pleasant. "I suppose you understood that we have a stopover for supper?"

"Supper!" Betsy cried with joy, and flushed because she had almost given herself away. "That is . . . I wasn't sure."

"We have only fifteen minutes. I'm familiar with this station, and the restaurant. Could I help you?"

"Oh, yes!"

"You'll need your coat," he said and helped her into it and off the train.

On either hand, snow-clad mountains climbed to the sky, and above them stars twinkled in a narrow lane.

"Oh, this air! It's like Minnesota," Betsy cried.

"Do you come from Minnesota?"

"Yes. I'm going to Munich. My name is Elizabeth Ray."

He hustled her into the station restaurant. It was as clean as that air had felt pouring down her throat. The cap and apron of the waitress were as white as mountain snow. There was a rich smell of coffee.

Mr. Brown ordered in German without consulting her, and the dinner was delicious. They didn't talk; they were too busy eating, and when they finished he paid the waitress, for which she was grateful. Foreign money was as bewildering as foreign languages, almost. But back at her compartment, she opened her purse.

"I'd like to repay you for my dinner."

"Why, all right!"

She took out a handful of mystifying coins. He selected one or two.

"And thank you very much," said Betsy, in a definite tone of dismissal. Mr. Brown smiled and retreated.

She didn't see him again until they were entering Zurich. Then, quite as a matter of course, it seemed, he came to her compartment door. He assumed the burden of her coat and suit cases, called a boy, and got her settled in the station waiting room.

"What train are you taking out?"

"It leaves about eleven-thirty. I have to get a berth on the sleeping car."

"Maybe I can get it for you now." But it developed that he couldn't.

"The office is locked," he said, returning. "They open in plenty of time, though, the porter says. And by the way, when you get a chance, better get rid of your Italian money. French gold is a good thing to carry. Well, good-by, Miss Ray." He held out his hand.

Betsy's heart dropped like a descending elevator. "Where . . . where are you going?" she faltered.

"To my hotel. I'm stopping in Zurich."

"You've been awfully kind." She tried to keep the despair out of her voice.

"It was nothing at all," he answered. "You're going to love Munich. It's a cozy little city." And he went jauntily out of the station, swinging his cane, and followed by a porter with some bags and . . . of all things . . . a pair of skis.

Betsy sat straight and still in the almost empty waiting room. Money to change! A berth to get! And she couldn't remember a word of German except *Spinat mit Ei.* Why did she remember that? What would she want with spinach and egg at this hour of the night? She burst into a trembling laugh, and the sound frightened her and caused some of her companions in the room to look at her curiously.

She drew her belongings closer—suit cases, umbrella, camera, and *Complete Pocket Guide.* She gripped her purse and waited.

It seemed like an eternity, although it was just half an hour later by the loudly ticking clock, when the door swung open and Mr. Brown came in, looking like a tweedy angel. He sat down beside her, folding his gloved hands on top of his cane.

"What are you doing here?" Betsy asked tremulously.

He grinned at her. "Looking after you. You need to get a berth, and you never could do it alone. After I got to my hotel I realized that if I didn't see you on that train, I'd have it to worry about all the rest of my life."

"Oh, Mr. Brown!" cried Betsy. "How kind you are!"

"Kind nothing! Pure selfishness! May I smoke?"

They did a lot of visiting in the hour and a half before the train arrived. Betsy told him about Miss Surprise, and her own plans for seeing the world. She told him about Minneapolis. He had never been there and he, too, was interested in Minnehaha Falls. She told him about the Rays.

"What you've done for me . . . that's just what my father would have done. He'll appreciate it awfully. He'll write a letter to thank you, if you'll give me your address."

"I have a card somewhere," he said, and fished in his pockets but he didn't bring one out. He didn't tell her much about himself. He didn't mention his home. Perhaps he, like Mr. O'Farrell, left his family behind when he went traveling.

"Are you married?" Betsy asked suddenly. It was apropos of skiing technique and not very subtle, but she didn't care. It was a question she planned to ask freely from now on.

Her frankness went unrewarded, for just at that moment the ticket window was flung up. Mr. Brown ran to get his place, and he spent a fevered fifteen minutes with the agent. He beckoned for her money and changed some to French gold. He got her a berth, and that wasn't easy. She could tell by his emphatic German and the way he was waving bills around.

"And I've found an English-speaking porter. He'll look after you." They ran for the train. It was moving when he jumped off. She had to shout her thanks.

"I don't know your address . . . and my father . . ."

"Never mind!" he said, and waved.

She was sleeping before they were out of Zurich.

The German customs officer came in, in the middle of the night. Betsy unlocked her suit cases and fell asleep again before he had finished with them. But in that short moment of wakefulness, she remembered Mr. Brown.

How heavenly kind he had been! This berth! She never could have managed it without him.

"You don't know how kind people are until you go traveling," she thought. "Travel is very broadening."

9
Miss Surprise's Surprise

WHEN BETSY CAME BACK TO her room after her first supper in the Pension Geiger in Munich, she shut the door behind her firmly, turned up the gas, walked to a capacious old-fashioned desk at the left of the window, and took Mr. O'Farrell's map out of a pigeonhole.

Lips quivering, she went to her bureau for pins, unfolded the map, and affixed it to the wall.

"Six days from Munich to New York," read the slogan across the top.

Only six days!

"I could be home next Sunday. I could be home for some of Papa's onion sandwiches. Maybe I will be, too! Nobody's making me stay here."

She took off the maroon silk dress which had been so completely wrong at the pension supper table and hung it in the huge dark wardrobe. She put on her bathrobe, and stood stiff and straight, looking defiantly around the empty room. Then with a wail she flung herself across the bed.

Surprise checked her tears, for she sank down alarmingly. But when she realized that it was only because of a feather bed, she kept on crying. Clutching a pillow, she cried in floods until her face was bathed in tears.

"I want to go home!" she cried, and kicked the feather bed, which wasn't much satisfaction because it was so soft and yielding. "I want to go home!"

She had been in happy spirits, although a little fluttery inside, when she reached Munich that morning. There was no sign of Miss Surprise, but Betsy hadn't really expected her at such an early hour. She had gone boldly into the station restaurant.

"*Guten Tag, Fräulein,*" the waitress had said, smiling, and Betsy was pleased that she understood,

"Good day, Miss." She did not understand anything further, but she received coffee, strong and delicious, with hot milk and little hard rolls and curls of unsalted butter.

An interpreter helped her get her trunk through customs; she wrote the address of the Pension Geiger on a card and, seated in an auto cab with her trunk on top and her bags around her, she rattled through the cold bright morning.

The streets were wide and very clean. They were being swept, she observed, by cheerful-looking old women in aprons. She saw a flower seller unpacking her basket. A group of soldiers in blue and scarlet uniforms passed at a dogtrot.

"I'm going to love Munich!" Betsy decided.

Nevertheless, she admitted to a feeling of relief that she was joining Miss Surprise. Independence was all very well, but it would feel cozy to be under somebody's wing for a while.

"Just until I begin to remember this darn language!"

Her heart was pounding when the cab entered Schellingstrasse and drew up before the Pension Geiger.

This wasn't too attractive. It rose straight from the sidewalk with a dreary courtyard at the side. Directly opposite, though, stood a wonderful house. Its walls were frescoed in lovely faded colors with kings and shepherdesses and cherubs.

"It's like a page from a picture book. Oh, I hope my room is on the front so I can look at it!" thought Betsy.

A servant girl came hurrying out. She was dark and stockily built with pinned-up skirts, rolled-up sleeves, a key ring at her waist, and gold hoops in her ears. Nodding, bowing, smiling anxiously, and saying things Betsy could not understand, she seized Betsy's bags and ran into the house.

She returned in a moment with a tall, hard-featured woman dressed in shiny black who greeted Betsy politely and helped her pay the cabman. But neither she nor the servant spoke English, and Betsy understood none of their guttural talk except for a Fräulein Ray now and then.

"I'll certainly be glad to see Miss Surprise," she thought, and began to repeat the name. "Fräulein Surprise, please . . . *bitte*, I mean. Fräulein Surprise."

The pension keeper said, "*Ja*, Fräulein," and continued with unintelligible jargon. But she led the way inside, and the servant girl, to Betsy's amazement, hoisted the heavy trunk to her back and followed.

Betsy didn't like the hall, which had high bare walls and uncarpeted stairs. It was cold and smelled of cooking. But she liked her room, up on the second floor. It looked cozy with its thick bright carpet and worn velvet curtains over lace ones. There was a green tile stove—such a foreign-looking stove!—and a magnificent desk. She went at once to the window, and to her joy looked out at the picture-book house. Now, if she could just find Miss Surprise.

"*Wo . . . ist . . .* Fräulein Surprise, *bitte?*" Betsy asked again, and her hostess picked up a letter lying on the desk. It was addressed in a large angular hand to Betsy, who opened it eagerly.

Miss Surprise, Betsy discovered, had lived up to her name. She wasn't in Munich at all! She had changed to a singing teacher in Italy. Maybe Betsy would join her there?

"But I just came from Italy!" Betsy almost shouted.

This room, Miss Surprise continued imperturbably, with board, of course, rented for one hundred and ten marks a month (twenty-six dollars and forty cents).

"And don't let Frau Geiger charge you any more! She's an old shrew, as you can see from her face. But the house is respectable. It's a student pension which is probably what you want since you are a writer looking for material, Julia tells me . . ." Betsy read that over, bracing herself with Julia's proud phrase. "The food isn't bad and the place is near everything . . . galleries, theatres, shops. I'll be writing you from Florence, Minerva Surprise."

Betsy put down the letter uncertainly. Frau Geiger looked expectant. The servant girl was watching anxiously like a dog awaiting the word of command.

"Oh, for Mr. Brown!" thought Betsy, groping vainly for German. She nodded her head in confirmation and Frau Geiger brought a formidable-looking book for her to sign. She summoned a Fräulein Minnie, a short young woman with bushy hair, who knew a little English and helped Betsy fill out the blanks. They gave her a massive key, and left.

The servant girl followed, but almost immediately she was back, and now she was smiling a different sort of smile . . . as though sure of her welcome. Her hands were overflowing with letters which she tumbled onto the green felt ledge of the desk.

"Oh, thank you! *Danke schön!*" cried Betsy, and without removing hat or coat, she began to tear them open.

But reading them was almost more than she could bear. Her father and mother were entertaining their bridge club. Margaret had been asked to a high school dance. The family was going to the Orpheum for a vaudeville show. Julia and Paige would be home for Easter.

There was a letter from Tacy. Betsy opened it with avid fingers, but she read only half a dozen lines. It was a funny letter—about how Harry had asked some men friends to a venison dinner, and Tacy had never cooked venison, but didn't like to tell him.

"It was awful! I certainly wished you were here to charm them with your indefinable Paris air . . ."

"See here, I can't stand this!" said Betsy, and pushed the whole snowy drift of letters back into the desk.

The servant girl, who was building a fire in the stove, looked up timidly. Betsy forced a smile. She buttoned her coat, picked up gloves and pocket book, and hurried out, trying to act as though she were late for an appointment.

She walked blindly up one street and down another. She didn't even pretend to look about. But gradually she became aware of broad, handsome avenues, pleasant squares filled with statuary, stately public buildings, and churches. One of these, with two round-topped towers, could be seen from everywhere.

Betsy walked on dizzily, and the streets began to seem theatric, as though she were seeing them on a motion picture screen—those old women still sweeping the pavements; policemen with shiny helmets; young men in flat, bright-colored caps; bare-headed girls carrying steins of beer, not one or two but half a dozen, foaming and spilling; and soldiers, soldiers, everywhere, especially officers whose blue and scarlet had an especial elegance and who wore swords at their sides.

Betsy walked and walked, and at last she realized that the sun stood overhead and she was very hungry. "I'd better find a restaurant," she thought, for she had no idea where she was or how to get back to the pension. "I remember enough German to read a bill of fare."

She found one and went in. But to her dismay the menu was in German script. She had forgotten that completely—what she ever knew of it—and was floored for a moment.

The Mullers were German. She thought back to all the savory dishes she had enjoyed at Tib's house. How did you say beef stew or roasted chicken or hot potato salad? She could think only of *Spinat mit Ei.* And she didn't even like spinach with egg!

But she said it, and she must have said it properly for spinach with egg was produced. Triumphantly Betsy added, *"Kaffee, bitte,"* and the waitress brought an empty cup over which she poised two steaming pitchers.

She asked pleasantly, *"Dunkel oder hell?"*

Now what could that mean? Betsy shrugged and laughed, and the waitress, smiling, poured twin streams of coffee and hot milk into the cup.

When the bill was presented, Betsy spread out a pile of coins and the waitress, still smiling, selected some and left the rest. One of these Betsy pushed toward her, and the girl said, *"Danke schön."* She accompanied Betsy to the door with a singsong of farewells in which the other waitresses joined. Betsy had noticed that all departing customers were sent on their way to this chorus. Nevertheless, it sounded friendly.

And she felt better after she had eaten—even spinach. She thought how funny her experience would read in a letter home. And Miss Surprise's surprise certainly left her in an adventurous situation. What would the family say?

But after a while she grew lonely again. Everyone else on Munich's spacious streets looked so happy and content; they made her feel like an outsider, homeless.

"But I've got a home. It's my own nice little room. I'll go back and settle it," Betsy decided.

How to find it, though?

She remembered what Miss Surprise had said about the pension being near the galleries. The Old Pinakothek was the famous one, of course. Stopping a woman who looked reassuringly fat, middle-aged, and plain, Betsy said, "Pinakothek?"

The kindly answer meant nothing, but the pointing

finger was fine. Betsy followed it. She stopped a succession of estimable-looking females. "Pinakothek?" "Pinakothek?" "Pinakothek?"

She passed bakeries and caught the smell of coffee and the warm fragrance of cakes. Probably Munich had the afternoon coffee habit. Betsy had acquired it, visiting Tib in Milwaukee. She adored it, but coffee would be no fun alone.

Besides, she realized with a twinge of apprehension, it was getting late. The sun had sunk into some western clouds. Betsy walked and walked, saying "Pinakothek?" "Pinakothek?" "Pinakothek?" and at last, just as dusk fell in earnest, she spied the decorated house.

She ran into the Pension Geiger gladly. A door on the second-floor corridor was open, and she saw an artist working at an easel. She admitted herself with the massive key, and her room did, indeed, seem a heavenly refuge. A fire was roaring in the tile stove, the velvet curtains had been drawn, and the gas was lighted.

She took off her wraps, and unpacked and settled. It was good to have her familiar things around her! Soon the little clock was ticking beside her Bible and Prayer Book on the commode beside the funny wooden bed. At the foot stood a marble-topped washstand; and next to that a dressing table bore her

❧ 148 ❧

jewel case, manicure set, comb and brush and mirror, and pictures of her father and mother. Then came her trunk with the steamer rug across it; and then the green tile stove.

Opposite, beyond the door, were ranged the wardrobe and a table covered with a spread on which were pictures of Julia and Paige, Bob Barhydt, Tacy and Tib. Mr. Burton's chocolates (what was left of them) sat there and her books: *The Beloved Vagabond, Little Women*, Emerson's *Essays*, some Dickens, Thackeray, and Dumas, and *The Oxford Book of English Verse*. Joe Willard had sent her that from Cambridge. There was another book Joe had given her, a limp leather copy of *As You Like It*.

Beyond a fat couch came the desk, which stood next to the window opposite the bed.

"At last," wrote Betsy, starting her letter home, "I have a big enough desk. It looks as though I were at least a congressman."

It had drawers and pigeonholes and shelves. Her writing materials were arranged with businesslike neatness inside. On top were "My Trip Abroad," and Margaret, and the American flag.

She told the family casually about Miss Surprise.

"I'll do whatever you think best but I'm sure I'm perfectly safe here. Miss S. said the pension was respectable, and I'm snug as a bug in a rug."

A piano broke in with a cataract of scales, and Betsy put down her pen to listen.

As in the early morning one bird is awakened by another into song, so was a violinist somewhere inspired by the pianist to start tuning up. A cornetist began to blow; a tenor began to vocalize; and a clear soprano note rose from the room below.

After a scale, the soprano broke into an aria, and then started to rehearse an operatic scene. Ignoring the discord of piano, violin, cornet, and tenor, she pleaded and sobbed and went off into gales of artificial laughter.

Betsy went off into gales of laughter, too.

"This is a student pension, all right," she said, and thought of the artist painting madly in the room across the hall. Tomorrow, she, Betsy, would be writing a story. She had read of Munich's student life. Now here she was in the midst of it!

With some excitement she began to dress for supper. It was served at eight, Fräulein Minnie had said. Betsy was very hungry and not only for food; she was even hungrier for the camaraderie into which she expected to be welcomed.

She wanted a bath after the day's wanderings, but when she rang for the maid and said, *"Bad, bitte,"* she wasn't taken to a bathroom. She received a small jug of hot water. She primped a bit, heating her curling iron over the gas flame, donning the maroon silk dress and spraying perfume with her usual liberality. When a hollow clangor announced supper, she went downstairs with a pounding heart.

But supper was a bitter disappointment.

The high-ceilinged dining room was cold. A tile stove stood in one corner but it didn't seem to hold any fire; it looked clammy. The plaster walls were cracked and the floor was bare, so that the chairs scraped dismally. Faded, discouraged-looking curtains hung at the single window.

This was flanked by two small empty tables. A long table in the center of the room was half filled with young people who scrutinized Betsy as she entered. The girls were wearing sweaters or woolen dresses, and Betsy was embarrassed by her silk.

Fräulein Minnie came rushing up to seat her.

"Does . . . does anyone here speak English?" Betsy whispered.

"*Nein*, Fräulein. At dinner, *ja*. We have many peoples den from outside. But dese peoples who live in de house do not speak English. Only me." She was Frau Geiger's niece, she explained.

Seating Betsy at the big table, she said something in German and there was an anonymous murmur. The men half rose for hurried bows. After a lull, conversation swelled up in a mixture of tongues: German and

French, but spoken too rapidly for Betsy's ear . . . Italian, she thought . . . Russian, maybe. German predominated, of course.

"This is the best thing in the world for my German," Betsy consoled herself, and tried to pick out phrases. But the enterprise lagged.

One girl looked German, another Italian, another was certainly Japanese. Which, Betsy wondered, was the aspiring prima donna? The artist, who was old and wrinkled, wore his hair to his shoulders, and a black Windsor tie. The other men were young with dark Slavic faces. They might be Bulgarians or Russians.

The tablecloth was not too clean. The dishes were thick and the meal was light. That dinner to which outsiders came in was clearly the substantial meal of the day. Supper offered only cold meat, bread and butter, a bit of salad, stewed fruit, and tea.

Fortunately, Betsy had lost her appetite. She was choked by that feeling of being an outsider. She cut the meat but couldn't put it in her mouth. She buttered the bread but returned it to her plate. She dipped a spoon into the sauce but carried to her lips only the smallest portion, and even that went down untasted.

One of the girls—the Italian—finished her supper and lighted a cigarette.

"She smokes it as calmly as—as Papa smokes his cigars," Betsy thought, shocked.

She rose as soon as she dared. Walking with leisurely dignity she left the dining room, but she ran up the stairs to Mr. O'Farrell's map on the wall.

Her pillow was soaked with tears when she heard a light knock. She didn't say "Come in," hoping that whoever was there would go away. Instead the door opened, and the servant girl who had carried up her trunk entered with a coal scuttle. Betsy turned her wet face back to the pillow.

But presently, after the rattle of coal subsided, Betsy felt a touch on her shoulder, and turned again. The servant girl stood looking down at her with a tender, pitying face.

She ran to the bureau and came back with Mrs. Ray's photograph. *"Mutter!"* she said, and thrust it into Betsy's hands.

She ran to the bureau again. This time she returned with Mr. Ray. *"Vater!"* she said.

She rushed across for Tacy and Tib. *"Schwester! Schwester!"* she cried triumphantly, pushing them all into Betsy's hands.

Betsy sat up, dashing the tears from her eyes.

"Nein! Nein!" She pointed to Margaret and to Julia. *"There* are my sisters. *Da . . . ist . . . Schwesters."*

The servant ran to get them, laughing.

She brought Bob Barhydt's picture. *"Schatz!"* she cried. But Betsy remembered this meant sweetheart, and shook her head firmly. That word brought only the image of Joe.

"Nein! Nicht Schatz! Freund! Freund!" she answered. Both of them were laughing now.

"Was heisst . . ." Betsy began, trying to ask, "What is your name?"

"Johanna," replied the maid, and added as though it were a nickname, "Hanni."

"Guten Tag, Hanni," Betsy said.

"Guten Tag, gnädiges Fräulein!" That meant "gracious Fräulein," Betsy remembered. How nice!

Hanni said something else with a rising inflection, but Betsy didn't understand. Hanni opened her mouth and put her finger in it.

"Ja, ja!" cried Betsy, bouncing off the featherbed. *"Ja,* I am hungry, *très* hungry. *Ich habe Hunger."*

Hanni beamed.

She rushed out of the room and Betsy jumped up and washed her face. She took down her hair and braided it, and sat down smiling beside the tile stove which was crackling now with heat.

"I just love this stove," she thought. "It belongs in a fairy tale, like that house across the street. And *what* a nice girl!"

Presently Hanni came back with a tray full of

cold meat, bread and butter, salad, stewed fruit, and tea . . . everything there had been at supper, and more! Pickles and jam!

Betsy ate ravenously while Hanni replaced the pictures, turned back Betsy's bed, turned over the wet pillow, and plumped it up invitingly.

She picked up her coal scuttle at last and stood in the doorway, smiling.

"*Gute Nacht*, Fräulein."

"*Gute Nacht*, Hanni," Betsy answered. But just "Good night" wasn't enough. She looked up from her bread and jam with grateful shining eyes.

"*Ich liebe dich*, Hanni!" she cried.

And Hanni chuckled. "*Amerikanische!*" she said.

Betsy could hear her chuckling as she hurried down the hall.

10

Betsy Makes a Friend

THE NEXT MORNING, of course, Betsy made a list.
Lists were always her comfort. For years she had
made lists of books she must read, good habits she
must acquire, things she must do to make herself
prettier—like brushing her hair a hundred strokes at
night, and manicuring her fingernails, and doing cal-
isthenics before an open window in the morning.

(That one hadn't lasted long.)

It was fun making this list, sitting in bed with her breakfast tray on her lap . . . hot chocolate, crisp hard rolls, and a pat of butter. Hanni had brought it to her after closing the windows and pushing back the velvet draperies. Betsy felt like a heroine in one of her own stories; their maids always awakened them that way.

1. *Learn the darn money.*
2. *Study German. (You've forgotten all you knew.)*
3. *Buy a map and learn the city—from end to end, as you told Papa you would.*
4. *Read the history of Bavaria. You must have it for background.*
5. *Go to the opera. (You didn't stay in Madeira because Munich is such a center for music and art???)*
6. *Go to the art galleries. (Same reason.)*
7. *Write!*

Full of enthusiasm, she planned a schedule. First, each morning, she would have her bath, and then write until noon. After the midday dinner she would go out and learn the city. She would go to the galleries, museums, and churches. She would have coffee out—for atmosphere.

"Then I'll come home and study German and read

Bavarian history. And after supper . . ." she tried not to remember the look of that dining room . . . "I'll write my diary-letter, except when I go to the opera or concerts."

It sounded delightfully stimulating. Having finished her breakfast and tacked the list beneath Mr. O'Farrell's map, she rang for Hanni and said, *"Bad, bitte."*

She had her towel over her arm and her soap in her hand. That ought to make it clear, Betsy thought, that she expected a tub bath. But Hanni said, *"Ja, ja, Fräulein,"* as before, and came rushing back with a jug of hot water again.

Betsy felt disgruntled. A sponge bath didn't take the place of a tub. It simply didn't! She must get out her German dictionary and make it clear that she wanted her bath in a tub. Tub! What the dickens was the word for "tub"?

"I'll ask Fräulein Minnie," Betsy decided. When she was dressed she sat down importantly at the marvelous desk.

It was pleasant to look over at the picture-book house and start a story. What should it be about? If it was to have an author in it, she had seen an author. If it concerned a New York debutante, she knew two ladies' maids. Not able to decide between an author and a debutante, Betsy made her heroine a woman of mystery. She wrote:

"Meet Miss So and So."

A cute title, she remarked judicially.

Hanni came in to clean, and Betsy tried to explain that she would like that work done early before she started writing. She picked up her pen and wrote in the air. She pointed to a book.

"*Ich verstehe,*" said Hanni, nodding eagerly, and tiptoed about, glancing at Betsy now and then with admiring awe. Evidently, thought Betsy, tickled, she wasn't the first writer to live at the Pension Geiger.

Going into Frau Geiger's office later (looking unsuccessfully for Fräulein Minnie to take up the subject of baths), Betsy met two officers coming out, resplendent in their blue and scarlet, with clanking swords. One was black haired, ugly, and thick-set; the other was young with blond mustaches twisted into peaks. He gave her a languishing look.

"I didn't suppose we had any of *those* gorgeous creatures here," thought Betsy, and looked for them at that one-thirty dinner to which Fräulein Minnie had said so many outsiders came. But they weren't there, that day or any other. Yet she saw them occasionally in the halls.

There was another mystery that grew as the days went by. At dinner, the two small tables in the dining room were occupied. Betsy still sat at the large table, listening in vain for the English Fräulein Minnie had promised, but the people at the small tables puzzled her.

Each sat by herself and neither spoke to the people at the big table. They bowed coming in, and said *"Mahlzeit"* going out. Everyone did that and Betsy soon learned to do it, too. But except for these formalities the two held themselves aloof.

One was a pleasant-faced lady in black who eavesdropped cheerfully and smiled when the people at the big table laughed. The other, at Betsy's first dinner, was a girl of about her own age with a most disdainful expression.

She was tall but delicately built, with black hair and eyes and a pale soft skin—like white rose petals, Betsy thought. She wore a gray suit, a white blouse, and a crisp black straw hat. White gloves lay beside her purse. Everything about her was fresh and immaculate.

"But what a superior manner!" thought Betsy, progressing through noodle soup, stewed meat with dumplings, Brussels sprouts, hot potato salad, pudding with chocolate sauce, and a small side-dish of stewed fruit such as she had had the night before. This was the first thing served and the last taken away.

After her meal the tall girl stood up, murmuring

"*Mahlzeit.*" She walked out, erect and arrogant, and when she was gone, everyone started talking at once in scornful voices.

The next day, to Betsy's disappointment, the girl's table was occupied by a dingy woman in a shapeless veil-swathed hat and a worn suit with a soiled lace blouse beneath. Her dyed hair needed re-doing. Her skin had blotches and her nails were ill-kept.

The following day the tall exquisite girl was back. After that, she and the dingy woman occupied the table on alternate days. It was certainly a mystery.

"Story material!" Betsy thought, as she too said "*Mahlzeit*" (whatever that meant!) and left on her afternoon rounds.

She followed her schedule rigidly—except for the tub bath which she had not yet achieved. Hanni continued to bring only a jug of hot water and Fräulein Minnie forgot all her English whenever Betsy mentioned tubs. After the morning's writing, and her dinner, Betsy set out briskly, armed with camera, notebook, pencils, and *Complete Pocket Guide*. But it was a false briskness. In spite of her list, in spite even of Hanni, she was miserably homesick again.

Whether the sun shone or went under a cloud, whether it rained or snowed, Munich was the same to Betsy. She read in her guidebook that this was one of the most charming capitals of Europe, that Ludwig the First had laid it out in magnificent avenues and decorated it with copies of famous buildings and statues in Greece and Italy. Betsy didn't care.

The city stood on the green Isar, she read—that "Isar, rolling rapidly" of Campbell's poem. The river was bordered by landscaped paths, spanned by snowy bridges. Betsy walked the paths and bridges, aching for the Mississippi.

She discovered a park called the English Gardens. Miles long, it was like a tract of country put down in the middle of the city. It had a stream, a lake, waterfalls. She sat on a bench and watched the people.

There were whole families together, enjoying the February sun. There were lovers with their arms about each other, and schoolgirls in giggling pairs, artists in soft hats, and those young men she had noticed before wearing colored caps. And of course there were soldiers, soldiers everywhere.

"What do they want all the soldiers for?" thought Betsy. "There isn't any war."

There were almost as many dogs as soldiers—aristocrats led by chains, and curs bounding joyously ahead of their owners. Bicycles, too, crowded the paths.

"This park would be nice if Tacy were here," Betsy thought wistfully.

She strolled past the Royal Palace and loitered in

its arcaded garden. She fed the pigeons in front of the Hall of the Fieldmarshals, but she felt self-conscious, doing it alone. She hunted up the Frauenkirche, Church of Our Lady, whose twin towers she had seen on the first day. This was to Munich what the Eiffel Tower was to Paris, she read. It was nothing to Betsy. But she sent flocks of post cards telling her friends that it was simply fascinating.

Americans were everywhere—smartly dressed, immersed in guidebooks, chattering. Some of them wore small American flags. They were all in twos or threes or fours and made Betsy feel lonelier than ever.

"I wander lonely as a cloud," she paraphrased Wordsworth, but she couldn't manage a smile. She felt desolate, even in the coffee houses. Oh, for Tib!

The guidebook made much of these convivial places, and of the overflowing beer halls. *"Gemütlich,"* it said, was the word for München, as the Germans called their city.

"Gemütlich!" That meant something like . . . cozy, which Mr. Brown had used in connection with the city. If there was anything Munich wasn't, Betsy thought bitterly, it was *gemütlich*!

Walking its streets was only better than being alone in her silent little room—at twilight when that din of practising began. The prima donna was learning Madame Butterfly, one of Julia's roles.

❧ 163 ❧

The familiar arias twisted Betsy's heart.

She still did not know which girl was the prima donna. The Italian? The Japanese? The plain little German with crimped hair? She looked too small, but Julia was small, and this girl carried herself like a singer.

In the evenings Betsy studied German fiercely.

"Ich bin, du bist, er ist . . ."

And she studied the history of Bavaria. It was quite distinct from Germany, she found, but its troops were at the Emperor's command. That Ludwig the First who had made Munich so beautiful had become infatuated with a Spanish dancer, Lola Montez. He had built her a palace and made her a countess. Finally, the people rebelled. She was obliged to flee, and Ludwig had to give up his throne. Not very edifying, Betsy thought.

She wrote notes to her *Columbic* friends and glowing letters home. She answered flippantly Margaret's reports on the stories she was sending out.

"It's too bad *Colliers* didn't appreciate 'Emma.' But let's be magnanimous and give them a chance at 'The Girl with Lavender Eyes.' You might try 'Emma' on *Ainslee's* next."

She stretched the evenings out and out, for bedtime was a time to weep.

Hanni always managed to drop in. She wasn't

much older than Betsy but she was as tender as a mother.

"Fraulein Ray *hat Heimweh*," she would say, bringing the family pictures one by one, and Joe Willard's picture—Betsy had found one pasted in a kodak book, and had steamed it off and put it in a frame.

On Sunday Betsy went to the American Church. But the hymns, the dear familiar ritual, reduced her to tears and she rushed out without even speaking to the rector.

A day or two later she returned, for she had noticed a book-lined library. Here, over tea and toast, you could read American magazines, and the Paris edition of the New York *Herald*. She went there the next day and the next.

"But I didn't come to Munich to read the *Saturday Evening Post*!" Betsy told herself furiously, and rushed outdoors again.

She went to the Hoftheatre and bought tickets for *Lohengrin* and *Tannhäuser*. She plodded through the galleries, beginning with the Old Pinakothek.

"But I don't know what to look for in these paintings," she thought despairingly, roaming past Raphael, Titian, Van Dyck, Rubens— The guidebook starred Rubens. She stared at his gigantic rosy figures.

"They're certainly fat!" she thought.

The New Pinakothek meant even less and the building wasn't heated. The Glyptothek had mostly sculpture, white and cold. In the Shack Gallery she found one painting she really liked.

A barefoot boy had thrown himself down on a hilltop. The sky was intensely blue, the grass was starred with flowers, and the boy was happily relaxed, one arm thrown over his eyes.

He reminded Betsy of herself and Tacy and Tib on the Big Hill back in Deep Valley. She could remember the warmth of the sunshine, the smell of hot grass, the hum of insects.

She bought a print of the Shepherd Boy—by Lenbach, her guidebook said—and put it up in her room. She loved it almost as much as Mr. O'Farrell's map.

Every night Betsy looked at that map and resolved to start home on the morrow. Every morning she decided to stick it out another day. But as though the situation weren't bad enough already, something happened to make it worse.

The street crowds began to grow fantastic. People were powdered, painted, masked; some were in costume. She ran into clowns, American Indians, court ladies, and girls in baggy trousers such as Betsy had seen in Algiers. Children were brownies and fairies. Even the dogs (and there were thousands of dogs, mostly squatty little dachshunds) had paper ruffs. Old men and women were selling bags of confetti. The air twinkled with dancing colored flakes.

It was the Carnival, Fräulein Minnie explained. It would last until Ash Wednesday. She herself had a shepherdess costume, she added, smiling broadly.

A carnival! But for a carnival . . . you needed to feel gay. It was awful if you didn't. And Betsy felt increasingly awful as the city turned into one huge masquerade ball. The crowds were laughing, shouting. They were orderly crowds, just childishly merry. But how could you be merry all alone?

Betsy tried. After half a dozen masks had showered her with confetti, she bought a bag and threw a handful. She didn't throw another. It was no good . . .

Giving her bag to a diminutive cowboy, she turned abruptly and walked toward the pension. She went faster and faster. She must, she must get home before she cried.

But back in her room at last, she didn't cry. She sat down and dropped her face despairingly into her hands.

"What I need is some friends," she said aloud.

She had never really appreciated friends before. Of course, she had always had them. Wonderful friends back in Deep Valley—Tacy . . . Tib . . . Carney. And at the University, Effie and Bob and the rest. She had always been surrounded with friends. She had taken them for granted. Never again, she thought, would she take friends for granted.

As usual at this hour the pianist with whose tireless fingers Betsy was all too familiar . . . the cornetist . . . the tenor all began to practise. The soprano struck a preliminary chord.

"Oh, not *Madame Butterfly*!" Betsy groaned. "Please! Not tonight!"

It wasn't *Butterfly*. The soprano began to sing a song so startlingly familiar that Betsy sat upright.

> *"From the land of the Sky-blue Water*
> *They brought a captive maid . . ."*

"Why, that's astonishing!" Betsy cried. She listened longingly. She could not tell whether the words were in English or German, but the tune was unmistakable. It was home itself put into song.

When Betsy went down to supper that night, she took along her German-English Dictionary. She slipped into her seat with the usual *"Guten Abend,"* and waited for a lull in the mingled German, French, Russian, Bulgarian, and Italian. Then she spoke boldly.

"Who," she asked in laborious German, "who sings the song about the sky-blue water?" She repeated

Wasser so many times that the waitress hurried to bring her a glassful, and everyone else looked bewildered.

Betsy began to sing it. *"From the land of the Sky-blue Water . . . ."*

She caroled as though she were standing beside the piano at home.

The girl with the crimped hair began to smile. She had a monkeyish, cute little face. She leaned excitedly across the table. "Me," she said. "I sing dat."

Betsy put a careful finger on her breast. "I," she proclaimed, "I come from there . . . from the land of the sky-blue water."

"Was? Was sagen Sie?"

She tried to say it in German but the Bulgarians, the Japanese, the Italian, the little German did not understand. Betsy had an inspiration.

"Minnehaha Falls," she said loudly. "I come from Minnehaha Falls."

She might have been back on the *Columbic.* "Minne-ha-ha," everyone repeated, with long "ah-h-hs" of interest, and Fräulein Minnie hurried up.

"Fräulein Ray. You have seen de Minnehaha Falls?"

Poetry, Betsy thought, was wonderful! Longfellow was henceforth her favorite poet.

"I live there," she proclaimed. If they thought she

went over the falls in a barrel every day, who cared?

She turned back to the small prima donna.

"Where . . . ?" asked Betsy, speaking in English slowly, "where . . . did you learn that song?"

The girl threw up her hands in laughing mystification, and the table broke into a babble of helpfulness. In German, in French, in Italian, and in what Betsy thought was Bulgarian or Russian, everyone said something.

The soprano called Fräulein Minnie and Betsy repeated her question. Fräulein Minnie turned it into German. The girl smiled and answered in German which Fräulein Minnie turned into English.

"After supper she vill explain. Vill you come to her room, please?"

The singer's room, too, looked out at the picture-book house. A grand piano stood in one corner and operatic scores and sheet music were scattered about. She was waiting with a calling card. "Fräulein Matilda Dienemann," it said. Betsy put her fingers to her breast again. "Betsy Ray."

Fräulein Dienemann went to the piano and took up a sheet of music. Before she put it in Betsy's hand, Betsy understood. Written across the title page in a black angular hand was the name—Minerva Surprise.

Fräulein Dienemann plunged into explanation, but Betsy got more from intuition than from the mixture of German and broken English. Miss Surprise had left this song behind, and Hanni had given it to Fräulein Dienemann.

"It was Miss Surprise who sent me here. She is a friend of my older sister. My sister is a singer, too." The two girls sat down beside each other on the couch, passing the German dictionary back and forth. A little French helped. In five minutes they were Tilda and Betsy to each other.

Tilda wasn't German, after all. She was Swiss. She showed Betsy a picture of a white stone house in St. Gallen, and photographs of her father and mother.

Holding her new-found friend tightly by the hand, Betsy led her upstairs to her own family photographs. Tilda was enthralled with Julia in her costumes as Cherubino and Elvira.

Betsy waved to the big desk. "I write stories," she declared. She could not understand Tilda's answer, but she understood her warm delight.

Hanni came in to turn back Betsy's bed and a smile spread over her broad dark face when she saw the girls together.

Presently Tilda took Betsy by the hand and they went back to Tilda's room. She made tea on an alcohol lamp, and brought out rolls and sausage and kuchen.

Tilda studied singing at the Conservatory, she said.

She took dramatic lessons, too. But there would be no school tomorrow; it was Shrove Tuesday. Could they spend the last day of Carnival together?

They could and did, and like the rest of Munich they were childishly merry. There was a parade with bands and flower-trimmed floats and carriages full of costumed people. Tilda and Betsy bought bags and bags of confetti and pelted passers-by.

They saw Fräulein Minnie, a happy, dumpy shepherdess, strolling home in the twilight. They saw even Hanni, who so seldom had a holiday. Everyone came out on the last day of Carnival, Tilda said.

Hanni wasn't in costume except for the confetti clinging to her hat and coat, but her face was shining with excitement and pleasure. She was with a soldier.

"He's her sweetheart," Tilda told Betsy. "But they can't afford to get married."

11

Betsy Takes a Bath

ONE MORNING FRÄULEIN MINNIE came into Betsy's room on some domestic errand, and Betsy closed the door and leaned against it.

"Fräulein Minnie," she said, "here . . . at the Pension Geiger . . . is there a bathroom?"

Fräulein Minnie, looking startled, nodded.

"A real, *echte* bathroom with a tub?"

"Sure, Fräulein! A beautiful toob."

"Then when, please," asked Betsy, "may I have a bath?"

Fräulein Minnie moved hurriedly toward the door. "Soon, *gnädiges* Fräulein."

"But I'd like one today," Betsy persisted, not yielding her strategic position.

"Ach, *Himmel*!" Fräulein Minnie looked around with a hunted expression. She was perspiring. "*Bitte*, Fräulein, not today! But it won't be long, I promise. Some day . . ."

"Some day! I can have a bath some day!" Betsy told Tilda that afternoon.

Their friendship had progressed by leaps and bounds. They spent their evenings in each other's room, usually in Tilda's because of the piano. She sang Betsy arias from the operas in which she had roles—*Madame Butterfly, La Bohème, Tales of Hoffman*—and Betsy taught her American popular songs.

"Peg off my hear-r-rt, I loff you . . ." Tilda sang.

They tried on each other's hats and looked into each other's books. Tilda had Goethe, Schiller, Shakespeare, George Bernard Shaw—but all in German.

She told Betsy about an artist who was in love with her. Wishing to be rid of him painlessly, she had invented a rich American fiancé. Betsy must tell her about rich Americans so she could convince August.

"Wonderful!" cried Betsy. "Say he comes from Pittsburgh."

"Pitts-burgh? *Warum?* Why?"

"Oh, the best millionaires do! Now, shall he be young and dashing or old and fatherly?"

Old and fatherly, Tilda decided when she understood. August was so jealous. "All gentlemens is jealous," she informed Betsy sagely.

And now, in turn, armed with the German-English dictionary and a French-English dictionary, Betsy brought the problem of her bath to Tilda.

At first Tilda was as horrified as Fräulein Minnie. "*Aber es ist unmöglich*. Impossible," she said.

Betsy leafed grimly through the dictionary. She stood up straight and slapped her chest.

"Nothing is impossible!" she declared grandiloquently, and Tilda burst into laughter.

"*Amerikanische!*" she cried.

She explained, while the books flew back and forth, that there really was a bathroom in the pension. There really was a tub. But it was downstairs in the officers' quarters. At least it was near their quarters.

"Is it their tub?" Betsy asked.

No, Tilda conceded, it was everybody's tub. But the officers didn't like anyone else to use it.

"Why shouldn't we all use it if it belongs to us all?"

"Oh, Betsy! *Offiziere!*" Tilda rolled expressive eyes. Springing up, she gave an imitation of an officer. She twisted mustaches, threw back a cape, put her hand on an imaginary sword.

"Germany is theirs," she said. "If Frau Geiger let you use their tub and they found out . . . !" Tilda drew the sword and ran it across her neck.

She spoke in German, but Betsy understood. She had noticed how important officers were in Germany. Germans stepped off the sidewalk to let an officer pass. Betsy didn't; and she heartily snubbed the young lieutenant who always ogled her when they passed in the halls.

"If it isn't their tub," she said stubbornly, "I'm going to have a bath."

"Very vell," said Tilda. "I vill speak to Frau Geiger. I vill tell her du bist Amerikanische und crazy. For you a yug off vater ist not enough."

"*Nein!*" cried Betsy. "Must be a toob for the crazy Amerikanisches Fräulein."

Wiping away tears of laughter, they ran down to the office.

Frau Geiger's smile vanished when Tilda explained. There was excited rebuttal and surrebuttal. Betsy didn't understand a word, but Tilda told her at last that Frau Geiger had promised to arrange things. When the officers went out, and she could be sure they would be gone for several hours, she would call Betsy.

"Then you must take your bath, *schnell, schnell!*"

"Like lightning!" Betsy agreed.

For several days she awaited a summons, but the officers seemed to be of most domestic habits. The days, however, passed quickly; Betsy's life was transformed because of Tilda.

To be sure, she was doing just what she had done before. She wrote in the morning and, after the noon dinner, went out to learn Munich. But what a difference, now that she had a friend!

Almost every day, she and Tilda met for coffee. Betsy learned what the waitress meant when she offered her steaming pitchers.

Dunkel meant "dark," and produced a brunette fluid. *Hell* meant "light," and resulted in an insipid pallor. Betsy learned to say, *"Mitte, bitte."* Then equal amounts of coffee and hot milk poured into her cup.

Choosing a cake from the rack of kuchen was a mouthwatering task, especially in the confectioners' shops, which were frequented chiefly by plump women.

Betsy and Tilda drank their coffee in all sorts of places. Austere resorts where orchestras played classical music. Smoke-filled rooms where chess games competed with racks full of German periodicals . . .

sometimes, the Paris edition of the *Herald*. Humbler hostelries; one was very cheerful with geraniums and a parrot that cried, *"Hoch!"* Here they saw coachmen, off duty, playing cards, and fat old women knitting.

One coffee house was popular with students. These proved to be the youths with colored caps. The colors denoted their clubs, Tilda explained, and their faces were scarred from dueling. That seemed to hold the place in German universities that football did at home!

The Café Stephanie was a haven of Bohemians.

"Why," Betsy asked Tilda, "do women have to cut their hair in order to paint and men have to let theirs grow?" For several women had their hair cut short, and others wore English bobs, like children, while the men affected flowing locks.

There were authors surrounded with inkpots and papers, writing busily. One man would pause, now and then, and rumple his bushy hair and stare wildly about and strike his brow. Betsy knew he was fishing for a word. She longed to lean over, fraternally, and suggest one.

"Oh, Tilda!" she cried. "Let's come here again! And I'll bring 'Meet Miss So and So,' and write."

Tilda agreed. But only in the daytime, she warned, and here Betsy must never come alone!

Betsy laughed. "Don't worry about me! I could never be a Bohemian."

She was too clean, and too systematic, and too orthodox, she wrote in the home diary-letter. "I can see a woman smoking now without batting an eyelash, but I wouldn't smoke myself. I like to get the atmosphere, though . . . for my writing."

She and Tilda always wandered a bit before starting home. There was no time for real sight-seeing; they planned to do that on Saturdays and Sundays which were Tilda's free days. But they patronized the flower sellers who stood on almost every corner. (Their baskets made little gardens in the February sun.) And they loitered near the Royal Palace hoping for a glimpse of the King and Queen, or even a princess. There were three princesses, all very plain, Tilda said. Plain or not, Betsy wanted to see one.

Sometimes there were errands. Tilda took Betsy to a shop where she could have her films developed. It was strange to see those breeze-blown snapshots from the *Columbic*.

"Which one is Mr. O'Farrell?" Tilda wanted to know.

She needed shoes, and the shoe shop fascinated Betsy. The owner's wife fitted Tilda. A grown daughter was fitting a man in the adjoining chair. A yellow-haired child, intent of face, buttoned and unbuttoned the shoes. The only one at leisure was the husband and father who strolled about impressively.

"Not much like *my* father and *his* shoe store!" Betsy thought.

Tilda always knew a good way home. Perhaps it would be through the Old City, those narrow streets around the Frauenkirche with tall, thin, high-peaked houses. On the nearby Marienplatz was the fourteenth-century Town Hall.

They looked in at the Hofbrau Haus, the Royal Brewing House. In this famous hostelry there was always a cheerful clatter. Maids were moving briskly about with racks of pretzels while men, women, and even children sat comfortably drinking beer.

München, Tilda told Betsy, strolling home along the Isar which reflected the first lights of evening, München was called the City of Art and Beer.

"It is *gemütlich,* München," she said, and Betsy was astonished to find that she agreed. Yes, knowing Tilda made a difference, and nowhere was this more apparent than at the pension table.

There was still that mixture of strange tongues, only now Betsy was trying to contribute to the conversation, and her efforts caused endless merriment. Again and again the company summoned Fräulein Minnie.

"Fräulein Minnie, was *heisst* . . . ?"

Slowly Betsy was straightening out the people. The Bulgarians were University students. There were several Austrians: a poet, the tenor, the indefatigable pianist. The Japanese girl studied composition at Tilda's Conservatory. The long-haired artist was the only German. The Italian girl was an artist, too.

She put a question to Betsy, via the poet who understood Italian and put it to Tilda in German who put it to Betsy in their peculiar patois.

There was an American boy at her studio, and he said continually, "Oh, how peach!" They had a pretty model, and he said, "She is peach." And someone sketched an old woman and when he looked at the picture he said, "It is peach." What, the Italian artist demanded, was "peach"?

"Here," said Betsy. "This is peach." And she took a spoonful of the ever-present compote. She chuckled to herself, remembering Maida who had asked a similar question.

So uproarious was the conversation these days that even the arrogant girl at the small table listened. Betsy kept intending to ask Tilda who she was. But she had not yet remembered to put the question, when one day at dinner the girl spoke.

Betsy had been to the Old Pinakothek, looking at Greek vases. She was trying to say that one beauty, covered with fanciful figures, had made her think of the "Ode on a Grecian Urn."

"You know. By Keats. It must have been translated into German. 'Beauty is truth, truth, beauty . . .' "

No one understood. And in the bewildered silence, the girl spoke.

"I don't know whether that has been translated or not," she said in flawless and beautifully articulated English. She gave the title in German, and there was instant recognition of the poem from Tilda, who nodded curt thanks. Betsy, too, expressed her thanks, and after the meal she paused by the tall girl's table.

"I didn't realize that you spoke English."

The girl smiled, and her smile made her look younger and sweeter. "I am only half German," she said. "My mother is English. Won't you sit down?"

Betsy complied gladly. "I've been wishing I knew you. Are you studying in Munich?"

"Yes. The piano, but I am only an amateur. I live with my parents. I've just come to stay with them after . . . a long time away. You know my mother, perhaps. She eats here the days I don't come."

Betsy was too taken aback to reply. That dingy woman and this exquisite girl!

"We never come together because we cannot leave my father. He is ill." For no reason that Betsy could see, the girl flushed. "My name is Helena von Wandersee."

"I'm Betsy Ray. Would you like to go for a walk?"

"That would be very pleasant."

But in spite of her perfect English, Helena wasn't easy to get acquainted with. She was excessively formal. She was trying to be friendly, though. When Betsy began to call her Helena, she reciprocated with a timid Betsy.

Like Betsy, she was just getting to know Munich. That long time away from her parents had covered not months but years. She had been living with cousins in some distant place.

"I can't get used to so much freedom," she confided. "My cousins and I never went out alone. If my aunt could not go, a maid took us . . . or a governess. It is very strange to go about like this."

They looked at the shop windows which were showing the spring styles.

"Do you like clothes?" Betsy asked, admiring a floppy flower-trimmed hat. She loved that picturesque kind.

"I have never picked out my own clothes. My aunt always bought what was suitable for us. It might be very interesting to make a study of one's own . . . type."

"You're the aristocratic type," Betsy volunteered. "I've never picked out my clothes either. My mother loved having three daughters to shop for. You must come up to my room and see my family."

"I'd like to, very much. Would you . . ." Helena's pale face flushed again. "I'm going to hear Gabrilowitsch, the pianist, Sunday night. Would you care to go?"

"I'd love it. Where do I go to get a ticket?" Betsy looked at her watch. "See here!" she said. "I'm meeting Tilda, Fräulein Dienemann, for coffee. I want you to get to know her. Won't you join us?"

"Thank you, but I really couldn't." In an instant the girl was stiff and cool again.

"I'm meeting her at the Hall of the Fieldmarshals. We always meet there because we can feed the pigeons if either of us has to wait."

"I'm sorry. I must go."

"I'm sorry, too," said Betsy, perplexed. "You can get a tram right here."

"I never take trams."

"You never take *trams*?" Betsy was astonished. How could anyone not take trams? And the streetcars in Munich were particularly nice. They were painted Bavarian blue, and the conductor lifted his cap and wished you good morning when you got on, and lifted it again and bade you farewell when you got off.

There was an awkward pause. Then Helena smiled, and that made her look sweet and friendly again. "I have so enjoyed being with you. And I'll pick up your ticket for Gabrilowitsch. Good-by . . . Betsy."

After coffee Betsy told Tilda about her. "I've been wondering why she came to dinner only every other day. Her father is ill; she and her mother can't leave him alone."

"So she can't leave her father!" Betsy was surprised to see Tilda's piquant face harden. "Ask Fräulein Minnie!" she added satirically.

"Why? What do you mean?"

"Frau von Wandersee gives Minnie English lessons to pay for one dinner a day, and she and her daughter take turns eating it . . . because they like to eat."

Tilda was speaking German and Betsy was sure she had not understood. But when the dictionaries were produced, the remark remained the same.

"She doesn't seem poor," Betsy replied thoughtfully. "And those cousins she's lived with all her life were certainly rich. But poor or not, she's awfully nice. Let's include her in some of our bats." Tilda had learned the word "bat," a favorite with Betsy.

"She wouldn't go," Tilda replied coldly.

"Why not?"

"Because she's a snob."

They paused on a street corner over their dictionary, to put "snob" into English.

She was much more of a snob than the princess, Tilda went on angrily.

"The princess? What princess?"

The woman in black at the other small table was a princess, Tilda said. But she was very pleasant. The girl was unbearable, and she was only a baroness.

Again Betsy was sure she had misunderstood. "Who's a baroness? Not Fräulein von Wandersee?"

"She's the Baroness von Wandersee."

Betsy was flabbergasted.

"Heavens and earth!" she said, and began to laugh. "Well, I told her she looked aristocratic!" But Tilda didn't smile, and Betsy sobered. Speaking slowly, in their mixture of tongues, she assured Tilda that Helena was not snobbish at all. She was lonely; she would be delighted to go about with them.

Tilda snorted.

They had reached the pension, and when they entered the courtyard they saw Frau Geiger standing in the doorway. Fräulein Minnie was behind her. The two called out in agitated voices.

"What is it? What has happened?" Betsy asked, thinking wildly of a cable.

It was her bath!

The officers had gone out, Fräulein Minnie explained while Frau Geiger and Tilda jabbered in German. They were going to a dinner, to a most important banquet. This was her chance.

Elated, Betsy pelted up the stairs, Tilda behind her. They rushed into Betsy's room and Betsy undressed swiftly. She screwed her hair into a knot. She put on her cherry-red bathrobe.

Hanni knocked with a pile of towels, although Betsy had plenty of towels already. Tilda ran down to her room for a bottle of cologne. Laden with towels, wash cloth, soap, bath salts, and cologne, Betsy stepped into the hall.

A sizable crowd had gathered. The Japanese girl said something in German to Tilda who exclaimed, *"Ach, lieber Gott!"*

"What did she say?" Betsy demanded.

The poet, Tilda replied, had taken a bath one time. He had told Susuki about it. When he came out, an enraged officer was lying in wait.

"You can't scare me!" Betsy cried and raced down the corridor, chanting,

> *"Half a league, half a league,*
> *Half a league onward,*
> *All in the valley of Death*
> *Rode the six hundred . . ."*

There weren't quite six hundred, but her bodyguard included all the servants, Frau Geiger, Fräulein

Minnie, Tilda, the Italian artist, the little Japanese.

On they went, downstairs and through a door, to the strange sacred wing of the officers. They escorted Betsy to the bathroom itself. There, everyone but Hanni left her.

A round heater had been lighted, but the tub was filled with boots and swords.

"Those officers don't appreciate their blessings," Betsy thought as Hanni pulled out the grim impedimenta and attacked the dusty tin catchall. There were even cobwebs in it!

Hanni scrubbed, and the heater roared and gurgled. Betsy glanced at it apprehensively, afraid it would explode. At last the water was drawn, and Hanni backed out. She would wait in the hall, she said.

"I will be here, Fräulein. I will not leave you."

"Und I am here," called Tilda.

Betsy peeped out. Fräulein Minnie, her eyes popping, stood guard at the door of the wing. "And Frau Geiger," Minnie called, "is waiting at the outer door . . . in case . . ."

But that "in case" was too awful to contemplate. Betsy closed the door.

The heater had done its work too well. And Hanni in her excitement had let only hot water run. The cold water came in a feeble trickle. Betsy tested it with a finger, with a toe. She dumped in rose geranium bath salts. At last she was able to step in herself.

Betsy loved baths. She soaped luxuriously, and then lay back in the hot scented water. Her nervousness receded and she was flooded with peace. She lay dreaming. Should she go to Rome next? To Paris?

"Fräulein! Fräulein!" Hanni called.

Betsy started upright.

"The officers!" This was Fräulein Minnie's voice. "They are coming back!"

"But why? What for?" They must have forgotten a sword or something, Betsy thought. Perhaps one of the very swords she was stepping over now as she climbed out. She rubbed herself frantically.

"Hurry! Make haste!" Frau Geiger was delaying them, Fräulein Minnie explained, her voice shaking with fright.

Betsy hurried into the cherry-red bathrobe. Gathering up towels, wash cloth, soap, bath salts, and cologne, she opened the door. A gust of warm perfumed air came with her.

With Hanni scurrying ahead she got safely to the door leading from the wing to the main corridor. But there she met the officers. She met them face to face—the thick-set ugly one and his handsome blond companion!

Behind them stood Frau Geiger, her face stricken.

Fräulein Minnie was a picture of terror and Hanni had that look Betsy had seen before, of a dog who has been ill-treated. Tilda had disappeared.

As for Betsy, there was no denying her guilt. The narrow passageway smelled of rose geranium, her hair was screwed into a knob, and her face, she knew, was moistly pink. In spite of herself, Betsy broke into a smile.

The young lieutenant who had ogled her so vainly smiled back in astonished delight. The dark, ill-natured-looking captain smiled, too. Both officers clicked their heels together. They bowed from the waist.

Betsy acknowledged this salute as graciously as she could, with soap, bath salts, and cologne in her hands and towels dripping from her arm. She trailed her cherry-red robe triumphantly up the stairs.

Tilda was trembling in a corner of the room.

"Look at me!" Betsy cried, revolving proudly. "Look at me! I have had a bath!"

12
Three's Not a Crowd

AT THE CONCERT, BETSY planned, she would see what she could do about bringing Tilda and Helena together. Tilda's attitude was most discouraging. She not only disliked the young baroness; she seemed stubbornly sure that Helena would never accept her as a friend. But how could that possibly be?

Tilda was engaging, well bred, well educated—her

interests extended far beyond music. If money mattered—her father was a prosperous manufacturer. She didn't have a title, of course, but neither did Betsy. Betsy liked Helena. She didn't like her arrogance, but it was easier to forgive now that she knew Helena's story.

"Eating dinner only every other day! When she's a baroness, too!"

Betsy had always thought she would be overwhelmed with romantic excitement by a title, but she wasn't. The baroness was just a nice girl whom she liked and wished she could help.

She must make Helena and Tilda and herself into a threesome, she decided. Three made a crowd, in more ways than the old adage indicated. It made a Crowd.

"Look at Tacy and Tib and me!" Betsy argued.

She thought about it all through the concert while the Polish Gabrilowitsch with dazzling skill played Beethoven, Chopin, Mendelssohn, and his pretty wife, once Clara Clemens, sang German songs. It was thrilling to be seeing Mark Twain's daughter.

Betsy planned to begin her campaign on the walk home, but Helena's mother was waiting, wearing the same rusty veil-swathed hat, the same worn suit, the same soiled blouse. "Doesn't she ever wash it?" Betsy wondered.

She didn't like Frau von Wandersee. Her manner

and her soft, purring voice were both insincere. On the walk home she asked questions about the concert . . . but not the music. She was curious to know what celebrities and society figures had attended. Had Betsy known any of them?

"Won't you sit at my table tomorrow?" she asked Betsy when they parted. "I should like to get to know you. My daughter is happy to have found a new friend."

"So am I," Betsy answered. "I've found two wonderful friends at the Geiger. Helena, and Tilda Dienemann."

There was no answer from Helena or her mother.

The following day, to Tilda's good-humored scorn, Betsy did eat dinner with Frau von Wandersee and, more than ever, Betsy did not like her. She had a sly way of manoeuvring the conversation to bring out that her husband had once been wealthy, that the cousins with whom Helena had been raised were countesses and lived in a castle.

All through dinner Betsy had the feeling that Helena's mother was trying to find out how much money she had. Every question she asked about Betsy, or anyone else, bore on financial standing. Yet she made it clear that Helena would never play the piano professionally, and that her husband did nothing at all.

"How can she love money so much and yet despise the good hard work which earns it?" Betsy wondered.

The next day Helena and Betsy made a plan to visit the National Museum. This time Betsy didn't suggest meeting Tilda.

"And afterward, let's go out for coffee," she said. For a coffee table with its atmosphere of leisure and relaxation would be ideal for a talk.

"I'm sorry. I never go into a coffee house."

This was even more amazing than the tram. "But, Helena! They're such fun! And we'll need nourishment after the museum."

"Mother will make us a little lunch," Helena replied. "If it isn't too cold we can eat it outdoors. There are some quite secluded places in the Gardens."

The National Museum was near the English Gardens. A rambling conglomeration of turrets, wings, arcades, and courtyards, it housed a renowned collection of Bavarian antiques.

"You'll love it, Betsy. Each room illustrates a period. They run from the Stone Age to the death of King Ludwig the Second. Let's go through them in order!"

"Oh, you Germans!" Betsy teased. "Such thoroughness! You know, don't you, that there are over a hundred rooms?" But she agreed and they passed through the Prehistoric Ages and the Roman invasion of Bavarian soil before they found themselves ready for Helena's lunch.

It was very dainty, with small linen napkins lying on top, each sandwich wrapped separately, and fresh cookies beneath. And they were able to eat in the Gardens for the sun was very warm. Buds were swelling; and robins, sounding just like those in Minnesota, were singing with abandon.

"Tilda would adore this," Betsy plunged. "You must get to know her, Helena. The three of us can have such good times."

The young baroness was silent for a moment. Then she said in a strained voice, "Betsy, I may as well tell you. We Europeans feel differently than you Americans do about some things. Fräulein Dienemann may be very nice but she isn't in my world and never could be."

"Why not?" Betsy asked. "She's studying music, just as you are."

Helena paused. "Betsy," she said, "I'll be frank. Her father is in trade."

Betsy burst out laughing. It was hard to take this remark seriously, but Helena looked as though she had just announced that Tilda's father was a murderer.

"Forgive me!" Betsy said. "It isn't funny, really. You may want to break off *our* friendship. *My* father is in trade. He runs a shoe store."

"I expected he did something like that," Helena answered calmly. "But you are an American."

"Do you really mean that you can associate with me and yet you can't associate with Tilda?"

"That is exactly what I mean," said Helena frigidly.

Betsy was angry. In their short friendship, she had come to love Tilda. If she had to choose, she would certainly choose Tilda. It might be best to choose now, and be done with it.

But when she looked up she saw something in Helena's face. It was an almost pleading expression. She was too proud to say, "Betsy, I'm lonely." But Betsy saw it shining in her eyes. And Betsy had learned since her trip started what it meant to be lonely. She reached over and gave Helena's hand a quick warm pressure.

"I wish you'd change your mind," she said. "But whether you do or not, you and I are friends. You must let me fix the sandwiches sometimes."

"Oh, no!" said Helena. "We have a kitchen." She turned her head and Betsy knew she was winking tears away.

"Helena," asked Betsy, "why do you object to a

perfectly respectable coffee house?"

"For one in my station," Helena answered stiffly, "it is not suitable. If I could afford a private room at a fine hotel, yes. But I could not eat with common people."

"And the tram?" asked Betsy gently.

"If I can't have a private carriage, I prefer to walk." Now tears rushed into Helena's eyes too freely for her to conceal them. She touched them with a snowy handkerchief.

"Betsy," she said, "you don't know what it is like to be in my station and be poor. At the castle I had my own bedroom, my own sitting room and bath, my maid. There was a coachman to take us everywhere."

"Do you like being in Munich?"

Helena spoke in a low voice. "It is wonderful to be with someone who loves me. My aunt was kind but I never came first. With my mother, I come first."

She did not refer to her father.

Betsy took her hand again and squeezed it. A feeling of thankfulness welled up in her at her decision not to choose.

And so Betsy's days came to be divided between Helena and Tilda. Tilda didn't mind. She only joked a little about decayed aristocracy, and when Betsy said that Helena was nice, Tilda made a face.

Betsy and Tilda began on the galleries, and the Old

Pinakothek was very different for Betsy with Tilda beside her. The German and Netherlandish pictures were the ones to study here, Tilda said—the Holbeins, the Dürers.

"The most important picture in the Pinakothek is Albrecht Dürer's portrait of himself."

She told Betsy stories about the Nuremberg goldsmith's apprentice who had made himself Germany's first great painter. Betsy looked at his self-portrait respectfully but she liked best Van Dyck's "Flight into Egypt." She bought a print of that and put it up beside Lenbach's "Shepherd Boy."

Tilda took her to an exhibition of ultra-modern paintings. She was interested in everything—like Julia and Joe, thought Betsy, watching her squint with lively curiosity at all the cubes and angles. Betsy remembered the *Columbic* dinner table, and how she had wished she knew something about the new art movements. She tried to understand these Cubist and Futurist pieces, but they seemed perfectly crazy.

They dropped into churches and sometimes Tilda explained the architecture. Often in the candlelit dimness they just knelt to pray.

Once they looked through an iron fence into a small enclosure with a shrine and two rows of graves. It had been a cemetery for some monks, Tilda said. Late sunlight lay on the plain black crosses, and green shoots of crocuses were pushing up from the graves. It was strange, thought Betsy, the stillness in there, when the world was so giddy with spring.

She did not speak, but Tilda pressed her arm.

"The spring . . . even there," she whispered.

One day they visited the golden Angel of Peace, poised atop a column beside the Isar, and afterward, they scrambled down to the river where children were wading and sailing boats. Betsy knew just the squashy, gritty, muddy, tired loveliness they felt. She remembered wading in the streams of melted snow that ran down the Big Hill.

"I wish I could go wading."

"I, also."

"I hate growing up."

And they fell into silence.

They made a trip to the gigantic statue of Bavaria and ascended into her head to get the view. That night Tilda got to talking about Bavarian history.

They always ate and made tea on the alcohol lamp before going to bed. This was quite in the German tradition, Tilda said. Germans in their homes ate six meals a day: breakfast, second breakfast, dinner, afternoon coffee, supper, and in the evening tea or beer with sandwiches and kuchen. Betsy, in the cherry-red bathrobe, and Tilda in a blue one, feasted merrily.

The second King Ludwig (a dull Maximilian came

in between) had been gloriously mad, Tilda said. He was dark and very handsome. On top of the Royal Residence in Munich he built a winter garden where, clad in silver armor, he used to float in a swan boat like Lohengrin's. This mad Ludwig was the patron of Wagner.

He built fabulous castles in lonely mountain spots. They often had French salons and gardens, for he was in love with Marie Antoinette.

"But, Tilda! She was beheaded before he was born."

"He loffed her," Tilda declared.

He used to ride through the mountains in a carriage drawn by four white horses. In the winter his golden sleigh was shaped like a swan. He would drive all night through snow and storm. The villagers in their beds would hear him rushing by. Or they caught glimpses of him, his face pale, his eyes blazing under a diamond-studded cap.

"Tilda! You're scaring me!" But Tilda kept right on. The peasants loved him, she said, in spite of his extravagances, and when he died . . .

"What did he die of?" Betsy interrupted.

He drowned himself, Tilda answered, because he was forced to abdicate. The peasants made a hero of him then. To this day young mountaineers wore his picture in their hats.

"There's a song about him," she added, and began to hum it. *"König Ludwig der Zweite . . ."*

"It's like a fairy tale," said Betsy. "A dark sort of fairy tale . . ." She paused uncertainly but Tilda understood.

"Ja," she agreed. "It is of the dark Bavarian mountains!"

History was less thrilling, more accurate, and much more arduously imbibed going through the National Museum with Helena. They proceeded slowly through relics of the Early Church, Guilds, the Reformation. Betsy liked the Knight Errantry room. It was lined with suits of armor, and there were life-sized models of armored men on horseback. She thought how much Joe would enjoy it.

Helena explained everything exhaustively. She was very well educated. In addition to German and English, she spoke French, Italian, and Spanish.

"You and Tilda make me feel so ignorant," Betsy said. She never lost a chance to bring Tilda's name into the conversation, but Helena always coolly changed the subject.

On rainy days they took their afternoon sandwiches in damp and drafty halls. But there were rewards. Betsy got Helena to talking about the castle in which she had lived . . . the powdered servants in livery, bowing on the terrace; the great entrance hall which was a bower of growing plants with statues gleaming through; Englander, her riding horse. Listening was like reading the beginning of a novel.

Frau von Wandersee took them to hear the orchestras. The concert halls were usually crowded with tables. During the music, the people were reverently silent, but when it stopped, everyone started smoking and eating and drinking beer.

Betsy was delighted one day when Tilda offered her concert tickets which she was unable to use. She rushed off eagerly to the von Wandersee apartment.

She had never been there before, and at first she wondered whether she had made a mistake. It was such a shabby place with dirty stairs and hall. But she found the card of the Baron von Wandersee tacked over the door.

His wife answered the bell. She was wearing a soiled bathrobe, and she didn't ask Betsy in. In fact, she pulled the door half shut behind her. Speaking in her usual purring voice, she said that Helena was out, but a strong odor of alcohol made Betsy suspect that the baron was in.

"Is that why Helena never mentions her father?" Betsy wondered. She felt sick inside.

Frau von Wandersee refused the tickets, and Betsy got away quickly. A few days later Helena, head high, told her that they would be moving soon.

"We have had such trouble finding a pleasant apartment. We've moved three times," she said.

Museums, galleries, concerts were all very well, but Betsy liked the opera best. She had awaited her first one with some trepidation. Julia loved opera so much, and had chosen it for her career. How awful, Betsy thought, if she didn't like it! But she liked it beyond words.

She went to the Hoftheatre straight from afternoon coffee, for the operas began early, sometimes as early as six. There was always a line of people waiting for "standing places"—shabby, humble-looking people, and soldiers, and students. Yet inside, the great auditorium glittered and shimmered with fashion. Everybody went to the opera in Munich.

The conductor was greeted with thunderous applause but there was a solemn silence when the lights dimmed. Betsy began to cry as soon as the overture started, and she never knew quite when she stopped. The music carried her off on a golden tide.

She was a Wagnerite from the moment when Lohengrin, godlike in silver armor, floated on stage in his swan boat.

"I don't blame the Mad King for trying it," she thought, munching sausages in a crowded lunchroom during the intermission. "I'd like to myself."

This opera and *Tannhäuser*—with its mountain

castle and shrine and the steep dark path down which the pilgrims marched, made her think of Tilda's stories.

Tilda always waited up for her, and they talked the opera over while Betsy ate her supper. Hanni brought it to her whenever she came in; that was the custom.

"You must hear something besides Wagner," Tilda said, and Betsy bought tickets for *Carmen, Madame Butterfly, The Barber of Seville*. She slipped in *Die Meistersinger,* too. She bought these tickets early Sunday morning when the cheap seats went on sale.

"You won't be a Münchener until you have stood in line with the crowd on Sunday morning," Tilda said. So Betsy got there at eight, but there were two or three hundred ahead of her. Some people stood from Saturday midnight on. Others hired street porters who would stand for them for a mark.

Betsy considered herself quite a Münchener now. She had seen the plain princesses going to church, and the King and Queen in a gala street procession, with martial music and gentlemen and ladies-in-waiting in carriages of vivid light blue. The royal carriage was drawn by eight black horses.

The King and Queen were old and dull. They hardly acknowledged the cheers of the crowd, just smiled in an absent-minded way. Nevertheless, when the Queen threw her bouquet, Betsy scrambled for some violets.

"I want to send them to Margaret," she told Tilda sheepishly.

On Sunday Betsy went to the American Church; now she knew the rector and his wife. Afterward she crossed to the Hall of the Fieldmarshals for the band concert, when all Munich promenaded. She met Tilda, who was a Lutheran, or Helena, who was a Catholic (but never both of them together), and they promenaded like true Müncheners.

And sometimes, also in München fashion, Betsy took her writing to a coffee house. It was "The Disappearing Dancer," now, for "Meet Miss So and So" had gone on its way to Margaret. Scribbling with a coffee cup beside her, she flattered herself that impressionable American tourists would write home that they had seen an authoress composing a masterpiece in public.

Betsy was devoted to the coffee houses. But she was disturbed by the little-boy waiters, wearing diminutive dress suits and running about with heavy trays. There was too much child labor in Munich. She could not forget that yellow-haired little girl buttoning and unbuttoning shoes, nor a pale little boy she had seen in a watch shop. Wearing an apron, bent over some delicate work, he had looked like a little old man.

She didn't like it that Hanni worked so hard and

that she couldn't marry her soldier. Hanni was so good to her! She polished Betsy's shoes, mended her clothes, and often brought little bouquets for her desk.

"Celeste is quite jealous," Betsy told Tilda, who knew all about Celeste.

Tilda was well acquainted with all Betsy's friends. She knew about Tacy's gay struggles with housekeeping, and Tib's affairs of the heart. Bob and Effie wrote from the University . . . about quizzes and spring track and who was leading the J.B.

"*Was ist* 'J.B.'?" asked Tilda, and received a glowing account of the Junior Ball.

Tilda admired Joe's picture, for even a snapshot showed how blond and muscular he was. She noticed also that although it stood at Betsy's bedside, there were never any letters from him.

"He used to be my beau, but he isn't any more. I don't have a beau."

It was true, and a strange situation for Betsy. But it was restful, she told Tilda, not to have to curl her hair. She hadn't curled it since the first night in Munich. And she was getting fat.

"Haven't I the most beautiful arms?" she asked, turning in front of the mirror. "And my shoulders aren't bony any more. I can hardly wait to wear a formal."

Munich agreed with her. But she must leave it soon to live in and learn another place. Her father and mother, aghast at first at Miss Surprise's surprise, had accepted the fact that Betsy seemed safe, living alone in Munich. But they didn't want her to try it in a second city. They had advised her to join a Thomas Cook party, make the Grand Tour, and come home. Betsy thought this would be horrible.

Fortunately the Wilsons had written, suggesting that she come to Venice. They were leaving for Greece, but the *Casa delle Rose d'Oro* was charming—run by three tiny old ladies, unmarried sisters, always dressed in black.

"You would put them into a story, Betsy," Miss Wilson wrote. "And they would be ideal as chaperones." Betsy could stay with them through May, and in June join the Wilsons for Switzerland and Paris.

Her parents approved this plan and Betsy loved it.

"Imagine me," she said, "floating along in a gondola and feeding the pigeons in St. Mark's Square!"

"For Venice," Tilda pointed out, "you will want a sweetheart."

"Pshaw!" said Betsy. "I'm going to study the stones like Ruskin did."

13
Dark Fairy Tale

TILDA WAS IN BED with a cold and Betsy was having supper with her. Hanni had set a low table between them. In the center was a bouquet of hyacinths from the corner flower seller, and that wasn't the only assurance of spring. The windows were pulled open to admit balmy air. And out in Schellingstrasse children were playing games with a joyful racket that took Betsy back to Hill Street.

"I remember," she told Tilda, "how I used to run in the house every two minutes and beg Mamma to let me take off my winter underwear."

"I have been thinking of summer clothes all day," Tilda replied.

"This weather is bad for work." Betsy sighed, for "The Disappearing Dancer" wouldn't disappear; she wouldn't dance; she wouldn't even budge. "No mail either," Betsy added as though this too could be blamed on April.

Tilda sat guiltily upright. "Betsy, I am a wretch! You were out, and Hanni brought a letter for you here." She fished it from the pile of books on her bed.

It was addressed in Mrs. Ray's dashing hand.

"Not very plump," Betsy observed. "Do you suppose my family doesn't love me any more?"

"*Ja,* I am sure! You should come and live in Switzerland. We will keep cows."

"'Cows, cows, beautiful cows!'" As Betsy ripped open the letter, an even thinner slip of paper fell out. She took it up. She stared at it. She threw her napkin into the air and shrieked.

"Tilda! Tilda! *Ainslee's* have succumbed!" Betsy spoke in English for she couldn't remember any German.

"*Was ist Ainslee's?*" Tilda cried.

"It's a magazine, Tilda. They've bought one of my stories, 'Emma Middleton Cuts Cross Country,' for one hundred dollars!"

Betsy flew over to the bed and they hugged each other until they were breathless. Hanni, coming in with fresh tea, stared in bewilderment.

"Hundred dollars!" Tilda cried. "Betsy, that's four hundred marks!"

"Is it? Oh goodie! Goodie!"

Tilda told the amazing news to Hanni.

Betsy looked up from her letter. "Papa wants me to spend this money for anything I like. Something I couldn't afford out of what he sends me. And, Tilda, I know what it will be! I'm going to travel around a little. I've been wishing I could, before I go to Venice."

"*Wunderschön!*" Tilda exclaimed. "Und to von place, I vill go mit."

"You will?" Betsy asked rapturously, and danced about the room.

"'Added hours had but heightened the wonder of the day,' tra la!"

"'His gray gaze was inscrutable,' yo ho!"

"Betsy, *bist du* crazy?"

"They're excerpts from the immortal manuscript," said Betsy. "One hundred dollars, Tilda! I never got more than ten before." She ran for Mr. O'Farrell's map.

When she returned Hanni had pulled the draperies

and lighted the gas and put a kettle over the alcohol lamp. This important discussion required more tea, of course. It was fascinating to take meditative sips over the rival charms of medieval Nuremberg and Wagner's Bayreuth.

"Pshaw! I'll go to both!" Betsy cried—after all, a hundred dollars! And she would go to a little town called Sonneberg which the rector had told her about. It was the doll center of the world.

Tilda was going home for the long Easter holiday, but afterward, they agreed, they would meet in Oberammergau. It wasn't a Passion Play year but they both wished to see the famous village.

"Will your parents mind your traveling alone?" Tilda asked.

"Not this tiny jaunt! Germany is as safe as my own back yard. And you know, Tilda, I speak the language now."

"*Ja,* magnificently! Of course, you call everyone *du,* even the policemen, and that is supposed to be only for family and friends."

"The way to talk German," answered Betsy, "is to talk German. If I bothered with forms, and genders and cases and tenses, I'd be tongue-tied. I just string along the words I want to say, and put *Nicht wahr?* at the end. Of course, I must have a new hat."

"With a hundred dollars? *Natürlich!*"

Next day Betsy cashed her big check at the bank where she cashed the checks her father sent each month. Then she bought presents: A pipe rack for her father, a pewter platter for her mother, carved bookends for Julia and Paige, a watch for Margaret, a pink enameled pin for Anna, the hired girl. She bought Tilda a print of Willem Key's "Pieta" which both of them loved, and Hanni, a lace collar and jabot.

Helena went with her, and she was a great help in shopping. There was something about her that made everyone jump. The milliner rushed for her finest creations, and Betsy bought a large black straw. One end touched her shoulder, the other shot off toward the sky, and under the skyward edge, next to her hair, was a luscious pink rose.

"It's a little extreme," she admitted, "but why shouldn't it be? I'm a famous lady author. You wouldn't like some coffee, would you?" But even to celebrate "Emma" Helena would not go into a coffee house. Betsy bought her a box of marzipan.

She and Helena finished up the National Museum. Betsy grew maudlin toward the end. Bavarian history, she said, was coming out her ears.

"But I do thank you, Helena! I wouldn't have missed it."

Easter was coming near. The streets were full of little girls in white dresses carrying candles. The shop windows showed rabbits, eggs, and chickens. Tilda

212

would be leaving soon. Betsy put aside "The Disappearing Dancer"; Tilda skipped all the classes she dared to; and they set forth exuberantly every day.

All Munich was out to celebrate spring. The squares were crowded with people, talking and drinking beer. The paths along the Isar were filled with loitering families.

"Nobody works in Bavaria," Tilda remarked.

"Except Hanni."

"Oh, *ja*! The servants!"

At Nymphenburg where the Mad King was born, they drank coffee out of doors. After that they did it every day. In the rustic English Gardens. In the Hofgarten, where the spring hats rivaled the tulips. In humbler parks where there were fewer tourists, artists, students, but more fat Müncheners, bicycles, and dogs.

Strolling home through the sweet spring twilights, Betsy and Tilda talked of their careers. They made plans for touring Europe in 1917. Sometimes Tilda talked about August. She liked him better than she admitted, Betsy perceived. Betsy at these pensive moments always thought about Joe.

In no time Tilda was packing for home. She and Betsy parted crying, "*Auf Wiedersehen!* Until Oberammergau!"

On Easter Betsy and Helena made the rounds of the churches. In the Frauenkirche, lofty and grim in spite of candlelight and lilies, the people sang while the organ rolled out paeans of gladness. Thinking of Easter at home, Betsy wept a little.

She was grateful for Helena, who ate dinner at the pension that day. Afterward they walked to the English Gardens and took snapshots under the trees. Helena had brought sandwiches as usual, but when four o'clock came, Betsy paused by the white-covered tables. Waitresses were rushing about with their moneybags jingling.

"Let's have coffee here! Please!" she pleaded.

Helena raised her pretty eyebrows. "They're very common people."

"So am I common. I'm terribly common. And, Helena, do you know what Abraham Lincoln said? 'God must love the common people because he made so many of them.'"

Helena laughed. "Come," she said, taking Betsy's arm. "I will drink coffee here. Not for the sake of your Abraham Lincoln, but because you are leaving so soon."

With their coffee they had sweet spirals of *Schnecken,* and above them birds were singing on frothy green boughs.

"I don't see why they call these *English* Gardens," Betsy grumbled. "The count who laid them out was born in Massachusetts. Of course, I know he was a

Tory and George the Third knighted him. Still, this is very like America."

"Everything good you claim for America."

"Come and see it, and you'll understand. Why don't you come, Helena? I'll matchmake you to a nice American boy. Of course, he'll be in trade," Betsy teased.

Helena smiled. But suddenly over the empty cups and plates and the white cloth on which blown maple wings were lying, Betsy saw that her eyes were full of tears.

"I am in love with my cousin Karl," she said.

"Why, Helena!" Betsy reached across and touched her hand. "Is he in love with you, too?"

"Yes."

"And will you be married?"

"Oh, no!"

"Why not?"

"My aunt wants a good match for him. It is quite right that she should. He is a lieutenant in the army."

"But you'd be a good match. You're pretty and clever and talented."

"I am poor."

"Well, he has plenty of money."

Helena shook her head.

"And Europeans were always saying that Americans liked money!" Betsy thought.

"Why don't you just get married?" she asked. "You could live on his salary."

But Helena, drying her eyes, did not bother to answer so preposterous a question.

"Helena," asked Betsy, "is this why you came to Munich?"

"Yes. There is talk at the castle of whom Karl will marry. My aunt thinks I behaved very well. I could go back. But, Betsy, I won't leave my mother."

"You could see her often."

"No, I couldn't." Helena's pale cheeks colored faintly. "I never saw my mother until I came to Munich. Not to remember her. You see . . . my father's family didn't like the marriage. My mother was English . . ."

And far beneath him, Betsy felt sure, the story unrolling like a scroll.

"They . . . cast him off. And it wasn't good for him."

Betsy knew. She had known since the day she went to their apartment.

"I didn't understand until I came to Munich, but now . . . I couldn't leave my mother. Things are hard for her, very hard. And she's so good to me . . . you can't imagine!" Helena's face glowed.

Betsy tried to remember that glow, for Helena's story left her with a heartache. Helena and her mother were so different. Tall and proud, Helena looked like a true aristocrat. She always made you think of something white—snow on a mountain, or moonlight, or lilies.

The next day Frau von Wandersee suggested that Betsy eat dinner at her table, and she was as dingy, frowsy, sly as ever.

"She must have something fine about her, and I ought to be able to dig it out," thought Betsy, but she couldn't seem to.

Frau von Wandersee talked on as usual about how much money people had . . . or didn't have . . . or used to have. But during the meal there came one moment of revelation.

She was saying that her daughter would miss Betsy. "She considers you a real friend. And she hasn't friends enough." The purring voice seemed to change, to strengthen. "Sometimes I'm afraid she ought to go back to her aunt."

"She doesn't want to, Frau von Wandersee."

"How do you know?"

"She told me. She said she would hate to leave you. She loves you very much."

Frau von Wandersee looked up. She looked straight at Betsy, which she didn't often do, and her eyes were luminous, beseeching.

"If I make her go back . . . it won't be that I want

her to go," Frau von Wandersee said. After a moment she added in her usual tone, "She will be over tonight to say good-by."

There was one last party in Munich. Betsy took Hanni out for afternoon coffee. She had to battle Frau Geiger, but the bath episode had given this lady respect for Betsy's perseverance. When she saw that the crazy American Fräulein was really in earnest, she gave in.

Hanni's face was one big smile. She wore a monstrous summer hat, several seasons old, and the lace collar and jabot Betsy had given her. She wouldn't say where she would like to go, so Betsy selected the zoo. Betsy was obliged to decide whether they would have coffee or tea and what kind of cakes. Hanni would only say, "As you will, Fräulein."

They discussed a favorite subject, Hanni coming to America. In the early days, Betsy had tried to plan how Hanni could marry her soldier. He could earn a little extra money, or leave the army and get another job.

"It is impossible," Hanni always said sadly. "I will come to America to you."

She loved to talk about this, telling Betsy over and over how hard she would work, how Betsy would have her clothes mended and her hair brushed and her breakfast in bed. She would live in Paradise, Hanni declared.

❧ 218 ❧

"Fräulein, when you are married, send for me, and I will come."

"And if I don't marry," Betsy said now, "when I get to be a famous author, we'll go around the world together."

"I'll have to write Tacy," she thought with a chuckle, "that I'm firing Celeste."

She took Hanni's picture, and the servant girl was transfixed with delight. She stood as straight as her soldier, smiling fixedly beneath the monstrous hat.

"I'll send you some prints from Venice," Betsy promised. Secretly she resolved to have one enlarged for Hanni's sweetheart.

For the last time Betsy heard the din of music practise at the Geiger. She said good-by to the cold bare dining room, to Susuki, and the Italian artist, the Austrians, the Bulgarians.

It was starting to rain and Betsy was afraid that Helena might not come, but she knocked at Betsy's door and came in smiling, wearing a raincoat glistening with drops. She carried a package.

"I can't stay. I know you are busy packing, but I wanted to say good-by. Betsy, I wish we could keep in touch."

"But of course we will! I'd love to correspond, and I write enormous letters."

Helena offered the package. Her sensitive face quivered with pleasure while Betsy unwrapped it.

219

There emerged a tall china cup, striped in pink and gold and blue.

"It is a cup the poet Goethe drank from."

"Why, Helena! How . . . how marvelous!"

"It's come down in our family. We haven't very many such things left; we've moved so much. But my mother and I thought you would like this because . . . you're a writer, too."

"I'm overwhelmed by it!" cried Betsy. "It will be one of my dearest treasures always." She threw her arms about Helena, wanting to cry.

For a second Helena's arms closed around Betsy. "You've helped me," she whispered, then drew back stiffly. She left soon after with *"auf Wiedersehen"* only, for Betsy assured her that she would be coming back.

While she packed, Betsy kept remembering that "You've helped me."

"I don't see how I helped her! Why couldn't I have liked her mother!" Betsy thought in self-reproach.

Packing was a complicated operation. Her trunk was being shipped to Innsbruck; only the bags were going on the fortnight of travel, and every article was shifted from bags to trunk and from trunk to bags, as Betsy decided now that she couldn't live without it and then that she would have to. Everything breakable had to be wrapped in something unbreakable, but there seemed to be more breakable than unbreakable objects. Goethe's cup had the steamer rug to itself. At the end the trunk would not shut although Betsy jumped on the lid. Hanni came in and sat on it.

The rain pounded, and in the wavering gaslight the dismantled room looked strange and unfamiliar. Ready at last to slip beneath her featherbed, Betsy opened the windows and looked out at the decorated house.

Helena had said she had helped her, but it seemed to Betsy that she hadn't helped anyone in Munich. Germans were hard to help. They were all so pessimistic, so sure that reduced circumstances could never be bettered nor difficulties solved.

Betsy remembered what she had told Tilda, that Bavaria made her think of a dark fairy tale. It did. In its wild mountains there were more sorcerers and ghosts and goblins than helpful fairies.

She thought of Helena locked in the prison of her title, and of that princess in the dining room who sat by herself, and of Hanni who worked so hard and couldn't marry her soldier. Although Munich was so *gemütlich,* it seemed to have a spell upon it.

But in the morning Hanni was smiling down at her above the breakfast tray. To the usual chocolate, hard rolls, and butter, she had added *ein bissel* marmalade. The rain had stopped and the air that the casement admitted was full of happy promise.

"A good journey, *gnädiges* Fräulein," Hanni said.

14
A Very Special Doll

BETSY WAS IN A BUS riding toward Krug's Hotel in Sonneberg deep in the Thuringian Mountains.

She had visited the festival city of Bayreuth. Opera was not sung at this season, but she had seen Richard Wagner's great Opera House, and his home, the Villa Wahnfried. In fact, she had trespassed in the garden there and had been ejected by no less a person than Wagner's son Siegfried.

At Nuremberg she had walked in enchantment around the old gray wall that encircled the medieval city. She had strolled the cobbled streets, looking up at the gable-roofed houses pierced by dormer windows . . . especially at the fifteenth-century house in which Albrecht Dürer had lived, and at the house of Hans Sachs, right out of *Die Meistersinger.* The cobbler poet had not always stayed at home, though. He had traveled the open road with a stick and a knapsack.

"Like I'm doing now," thought Betsy, ignoring the bulging suit cases piled around her feet. She was all alone in the bus and bounced like a piece of popcorn.

She had been surprised, at the Sonneberg station, to see a uniformed driver from Krug's Hotel. She had expected only a primitive inn in the little Doll Town and looked out curiously as the bus joggled along through a wide mountain valley. But the town was at some distance from the station.

Betsy caught her reflection in the bus mirror. She was beaming like Hanni at the coffee party.

"Pretty pleased with yourself, aren't you?" she asked. "Well, no wonder! I'm pleased with you myself."

She was pleased, for one thing, because her mail was being forwarded from Munich. There should be lots! Since leaving Munich she had had her twenty-second birthday. A strange birthday with no cake or presents, just the wine of traveling alone . . . seeing strange places, meeting new people, struggling with a foreign language! Her present, the family had written, was a check to be spent for new clothes in Paris. But there would certainly be some letters here.

"What a place," Betsy thought, "to be getting mail from Minnesota!" A town in the Thuringian Forest that had been making dolls since before Columbus!

But Sonneberg was a little like Deep Valley, she discovered as they entered. The mountains seemed no taller than the Big Hill and its companions had seemed to her and Tacy when they were little girls.

"Tacy would love this crazy expedition," Betsy thought.

Krug's Hotel was something of a shock. It was an imposing white stone building with gardens and shaded verandas. Betsy's room had electric lights, and steam heat flooded it with summery warmth, quite different from the limited circle of heat thrown off by porcelain stoves. Most surprising of all, there was a bathroom.

"Glory of glories!" Betsy cried. Her one and only bath in Munich was a long time behind her now. "What? No boots?" She smiled down at the gleaming white tub.

She was in wonderful spirits, in spite of the fact that there had been no mail awaiting her. It would come! And the clerk had spoken English!

"I might be in the Radisson Hotel in Minneapolis," Betsy thought.

The reason for this cosmopolitan atmosphere was, of course, that Sonneberg was the center of the doll trade. It drew buyers from London, Paris, New York. Betsy was made aware of this again, when, having freshened up, she went for a walk before supper.

On cobblestone streets, where oxen were more common than horses, she passed well-dressed, clean-shaven men wearing Derby hats, swinging canes.

"Heavens!" she thought. "I should have curled my hair!" But even with straight hair, she attracted attention enough. In her smartly cut suit and the big slanting hat with the rose—and, of course, the debutante slouch which she did not forget to assume—she seemed as surprising to the buyers as the buyers did to her. The Americans especially looked at her unbelievingly, and some even seemed on the point of speaking. But Betsy was cool and unresponsive.

The air, piney and fresh, was as stimulating as the unwonted admiration. The streets ran up the side of a mountain, but just a little timid way. Above them, where a stretch had been cleared of trees, old women with baskets on their backs were stooped over, gathering fuel. Higher still, the slope was darkly wooded and a bench had been placed to catch the view.

"Like the bench on Hill Street where Tacy and I used to take our suppers when we were little. Dear me, Tacy ought to be here!" Betsy mourned.

The newer streets had modern shops and villas, carriages, and even a few automobiles. But there were old streets, too. Streets so narrow that the gable-roofed houses almost touched overhead. Streets that were nothing but winding paths or steps up the side of the mountain.

Many people wore baskets, such as the old women had worn, fastened to their backs. Some of these were filled with wood; others, with groceries. But most of them were covered with white cloths and Betsy could not see what they contained.

Some of the women carried their babies tied on with shawls. Betsy smiled at them but they looked blank.

"People don't seem very friendly," she observed. Tilda had told her that the North Germans were different from the dark, vivacious, warm-hearted Müncheners, and it was certainly true.

Not the children, though! They gathered about her, smiling and nudging one another. Betsy tried out her German, and they bent their heads to conceal de-lighted chuckles. They were rosy and fat. All the little boys seemed to be outgrowing their jackets. The little girls wore aprons over their dresses, and thick black stockings, and stout shoes.

"But none of them are carrying dolls!" Betsy was puzzled. There certainly ought to be dolls on the streets of the doll metropolis! She couldn't look into the matter, for now the quick upland twilight fell. It was cozy to return to the warm luxurious hotel, but there still wasn't any mail.

The dining room was spacious with glittering chandeliers and potted palms, and the traveling men were already eating when Betsy came in. Her entrance caused a flattering commotion, and although she strove for a bored air, she was charmed with the proximity of the American men. Their voices, their slang, took her across the wide Atlantic—to her father, to Joe, to college dances and gaieties at the Ray house.

Eavesdropping as intently as she could while remembering to act blasé, she heard them discussing the States. They even mentioned Duluth, Minnesota. Betsy wanted to lean over and say, "Boo! I come from Minneapolis!" But she resisted.

After sauntering out like a woman of the world, she hurried to her room lest she be tempted into some indiscretion. She knew the rules for safety in traveling alone, and they didn't include picking up strange men acquaintances—even Americans!

She wrote home jubilantly, pouring out the day's adventures. And naturally she took a bath. She had had one before dinner, but she took another now and planned a third in the morning.

"Goodness knows when I'll see a bathroom again!"

She was glad, though, that Krug's Hotel was not too modern for a featherbed and slipped beneath it gratefully for the night air was sharp. In the morning the snug warmth of steam heat returned. She ate breakfast in her room, and presently in suit and hat with camera, notebook, and pencil, she was down in the cool invigorating morning.

Everyone was either at work or going to work. Sonnebergers, both men and women, hurried along with those large wicker baskets on their backs. All the baskets now seemed to be covered with white cloths. The buyers, freshly pressed and shaven, were heading for the doll factories—*Puppen Fabriken,* the desk clerk had called them.

There weren't many factories here; that was the reason the air was so pure, he had said. No smoking factory chimneys as in Nuremberg where they made their toys by machinery. In Sonneberg, manual work in the homes was most important.

Betsy, too, headed for a *Puppen Fabrik.* The large

modern buildings were easy to identify on Sonneberg's picturesque streets.

A crowd of children had already gathered behind her. "I feel like the Pied Piper," Betsy thought, turning to smile at them. One little girl put her hand shyly into Betsy's. She was the only thin one in the lot, elfishly thin, with a shock of pale straight hair and vivid eyes. Her name was Gretel.

At the door of the *Fabrik* a youth of tender years stood moodily with folded arms. Betsy asked in her best German if she might go through the factory. Before replying he astonished her by going through all the motions of brushing up a mustache, although his pink and white face looked as smooth as a girl's. Studying him closely she did catch a bit of fuzz.

A trip through the *Fabrik*? Impossible, he said, and brushed up the mustache again.

Betsy explained in a torrent of bad German that she came from the United States, that she was a writer, that she loved dolls and expected to have a large family of children who would also love dolls. Surely he would like to have her able to tell her children that she had seen the famous dolls of Sonneberg—*nicht wahr?*

He blushed. "Oh, I was calling him *du!*" Betsy thought in consternation. Tilda had warned her over and over that *du* was only for family and intimates.

He said something, bowed, and went inside. He would be back, the children told her, jumping up and down and laughing. They all waited.

He returned accompanied by a larger and more substantial young man with a florid face. Betsy repeated her speech, watching out for *du*'s. At the end he bowed again and now both youths disappeared.

The pair returned with an older man. He had a paunch with a gold watch chain across it and piercing eyes behind thick spectacles.

"I must be careful not to call him *du*," Betsy warned herself, repeating her speech with care.

When she finished he too bowed. He turned upon the two young men with rapid words; she thought he was calling them donkeys. Then he said in careful English, "Gracious young lady, it makes us very happy that you wish to see our dolls. Have the goodness to let these two young men accompany you!"

So the two young men took her through the factory. It made dolls' heads, she found. These were sent to the homes.

"In baskets!" Betsy cried.

"*Ja*, in baskets, covered with clean white cloths!" In the homes the eyes were put in, the hair was pasted on, bodies were attached; the dolls acquired dresses, hats, and shoes.

"Do the children help?"

"*Ja, natürlich!* Whole families."

"And do the children . . . still like dolls?" It would be too sad, she thought, if they didn't; if that was the reason she had not seen any little girls playing with dolls!

But the young men were baffled by this question and hurried her off to the showroom. Here she saw finished products, samples of dolls that would come out next Christmas. There was a dazzling array! Blond dolls and brunette dolls, large dolls and small dolls, dolls of every kind, type, and costume.

"Oh, what a beauty!" Betsy cried, reaching for a large, yellow-haired charmer. It was dressed in pale blue and wore a straw hat with a high pink plume, pink gloves, and pink shoes and stockings!

"Tacy and I would certainly have bonied this one," Betsy thought.

When she and Tacy were children they had loved to look at the dolls in the Christmas shop windows, pressing their noses against the plate glass while snow fell and sleighbells tinkled all up and down Front Street.

"I bony this one!"

"I bony that one!"

"So do I."

Betsy stood with the big doll in her arms thinking about Tacy. At last she put it down. "I really must go now. Thank you for showing me the factory." The two young men glanced at each other, and the slender one began to twirl his invisible mustache into fascinating spirals.

"And this evening?" the florid one asked softly. "Would the Fräulein enjoy a ride?"

"Or a little walk?" suggested his companion.

"A glass of beer, perhaps?"

Betsy shrugged as though she did not understand. *"Ich verstehe nicht,"* she said brightly. "Good-by. Thank you again."

The children had disappeared. Were they making dolls? she wondered, walking back to the hotel. She hoped Gretel had a doll. There was still no mail, and after dinner, during which she happily impressed the buyers with her aloof sophistication, Betsy went to the Historical City Museum.

She saw the dolls that over past years had won prizes for the Sonneberg makers. A life-sized Gulliver covered with tiny Lilliputians. A miniature Kirmess, complete with merry-go-round, fortuneteller, dancing girl, clowns, fruit vendor, crowds of people, even dogs.

There was a display of period dolls beginning with rude figures cut from wood. Each successive generation was dressed like the children who had played with them, and Betsy saw dolls in costumes of the

Civil War era who looked like Meg, Jo, Beth, and Amy. She saw dolls in accordian-pleated skirts, in long-waisted dresses that looked like herself, or Tib, or Tacy.

She and Tacy had been funny about dolls, Betsy reflected. The most important thing to see on Christmas morning, poking out of a stocking, or sitting under a tree, was a big curly-haired fancily dressed doll. But after Christmas they used to put these dolls away. They preferred paper dolls cut from magazines. And Tacy, of course, preferred real babies.

Tacy had always been crazy about babies. She used to help Betsy take care of Margaret, and Tib take care of her little brother Hobbie. She even used to ask the neighborhood mothers to let her take their babies out riding in their carriages—just for fun!

"Why am I thinking about Tacy all the time, for goodness' sake!" cried Betsy, and went out into the sunshine. She wished to get a peek, if she could, of the doll-making in the homes, and in the old part of town the streets were so narrow that you couldn't avoid looking in the windows.

She made her way to those ancient houses with dormer windows sticking through the roofs. The streets were clean and cheerful. Ducks waddled along the cobblestones. There were pink and white fruit trees at every turning and multitudes of children.

The children made a rush for her. Gretel put her hand into Betsy's as a matter of course, smiling elfishly through pale wisps of hair. Betsy took snapshots of them all and asked an older boy to write down their names and addresses so that she could send them pictures.

Loitering along with her bodyguard, she saw men and women sitting in the windows, and they *were* making dolls. One flaxen-haired woman was gluing on a flaxen wig. Another was seated at a table covered with doll hats. A man wearing an apron was wiring eyes into rows of china heads.

Betsy turned to the children. "Do you have dolls?" she asked. *"Puppen?"* She rocked one in her arms.

They stared at her for a moment. Then the little girls turned and ran. Gretel ran into the house where the woman was gluing on wigs. They all returned with shining faces, and each one was holding a banged and battered doll.

"Look, *gnädiges* Fräulein!" Gretel's vivid eyes were snapping as she exhibited a headless treasure. *"Meine Puppe.* She is called Victoria."

So! That was settled. It was all right. But returning to the hotel in the late afternoon Betsy admitted a craving that had been growing all day. She wanted a doll! She wanted one even though she *was* twenty-two years old. Moreover, she knew the very doll she wanted. The yellow-haired charmer with the pink plume on her hat.

It wasn't easy to buy it, although she found her two cavaliers without difficulty. They were delighted to see her, thinking at first that she had reconsidered about the drive, the walk, the glass of beer. But when she explained her real reason for returning, the florid one frowned and the slender one tugged sternly at his mustache.

"Please! *Bitte*!" Betsy waved her purse. "I can't leave Sonneberg without a doll. The gentleman who spoke to me this morning . . . maybe *he* would sell me a doll." She hoped they would remember that he had called them donkeys.

She won, and marched out triumphantly with the pink and blue beauty. "She looks just like Lillian Russell," Betsy thought. But before she reached the hotel she began to feel a little foolish. A doll did look strange on the arm of a girl in a picture hat with long rustling skirts.

"Crazy *Amerikanisches* Fräulein!" she could imagine people saying.

"Of course," she told herself, trying to find a sensible motive, "of course I bought her for someone. My little sister . . . ?" But Margaret, in high school now, was more interested in boys than dolls.

"Who could she be for?" Betsy wondered. She

couldn't seem to remember a single child of doll-playing age.

What made it worse, the buyers were in the lobby smoking and reading their newspapers. They all looked up and some of them grinned. It was hard to saunter by like a lady author with your arms full of pink and blue doll. Betsy blushed crimson and thought she would never reach the desk.

Once there she forgot her chagrin. She forgot the doll, everything! For there was an enormous stack of mail—from her parents . . . Julia . . . Margaret . . . Cab . . . Tib . . . Tacy . . .

"I'm going to open Tacy's first," Betsy planned. "I've been thinking about her all day."

Up in her summer-warm room, she put the big doll against the pillows of her bed and established herself blissfully in an armchair by the window. Smiling in anticipation, she opened Tacy's letter and started to read. But in a moment she put it down on the bed. She clasped her hands in her lap and tears came into her eyes.

Tacy was going to have a baby!

Tacy! Betsy could hardly take it in. Why, she could remember Tacy at her own fifth birthday party, bringing a gift of a little glass pitcher, so shy that she held her head down and her long red ringlets fell over her face! But it was wonderful. It was just right. Tacy had always loved babies. Betsy had been remembering that all day.

"Only, I wish I could be there! I wish I didn't have to be so far away!" said Betsy, and she leaned her head on the bed and her tears flowed over Tacy's letter, making it quite soggy. Betsy sat up when she realized that, for she hadn't finished reading it yet, and her gaze fell on the big doll with its pale blue dress and coat, and its hat with the pink plume, the pink gloves, and the pink shoes and stockings.

Betsy caught it into her arms.

"*That's* why I bought you!" she cried, and her tears came faster and faster, but they were happy now. "*That's* why I bought you! I knew you were a very special doll."

A very special doll, for a very special baby! Tacy's baby! Maybe she would have red curls like Tacy's?

Betsy had an awful thought.

"But what if it isn't a girl?"

"Well! It had better be!" cried Betsy.

15
A Short Stay in Heaven

TILDA WAS WAITING at the Oberammergau station. She and Betsy flew into each other's arms.

"Betsy!" Tilda whispered ecstatically. "Here is Heaven!"

Betsy breathed deep of the mountain air. She looked around at the houses—white-plastered, green-shuttered, red-roofed—and up at the rolling hills that were buttressed by pine-covered slopes. On a rocky height overlooking the village stood the famous Cross of Oberammergau.

"So it's Heaven!" Betsy replied. "Well, I've certainly been climbing to reach it!"

She had come by way of Munich, and her train had started climbing soon after the towers of the Frauenkirche melted into the blue. It had wound around mountainsides, past shining lakes and waterfalls, higher and higher, until the skyline wore royal crowns of snow. Far below, the valleys were dotted with villages, each one a cluster of red roofs about a spire. Oberammergau was swung like the others in a green hammock of valley.

Betsy had heard of it all her life. She knew that almost three hundred years before, when the Black Death was ravaging the Bavarian highlands, these villagers had promised that if God would spare them they would perform every ten years the drama of Jesus' Death and Passion. No man, woman, or child had fallen to the plague after the vow was made, and it had been faithfully kept by succeeding generations. Given at first in the churchyard, the play now required a huge auditorium. Every tenth year, from May to September, throngs of people from all over the world poured into the village—and then went away, leaving it to the peaceful isolation which

Tilda and Betsy now disturbed.

The girls had engaged rooms with Herr and Frau Baumgarten. They were already, Betsy found, Uncle and Aunt to Tilda who had arrived the day before. *Tante* Else was a spindling old lady with a smile almost as broad as her white cotton umbrella. *Onkel* Max was tall, too, and knobbily thin.

"And that's Hedwig!" Tilda smiled at an apple-cheeked servant girl who was bundling Betsy's belongings into a handcart.

Accustomed to the geometric arrangement of an American middle-western town, Betsy was charmed by Oberammergau's streets. They ran without rhyme or reason under flowering fruit trees, pink and white. There were no sidewalks.

On many of the whitewashed houses Biblical scenes were frescoed in bright colors. Shrines looked down from almost every door. Crosses spread benignant arms above rooftops, in gardens, at street corners. The people looked Biblical, too. Many men wore their hair long, and beards were everywhere—black, brown, yellow, gray.

"*Natürlich!*" Tante Else said. "In the Passion Play, the actors would not wear wigs or false beards, any more than they would powder and paint."

"And Betsy!" Tilda said. "They call each other often by their names from the Passion Play . . .

Judas, Pilate, even Christ."

"*Ach, ja!*" said Onkel Max. "Christus Lang. You must meet him this afternoon."

Even more suggestive of holiness than the Biblical scenes, and beards and names, were the smiles that welcomed Betsy and Tilda. "*Grüss Gott!*" everyone said.

"God bless you!" What a wonderful greeting!

Children ran out to take their hands and curtsy. There was a pervading air of friendliness, of love.

"Maybe there's one place in the world where people really live up to their religion," Betsy thought, looking around.

"Wait until you see our *Haüschen,*" Tilda kept saying. At last she cried, "There it is!" And Betsy let out a joyful cry.

The lawn was smartly green. White stones edged the graveled paths, and peach trees in radiant bloom stood out against the lath and plaster walls. A balcony ran around the second story, and a smaller one stretched across the front, up under the eaves.

"Oh, that sweet balcony! The little one!"

"It's outside your room," said Tilda. "I remembered you liked balconies."

Onkel Max and Tante Else smiled proudly.

Up two flights of stairs they clattered, followed by Hedwig with the suit cases. They went through Tilda's room and into Betsy's, which had a puffy white bed and a *Herr Gott* worked in brightly colored yarns on the white-washed wall. They pushed out to the little balcony.

"Nice! *Nicht?* " asked Tilda.

"Darling!" Betsy looked down in delight.

Sunlight danced on the clear River Ammer winding through the village. Out in the fields oxen were dragging ploughs and old women with white scarves on their heads bent to their work. Beyond the fields, blossoming meadows climbed to dark masses of pines, and in the distance the skyline was topped with a white meringue. The balcony faced the towering cross.

"How it glitters!" Betsy exclaimed.

"It is covered with zinc," Tante Else explained. "It catches every ray of light. We can see it before dawn and after sunset, even. But now you must have second breakfast. Here on your balcony."

She and Onkel Max retreated. Hedwig of the apple cheeks brought hot water in a thin-necked pitcher. And while Betsy washed, and drank coffee and ate *Pfannkuchen,* and finally unpacked, she and Tilda talked, talked, talked.

"Whatever are you doing with that doll?" asked Tilda when Betsy lifted the radiant creature out of its box.

Betsy told the great news of Tacy's baby.

"And me unmarried at the ripe old age of twenty-two!"

"You had your birthday all alone!"

"I felt very philosophical. I planned out my future all the way to when I'm an old lady. I'm going to wear a cap and sit by the fire."

"We'll fatten you up for it," said Tilda. "Here we eat all day. And never did you taste such cooking!"

Running downstairs and outdoors, they crossed a rustic bridge to those slanting meadows strewn with daisies, forget-me-nots, violets, and buttercups. They sang "Peg o' My Heart." They raced through the grass like children.

"This air goes to my head," said Betsy, smoothing her hair as they walked back, more sedately, to dinner. It was such a meal as she remembered from the Mullers, rich, heavy, and delicious. Tante Else loved to work in her kitchen as her husband loved to pull weeds from his velvety lawn and whitewash the stones along his graveled paths.

After dinner they all went over to the Langs'.

Anton Lang lived in a rambling house, plastered in white like its neighbors and bearing above the door a shrine and the scrolled name of its master. He was a potter and his workshop was attached.

In the yard, which was full of fruit trees, children,

and confusion, they met Frau Lang, a small plump woman with rolled-up sleeves who greeted them in English. She had bright black eyes, ready dimples, and a chuckly voice.

Cheeriness seemed to be the keynote for the family. There was Anna, Anton's sister, tall, energetic, and overflowing with fun. She was one of the Three Weeping Women in the Passion Play.

"But I can't imagine her weeping," Betsy whispered.

There was Matilde's father, a one-time director of the Passion Play chorus, and little Martha, the baby and pet of the family. The white-haired old man and the toddler were as jolly as the others.

Anna said, "Come on in and see Tony!" And they all trooped into a workshop filled with the tile stoves, plates, jugs, and vases that Anton Lang made. There were several men in the shop, but Betsy recognized the Christus before he put down his tools and turned to greet them.

Back home, the pictures of this large bearded man had aroused in her a slight unreasonable resentment. It had seemed presumptuous in any human being to appear in the role of Jesus. This feeling melted before his warm unaffected smile.

He was slightly stooped, and wore work clothes, dusty from his craft. He had flowing light brown hair and beard, and a strong face with keen, humorous, light-blue eyes. His stoop was humble but his whole manner expressed a simple natural dignity. Like his wife, he spoke in English.

"What a happy family!" Betsy commented as she and Tilda and the Baumgartens walked home.

"Tony is a good man," Onkel Max said. "No man is chosen for the Christ unless his life is blameless."

"In Passion Play summers," Tante Else added, "he goes into another world. It is very hard, the part . . . so full of strain. Imagine the fatigue of hanging for twenty minutes to the cross! And the self-control he must exercise when he is taken down for dead, and the blood comes rushing painfully back into his arms."

"There are other times when he must show self-control," Onkel Max broke in. "The adoration of the crowds would spoil some men. People besiege him; often he hides out in one of the mountain grottos to escape them and Anna brings him his meals."

They spoke in German, but Tilda quickly translated the words Betsy did not know. For both of them, the Passion Play had come out of books into life.

Tante Else went on to say that Herr Lang had refused huge sums to play his role elsewhere. Once, an American manager came all the way to Oberammergau to ask him to star in a play, "The Servant in the House."

"Tony would not think of it, of course. And the manager was astonished. He thought every man had his price."

Through coffee in the garden and supper back at the dining-room table, they talked about the Passion Play. They kept on talking until they grew sleepy, and then Tante Else urged cookies and milk. Out on their balcony before going to bed, the girls drank in the country dark and silence.

Breakfast was served back in the garden, dazzling in morning freshness. Second breakfast, Tante Else announced, each one took where he pleased.

"You'll never again be able to lament that I haven't seen German home life," Betsy told Tilda. For they were treated like daughters. They scattered their belongings from end to end of the Haüschen, and if they went across the Ammer they were given picnic lunches and enough cautions to have brought them safe out of Daniel's fiery furnace.

Kindly proud guides, the Baumgartens took them to the church and the great Passion theater that stood on the edge of the village. The stage was in the open air with the natural background of mountains. They went into the dressing rooms. They saw the basin in which the repentant woman bathed the feet of Christ; the table and chairs used for the Last Supper; the cross. They inspected the costumes which were all of the finest materials.

"They are made by the villagers themselves, copied from famous paintings," Tante Else said.

They called on Ottile Zwink, the Virgin Mary of the last Passion Play. Married now, she would not play the part again. She met them at her door in a spotless apron. Betsy, who had expected a pink and white beauty, was surprised.

"You'd hardly even call her pretty," she and Tilda agreed later. But she had a sweet tender mouth—like Tacy's—blue eyes and wavy brown hair.

Her little parlor was full of Passion Play mementoes. Shyly, she showed them pictures of herself as Mary and autographed one for each.

As the days went on the girls met many of the actors. They even met the ass used in the entry to Jerusalem. In every home they were shown photograph albums.

"Family albums, Oberammergau style!" Betsy wrote in her diary-letter. "Instead of 'This is my aunt's cousin who was killed falling off a step-ladder,' we hear, 'This is my brother-in-law. He played Herodotus in 1900.'"

Only natives of the village were allowed to take part in the play.

"How sad for a little girl whose family just moved

in!" Betsy exclaimed. "All her playmates would probably be seraphims with three sets of wings apiece, and she couldn't be even a little old baby angel with one pair."

"*Ach!*" said Tilda. "You're always making up stories."

Every day, wherever else they went, Betsy and Tilda walked through the twisting streets, past curtsying children and their smiling elders, to Anton Lang's house which was the friendly center of the village. Here too, in Herr Lang's workshop or Frau Lang's shining kitchen, the Passion Play was discussed.

In Oberammergau time was marked not by years but by tens of years. As the villagers made their pottery, or their fine wood carvings, or tilled their fields and gardens, they talked of the Passion Play summer that was fading into the past and of the one that was looming ahead. They presented minor plays now and then.

"Fine training," Onkel Max explained, "and a good way to discover talent. It helps the judges decide who shall be picked for the great Passion Play."

For this purpose, every tenth year a committee of villagers met in the Town Hall in secret session. It was a solemn religious occasion. Betsy felt prickles along her spine as she listened to Tante Else tell how Anton Lang had been chosen.

"Nobody expected it. He was only twenty." His modest hope, Tante Else said, rose no higher than the part of St. John. And he only dreamed of that, talking in secret with his father of how wonderful it would be to play the Beloved Disciple.

He was at supper in his father's house. The committee had been in the Town Hall all day. Everyone was on edge. And suddenly shouting neighbors were tapping at every window, and others were crowding through the doorway.

"Tony is to play the Christus!" they cried. "The committee has picked Tony."

Tony's face went white, Tante Else said. Without a word he rushed into his bedroom.

One sparkling morning, Betsy and Tilda set off for the monastery of Ettal. It was from Ettal, Herr Lang had told them, that the Passion Play had sprung. The monks had written the earliest known version in 1662.

Their way led up piney mountain paths. Betsy and Tilda picked flowers and laid them on the roadside shrines. Once they stopped in a meadow for Betsy to teach Tilda the tango. And when the lesson was ended, Betsy ran to an apple tree and broke off blossoms for their hair.

"These make me think of Joe Willard."

"Vy?" Tilda wanted to know, for she was always interested in Joe. "Betsy," she said in English. "You loff him. For vy you fight?"

But instead of answering, Betsy swung Tilda into the tango again.

At Ettal their mood changed. The ancient monastery with its enormous church was startling in this lofty solitude. And the cool hushed cloisters were strange after the blazing spring sunshine.

The monks who had lived here long ago had done more than write the Passion Play. They had taught the villagers to act by putting on those miracle and morality plays so popular in the Middle Ages. They had taught them music. They had taught them to carve in wood and ivory. The library with its thousands of volumes had been a source of culture.

"Ettal explains a lot about Oberammergau," Tilda said thoughtfully, walking homeward, and Betsy agreed. It explained why the people of that village were so different from the run of mountaineers. It explained their gentle manners, their dignity, their cultivated voices. They were even unusually handsome.

"It doesn't explain everything though," Betsy added, and Tilda understood. How about that simple goodness that filled the village like soft air?

Betsy remembered something Onkel Max had told them. "Generations of boys have grown up here with just one ambition, to play the Christ."

They walked on silently for they seemed to be touching the hem of a mystery.

Tilda said at last, "I wonder how long Oberammergau can keep itself unspotted from the world."

"Always," Betsy answered confidently.

"Could it survive a war?"

Betsy faced her, laughing, hands on hips. "You Europeans! There's never going to be another war."

On the last day, of course, they went to say good-by to the Langs. They were in the workshop talking, when a clatter sounded in the street. Excited voices lifted, and Betsy looked out to see a cloud of dust and a low-slung expensive-looking automobile.

For a moment she was delighted. The young man in the car was obviously American. She was reminded happily of dating and dancing. "Of my gay young days," she thought and wondered where he came from. But when children ran in shouting that the foreigner wished to speak with the Christus, Betsy's pleasure fled.

The young American sprawled behind the wheel, smoking a cigarette, waiting with condescension for Oberammergau's world-famous Anton Lang to come out into the street and greet him.

"*I'm* going out!" Betsy said furiously. "I'll tell him to go home and learn some manners!"

But Herr Lang smiled and said, "No, please!" He put down his work, dusted off his hands, and went out to stand bareheaded in the sun and chat with the young tourist who did not remove his hat, did not unsprawl, and acted, Betsy thought, as though he were inspecting animals in a zoo.

"I'm ashamed!" she raged to Tilda who, although she was indignant, too, was a little amused at Betsy.

"It is the first time you have ever admitted that anything American was less than perfect," Tilda said.

Betsy kept looking through the window, at Anton Lang in his rough clothes standing in the dust beside that automobile. He didn't even seem annoyed, although there was a quizzical look in his eyes.

Anton Lang gave Tilda and Betsy each an autographed picture, and a little pottery angel signed with his name. The Baumgartens loaded their charges with flowers, and presents, and packets of lunch, and half of Oberammergau took them to the station behind Hedwig's rattling cart.

The girls weren't leaving together. Tilda, who had to get back to her school, was going by train. Betsy was going by bus, for she wanted to see the Mad King's castle of Linderhof nearby, before she went over the Brenner Pass to Italy.

"*Liebe, liebe* Betsy!" Tilda kept saying as they waited for the train.

"Dear, dear Tilda!" said Betsy. "But I'll be coming back in 1917." That was the date of their planned re-union.

To keep from feeling weepy, Betsy started a chant such as they used at football games at home.

"*Neunzehn siebzehn! Neunzehn siebzehn!*" Nine-teen seventeen! Tilda fell in with it, of course.

Her train arrived; they hugged and kissed, and in a flurry of good-bys she climbed to the platform. Short, erect like a singer, very graceful, her plain little face made lovely by a smile, she called her last farewell. And as the train pulled out, she and Betsy took up the chant again, waving, laughing, crying a little.

"*Neunzehn siebzehn! Neunzehn siebzehn!*"

Yes, Betsy resolved, she was coming back in 1917 and nothing could stop her.

16

Betsy Curls Her Hair

IT WAS NOT QUITE EVENING when Betsy's train shot out between sky and water to the City of the Sea.

She was tired, having left Innsbruck early that morning. She was exhausted, too, by her enthusiasm over the Alpine scenery. And there had been an emotional wrench when she left Austria (which seemed just like Bavaria) and descended to Italy's vineyards and olive orchards, and the air grew warm, sweet, and lazy.

She had changed trains at Verona. Grateful to find that she shared her compartment with nuns, she had relaxed completely, fully believing that she would not begin to savor Venice until after a good night's sleep. But sweeping across this bridge into a crystalline world jolted her awake.

In a moment they were in a bustling railway station and Betsy, clutching her handbag, camera, umbrella, and *Complete Pocket Guide*, looked about for one, two, or three Signorinas Regali.

"They shouldn't be hard to find," she thought. "Little old ladies in black." But while she still stood looking around, a young Italian approached, his straw hat in his hand.

He was very good-looking, with thick black hair, just slightly wavy, and expressive dark eyes that seemed darker and brighter because of heavy brows and lashes. He was olive skinned, clean shaven; white teeth shone when he smiled. To her surprise he spoke in English.

"Are you Miss Ray?"

"Yes, I am."

"I am Mark Regali. My aunt asked me to meet you, and some other guests for the *Casa delle Rose d'Oro.*"

They shook hands and he beckoned the boy with her bags.

Emerging from the station, Betsy gasped. Of course she had known that Venice had streets of water. Yet it was a shock to see gondolas and motor boats crowding about the quay like hacks and auto taxis and to hear boatmen crying out for fares. She flashed a delighted look at Mr. Regali.

They joined two plump ladies—Miss Cook and Mrs. Warren from Philadelphia—and Mr. Regali helped them all into a gondola. This looked excitingly familiar, curving out of the water at both ends, with a small covered cabin in which they seated themselves. The gondolier stood at the stern, his oar in his hands.

They glided off into the Grand Canal. Dusk had fallen, but there was a moon. It turned the street of water into an even more incredible street of trembling silver. When the clamor of the station died away, there was no sound but the soft plash of an oar and some distant music. Betsy spoke of the silence and Mr. Regali said, smiling at her, "The Grand Canal is in the shape of an *S*. Italians say this stands for Silenzio."

At that moment a shrill whistle blew and a loaded steamboat hurried past, churning up a noisy wash of water. He and Betsy both laughed.

"That's a *vaporetto*. They are our streetcars. They're

very convenient even though they do spoil my story."
He was nice, Betsy thought. She wondered how he
happened to speak English.

Moonlight shimmered over the snowy palaces that
rose on either side. They rose straight from the water.
Betsy had expected a scrap of lawn or sidewalk in
front, but there was none. Just steps, lapped by the
waves, and some tall striped posts. These were hitching posts for gondolas, Mr. Regali said.

As they glided along he pointed out houses in
which Wagner had lived, and Browning and Byron.
The ladies from Philadelphia peered out and asked,
"Where? Which one?" But Betsy was speechless with
rapture. She sat with her hands squeezed together,
looking at the glimmering city. Byron was right. It did
seem to have come from the stroke of an enchanter's
wand.

"Oh, I love it! I love it!" she thought. "How lucky
I am to be here."

Mr. Regali looked at her now and then.

They traversed a network of shadowy small canals
and arrived at the House of the Yellow Roses. It was
one of a row of white houses and had iron window
grilles through which lights were streaming. There
were no yellow roses in sight, but there was a sidewalk!

In the tiny office, crowded with new arrivals, all

was confusion. The three Signorinas Regali—small, dark, and dressed in black, as described—welcomed Betsy kindly. One spoke English, and asked her if she would have dinner. She had dined in Verona, Betsy answered. All her fatigue had come back. She was longing for her room—and her mail.

"Miss Ray has a great deal of mail," Mr. Regali reminded his aunt and brought it out from the desk at which Betsy was registering. There was a glorious thick pack, bound with a cord. Betsy smiled luminous thanks, and clutching her treasure, she followed the maid up to her room.

She didn't even take off her hat before diving into the letters . . . the first she had received since Sonneberg. Having finished them, she undressed and dropped into bed without even unpacking. It seemed no time at all until sunlight was flooding into her windows along with the hum of bees and a sweet, sweet scent.

Betsy jumped up. Her room overlooked the garden! And the white walls that enclosed it were covered with climbing roses. *There* were the yellow roses, and pink and red ones, too! Below her, little paths intersected flower beds, and in a patch of lawn, tables were ready for breakfast.

Her room had a desk. "Hooray! I'll lay a story in Venice. A love story, of course."

She could hardly wait for her trunk, to get out her books and writing materials. She would go to the Custom House this morning, she planned. Meanwhile she unpacked her suit cases and ran downstairs to breakfast.

The House of the Yellow Roses was different from the Geiger. Here were no impecunious European students but prosperous American tourists, with flags in their buttonholes and guidebooks open on the table—Miss Cook and Mrs. Warren, four college girls, a doctor with his family, a young man from Harvard and another from Princeton. There was one lone Englishman.

"Sort of broken down," Betsy decided. He was well into middle age with a red dissipated face which had once been handsome but wasn't any more.

They were all talking of what they would see today—cutting up Venice as though it were a sausage and their days were sandwiches, Betsy thought. No one planned to stay more than a week. Half that time was more common. She was offered numerous sightseeing schedules, and people acted astonished and almost resentful when she said she planned to stay six weeks.

Mr. Regali, who ate with his aunts, strolled past and said good morning.

"Don't get a crush!" one of the college girls warned

Betsy. "It won't do you any good."

"What made you think I was going to?"

"Everyone does. But he's not susceptible."

"And he's busy making drawings."

Harvard turned to Princeton. "Do you suppose they talk *us* over like that?"

Mr. Regali strolled past the table again.

When they rose, the Englishman said to Betsy, "May I offer my services, Miss Ray, in introducing you to Venice? I have a gondola ordered for ten."

"Oh, no thank you!" said Betsy hastily. She groped for an excuse. "I have to go to the Custom House to see about my trunk."

"I'll take you there. It will be a pleasure." He bowed quickly as though the matter were settled.

Flushing, Betsy glanced around. Mr. Regali was listening, his black brows drawn together. She would consult his aunts, Betsy thought, and went to the office, but it was empty. Mr. Regali followed her inside.

"See here!" he said. "Excuse me! But you can't go out with that fellow."

"Oh, dear! I know it. But what am I to do?"

"You are in my aunts' care. They would never permit it."

"Of course not. But what can I *say*?" Betsy wailed.

His answer was stern. "Go back and tell him that you've changed your mind. Tell him you don't *think*"—

he stressed the word—"you'll be going out today. Then as soon as he's out of the way, I'll take you to the Custom House myself."

"All right," said Betsy meekly. It was wonderful to have broad shoulders to drop her problem on.

When the Englishman had departed, she and Mr. Regali took a *vaporetto* to the railway station. It was a sunshiny morning with a breeze, and Betsy's spirits rose like a balloon in the bright Venetian blue. Mr. Regali's kept pace. Leaning over the rail, they laughed together at the neatness with which they had extricated her from her predicament.

The Grand Canal was crowded with watercraft, and all around them was a babble of Italian.

"How do you happen to speak English?" Betsy asked.

"I lived in the States until I was fifteen."

"*You did?* Where?"

"Princeton, New Jersey. My father taught in the University. When my parents died, I came here to my aunts. So Venice has been my home for eight years."

Then he was twenty-three. Just a year older than she was!

"Of course, I've been off at college," he added. "Rome."

"Finished?"

"I'm an architect. And I was lucky enough to be

put on a research project. I was sent right back here with some very interesting work laid out. I'm making drawings now of the choir stalls at San Giorgio Maggiore."

"Do you . . ." Betsy broke off, laughing. "Really," she said, "I was brought up not to ask personal questions. I know I shouldn't be hurling them at you. It's just so wonderful . . . to be out with someone my own age who speaks English. I'm so happy!"

"So am I," he answered.

After getting her trunk through customs, they ordered it sent to the pension and Mr. Regali said, "Why don't we look around Venice a little before we go home?"

Because it was near, they went first to the Rialto. The old marble bridge was lined with cheap little shops. The proprietors stood in front haggling over prices with women in black shawls.

"All the treasures of the Orient used to be spread out here," Mr. Regali remarked.

"And Shylock used to come!"

They took another *vaporetto* to St. Mark's Square . . . the Piazza, Mr. Regali called it. It looked just as it did in all the pictures, except that the colors of the marble buildings were richer and the Grand Canal sparkled as it never did on canvas.

Tourists were going in and out of the rosy Doge's Palace and St. Mark's Cathedral with its oriental-looking domes. They were looking up at the clock tower and the golden angel on top of the Campanile. They were lunching at the open-air cafés, and feeding the pigeons that kept circling down in glossy waves.

"Oh, I wish we'd brought my camera! I want my picture taken feeding the pigeons."

"If you really do," said Mr. Regali, "I'll take it the next time we come. I believe we've passed lunchtime. How about stopping here at Florian's?"

They lunched at that famous café, outdoors. Betsy kept looking around at the brilliant busy square.

"They have music in the evenings."

"Oh, that would be too celestial!"

"You must let me bring you soon."

They walked from the Piazza to the Piazzetta, and between two stately columns, topped by St. Theodore and the famous winged Lion of St. Mark, down to the quay. The Grand Canal was full of gondolas, barges, yachts, and ferries. The gondoliers began to call: *"Una gondola, Signor! Una barca!"*

Mr. Regali nodded across the water. "See that tower? It's on the church of San Giorgio Maggiore."

"That's where you're drawing the choir stalls."

"Yes. And the view from the tower is the finest in Venice. Let's go over; shall we?"

"Oh, yes!" Betsy said.

So they took a gondola to San Giorgio Maggiore. The gondolier wore white with a green sash. They swept gently over the water and landed at another domed church. Palladio had built it in the sixteenth century, Mr. Regali said, and going inside he showed her pictures by Tintoretto, and the choir stalls. "Magnificent baroque!"

They climbed what seemed like a hundred thousand dark steep steps, but when they came out into the sunshine, Venice was spread out below like a map, glistening white, the water dotted with the orange sails of fishing vessels.

"Oh, oh!" cried Betsy.

"Ripping, isn't it?" came a British voice. There was another visitor in the tower. The Englishman of the House of the Yellow Roses lifted a soft hat.

"Why . . . how do you do? I *did* go out after all," said Betsy.

"So I see."

"We attended to the trunk," said Mr. Regali.

Then, forsaking the view, he and Betsy turned and clattered down the stairs. Laughing, they ran as though pursued, down through the vertical darkness and out into the light and back to their gondola.

"Wasn't *that* a horrible moment?" Betsy asked.

"He's a horrible person. The idea of his thinking he could take you out all alone on your first day in Venice!"

Simultaneously they realized that it was just what he himself had done, and they broke into laughter.

❧ 264 ❧

It dawned on Betsy that they had been laughing all day.

"I laugh with him like I do with Tilda, and Tacy and Tib," she thought. She felt as though she had known him forever. It seemed completely natural to be wandering around with him, but it came to her now that perhaps it hadn't been quite proper.

"I was having so much fun I forgot about everything."

She had even forgotten how she looked. She hadn't so much as glanced in her pocket mirror. Taking it out now, she tucked her hair beneath the red and green cap, buttoned her red jacket, and smoothed the skirts of her pale green cotton dress.

"If I'd known we were going to stay all day, I'd have worn a hat, at least."

"I like you the way you are," said Mr. Regali. "Do you know," he added thoughtfully, "there's a full moon. *This* might be a good night to go over to St. Mark's Square."

"And it might not," said Betsy, and laughed, and he laughed, too. He knew she had realized belatedly that they had been together for a very long time.

Reaching the pension, Betsy went straight to her room. She rested and bathed and changed into a white dress. At dinner she talked animatedly to her fellow Americans. (The Englishman ignored her.) And in the evening she took pains to join the college girls in the garden. Mr. Regali walked past them once or twice.

She went to her room early, for her trunk had arrived. She unpacked, and settled her desk, and got out her photographs and Goethe's cup and Tacy's doll, and put the American flag over her mirror. She wrote her home letter and told the story of the day, not forgetting the embarrassing situation on the tower at San Giorgio Maggiore.

"Mr. Regali is a perfect dear," she was writing when she heard a knock. She opened the door to find one of the maids with an enormous armful of pink roses.

"Oh, thank you! *Grazie!*" Betsy cried. But she knew from whom they came. She put them in her water pitcher, for none of the vases in the room would hold them. They filled the entire room with fragrance.

Standing before the mirror in her pink summer kimono, brushing her hair, Betsy's expression grew thoughtful. She opened a drawer in which she had arranged her toilet articles and began to hunt for something she had not used for a long time.

A short time later, chuckling, she went back to her letter and added a postscript.

"I just put my hair up on curlers," she wrote, "for the first time in Europe. You've heard about emotion coming in *waves*??? "

17
Forgetting Again

IN EXACTLY FIVE DAYS Mr. Regali told Betsy that he loved her. And after that he told her every day in Italian, French, and English.

"When I saw you standing in the railway station," he said, "with all those bags, I fell in love. I didn't admit it, though. I said to myself, 'Oh, I hope she will be stupid!' But in the gondola I could see that you weren't. I knew I was a goner."

"It's perfectly ridiculous," Betsy replied with a joyful sensation spreading through her body. "You only imagine it!"

"I wish I did. I didn't want to fall in love. Why couldn't you have stayed in Oberammergau?"

Until this revelation he had continued to be only an extremely kind friend.

"He's my guardian angel," Betsy wrote home.

He explained the monetary system and helped her change her money. He pointed out the American Express Company, and Thomas Cook's, and the English Church. He bought her a map of Venice and checked the steamboat stations and the ferries.

"But getting around Venice on foot is complicated," he said. "I'd better show you in person."

There were no streets except canals. Walking, you went up and down bridges, and along tiny alleys, spanned by clotheslines full of washing, and across picturesque courts where people were always hanging out the windows in vigorous conversation. They shouted; they gesticulated.

"What's the matter with them anyway?" Betsy asked.

Mr. Regali laughed. "Oh, they're just saying it's a beautiful day!"

You dodged around old houses, time-stained to

mellow hues. You went through lanes with vines climbing over the walls and hints of gardens behind. With Mr. Regali, Betsy explored every tantalizing nook.

And always in the end they came out on the Grand Canal. The palaces lifted their airy arches, balconies, and columns above water that changed color all the time. It was oftenest a vivid blue, but it could be sapphire blue and lilac blue. It could be grass green and emerald green and bottle green. It could be iridescent, enameled, pearly, silky.

"I don't see how you put up with me!" cried Betsy. "All my raving and ranting! I know I bore you, but I just can't help it."

"You don't bore me."

He took pictures of her feeding the pigeons. They bought a paper bag full of corn, and the pigeons perched on her shoulders, her arms, her fingers! The Harvard man passed by and yelled something scoffing.

"I know it's a touristy trick, but I don't care," Betsy said.

"He's only ignorant," Mr. Regali assured her. "He doesn't know how important these birds are. They're direct descendants of carrier pigeons that helped us win a victory over the Greeks five or six centuries ago."

They peeked in at St. Mark's Church, dim and

glittering. St. Mark was buried here, Mr. Regali said. His body had reached Venice after many strange adventures which were told in mosaics over the entrance door. They went up to the galleries to see them, and on a balcony overlooking the Square stood four bronze horses.

"The only horses in Venice!" he announced. They were trophies from Constantinople. Napoleon had taken them off to Paris, but after his downfall they had been returned. Betsy had her picture snapped beside them.

They went next door to the rosy Doge's Palace. Its stones were red and white, but the effect was pink. Going inside, they climbed the Giants' Staircase and wandered through lofty halls which were carved and gilded, with gigantic paintings by Tintoretto, Titian, and Veronese covering the walls and even the ceilings.

They walked through the Palace to a bridge which led to an ancient prison next door.

"Recognize this?"

"The Bridge of Sighs! But, oh dear, I don't feel like sighing!"

"Neither do I. There isn't a sigh in me. I think Florian's would be more suitable for us."

So they went back to the Square and drank coffee and ate *casata di Siciliano,* a delicious concoction with chopped fruit and nuts and layers of chocolate in it. They talked about the Wilsons, who were having a fine studious time in Greece, and about Betsy's travel plans, and—of course—her family.

"All those letters that were waiting for you. Were they from your family?"

"Not all of them."

His expressive eyes grew thoughtful.

New sets of tourists were feeding the pigeons now, and going in and out of the Palace and the Cathedral, and shopping in the arcades of other marble buildings around the Square.

"I just adore this place," said Betsy.

"Then when are we coming in the evening?"

"Oh . . . . sometime!" She wasn't sure it would be proper to go out with him alone at night. And she was trying to be very discreet.

Partly because her *Italian Self-Taught* proved to be inadequate, and partly because study took time which might otherwise be indiscreetly spent, Betsy had started Italian lessons. One of the aunts, the one who spoke English, was her teacher.

Mr. Regali spent her lesson hours in his rooms, a few houses away. He had been climbing around Venice gathering data, he said. Now he was working on his drafting board, transcribing notes.

"The sort of notes an architect takes . . . with pencil, scales, and caliper."

Betsy alternated walks with him and sight-seeing trips with her fellow Americans . . . to the Accademia to look at masterpieces or to Murano to see the glass works. If she went out with him in the morning, she was careful not to do so in the afternoon. But every evening they walked down to the nearby Giudecca Canal to see the sunset.

Sunsets in Venice were twice as beautiful as ordinary sunsets because they were doubled. All the splendor of the sky—the flaming crimson, violet, and gold—was spread on the water too. And all the tender after-colors, the pastels, the fading silvers were repeated.

Battleships, merchant vessels, yachts, and gondolas were moored on the Giudecca. Artists were sketching on every bridge and barge.

"They'll be putting us into their pictures," Betsy said.

"Let's fool them Sunday night and go to the Piazza."

Betsy hesitated. "I'm not sure we should go out at night unchaperoned. In America, of course, I'd think nothing of it. But in Italy . . ."

"You're an American."

"Yes, but your aunts . . ."

"We'll ask them," he said, and when they returned to the pension they hunted up the Signorinas Regali.

Betsy had straightened them out now, although

they looked much alike. All were small, and submerged in black garments, and had their nephew's thickly lashed dark eyes. They consulted each other on everything, like chattering birds.

Signorina Eleanora was a little shorter than her sisters but she was more forceful. Signorina Beatrice was a little taller but she had a quicker sense of humor. Signorina Angela, Betsy's Italian teacher, had the softest heart.

"We'll ask Aunt Angela," Mr. Regali said as they walked back to the House of the Yellow Roses. But they found all three in the little family parlor.

The aunts, whose home was full of Americans from one year's end to the next, understood American ways. They made no objection to Mr. Regali's plan.

"Americans think nothing of such things!" Aunt Beatrice tossed it off.

"You must bring her home early," Aunt Eleanora warned, looking at her nephew.

"Marco is a good boy," said Aunt Angela lovingly.

It was agreed that they might go. But as it happened Betsy did not, after all, have her first glimpse of St. Mark's Square by night with Mr. Regali. He received a telegram from a group of professors under whose direction he was doing his research. They were visiting at Padua and they wished him to come on Sunday for a conference.

Betsy was surprised at how much she missed him. She went to the English Church in the morning, and after dinner she went to the Frari and looked at Titian's tomb. At supper Miss Cook and Mrs. Warren asked her if she wouldn't like to go over to St. Mark's Square; they had heard it was delightful in the evening. Betsy accepted, and then she had a miserably guilty feeling.

"Why under the sun should I feel guilty?" she asked. "Mr. Regali didn't invent Venice."

But while she was putting on her hat in her room, she heard a whistle from the garden.

"For, I adore,
I adore you, Giannina mia . . ."

It was their signal, formally adopted several days before. He had heard her humming the song and had been charmed with the Italian phrases. She went to the window and there he stood, looking hot, rumpled, and triumphant.

"Ecco!" he cried. "I had to run out on a whole flock of bigwigs, but here I am! And there's going to be a band concert."

"Oh, Mr. Regali!" Betsy faltered. "I'm so sorry! Miss Cook and Mrs. Warren asked me to go with

❧ 274 ❧

them, and I didn't know you were coming back . . ."

The joy went out of his face. He didn't speak.

"I'm so terribly sorry!" Betsy repeated. She was. She wanted to cry.

He said something in Italian; it sounded despairing. And he pushed his fingers through his hair. But then he looked up with his shining Italian smile.

"My fault!" he said. "But will you promise not to look at a thing?"

"Not a thing," answered Betsy tremulously.

"And not to listen to the music?"

"I won't listen."

"And tomorrow," he said, "you'll go out with me on a bat?" Like Tilda, he had picked up Betsy's favorite word. "And no talk about hurrying home to write letters or study Italian!"

"But I have a lesson in the morning," Betsy reminded him, laughing.

"*Bene!* You may take it. But I'll be waiting for you when it's over." And he picked a rose and threw it through the window, and Betsy went slowly out to meet Miss Cook and Mrs. Warren. They were nice; they were very full of fun. But Betsy wished they had never started traveling.

At St. Mark's Square she tried not to look or listen, although on a platform in the center a band played rousingly. Everything was brightly lighted, and there were crowds of people promenading across the marble pavements, strolling in the arcades, and eating and drinking at little tables. It seemed as though the rest of Venice must be entirely deserted, and no one anywhere sleeping.

The Grand Canal doubled all the lights and the beauty and the fascination. It was full of gondolas, some of them strung with lanterns, and their occupants were singing and strumming guitars.

"Oh, dear!" mourned Betsy while she ate ices with the jolly middle-aged ladies. "It would have been so nice to see it with him!"

The following morning she put on her prettiest dress, white, with a tiered skirt, green buttons down the front, and a flat green bow at the collar. She wore the green bracelets she had bought at Gibraltar, and her jade ring, and her slanting black hat with the green leaves and the rose.

Mr. Regali was waiting when her lesson was over, and they took a steamboat to the Lido.

The large island contained a city of hotels and bathhouses. Smartly dressed crowds strolled its walks, while vendors of flowers and fruits called their wares. The beaches were scattered with bathers, and children were digging in the sand.

Betsy and Mr. Regali sat down on a bench and looked out at orange sails floating on the water. It was here he told her that he had fallen in love.

She was astonished, delighted, and half-unbelieving. How could even a romantic Italian fall in love in five days! But with the sun flooding down on the Lido, she wanted to believe him, even though she realized that she didn't know—now that he had ceased to be a friend—how she felt about him. He relieved her by not asking for an answer.

"Understand," he said, "I don't expect you to feel as I do! Not yet! But you're going to be here six weeks. That ought to be time enough . . . in Venice."

He asked her again about the letters. "The ones that didn't come from your family. Were quite a few from some one person?"

"No," answered Betsy, smiling.

"You aren't in love with anyone?"

"No."

"Have you ever been in love with anyone?"

"I thought I was one time." She told him about Joe. "He's a wonderful person. I liked him all through high school and college. But we quarreled."

"How could anyone quarrel with you?"

"It was my fault."

"I don't believe it."

"It really was, Mr. Regali . . ." But he didn't want to be called Mr. Regali any more.

"I am Marco for the Saint, and the Cathedral, and

the Square, and Marco Polo. He was born in Venice; I'll show you the court."

"All right, Marco. My name's Betsy."

"It's Elisabetta, and I shall call you Betta." He had another inspired idea. "After this, I shan't whistle just two lines of our song.

> *"For, I adore,*
> *I adore you, Giannina mia . . ."*

"I shall always whistle four lines.

> *"More, more and more,*
> *I adore you, Giannina mia."*

Betsy was enchanted.

But that night when the whistle sounded . . . unexpectedly, for she thought he was working . . . there were only two lines.

> *"For, I adore,*
> *I adore you, Giannina mia . . ."*

"He forgot!" Betsy thought in disappointment. Glancing at the mirror, she went to the window. But when she put her head out, the four college girls were grinning up at her.

Fortunately, they moved on the next day to the Italian Lakes, and after that there were always four lines whistled, and it was always Marco, leaning against an arbor, gazing up.

"Only an Italian could do it," Betsy often thought, for he was never awkward or self-conscious but always graceful and at ease.

He was usually asking her to come down and go some place, and she usually went.

They saw a wedding—and a funeral. The funeral had a band, and the mourners carrying the casket to the black-draped gondola marched in time to the music, followed by boys with candles, and a priest. The silent gondolier, standing behind the casket, dipped his oar and Betsy thought of the Lily Maid of Astolat floating downstream. But this boat was one of a long procession. The cemetery was on a nearby island, Marco said.

"I believe we've seen every one of those hundred islands you told me Venice was built on," Betsy remarked, for on foot and by gondola, steamboat, and ferry, they had traversed the city from end to end. "I'm glad people thought of building this heavenly place. They were running away from the Huns; weren't they?"

"Yes. Back in the fifth century. And they built a cluster of reedy little islands into a great Republic.

I wish we could have seen it in the days of the Doges, Betta."

"It couldn't," Betsy answered positively, "have been any nicer than it is right now."

She was happier than she had been since she left home. Up to now a nagging homesickness had been with her all the time . . . except when she was with Tilda or Helena. But here she was completely free of it.

And how grand, she thought, to have a man to bat with! Because she had known no men in Munich, she had seldom gone out at night and hadn't had a single party. It was glorious to dress up and curl her hair and go to St. Mark's Square in the evening with Marco.

They went whenever the band played, and they drank coffee, and ate *casata,* and watched the crowd. Marco knew many of the people who went by, artists and musicians and some architects like himself.

They always took a gondola home. From the Grand Canal the lighted Square stood out like a stage setting. People floating around them were singing . . . everything from *Il Trovatore* to "Funiculi, Funicula." Betsy and Marco sang with them.

When their gondola left the Grand Canal and went gliding down dark waterways to the House of the Yellow Roses, they kept on singing.

Although he had told her he loved her, and repeated it every day in Italian, French, and English, Marco never touched her, which pleased Betsy, for if he grew mushy she would have to stop seeing him. And oh, she didn't want to have to do that!

"Dear darling family," she wrote home. "To say that I'm happy as the day is long doesn't express it. I wake up happy. I go to bed happy. Oh, my beautiful, beautiful Venezia! (As Marco likes me to call it. That's the Italian name.)"

She liked her Italian lessons and studied two hours every day. She tried this new language on the maids and in the shops. (German seemed like an old friend now. One day at Florian's she heard some people speaking German and for a second she thought they were speaking English, because she could understand.)

She loved the garden at the House of the Yellow Roses, and often had it to herself. She sat in a low wicker chair, pretending to write, but really dreaming, enjoying the scent of the flowers, the buzzing of the bees, and the circling of white butterflies.

The other guests were out sightseeing, of course . . . rushing about in the heat, staring up at the ceilings of the Doge's Palace, marching through St. Mark's Cathedral with their Baedekers in their hands. How sensible she was, thought Betsy, just to live in Venice, to dawdle about this sunny garden, and take walks and stroll down with Marco to watch the sun set over the Giudecca!

They were doing that one evening when they saw a steamer starting for Fusina, the nearest point on the mainland, and on an impulse they boarded it. They didn't get off at the little town but came directly back. Venice was outlined by lights against black sea and sky.

Betsy and Marco stood out in the bow gazing.

"What is it like at Fusina in the daytime?" Betsy asked.

"I'll take you someday, and you'll see."

18

The Second Moon in Venice

ONE MORNING WHEN BETSY was studying Italian, she heard "Giannina mia" under her window and looked out to see Marco smiling up at her. The sun was shining on his wavy black hair, his eager face.

"How about a walk?"

"I'm working."

"So was I, but I stopped. Besides, I can teach you Italian down on the Giudecca."

"Will you hear me say verbs?" asked Betsy, and she caught up her red jacket and ran down to the garden where the aunts were shelling peas, looking as alike as peas themselves. Smiling at Marco, Betsy said *"buon giorno"* nicely as Aunt Angela had taught her.

"Bene!" cried Marco, and Aunt Angela gazed at them fondly. Aunt Beatrice twinkled at them, but Aunt Eleanora, Betsy thought, looked a little grave. Aunt Eleanora liked her, she felt sure. And she had done nothing the aunts had not approved. Could Aunt Eleanora be worried for fear she and Marco were getting serious? Didn't she know it was just that they were young, and in Venice in June?

On the Giudecca there was a lively breeze. The water was rippling, boats were rocking. The clouds, Betsy remarked, all seemed to be going some place.

"We ought to do the same," Marco replied. And just as before, they heard a steamer whistling its departure. "Here's your chance to see Fusina in the daytime."

"Marco Polo! I'm not even wearing a hat!"

"We'll just make the round trip. Be home for lunch," he said.

But when they reached the little town they got off for a moment. And beside the station, a meadow rolled down to the sea. It seemed to belong to the sea, although its grass was sprinkled with poppies, and a goat was browsing. But the small trees were wind-blown; there was salt in the air. Children were playing down on the beach.

"Let's stay!" Marco pleaded.

"But your aunts would be worried."

"I can telephone from the station house."

"Well, I'm starving, and I don't see any restaurant!"

"Restaurant!" said Marco scornfully. "We're going to eat in this meadow. You pick the spot."

"*Ecco!*" said Betsy, dropping down. Her green skirts spread out around her. Marco looked at her, nodded judicially, and strode back to the station.

The sea spread a fan of cerulean blue, and Betsy looked off in great content. The steamer whistled two or three times.

"It won't do you any good," she said.

Marco returned, smiling. "The Signora Station House is killing a chicken."

"For us?"

"For us. We're going to eat it on this identical spot. 'Exactly where the signorina is looking so beautiful among the poppies!' That's what I said, and she understood."

He sat down beside her and the steamer with a last reproachful whistle sailed away.

"If they want passengers," said Marco, "why do they build their station house so close to this meadow?"

"Isn't it stupid of them?" Betsy asked. "I feel a thousand miles from Venice."

"So do I. I feel as though you and I were alone in the world."

"Except for a goat."

"Oh, yes! The goat."

"And a station master." For he was approaching with a table. His daughter followed with two chairs. Laying the cloth, she turned her eyes wonderingly from Marco to Betsy.

The children too had come within staring distance. The goat was indifferent for a time. But when the chicken appeared, trailing savory odors, he galloped around on his small hoofs.

"I'm astonished. I thought goats were herbivorous," said Betsy. This one didn't seem to be. Marco brandished a chair. The children jumped and squealed with delight. Betsy laughed until she was weak.

The station master's daughter came out with a stick at last and drove the beast away.

"My family," Betsy said, "writes me that they are always saying, 'I wonder what Betsy is doing now.' Well, if they're saying that this moment they'd have a hard time guessing. They'd never think of me eating lunch with you in a meadow by the Adriatic."

The chicken was served with rice, and peas, and

little hard rolls. Marco had the sour red wine Italians are so fond of, and Betsy had very strong coffee. For dessert there were strawberries, and the sun shone down on the little sea meadow.

"This is just about the loveliest time I ever had in my life," Betsy said.

After the table was taken away, Betsy and Marco went down to the point where the rough grass met the sand. There they could look out at the orange-colored sails, dancing over the sea. Betsy was feeling as gay as the waves, but Marco grew serious. He stopped talking. Sprawled on the grass, he pulled out rough blades and chewed them moodily.

"Betta," he said at last, sitting up and turning toward her. "I've been thinking for several days that I'd better have a talk with you."

"What about?" Betsy asked.

"About us. About loving you. I can't go on this way."

"This way? But we're so happy, Marco . . ." Betsy didn't want him to say any more.

But he cut her off short, and went on grimly, "All I want to know is whether I have a chance."

"You couldn't really expect me to be in love with you in three weeks," she answered in a small, weak voice. "I don't believe you're really in love with me."

"I can answer for myself," he said shortly. "As for

you, I know you couldn't tell me you love me and promise to marry me so soon. I've not yet had a chance to meet your family. But you must know whether I have a chance or not. You see . . . . if I haven't, I'd better go away. If I let myself go much farther, I may never get over it."

At his mention of marriage, Betsy was suddenly panic-stricken. She didn't know what to do or say. Staring off at the water, she thought of how much she liked him. She had written her family that he was her guardian angel. He had taken her in charge from the very first, and had been so immensely kind and thoughtful.

Perhaps because they were both artists, they were completely congenial. Betsy never tired of him and he never tired of her. He didn't care how she looked, or if she was tired or quiet or had a headache.

"He loves me the same way Tacy does, and Tib and the family," Betsy thought. And yet not exactly that way or he would be content to keep on being friends, and plainly he wasn't.

She had noticed him with his aunts, and knew his affectionate disposition. She loved that about him. It was one of the things that made her so happy with him. It was one thing that had driven her homesickness so far away that it seemed strange now to think she had ever had it. And yet . . .

Something wasn't there. Something she had felt for Joe Willard—and maybe still felt, although she had hardly thought of him since she got to Venice.

She glanced at Marco's strong, handsome profile. He looked more serious now than she had ever seen him. She had to be careful what she said; she had to tell the truth. It seemed to her that her heart would break if he went away, but maybe it would be better for him if he did. She drew a deep breath and squared her chin.

"You know how much I like you," she said. "That's so obvious it isn't worth mentioning, but that's all I feel. Just liking you an awful, awful lot."

He didn't turn. "Do you think that liking will ever change to anything else?"

"I don't think so."

"Why not?"

"I don't know."

They sat in miserable silence and stared out at the Adriatic.

"Is it because I'm not of your nationality?"

"No . . . I don't think so. I love your being an Italian. But . . . I can't imagine you outside of Venice."

"I like the United States. I've lived there. I may go back some day. I would, if you wanted me to, Betta. You could live right next door to that family you're so crazy about. I could practise my profession there.

They have architects, don't they, at the Minnehaha Falls?" Which made Betsy smile a little, but there were tears in her eyes.

"Are you in love with anyone else?"

"You asked me that before, Marco, and I told you all there was to tell. That boy I used to go with, Joe Willard. I think I was in love with him, but we don't even correspond any more."

"Is he the reason you can't love me?"

"I don't know," said Betsy wretchedly. "The way I feel now, I don't want to marry you or Joe or anybody else for years and years."

She put her head down on her knees. She had told the truth; but now he would go away. And at the thought, all her homesickness came back. Her tears began to flow.

Marco didn't notice for a minute, because he was still looking at the Adriatic with a frozen face. But when he heard a sniffle he turned, and he changed at once.

"Betta mia! You mustn't cry. I won't have it. I can't stand it." He put his arms around her. He found a wet cheek and kissed it.

"Don't be so sorry for me! I'm not feeling so badly. You have been so sincere in saying no, that I'll know you are sincere when you say yes. And the next time you'll say yes."

"No, I won't," said Betsy, thinking that if it had to end, it might as well end now. She might not be able to be so firm again. "I wish I would. But I know I won't."

"Why do you wish you would?"

"Because I like you so much."

"Is that the only reason?"

"Because . . . I don't want you to go away."

"Do you think you could drive me away?" he asked. He jumped to his feet and pulled her after him, laughing down at her. "You are going to be here for three weeks and a half! In Venice! And, Betta, there's going to be a moon! What kind of a man would I be, not to take advantage of that opportunity to get something I want as much as I want you?"

Betsy dried her eyes. Her hair was loose, her nose was red, and she knew she looked awful. "I'm going to the station house and ask if I can wash up, and let's take the next boat back to Venice."

"All right," he answered.

"It was a wonderful picnic, Marco."

"Yes, it was. And now, please be happy again, *carissima*. We won't talk about this any more for a while."

He put his arm about her shoulders and kissed her wind-blown hair as they moved off through the waving grass.

When they got home, it was dinner time, and after dinner Betsy went straight to her room. She had stopped crying at Fusina, but she wasn't through crying. She flung herself on the bed and sobbed. She felt guilty. She wanted to talk with her mother. She didn't know if she was doing wrong or right in staying on in Venice, in letting Marco stay.

She heard Marco's whistle, but she didn't answer it. She had not turned on a light; perhaps he would think she had gone for a walk. But after a moment she heard a soft thud on the floor, and then another, and another, and another! Betsy jumped out of bed. Coming through the open window were roses and carnations, roses and carnations. By the time the shower ended there were enough to fill her water pitcher to overflowing.

"He knows how I'm feeling," she thought.

She put on her pink kimono and poked her head out of the window.

"*Grazie,*" she said in a small voice.

"Good night, Betta mia," he answered.

But Betsy could not sleep. The room was full of the scent of flowers, and she was very troubled. After an hour or two, she went to the window again. He was still standing there in the garden, looking at her window.

"An American man would never do anything like

that. He couldn't," Betsy thought. "And if he did, he would look silly."

But not Marco, standing down in the garden with folded arms.

Betsy went back to bed and cried some more.

After that they were together even more than before. The aunts understood; Marco had told them. And sometimes he and Betsy still had fun together. Swinging hands, they went through the lanes and over the bridges of Venice. They went to the Rialto and watched the bargaining. They went to St. Mark's Square and ate *casata*. They took the steamboat to the Lido.

But now there was a weight on Betsy's heart. She wasn't so carefree any more. He had told her that if he stayed and fell more in love with her, he would never get over it. Was she doing wrong to keep him with her? She had written her mother all about it, but there wasn't time for an answer that would help.

Sometimes he was very unhappy. When he asked her if she loved him and she had to say no, he flared up: "Oh, you Americans! You can't feel! You're like ice!"

But Betsy did feel. She felt like a murderess.

"I think you ought to go away," she would say. "I really do." But then she would begin to cry, and he would take her in his arms and beg her to forgive him.

The moon came, and poured its golden-silvery light over the pearly buildings and along the canals of Venice, but Betsy didn't change her mind. And the weeks were slipping by fast. They went to the Accademia and looked at the Titians, the Tintorettos, the Bellinis. They went to the Church of San Zaccaria, because her favorite picture was Bellini's "Madonna with Saints."

"You and Ruskin!" he said. Ruskin, it seemed, had called that one of the two most beautiful pictures in Venice.

"Me and Ruskin! I must write that to Tilda."

One morning the King and Queen came to Venice. Betsy was awakened by cannons which announced the arrival of their train. She dressed hurriedly, and after a bite of breakfast ran over to the Santa Maria della Salute with Marco to see their boat go past.

Flags and banners were hung out of the windows of the palaces along the Grand Canal. But it was drizzling and the crowd was so thick that Betsy could hardly see Victor Emmanuel and Elena through the dripping forest of umbrellas.

"Won't they appear again? I want to get a good look at them."

"They'll come out on the balcony of the Palace tomorrow night," Marco answered. "I'll take you, unless it looks as though there is going to be trouble."

"Trouble?"

"I think the monarchy is tottering," he answered. "The Socialists are very strong; there may be riots."

But there were no rumors of riots the next day, and although by nightfall it was raining harder than ever, Betsy and Marco went to the Palace. The square in front was a sea of bobbing umbrellas and filled with a roar of voices.

Betsy doubted that royalty would really appear in such a downpour, but suddenly they were there above her, the little king and the tall, bejeweled queen. They seemed extremely nervous, and bowed hastily to the cheering throngs as though they were anxious to retreat into the room behind them.

The crowd certainly seemed loyal and enthusiastic. A woman beside Betsy almost lost her head with admiration. She kept tugging at Betsy's arm and shouting, "Ah, signorina! *La regina!*" But there were ominous lines of soldiers and armed police guarding the square.

A few days later, when the sun was shining again, they went to Chioggia. By special request Betsy wore the red jacket. Chioggia, which guarded the entrance to Venice, had been a most important place in the great days of the past, Marco said. Now it was a fishing town, remarkable only for its picturesqueness.

Betsy and Marco took a walk and admired the

forests of rigging. They took pictures, surrounded all the time by an interested, amused, sympathetic, and chattering audience of children.

"Like in Sonneberg," Betsy said. Marco was always ready to listen to her tales of Germany.

They ate dinner in a little café with a view of the sea. Their friends the children stood outside in the twilight and Marco and Betsy tossed them sweets. They were handsome little ragamuffins. All Italians were handsome, Betsy thought, glancing at Marco.

They were happy all day, but on the boat ride home they grew quiet. Up in the stern men were singing strange, fantastic songs. They kept passing quiet groups of fishermen, and by and by the full moon came out.

"My second moon in Venice!" Betsy said.

"Oh, Betta!" Marco answered. "Aren't you going to change your mind? How can I bear it after you go?"

"And how can I bear to go?" thought Betsy, but she didn't say it. She only pressed back tears and shook her head.

It was almost time to leave Venice now. Marco helped her buy her presents—mosaics, laces, leatherwork, beads of Venetian glass. They bought a special print of St. Mark's Square for Betsy.

They went to Thomas Cook's and planned her trip.

She was joining the Wilsons in Lucerne. They cashed her father's travel check and shipped her trunk to London. Betsy wondered how she had ever managed to leave Munich without Marco.

He went with her while she said good-by to Venice. Venezia! She would always remember the varying colors of the sky and water; the time-worn marble palaces with their barred windows and their wave-washed steps and the colored hitching posts in front for gondolas; the little courts and alleys with the swarms of gesticulating people; sunsets in the Giudecca; the Lido with its golden beach and turquoise sea. But, above all, the Square: St. Mark's and the Doge's Palace, the bric-a-brac shops under the colonnades, the streams of people, the little outdoor tables, and the fat glossy pigeons circling down.

On her last afternoon, Betsy got into her kimono, wadded up her hair, and approached her packing. Every other moment Marco knocked and offered to help, but he was refused. He asked her to open the door a crack and handed in some cherries. He threw flowers through the window.

About six o'clock she freshened up and slipped into the white and green dress for dinner. Afterward she took the red blazer and she and Marco went down to the Giudecca.

They had planned to go to the Square again, but

somehow they didn't want to. They watched a last sunset over the crazy quilt of water craft, and then he got a gondola. In the darkness on the Grand Canal, people were singing as before, everything from *Il Trovatore* to "Funiculi Funicula." But tonight Marco and Betsy didn't sing. They floated silently, sadly, her hand in his.

In the morning Betsy got up early and finished packing. Then she walked toward Marco's room to meet him. It was misty. The canals were pale, but no paler than Marco, although he smiled his eager, vivid smile when he saw her.

The little aunts gave Betsy a lunch. (They had printed—or Marco had—*Arrivederci* on the eggs.) After breakfast, which neither Marco nor Betsy ate, she said good-by to the little aunts and a gondola carried them heartlessly through the mist to the station.

Marco helped her buy her ticket. He took her to her compartment. He was behaving cheerfully, but his eyes, Betsy thought, were liked burned holes in a blanket. Yet she didn't think he felt any worse than she did. How could she bear to go out into the world and leave this love, this thoughtfulness, this protection? Loneliness flooded over her and she began to cry.

"Maybe I do love you," she said.

"Don't say it unless you do. I couldn't bear it if you changed your mind."

"Then I won't say it," she answered. "But oh, Marco! I'll never forget you!"

He kissed her, and she clung to him, while whistles blew and bells rang. The train was moving when he jumped off.

It crossed the bridge and reached the mainland. It ran through meadows full of poppies like the ones at Fusina. It ran past white plastered houses with flapping washlines, olive orchards, vineyards. Betsy was still crying.

The bad thing about traveling, she thought, was leaving people you got to like—or love. Maida, Mr. O'Farrell, Tilda, Helena—now Marco.

She certainly loved Marco, but not—she still believed, in spite of her tears—the way she ought to love him if she were going to marry him.

Maybe she would have if it weren't for Joe. She didn't know.

19
Betsy Writes a Letter

"ONZE RUE SCRIBE," said Betsy, smiling up at the little old driver who was perched jauntily on the seat of his horse-drawn hack. She was standing in front of the Grand Hotel Pension in the Latin Quarter, where she and the Wilsons had lived for the past two weeks, and the address she now gave in her best French was that of the American Express Company office.

"*Pardon, mademoiselle, je ne comprends pas,*" the driver answered politely.

Oh, no, not again! Her next-to-last day in Paris, and she still couldn't make herself understood!

"*Onze Rue Scribe,*" Betsy repeated in a loud voice.

"Mademoiselle?" He threw out his hands in apologetic bewilderment.

Betsy drew a deep breath.

"*Onze Rue . . .*" But she knew from experience that this could go on for hours. She'd better give up. Pulling from her purse the little notebook she always carried to jot down a bit of description or an idea for a story, she printed the address in large letters and handed it up.

"Ah!" Relief flooded the driver's face. In a torrent of words he begged the mademoiselle's pardon a thousand times for having misunderstood. If she would do him the honor of entering his humble conveyance, they would set forth immediately for *Onze Rue Scribe,* the home of the so-distinguished American Express Company—unless perhaps the mademoiselle would first like a little drive about Paris?

Betsy climbed to the back seat of the hack and vigorously nodded her assent. Patient Miss Wilson wouldn't mind waiting a little longer, and Betsy had wanted to drive through the city and take what might be her last look at it—alone.

But as the sturdy old horse began to move at a gentle clip-clop through the twisted streets of the left bank, she sank into a brown study. The last month had been a disappointment. Ready to leave for London, which would be practically home, she knew she couldn't count Paris as one of the places she had lived in, or Switzerland either.

Of course, in Switzerland she had been bitterly unhappy. The nagging homesickness had returned, mixed with loneliness for Marco. There had been letters and telegrams from him at every stopping place. Sometimes, falling asleep in strange hotels, she had thought again that she was mistaken, that she did love him after all. There was every reason in the world why she should, and it would be so easy to write and tell him so! She had imagined his overflowing happiness on receiving her letter. He would probably join her, she had thought; they would see Paris together, she would give up London and they would go home to be married. But there, somehow, her imagination had always rebelled. Something inside you told you when you didn't love a person, just as . . . something . . . told you when you did, even though he was thousands of miles away and you could hardly bear to think about him because you'd probably lost him.

Betsy and the Wilsons had left Switzerland behind

on the twenty-eighth of June. She remembered how, reading in a newspaper about the murder of an Austrian archduke in the Balkan town of Sarajevo, she had amused herself as the train sped through the night by plotting a romantic novel full of titled corpses, spies, and intrigue.

Then, as she tried to sleep in a jiggling upper berth, she had thought about Marco and Joe—or rather, she had suddenly ceased to think about Marco and had begun to think about Joe, with persistent, painful intensity. Venice was fading away—home was coming closer—and how she wished that Joe were waiting for her there!

But it was over a year since she and Joe had written to each other. Betsy wished that night that she had written him about Julia's wedding; she wished that she had written him about her trip to Europe, or from the *Columbic* to explain not having seen him in Boston. Now she had no excuse at all for writing, and she couldn't write without one. She was too proud for that.

The next day, her first in Paris, she had slipped out of the drab little Grand Hotel Pension and had walked out in a soft gray morning to the Pont Neuf, one of the bridges spanning the Seine. She wanted to do something the Wilsons certainly would not understand. Neither of them had read *The Beloved*

Vagabond and knew how Paragot, with his world crashing around him, had gone to ask advice of the statue of Henri Quatre on the Pont Neuf . . . or how the king had nodded and pointed to the Gare de Lyon.

Betsy didn't expect Henri Quatre to do the same for her, but she wanted to take a snapshot of him to send to Tacy. And she thought he might, he just might, give her a little hint about how to get in touch with Joe again. He sat on horseback looking out over the Seine, and didn't even seem to know she was there. But just the same she'd been glad she'd gone. And from that day to this, the sixteenth of July, she'd put the problem stubbornly out of her mind and tried to enjoy Paris.

Her hack was approaching the Pont Neuf now, jolting along the cobbled streets, lined with open-air bookstalls presided over by old ladies who sat knitting as implacably as Madame Defarge, or by old men as yellow as their oldest manuscripts. As she crossed over the bridge, she leaned out of the hack impulsively and waved to Henri Quatre. Her only Parisian friend! she thought. No, not quite; she had made others, and equally notable ones.

One was in the Louvre, which they were passing now; her cabby turned to indicate it with a wave of his whip. She would never forget the moment when, down a long avenue of statues, she had glimpsed against a dark velvet background the white gleam of the Venus de Milo.

"I never dreamed she would be so beautiful," she had said to Miss Wilson. "I never expect to like famous things! But I guess they're famous because they give everybody this wonderful feeling."

Victor Hugo was another friend. He had been with her on her first visit to Notre Dame. Gazing up at the great church, she had imagined his little dancing girl among the bells; and inside she had seen the Hunchback lurking in the shadows.

It had been fitting afterward to go to Hugo's tomb in the domed Pantheon. It was down in a dark, gloomy vault, in a small stone cell behind a grating. She had wished that she had brought him some flowers; it seemed sad for such a lover of life to be shut up in musty obscurity.

Napoleon wasn't a friend, exactly; Betsy had never been an admirer of his. But she had been unexpectedly stirred by the sight of his last resting place. In the silence of the room, awed crowds looked down at the sarcophagus which held the small body of the man who had made all Europe tremble . . . returned from exile as he had wished to be, and buried among the French people.

Fully half the onlookers were Americans, but Betsy

had wondered if Germans ever came, particularly when she read the inscription on the fresh wreath prominently displayed: "Let no French soldier rest, while there is a German in Alsace."

The French and Germans really hated each other, Betsy thought, as the hack bounced on past the Tuileries Gardens. Marie Antoinette was there; another friend. And also the Empress Eugenie, who Betsy's grandmother had once seen with her own eyes, sitting on one of these benches.

The hack passed through the Place de la Concorde, spacious and brilliant, with the Obelisk in the center surrounded by fountains, and the eight colossal statues symbolizing the queen cities of France. It swung down the broad, tree-lined Champs Elysées; and the Arc de Triomphe, the Eiffel Tower, came into full view. The tea gardens and Punch and Judy shows were crowded; the nursemaids and charming French children were out in full force among the strolling crowds.

Betsy felt a lump in her throat. "Paris is so beautiful! A little of it ought to belong to me by now, and it doesn't, any more than it did when I read the *Stoddard Lectures* at home!" She needed someone to share it with, someone who would love the same odd, romantic things that she loved.

Tilda would have understood about Henri Quatre

and Victor Hugo. Tib would have wanted to go to the smart restaurants, and shop at Paquin's or Worth's, and see the models parade at Longchamps. Tacy would have liked to picnic in the Bois de Boulogne, and Marco would have appreciated the sidewalk cafés.

She and the Wilsons had never once eaten in a sidewalk café! Dr. Wilson felt sure that none of them would supply his carrots and whole-grain bread, and while Miss Wilson would really have enjoyed going, Betsy felt sure, she had noted Baedeker's warning that unattended ladies didn't eat in such spots.

"French women must think it's all right," Betsy had thought, noticing many of them alone or in twos and threes at the gay little outdoor tables.

It wasn't that she didn't like the Wilsons; on the contrary, she had grown fonder of them every day. The erect little professor with the pointed beard was amusing and often stimulating, and Miss Wilson was wistfully lovable.

Miss Wilson would have liked to have some fun in Paris, Betsy thought now. It was just that she had been brought up so strictly that she didn't know how. Betsy had wished time and again during the past two weeks that she could find a way to give Miss Wilson one good bat. But she had never felt that she should take the initiative in making plans, or urge her chaperones to do anything they hadn't done before.

So she had dutifully gone sightseeing. And she had gone with Miss Wilson to sensible, medium-priced stores like the Bon Marche to buy perfumes and gloves for gifts and to spend her birthday money on a dark blue suit with a soft, wide belt of crimson satin. With a black hat and a crimson veil, it made a stunning outfit.

She was wearing it now, as the hack pulled up in front of the American Express office. She tipped the driver generously, and watched him clip-clop off down the crowded, busy street.

Stopping at a sidewalk kiosk to buy the Paris edition of the *Herald,* Betsy entered the office.

As she saw Miss Wilson standing at the cashier's window, she felt a sudden wave of affection for the kind, reserved little spinster.

"Oh, I wish I could do something nice for her!" she thought again.

Miss Wilson waved. "Here you are, my dear! My, it took you a long time to finish that letter!"

Betsy felt guilty, and she hugged her companion's arm. "I finished the letter half an hour ago, Miss Wilson . . . I let the driver take the long way around. I sort of wanted a last look at the Champs Elysées."

"Of course you did! You have so much imagination, Betsy; you really know how to enjoy things.

Let's you and I do something pleasant this afternoon. It's our last. You'll soon be at Mrs. Heaton's boarding house in London, and we'll be off to the Lake Country."

Betsy agreed warmly. They had both exchanged some travelers' checks for shillings and pounds, and were turning away, when Betsy suddenly caught sight of a moving flower garden—purple, yellow, blue, and pink—atop the head of a short, stout woman in a yellow silk suit. She heard a familiar voice raised in animated argument with an American Express attendant.

"Mrs. Main-Whittaker!" Betsy cried, as happy as though she had found a friend from home.

To her astonishment, Mrs. Main-Whittaker not only turned, but bounced over and embraced her. Betsy almost choked on a deep wave of perfume.

"Why, it's little Miss . . . Miss . . . Ray, from the *Columbic*! The one who plans to be a writer!"

"How did you know?" Betsy asked in delight.

"That nice Mr. O'Farrell told me. Well! I suppose you've been to the Ritz? To the Comédie Française? Out to Montmartre where our Bohemian friends are gathering these days? All excellent background for modern fiction."

"I've been concentrating more on background for historical novels," said Betsy, smiling at Miss Wilson.

A flash of understanding crossed Mrs. Main-Whittaker's face. "Well, what are you doing today?"

"We really hadn't made up our minds."

The author chuckled. "You come with me, and we'll do the town together. But first, have you had lunch? How about a sidewalk café?"

In the dazzled silence that followed, Betsy almost prayed that Miss Wilson would say yes.

"Do come!" Mrs. Main-Whittaker urged Miss Wilson. "I've just been wishing I had some good company. And Miss Ray and I can talk shop." She almost seemed lonesome, canary-colored suit, perfumed sophistication, and all.

Miss Wilson's smooth cheeks flushed. "Why, certainly! Betsy and I have never eaten in a sidewalk café."

"I suppose," said Mrs. Main-Whittaker, "you're afraid of the wolves in sheep's clothing. I'd say there were more sheep in wolves' clothing around, at least for an old lady like me!" She laughed exuberantly, and with Betsy on one arm and Miss Wilson on the other, sailed out into the sunny Paris afternoon.

The sidewalk luncheon was the beginning of a perfect day. Mrs. Main-Whittaker, who delighted in spending her money as much as she delighted in talking, ordered the meal, which began with shrimp and ended with *baba-au-rhum*, while Betsy and Miss

Wilson beamed at each other and at the occupants of the other tables under the bright awnings.

"Now," said Mrs. Main-Whittaker, after their waiter had bowed to the sidewalk over her tip, "we have just time for two sights no novice writer should miss. We'll go to Longchamps for a look at the models. Then how about dinner at the Ritz?"

Miss Wilson, who had half risen, sat down as though she were suddenly faint. Betsy looked away, and wondered how she could bear it if they didn't go. Miss Wilson adjusted her spectacles and managed a faint whisper.

"Is Longchamps very far away?"

"We won't be walking," Mrs. Main-Whittaker chuckled. "But . . . pardon me for saying so . . . and believe me, I do say so only because I've just had a check for royalties big enough to float a bond issue . . . this is all going to be my treat. Please don't say no."

Miss Wilson, with a common sense and dignity that made Betsy want to hug her, gave a chuckle not unlike Mrs. Main-Whittaker's.

"A teacher's salary," she said, "is definitely no royalty check. But at least I'll pay for the cab."

And the next thing Betsy knew, they were racing through the crowds of fashionable carriages and enormous black automobiles, some of which bore crests, toward the Longchamps promenade in the

Bois de Boulogne. There Miss Wilson paid the charge and gave a tip big enough to bring the driver's head down to his very feet.

They made their way down to the benches where spectators were settling themselves for the fashion show, and found front-row seats, Betsy drinking up the sights and sounds of the crowd for repeating to Tacy, Tib, and the family.

Beautiful models began to saunter past with the fashionable limp look.

"And I thought *I* had a debutante slouch!" Betsy whispered to Miss Wilson, whose face was alight. This really was the bat she had wished they could have together, Betsy thought joyfully. Miss Wilson didn't even look shocked, although as the parade progressed the skirts, slit to the knee, revealed long lengths of lavender, yellow, green, and even pink stockings.

"And what heels!" Betsy gasped. They were inches and inches high.

The make-up astonished her, too. She had never seen such make-up, even on the chorus girls of the musical shows that came to Minneapolis. Lips were crimson; eyes were painted with thickly drawn shadows. Hair-dos leaped straight up or spread straight out, and hair was every color of the rainbow.

Capes seemed to be coming in, Betsy noted . . . if

you could judge by these fantastic styles. Hats were smaller and the suits had vests and pleated, knee-length overskirts. Looking at one, Betsy heard Miss Wilson gasp, and she could have gasped herself. Beneath the overskirt were trousers! Trousers! On a woman in broad daylight in a public place!

The sun was setting behind the tall trees of the Bois de Boulogne when the parade ended.

"The fashions are really exciting this year, don't you think?" Mrs. Main-Whittaker remarked as she led her charges through the animated, well-dressed crowds. "You'd look stunning in one of those suits, my dear," she added to Betsy.

"With trousers, I suppose!" Betsy thought. She was feeling lightheaded. The ride to the Ritz went like a ride on a roller coaster.

And the dinner opened new vistas of luxury. The attentive waiters she remembered from the *Columbic* were quite outdone by the waiters here who leaped to obey Mrs. Main-Whittaker's waving, sparkling hand. For the party of three there were two waiters, and behind these a captain of waiters hovered, and behind the captain, a maître d'hôtel. He was most attentive of all.

Mrs. Main-Whittaker seemed to know everybody. She waved and called greetings in every direction.

"Cornelia, my dear!" "May, how nice!" "Adele,

where have you been?"

Vastly important as she seemed to be, Mrs. Main-Whittaker was really interested in Miss Wilson and Betsy, and in their plans. Over the onion soup, thick with bread and grated cheese, the frogs' legs, the salad which a waiter mixed at their table, they discussed England.

"You must be sure," the author said to Betsy, "not to miss the Agony Column!"

"The Agony Column?" asked Betsy eagerly.

"It's on the front page of the London *Times*. So astonishing that such a paper would give its front page to personals! John asking Mary to write him, Mary warning Eloise to leave John alone, the gentleman who noticed a lady in the bus asking her to let him see her again. There's a plot in every item."

Betsy was enormously flattered that Mrs. Main-Whittaker should talk shop with her!

When they had finished their crêpes suzettes and were lingering over their coffee, Mrs. Main-Whittaker opened a jeweled cigarette case. She extracted a cigarette, beckoned to a hovering waiter to light it for her, and was about to put the case away. But perhaps she noticed that Miss Wilson's gaze had a peculiar intensity.

"Will you join me?" she asked, and passed the case.

Betsy's pride in Miss Wilson's new aplomb soared to the heights.

"No, thank you. I . . . I . . . I was just admiring your cigarette case."

Mrs. Main-Whittaker puffed luxuriously. "It is nice, isn't it?" she said. "But smoking is a terrible habit. Do try not to take it up, my dear," she added to Betsy.

A few minutes later Betsy found courage to open a topic that had been on her mind all day. She mentioned her first sight of Mrs. Main-Whittaker surrounded by reporters on the *Columbic*.

"One of those reporters was an old friend of mine, Joe Willard. He was covering the story for the *Boston Transcript* . . ."

"Oh-h-h-h!" Mrs. Main-Whittaker interrupted, almost cooing. "The *Transcript* young man! I remember him very well. Extremely handsome!"

"Yes, he is," said Betsy softly.

"And he wrote an excellent story. I received it in my clippings. I subscribe to a clipping bureau. You must do it, too, when you're established, my dear. His story was entertaining, and he got the facts right . . . all my plans and ideas. It was the best story of the lot."

Henri Quatre had helped her at last! Betsy thought, back in her room at the Grand Hotel Pension. She climbed into bed, but she couldn't sleep. She was too full of the promenading models and the bowing waiters and especially of what Mrs. Main-Whittaker had said about Joe.

Here was her chance! It was now or never, if she was going to write to Joe.

Lying there in the darkened room, she thought about Joe, as she hadn't thought about him for months. She thought about the first time she had seen him, a cocky blond boy of fourteen, eating an apple and reading *The Three Musketeers* in Willard's Emporium, in Butternut Center, Minnesota. She remembered him running up and down the sidelines at the high school football games he'd covered so well for the Deep Valley *Sun*, and the evenings they had sat side by side in the library studying for the essay contests.

She remembered the first letter he'd written her, the summer after junior year, and how she had slaved over her replies, copying them onto scented green note paper. She remembered the first time he'd come to see her, in the fall of their senior year, and all the times after that, when they'd made fudge in the kitchen and talked in front of the dining-room fire.

They had had a quarrel in their senior year, but she remembered the beautiful spring when they made up. She remembered when he had first kissed her up on the Big Hill. She remembered the few months they'd had together at the University, and how proud she had been when he went away to Harvard.

She thought about him in quiet adoration. She loved him. She'd loved him for years. He was the finest person she'd ever known—he was bound up with almost her whole past life, and she didn't want to live the rest of her life without him.

Of course that was why she hadn't loved Marco! Deep inside herself, she must have known. She should have drawn the truth out sooner. But at least now she knew what she had to do.

Betsy got up, turned on the light, put on her pink kimono, and got out her fountain pen. But the only letter she wrote that night went to Marco. It told him gently that they must stop corresponding with each other.

Next morning after crescent rolls and *café au lait,* she dressed and went out of doors, taking her fountain pen and box of scented green stationery. She went out to a little square and found a bench, and there at last she wrote to Joe!

It was a carefully casual letter.

"If he's already married to his roommate's sister, he can show it to her without a blush," Betsy thought grimly.

It didn't offer any apologies or excuses, or any

explanation other than the desire to tell him about Mrs. Main-Whittaker's compliment.

"I have a t.l. for you, Joe. That charming Mrs. Main-Whittaker from the *Columbic* (I met her in the American Express office today) said that your story was the best one to come out of that interview."

Betsy described her day with the author in sprightly style—the sidewalk café, Longchamps, dinner at the Ritz.

"She really takes an interest in young writers. She gave me all kinds of advice. I'm going to be sure to take a look at the Agony Column in the London *Times* . . . she says it's full of story material."

The letter went on to sketch her trip in three or four well-chosen lines.

"And a story I wrote last summer sold to *Ainslee's* while I was over here. That was how I financed the trip to Sonneberg and Oberammergau."

Betsy wasn't sure whether it was a good letter or not. Maybe it sounded too self-centered, but she didn't want to seem to be prying or hinting for an answer if she asked Joe too much about himself.

She didn't read it over for fear she wouldn't mail it. She put it into an envelope and sealed and stamped and addressed it and found a letter box.

She held the letter between her hands a moment, and prayed . . . then quickly let it go.

That afternoon, rolling toward the English Channel, Betsy remembered that she had not included the address of her London boarding house. Joe could not answer even if he wanted to. It was too bad! But on the other hand, he would know that she wanted to make up. He could write to her in Minneapolis . . . and somehow, she believed that he would.

20

The Roll of Drums

"There's a barrel-organ caroling across a golden street
In the City as the sun sinks low;
And the music's not immortal; but the world has
made it sweet . . ."

Kneeling beside the window of a small white room
in which her trunk, steamer rug, flag, books, photographs, Goethe's cup, Tacy's doll, and a print of St.

Mark's Square were tastefully arranged, Betsy looked down four stories into Taviton Street where a barrel organ was caroling indeed.

She continued saying the Noyes poem to herself after she had thrown some pennies and the Italian had bowed over a velvet cap and trundled his organ away from Mrs. Heaton's boarding house. This overlooked a green square. It was one of a row of attached houses, all tall and thin with neat door plates, bells, and knockers.

> *"Come down to Kew in lilac-time,*
> *in lilac-time, in lilac-time;*
> *Come down to Kew in lilac-time*
> *(it isn't far from London) . . ."*

This wasn't lilac-time. It was July, 1914. But it was London, and Betsy loved it.

She hadn't expected to love it so much. She had known it would be pleasant to hear English spoken again, and moving to be in the land from which her own country had sprung, a land peopled for her by long-familiar figures of history and fiction. But she hadn't known it would be so . . . heart-warming. The Wilsons had gone on, and although Betsy had been sorry to part from them, she didn't feel lonely. In this vast, ancient city she felt completely at home.

She was happy because she was getting nearer her

family. She was happy because she had written to Joe.

She drew satisfaction, too, from the thought that she was *living* in London, not just sightseeing, as in Switzerland and Paris.

She was writing again; she had already finished "The Episodes of Epsie." Search for a shop where she might get it typed had taken her on a legitimate errand to Fleet Street, for generations the stamping ground of publishers and booksellers and anxious young authors like herself.

Of course, while there, she had peeked into old St. Paul's which dominated the region from its little hill. She had browsed down bookish Paternoster Row to Amen Corner and hunted up the Inn of the Cheshire Cheese where Dr. Johnson used to dine while Boswell took worshipful notes. She had only walked up and down in front of that and gazed, for ladies didn't eat there alone.

She attended church every Sunday at Westminster Abbey. "Why not?" she defended herself at the storied portal. "That's what it's meant for." You soaked in more of the dear gray old place, kneeling in the candlelight, than you did walking around with a guidebook.

She did that too, of course. Dick Reed, a law student who lived at Mrs. Heaton's, came along sometimes. He wasn't another Marco, but he was very nice. They wandered about the Poets' Corner, reading inscriptions to Goldsmith, Gray, Shakespeare, Dickens . . .

Afterward they often prowled around the Parliament buildings. Betsy loved the great song of Big Ben because it reminded her of the chime clock at home. And they always walked to Number Ten Downing Street where the Prime Minister lived. Mr. Dick, as the other boarders called him, because his older brother Leonard also lived at Mrs. Heaton's, wanted to be Prime Minister some day.

Number Ten was very dingy. "But it will be fun living there anyway," Betsy consoled him.

When not accompanied by Mr. Dick or her other new friends, Betsy was guided by bobbies. She adored these obliging London policemen. Directing traffic, they would stand as cool as cucumbers, gloved hand in air, to listen to your problems, and advise.

"Take bus Aighty-Aight, Miss."

Betsy consulted them mostly about buses. A top front seat on a bus was a grandstand seat for London. Of course, you had to scramble down, now and then, to view Hyde Park or Trafalgar Square, or perhaps to watch a sidewalk artist. These amazing peple made their living by drawing pictures in colored chalk on the sidewalk and passers-by stopped and dropped tuppence. Naturally you came down from any bus at teatime.

The English were even more devoted to their tea than Germans to their coffee. Tea was served at His Majesty's Theatre where Betsy saw Mrs. Patrick Campbell in *Pygmalion* and became a Shaw devotee. A tray was brought right to her seat for sixpence. It was the same at the movies, or "the pictures" as her friends from Mrs. Heaton's called them. Yesterday, seeing Mary Pickford, they had all had trays of tea.

It was amusing, Betsy thought now, how well you knew when four-thirty came. She glanced at her watch, and simultaneously heard a call.

"Hello up there! Yankee Doodle!"

"Hello!" Betsy ran to the door.

"Tea in the garden!" called Mr. Dick.

"Right-o," answered Betsy, very British. Giving a pat to her hair and brushing a chamois skin over her nose, she skimmed down past the second-floor drawing room to the first-floor dining room and back to the garden.

This was a bit sooty . . . no white, rose-draped walls as in Venice. But there were vines and a snowy tea table, and behind the pot Mrs. Heaton's sweet care-worn face. She mothered everybody, and most of her boarders could use mothering. They were almost all young.

Jean Carver was an actress. When Betsy first arrived Jean had been out of work and her eyes were often red. But now she was engaged for the chorus of *The Arcadians,* and busy with rehearsals.

"Glad to see you home," said Betsy. "Dolly needs your legs!"

Little Dolly Cohen was an artist. Her room was just below Betsy's, wildly untidy, with drawings scattered everywhere, and tubes of paint and brushes about, and an easel in front of her window. She was illustrating a new edition of *Helen's Babies* and everyone in the house had posed for her. Betsy was modeling the lady who listened to Toddy's recitation. Mr. Leonard had posed as Toddy spilling soup. This showed how much everyone liked Dolly, for Mr. Leonard, who was studying to be a doctor, was a most dignified young man, slenderly erect, with eyeglasses. He never went out without a cane.

Mr. Dick was larger and more casual.

"Here's your Agony Column," he said as Betsy dropped down beside him. He clipped it for her every day. It was even better than Mrs. Main-Whittaker had promised. Consuming their tea, Betsy and Mr. Dick read with interest that if I.J. would come home all would be forgotten. Now and then they read an item aloud to the crowd.

This group was really a Crowd, such as Betsy had hoped to start in Munich. Only they called themselves The Crew. And one member was missing today.

Claude Heaton, a broker's clerk, was off with his regiment. The Territorial Troops (something like the National Guard at home, Betsy understood) had a period of training over the August Bank Holiday which was impending.

Most of the boarders, like Betsy, were new to London, and The Crew had made a number of expeditions, chaperoned by Miss Dodge, a merry elderly spinster. They had gone to Windsor Castle, but only into the gardens. The palace was closed to the public because of the militant suffragettes who were now starting fires, throwing bombs, and slashing pictures. The suffragettes had closed many places Betsy wished to see.

"Them wild ladies!" a bobby had mourned, turning her away from the National Gallery. But Betsy was in sympathy with their cause.

And the out-of-door places weren't closed. The Crew had gone to Hampstead Heath; to Stoke Poges, where they saw the country churchyard of Gray's "Elegy"; to Epping Forest. (That had gone into "The Episodes of Epsie.") And they had gone boating on the Thames which was crowded companionably with rowboats, houseboats, punts, canoes. Tied up beneath an overhanging tree, they had eaten apple patties with tea made over an alcohol lamp.

At tea in the garden now, Jean said, "Where are

we going to go on Bank Holiday?" And Betsy cried, "Oh, let's go up the Thames again!"

"We could take a boat from Richmond," Mr. Leonard volunteered, "to Kingston-on-Thames."

"I'll provide more apple patties," Mrs. Heaton offered. "I only wish Claude could be with you."

"What is a Bank Holiday anyway?" Betsy asked.

"It's a holiday when the banks close," Mr. Leonard explained. "We have four a year. And one is the first Monday in August."

"Then it's almost here. Today is the twenty-ninth."

"And not a very good day," said Mr. Heaton unexpectedly. He had just come in with a newspaper under his arm. His appearance, like the remark, was unexpected for he worked in the city and seldom came home for tea. He was a large man, fiercely mustachioed but as gentle as a lamb.

"Austria-Hungary," he went on, "has just declared war on Serbia."

"Why? What for?" asked Betsy.

"Oh, it's on account of the murder of that Austrian Archduke last month," said Mr. Dick, helping himself to marmalade. "They'll probably settle things before any shooting starts."

"And it looks as though Germany is going to declare war on Russia," continued Mr. Heaton.

"But why Russia?" Now Betsy was really confused.

"Russia is pledged to help Serbia and Germany is tied up with Austria. France could be drawn in, too. She and Russia are allies."

This was too complicated to follow. And the news was so disquieting that talk of the boating trip died down. But it sprang up again at dinner.

Dinner at Heatons' charmed Betsy. There was a butler (as fascinating as Mrs. Sims' and Mrs. Cheney's ladies' maids). And Mr. Heaton carved with dignity. There were always two kinds of meat and two kinds of dessert.

"Will you have hot or cold, Miss Ray? Hot? A slice off the joint?"

"Miss Cohen, would you prefer cold shape or cherry tart?" Cold shape was gelatin.

English food, Betsy thought, sounded better than it tasted. (The meat pies of which she had read such mouth-watering descriptions in Dickens were cold and clammy.) But dinner at Mrs. Heaton's was very nice anyway, and it was such fun afterward up in the drawing room. (Betsy rolled that word over her tongue.) They often had music, for Claude had a fine bass voice. Since he wasn't here, they talked about the river trip, making enthusiastic plans.

This holiday expedition was never mentioned again.

The next afternoon Mr. Leonard had no classes,

and he and Betsy made a planned visit to the Tower. Within these gloomy walls they were carried from modern perils back to old ones. Betsy could almost hear the ghostly voices of the murdered princeling sons of Edward IV. Mr. Leonard stared at the ax which had struck off Raleigh's head.

"My word!" he said, adjusting his eyeglasses as though they had been a monocle, "Extraordinary!"

"My word!" he said again, over tea and cherry cake, "think of Mary, Queen of Scots, and Anne Boleyn! Their heads chopped off just like snick!" He adjusted his glasses again to frown at Betsy's soft white neck. She closed her hands protectingly about it.

"It couldn't happen today," she said. "I guess the world is really getting better."

"Let's hope it is better enough to keep out of real war."

"Why, of course it is! A war in these civilized days is absolutely unthinkable."

But when they got out into the streets they saw the big news posters crying out that armies all over Europe were mobilizing. And London was suddenly full of soldiers. Dinner that night was quiet, for it looked pretty certain that the Territorials would not go back to their shops and factories, their offices and universities, when the training period was over. The table missed Claude's deep voice.

"My brother is a Territorial, too," said Dolly.

The newspapers next day, and the next, said that a state of war existed between Germany and Russia. Americans were rushing off the continent like leaves before a storm. They were pouring into London by the thousands, telling of the cold war purpose in Berlin and the fever of excitement in Paris. Crowds there were singing and marching in the streets.

"Oh, I'm lucky to be here!" Betsy cried as each new edition brought more tales. Americans were traveling day and night to get to England. They weren't allowed to leave the railroad stations, even to eat. They were locked into the cars. They couldn't get money. Many who arrived in London had left all their luggage behind and had only the clothes on their backs.

On the eve of the Bank Holiday German troops goosestepped over the French border. The barrel organs began to play the "Marseillaise," but what stunned Mrs. Heaton's even more was Germany's ultimatum to little Belgium demanding permission to send her armed forces unopposed across the Belgian border.

"Why, that's outrageous!" Dolly cried. "Belgium has a guarantee of perpetual neutrality."

"And England has guaranteed the sanctity of Belgium."

"We're as good as in," Mr. Leonard said, but Mrs. Heaton put in briskly, "We may be in, but we'll be out in a jiff. The fighting will be over in a month or so at most."

Everyone looked anxious.

"I'll sign up," said Mr. Dick. "But you ought to finish at medical school, Len."

Mr. Leonard looked thoughtful.

"I don't believe *The Arcadians* will ever open," said Jean.

"I wish I knew what this would do to my brother," Dolly said.

"And your book!" It seemed unlikely that a new edition of *Helen's Babies* would be wanted now.

Betsy, Jean, and Mr. Dick went to vesper services in Westminster Abbey. When they returned, the streets seemed to hold twice as many sailors and soldiers as before. An artillery regiment, complete with cannons, shouted boisterous jokes. A company of Territorials marched by singing.

They were very young and slim, with fresh pink cheeks. The German soldiers had been so big and capable! The memory made Betsy apprehensive, and newsboys were shouting that the last train, the last boat, had come from the continent.

"Perhaps, Betsy," Mrs. Heaton said at tea—it was high tea on Sunday night—"perhaps you ought to be thinking about getting home. Your parents must be worried."

Betsy was sure they were and she was sorry. But she didn't really want to go home. It was partly that she had come to love these people and didn't want to go back to comfort while they were in peril. But it was also because of the great events that seemed to be impending. As a writer, she hated to miss them.

No one at Heaton's slept much that night, and in the morning everyone was down to breakfast early. This was Bank Holiday. Could it really be that they had planned to spend it boating on the Thames?

The crowds on the streets were restless instead of merry. All holiday excursions had been canceled to provide trains for troops. And Germany made her formal declaration of war against France.

Betsy's thoughts went back to the line cut into Napoleon's tomb. It would have to be recarved.

"Let no French soldier rest while there is a German in *France*."

"I can't take it in," Jean stammered. "Thousands of men marching off to be slaughtered. Ruin, terror, misery, sweeping us all. Why?"

No one knew. But Betsy kept remembering the marching soldiers she had seen everywhere in Germany and all the talk of war.

She thought of Tilda. What would this do to her

career? She thought of Helena and Hanni. Each loved a soldier who would now be going to war. And how could she ever get Hanni over to the United States?

She thought of Marco. Italy had declared her neutrality, but Italians by the thousands were enlisting in France. Marco might do that.

Down at Buckingham Palace, Mr. Heaton reported, a huge crowd was gathering, singing and cheering. Now and then King George and Queen Mary came out on the balcony.

"Why do the people go to the Palace?" Betsy asked.

"They want to let the King know they're behind him," Mr. Heaton said.

"We talk, eat, drink, and sleep war," Betsy wrote home. It was strange. Belgium had been hardly more to her than a spot on the map, and now she was shaken with pity, excitement, and pride in the human race by the little country's answer to big Germany. The forts at their border were to be defended—to the last man.

On the morning of August fourth the conviction that war would be declared before nightfall was as strong around Mrs. Heaton's breakfast table as it was in the *Times*.

It was strong even in the Agony Column. A penitent Nan begged her Jack—fifth advertisement down— "if you love me, don't enlist until we make up."

In the middle of breakfast Betsy received a cable from home.

"ARE YOU ALL RIGHT? BEST RETURN AT ONCE. WORRIED. LOVE. DAD."

Tears rushed into her eyes. She knew how anxious they must be. She still didn't want to go home, but she knew she would have to if England really did get in.

Shortly it became clear that England would get in. Six German columns crossed the Belgian frontier. The Belgians were waiting for them at the Meuse.

"Good little Belgium!" Mr. Leonard cried.

The Crew went out to roam the streets with the rest of London. Soldiers were everywhere—alone, with sweethearts, with wives hanging to their arms, carrying their children. Some of the boyish Territorials were walking with red-eyed girls. Others went alone, cockily or forlornly.

In front of the German Embassy a long line of people—many tearful—waited for passports. "Some of them have lived here a long time. They've just neglected getting naturalization papers, and now they must go back to fight us," Mr. Dick said.

Peddlers were hawking flags. The sidewalk artists were drawing battleships and the royal family.

By teatime Great Britain had delivered her ultimatum

to Germany, and midnight was fixed as the time limit for Germany's answer.

At the Houses of Parliament, crowds cheered as the members came out. At Buckingham Palace was such a throng as Betsy had never seen or imagined.

"I'm so glad I'm with you," Betsy told The Crew. She was very fond of them, and proud, too, because they made her seem a part of this great spontaneous demonstration.

Dinnertime came and went. The Crew didn't wish to go home without seeing the King and Queen. Both had been coming out frequently, everyone said, but now only Princess Mary appeared briefly, taking snapshots.

"She has her hair up!" Jean cried. "It's the first time."

The young, slim, handsome Prince of Wales, wearing a silk hat, crossed the courtyard to cheers and applause. He disappeared inside.

"But he wiped his feet on the doormat!" Betsy cried. "His mother brought him up well."

Hungrier and hungrier, they waited until almost nine.

"Mrs. Heaton will be worrying," Mr. Leonard said. "I ought to take you girls home. Claude is enough for her to worry about. I'll be back," he added to his brother. They made plans to meet.

"I thought I was tired," Betsy said, when they were

raiding Mrs. Heaton's kitchen. "But I'm absolutely wide awake. Let's have a kimono party up in my room, and wait for the news at midnight."

Dolly and Jean agreed enthusiastically and so did Mrs. Heaton. Her husband had returned with Mr. Leonard to the Palace. With a big pot of tea to keep them company, the girls crowded Turkish fashion on the bed, leaving the easy chair to their hostess.

They talked a little, but mainly they listened to the noise outside. Rarely did all of them together look away from the clock.

"And this," Betsy thought, "is what the start of a war is like!"

"A quarter after eleven," Mrs. Heaton said.

A searchlight poked a bright finger into their room, but withdrew as though embarrassed.

"A quarter of midnight," Mrs. Heaton said.

"I'll wager," said Jean, "that if it lasts long enough, they'll enlist girls."

"Tosh!" said Mrs. Heaton. "Never!"

"I'd go," said Dolly. "A girl could be a messenger. She could operate an army telephone."

"Tosh!" said Mrs. Heaton again. "And listen! Just a minute to go! If Britain declares, there'll be a roar that will carry to Ireland."

They all fell silent.

The minute hand of the clock suddenly stood

upright, and St. Paul's chimes began to count twelve.

Then Mrs. Heaton's predicted roar came. It could have carried to Ireland. For long minutes it swelled like the sound of the sea. Then it changed. Betsy caught Dolly's arm.

"It's singing!" she cried.

It was singing. First it was singing far off. Then it was singing outside the window in Taviton Street. Then it was singing right in the room. Mrs. Heaton was up from her chair. Jean and Dolly were off the bed. The three of them joined, it seemed to Betsy, with all London.

> "When Britain first at Heaven's command,
> Arose from out the azure main,
> This was the charter of the land,
> And guardian angels sung this strain,
> R-u-l-e B-r-i-t-a-n-n-i-a . . ."

That was Betsy's cue. The next two lines, at least, she knew. Her arms went out. Mrs. Heaton's arms, and Dolly's, and Jean's replied. In a weeping, valiant line, the four stood at the window and sang with the crowd below.

> "Rule Britannia! Britannia rule the waves,
> Britains never, never, never, shall be slaves."

Mrs. Heaton broke free, clapped hands to her face, and ran from the room. Dolly followed, and Jean. Betsy continued at the window, fixed there by the magnet of the singing.

But presently, as before, her ears caught a change. The singing became words, two words, intoned over and over. Newsboys were running up and down crying them.

"War declared! War declared!"

Finally it was fused into one word.

"War! War! War!"

Betsy did the only thing she could do at such a moment. She got down on her knees.

21

The Agony Column

"WHAT A TIME," grumbled Betsy, settling herself and her umbrella on top of a bus, "what a time to have to think about money!"

She was going to the American Express Company, but this time not to *Onze Rue Scribe*. It was to Six Haymarket, S.W., in London, to her everlasting thankfulness.

Breakfast had brought a rumor that the invaluable offices were to reopen for the benefit of stranded tourists. The banks had been closed for several days by government moratorium, and money was growing scarce. The boarders at Mrs. Heaton's had been making a great joke of borrowing shillings and pence. But Betsy, needing a ticket home, could not be helped by such small change. Everyone had rejoiced with her over the morning's report.

"You must jolly well go right down!" Mr. Heaton had said. "Get some money and book your passage. Only the early birds among you Americans are likely to get home by Christmas."

"Here goes Early Bird Ray," Betsy murmured. "Jolly well going right down as fast as the bus will take her."

But she was aware that even if she found the Express Company open, the purchase of her passage home was going to take some doing.

Betsy had only one lone American Express Company check, and it was for just fifty dollars. Unless a certain piece of paper in a chamois bag, which she wore carefully pinned to her innermost garments, proved negotiable, she was, she warned herself adventurously, likely to be marooned, far from kith and kin.

Until now Betsy had always had all the money she

needed. Her father's monthly remittance had been a modest but dependable mainstay. Extras had been cared for by her American Express checks, now reduced to one. And as a last resource she had always carried, in the chamois bag, a check signed in blank by her father.

"Strictly for an emergency!" Mr. Ray had warned. "But in any real jam, fill it in for whatever you need. Any bank'll cash it if you give 'em time to cable my bank in Minneapolis."

The trouble was that Mr. Ray hadn't reckoned with a war. With the war on, if Betsy gave any bank much time, she was likely to miss out on her ticket home.

"Oh, well!" she thought. "The American Express Company will just have to cash Papa's check for whatever I need!" She refused to worry, but she did object to having to think about anything so mundane as money . . . when the world was in flames, and she should be back at Heaton's, helping the other women. They were going to make shirts for soldiers.

"We'll start this very afternoon," Mrs. Heaton had planned at breakfast where there had been no sugar and no butter. "We women will sew, and one of the young men can read aloud."

That, Betsy realized, was being optimistic. Mr. Claude was already gone; Mr. Dick had enlisted;

and Mr. Leonard was only waiting.

"I could certainly be doing something more useful than thinking about money!" Betsy said disgustedly. But alighting from the bus she soon saw that plenty of other people had to do it, too.

An impatient queue already stretched two blocks from the American Express Company's office. Bobbies were patrolling it; one of them waved her into line.

"You'll save yourself a lot of trouble, Miss, if you just fall in. The door's not even open yet."

His eyes twinkled, and as she took her place, Betsy's eyes began to twinkle, too. Here were all those Americans—or most of them—who had been rushing about Europe so happily with guidebooks and cameras and usually well-filled purses. Here they were, blown by war to England and longing to be blown still farther across the wide Atlantic to their own United States.

"We lost every scrap of our baggage."

"I had my letter of credit, but a lot of good it did me."

"Uncle Sam will get us out of this hole," a booming voice proclaimed. "He looks after his nieces and nephews."

Everyone wanted to talk . . . about past adventures, or the present situation, or the gallant little Belgians, or President Wilson's neutrality proclamation.

"We won't stay neutral long!"

The door did not open and the line grew longer. It started to rain, which struck Betsy and some of the other light-hearted ones as funny. Looking around, under the bobbing umbrellas, she thought she saw Mr. Glenn of the *Columbic*, but he was too far away to be hailed.

"And probably Mrs. Sims and Mrs. Cheney are in this line somewhere. Maybe even Miss Surprise!" But not, Betsy felt sure, Mrs. Main-Whittaker. She would be dashing about Paris scooping up material. And the Wilsons, Betsy knew, were still in Derwent Water. Their last letter had sounded serene, except for concern about her.

"If worse comes to worst," she thought, "Dr. Wilson will cash a check for me." But she was reluctant to burden anyone with her problem. Everyone, it seemed, had problems enough of his own.

These seemed to lessen, however, as the doors of the Express Company opened at last.

"Don't push, laidies," the bobby urged gently. "Remember, laidies and gentlemen, you've got all day."

Some people talked about dropping out.

"But I can't drop out," said the booming voice which had once praised Uncle Sam. "I've got to get at least a thousand dollars."

"But I hear we won't be allowed more than a hundred."

"A fine note!" Uncle Sam's nephew roared. "They sold 'em to us; didn't they?"

A lady standing ahead of Betsy turned around.

"Do you have a passport?" she asked.

"No," Betsy replied, surprised. Very few people bothered with passports for a mere trip to Europe.

"Do you suppose someone might ask us for them?"

"Of course not," Uncle Sam's nephew cut in.

Betsy reached the door at last. The queuers, once inside, were being directed to various windows. Halfway to hers, Betsy stopped short at sight of a familiar figure.

"Oh, Mr. Brown!" she exclaimed.

It was, indeed, her kindly friend from Zurich. He wasn't in any of the lines. Jaunty as ever, even in a raincoat, swinging an umbrella instead of a cane, as thin as ever, too, and no less bald, he was inside an imposing railing, leaning against an imposing desk, talking with the desk's imposing occupant.

"Mr. Brown!" Betsy called again. Except for her own father there was no one, she told herself, she'd rather see.

Mr. Brown turned. His questioning gaze carried along the line from which the call had come, and his thin face broke into the pleasant smile Betsy remembered.

"Miss Ray!" he exclaimed and was alongside her in an instant. "The girl who would to Munich go! How grand that you got out! How are you?"

"I'm fine." Betsy smiled back. She took a step forward in her window line and Mr. Brown followed. "I don't suppose that Munich is very *gemütlich* now."

"I take it," he said, "that you're here for money. But I understand they won't give you much."

"Oh, I only have one fifty-dollar check!"

"Only . . . . fifty dollars?" He sounded startled.

"My father's allowance comes monthly, and it hasn't come yet for August," Betsy explained.

"Do you have your passage home?"

"No. And it's sort of complicated." How wonderful, how comforting, to talk it over with Mr. Brown! "I'll have to pay by filling in a blank check my father gave me. He signed it before I left home, and said I was to save it for an emergency. I guess this is an emergency all right."

"Where do you think you can cash it?"

"I thought I'd try here. And in any case I'll cash my fifty dollars."

Mr. Brown in sudden decision drew her out of the line. "Never mind about that fifty dollars!" he said. "Let's think about getting you passage home."

He led her outside. The rain had stopped, and he swung his umbrella thoughtfully.

"The *Arabic* is sailing, I think," Betsy suggested.

"No. Not a British boat. I know. Come along." He took her arm, and they headed for the offices of the United States Lines.

Tourists were besieging it, but Mr. Brown got to an attendant who broke into a broad grin of recognition.

"Mr. Brown!"

"Good afternoon, Joe," Mr. Brown replied. "Tell me where I can find . . ." His voice died away and Betsy could not catch the name he gave. But Joe did. He grinned more broadly and led Mr. Brown, with Betsy trailing, up to a second-floor office and a desk even more imposing than the one at which she had first seen him today.

The desk's occupant looked up, and leaped to his feet in welcome.

"Van!" he shouted. "I thought you sailed a week ago."

"Hi, Petey," said Mr. Brown. "Nope! I didn't sail. And now how glad I am! Because I can let you be kind to this very good friend of mine. Miss Ray, this is Petey Conant, a man who'll do anything for me because without my help he'd still be a Princeton freshman."

"A slander, Miss Ray," said Petey. "The truth is

that I pulled Van through. My coaching got him honors in history when alone he couldn't even have told you that the Civil War was uncivil."

"Look, Petey!" said Mr. Brown. "Can you squeeze Miss Ray into the *Richmond*?"

"Gosh!" Petey said and turned serious, but Mr. Brown cut him short.

"'Gosh, yes!' you were going to say. Good old Petey! And don't bother about doing anything special. Miss Ray knows there's a war on."

"Gosh, Van!" Petey began soberly once more, but again Mr. Brown broke in.

"Just standing room, sort of, will do in any stateroom. Won't it, Miss Ray?"

Betsy nodded, a little embarrassed, because she didn't, she felt, merit special attention . . . especially when she was in no hurry to go home. She was about to say so, when Petey gave in.

"All right," he said grudgingly. "For Miss Ray I'll do it. But while she's sharing a stateroom with three or four or more, ten thousand disappointed Americans are going to be trying to cut my throat."

"A detail!" said Mr. Brown. "Miss Ray, may I have your check?"

Betsy blushed. She looked around. "I'll have to . . ." For the chamois bag was concealed beneath many layers of undergarments . . . even her corset.

"Of course!" said Mr. Brown consolingly. He too looked around, and so did Petey. Petey beckoned to a pretty clerk and she led Betsy down a corridor and opened a door. There in the necessary privacy Betsy extracted the chamois bag and the check. She also seized the opportunity to powder her burning cheeks.

She trailed the pretty clerk back to the desk where Mr. Brown and Petey waited, smiling.

"Will you have enough, Miss Ray," Mr. Brown asked, "if Petey gives you five hundred?"

"I don't need half that," Betsy gasped. Did the man think her father was made of money? "The fare is under two hundred; isn't it?"

Petey nodded.

"Let's say two fifty then," Mr. Brown suggested. "And Petey will cash your American Express check, too. You must have something extra."

"Thank you so much!" Betsy cried when the tickets and money were safe in her purse and she and Mr. Brown were out on the street again. "My father will never be able to thank you enough. But he'll want to try." She remembered something. "You jumped off that Zurich train so fast that you didn't give me your address. This time you really must."

"Of course," said Mr. Brown, and stopped a hansom cab.

Betsy was shocked. "I don't ride in hansom cabs,

for goodness sake! They're awfully nice, of course. But I bus everywhere."

"Not with that ticket in your purse," Mr. Brown replied, helping her in. "We can't have your pocket picked today. We'd never be able to squeeze another ticket even out of Petey." He stepped back to say something to the driver, then returned and held out his hand.

"Good-by," he said. "And take all your fences boldly, but not too boldly."

"Good-by," Betsy answered. "Oh, you've been so good!" Then she remembered again. "But you haven't given me your address for Papa."

The driver overhead clucked to his horse.

"To be sure," Mr. Brown said hastily. "Of course." He started fishing in his pockets as he had done before, and just as the cab rolled forward he found a card and thrust it into Betsy's hand.

Rolling off toward Taviton Street, she looked at it. She looked at it again.

"For goodness sake!" she exclaimed aloud. "Just wait until Tib hears of this!"

For the full name of Mr. Brown was as familiar (or even more so) to Betsy and Tib as President Woodrow Wilson's. Just Mr. Brown could be anybody. But this Mr. Brown! They had read about him in society pages for years and years!

"Imagine!" Betsy murmured. "Van Rensselaer Brown!" The eligible bachelor who was angled for by debutantes, and considered suitable for European princesses, even.

Betsy leaned back in the cab. "Tib said it for a joke . . . that I'd meet an American millionaire. But I have. And who would have thought he'd be so plain ordinary nice!"

He was even nicer than she had thought. Arriving at Mrs. Heaton's boarding house, she found he had paid the cab fare.

Her ticket was stamped for September 1, and Betsy was glad that she did not have to hurry away from London. She was grateful to be able to share a little longer in the troubles that had befallen the old city.

She shared the sorrow of the fall of Liège. Betsy and Mrs. Heaton joined the crowds that thronged St. Paul's Church for the Service of the Intercession. They sang "Rock of Ages" and "God Save the King." They sat next to a mother and daughter who held hands and wept. On the other side was an over-dressed girl with a round, almost silly face. She cried until her lacy handkerchief was a soggy ball.

Going out, Betsy touched her on the shoulder.

"Good luck!" she said.

"Thanks, ducky!" answered the girl. "And bad luck to the Kaiser! And it will be bad luck for him, all right, if he gets in my Bob's way."

Everywhere in London now there were huge placards saying, "Your King and Country Need You." Sidewalk artists were picturing Earl Kitchener, who had become head of the War Office. As the congregation melted out of St. Paul's, a street organ began to grind out the tune that all the slim young soldiers were marching to these days.

> *"It's a long way to Tipperary,*
> *It's a long way to go . . ."*

They had played that, Betsy remembered, on the *Columbic* on the first night out. She had been so blue because she was leaving home . . . and because of Joe!

She still hadn't heard from him. Of course, she hadn't given him an address, and not much mail nor many cables were getting through. Still, it wasn't like Joe not to find a way—if he cared to.

Maybe, Betsy thought, he had stopped loving her. Maybe she was going to have to build her life without him. She took brave little Mrs. Heaton's arm.

They had a very special tea that day. Claude was home on leave. Mr. Dick, now in uniform, was coming. And Jean and Dolly would be there, but tomorrow they would both leave for their homes.

Dolly's book had been canceled. Jean's show would

not open. Their careers were over for the duration.

"But I've done the best I could for them," Mrs. Heaton whispered to Betsy. "I've baked plum tarts."

Everyone tried to be cheerful. Claude, on the arm of his mother's chair, told some stories about new recruits. Jean and Dolly and Betsy laughed.

Mr. Dick came in, wearing his new ill-fitting uniform. He walked over to Betsy, smiling.

"Still keep up with the Agony Column?"

"Heavens, no!" Betsy answered. "I'm trying to learn to sew."

"Well, it's a good thing I clipped this," he said and reached into his pocket. "Of course," he added, "I know you aren't the only Betsy in London. But do you know anyone named Joe?"

Betsy stared at him for a long unbelieving moment. Without a word she put out her hand.

Joe hadn't forgotten her! And he had found a way! Holding the clipping fast, she ran out of the garden and up to her little white room. She sat down, with tears running down her cheeks.

"Betsy. The Great War is on but I hope ours is over. Please come home. Joe."

She would cable a reply, Betsy thought, pushing the tears out of her eyes so she could read the wonderful words again. Perhaps she could think of something clever to say? But no, she didn't want to! She was too aware of the worry, the dread, the grief down in the garden . . . the danger hanging over her friends down there, and over London and all of Europe. She was just full of thankfulness and love.

She found a pencil.

"Joe. Please meet S.S. Richmond, arriving New York September 7. Love. Betsy."

She hadn't forgotten him! And she hadn't lost him! "Oh, Joe! Joe!" said Betsy.

Betsy's Wedding

Acknowledgments

The verse on page 516 was written by Darragh Aldrich and appeared in the *Minneapolis Tribune* in 1914. The verse on page 630 is adapted from a verse by Earle Buell which appeared in the *Minneapolis Tribune* in 1917. The epigraph is from "For Katrina's Sun Dial" by Henry Van Dyke, and the lines on page 366 are from "America for Me" by Henry Van Dyke; both from *The Poems of Henry Van Dyke*, copyright 1911, 1939 by Charles Scribner's Sons, New York. The lines from "Silk o' the Kine" by Alfred Noyes, which appear on page 444, are from *Poems*, copyright 1906, 1934 by Alfred Noyes, reprinted by permission of J. B. Lippincott Company, Philadelphia, and A. P. Watt and Sons, London.

For
LILLIAN HAMMONS WAKEFIELD

Contents

Hours fly,
Flowers die.
New days,
New ways,
Pass by.
Love stays.

—HENRY VAN DYKE

1

Home Again

ALMOST CHOKED WITH excitement and joy, Betsy Ray leaned against the railing as the S.S. *Richmond* sailed serenely into New York City's inner harbor. The morning was misty, and since they had passed through the Narrows, she had seen only sky and water—and a gull, now and then—as though they were still out in the Atlantic. But she knew she had come home.

❧ 365 ❧

> "... *home again, and home again, America*
> *for me!*
> *My heart is turning home again, and there I*
> *long to be ...*"

Betsy chanted softly to herself. She gripped the rail hard.

And Joe's waiting for me! she thought. Oh, I hope he's going to like me as well as he used to! I hope I look nice.

It wasn't her fault if she didn't. She had beautified herself as thoroughly as possible, but that wasn't much, for she shared a stateroom with three older women—and had been lucky to have one at all. The outbreak of war in Europe had crowded to over-flowing all American-bound ships. On the *Richmond* many men had slept on deck. There had been three sittings at table—the dishes were barely washed between—while talk went on and on about the adventures, the mishaps, the dangers the passengers had encountered in getting out of Germany, or France, or England. Talk was the only diversion for the vessel had sailed its fearful way in darkness.

It had been a contrast to the gay trip on the *Columbic* which had taken Betsy abroad in January. This was September, 1914. She was twenty-two years old.

I'm glad of my new Paris suit, she thought. The suit, of dark blue wool, was flattering to her slender figure. The skirt was long; the jacket belted with crushed crimson satin. A dark hat framed her shining face. Not just her eyes were shining. Something inside was shining because she was meeting Joe.

Joe Willard had been important to Betsy since high school days in Deep Valley, Minnesota. He had not gone with her Crowd—by his own choice, for his good looks, humor, and warmth drew people to him. But he was an orphan with scant pocket money and no time to waste. He had worked after school on the *Deep Valley Sun*.

He had worked on the *Minneapolis Tribune* during the following two years when he and Betsy attended the University of Minnesota. They had considered themselves almost engaged. But then Joe had won a scholarship to Harvard. He had gone East, getting work on the *Boston Transcript*—for Joe was always working. And they had quarreled.

"It was my fault," Betsy said to the gulls, swooping past her toward the foam that boiled up along the vessel's side. "Flirting with someone I didn't give a hang for! No wonder Joe stopped writing!"

She had felt very badly about it but she had been too stubborn to try to make up.

When her trip abroad was planned—because she

wanted to be a writer, and her father had thought she would profit from foreign travel—Betsy had not even let Joe know that she was sailing from the port of Boston. As it happened, however, she had caught a glimpse of him there.

He had been one of a group of reporters interviewing Mrs. Main-Whittaker, the author, and Betsy had recognized his walk. Joe Willard met life with a challenge which showed in his swinging walk. His blond hair had looked the same too, brushed back in a pompadour. The close-cropped mustache had been new. But Betsy had known him, and the sight of him had brought all her heartache flooding back.

She had sailed away determined to forget Joe Willard but she had not forgotten him, during her journey into the Great World.

"I didn't forget him and I didn't stop loving him," she said. She spoke softly for there were people at her elbows now. The sun had come out, and the bay which had been gray was greenish-blue, full of dancing whitecaps. Suddenly a murmur ran along the railing, rising to glad cries and long-drawn-out "Ahs!" of admiration and wonder. Through a crack in the misty clouds ahead, the towers of Manhattan had come into view.

They looked unreal, white and glistening among the clouds, like the towers of a city in a fairy book—

or the holy city in the Book of Revelation, Betsy thought, gazing.

"Why, it's Lilliput! You feel you could take it up on the palm of your hand!" a man near her exclaimed.

As the ship churned forward, the buildings grew more substantial, but still they were only white pencils standing on end. It did not seem possible that these could be powerful masses of steel and concrete and stone, the celebrated skyscrapers of New York.

"There's the Woolworth Building!" someone shouted, and everyone stared at that world-famous pile, the highest one of all.

New Yorkers all around her were eagerly identifying other famous buildings, but these cries died down. Gleaming in sunlight, majestic, benign, the Goddess of Liberty had come into view.

That figure with the upflung arm caused silence to fall along the line of travelers returning to their peaceful homeland from a Europe blazing with war. France, Betsy remembered, had given the United States this statue in tribute to the American fight for freedom. And now France was fighting for her freedom!

Tears blurred Betsy's eyes but they weren't just for France. They were for America, and Joe, and because she was so glad to be back. She cried and cried, wiping away the tears with both her hands, so she could look ahead.

Now everyone was shouting frantically again, above the din of whistles and hollow-sounding horns. They were exclaiming that a phantom bridge at their right was the wonderful Brooklyn Bridge. They were pointing out Ellis Island where immigrants stopped before entering the United States.

There were ferries, ploughing placidly between Staten Island and the Battery, and more ocean-going steamships, and grimy freighters, and busy little tugs. There was even a delicate four-masted schooner, speaking in silence of a gentle past.

Joe would like that schooner, Betsy thought, as she had thought so often when seeing lovely things during her travels. And then it came to her that in a few moments she could tell him about it, about anything she cared to, and she started crying again.

They had turned up the Hudson—it seemed to be called the North River—and the waterfront was lined with ships, flying flags of many nations. A pair of tugs began to nudge the *Richmond* into one of the rows of jutting piers. The water was quieter here although it still smelled salty and fishy. All mists had gone, and the sky above the waiting city was lavender blue, full of light spirals of cloud.

Betsy looked at the barnlike structure rising at the end of the pier. Joe was in there!

And I must look like an absolute fright! she

thought, wiping her eyes with new determination. She took a powder puff out of the handbag swinging from her arm and powdered her hot cheeks. She found a tiny bottle and touched her earlobes with a new Parisian scent.

Joe would be waiting, strangely enough, because she had met Mrs. Main-Whittaker in Paris. Betsy had been too stubborn to write and make up their quarrel until that famous lady had inadvertently shown her a way. Mrs. Main-Whittaker had praised the story of her departure from Boston which Joe had written for the *Transcript*, and that had given Betsy the excuse her pride needed. She had passed along the compliment in a carefully casual note.

To be sure, she forgot in her confusion to include any address. But she had told him that she was bound for London and had mentioned chattily something Mrs. Main-Whittaker had said: that Betsy, because she liked to write stories, should be sure to read the column of Personals—the Agony Column, it was called—in the *London Times*.

That had been enough for Joe, who always knew how to find a way. After the Germans marched into Belgium he had cabled to the Agony Column.

"BETSY. THE GREAT WAR IS ON BUT I HOPE OURS IS OVER. PLEASE COME HOME. JOE."

And Betsy had cabled in reply:

"Joe. Please meet S.S. Richmond arriving New York September 7. Love. Betsy".

She had been bold, she thought now, color flooding up into her cheeks, to put in that "love." And she had been assuming a good deal when she asked him to meet her in New York. He had been graduated in June, but she felt sure he was continuing on the *Transcript* in Boston.

A girl named Victoria came up and tugged at Betsy's arm. "Have you remembered everything?"

"Everything. Even the doll for Tacy's baby." Betsy's smile which showed white teeth parted a little in front was friendly like Betsy herself. Victoria knew all about Tacy, Betsy's best friend, who was expecting a baby which Betsy was expecting to be a girl.

The doll, bought in Germany, was a bulky package piled, with Betsy's suitcases and steamer trunk, out in the passageway. Her umbrella and camera were on the steamer chair behind her. She picked them up, for the liner was bumping now, conclusively, against the pier.

Betsy and Victoria were caught up in the crowd pushing toward the gangplank. Betsy went with deliberate slowness for her heart was thumping. She was even trembling a little. And she mustn't, she told herself, act excited. Joe would expect her to be poised and dignified after almost a year in Europe.

She and Tacy had joked in their letters about Betsy's acquiring "an indefinable Paris air."

"But it's no joke! That's just what I ought to have," Betsy declared firmly. She adjusted her hat to its most effective slant and patted her curls—she hoped they were still curls, but the sea air didn't agree with Betsy's hair. She remembered the models she had seen parading at Longchamps. They had that fashionable, spineless look called "the debutante slouch." Betsy let herself slink into it now.

Victoria understood.

"No need to get fixed for him yet," she said. "We have to go through Customs, you know. People aren't allowed to come in without passes, and with the war on, they'll be hard to get."

But Joe, Betsy knew, was the kind to get a pass no matter how strict regulations might be, and she continued to saunter like a Longchamps model down the gangplank and into the barnlike warehouse. This was divided into sections with the letters of the alphabet posted above to indicate where the passengers might find their luggage and open it for waiting Customs officials. Bidding Victoria an affectionate good-by, Betsy sauntered toward the "R's."

But suddenly she stood up straighter than an arrow. Not standing under the "R's," but swinging toward her with a cane hung over his arm, came a stocky blond young man.

Betsy ran toward him.

The next thing she knew he had his arms around her. She had dropped her umbrella and her new hat was knocked off but she didn't care. He was holding her close and saying over and over, "Oh, Betsy! Betsy!" And Betsy, when she could lift her tear-wet face from where it was crushed into his woolly shoulder, tried to say "Joe! Joe!" but she couldn't because he was kissing her and she was kissing him.

Joe held her off at arm's length. Under his blond pompadour and tufted golden brows, his eyes were blazingly bright. Blushing, Betsy rescued her hat, and Joe picked up her umbrella.

He took hold of her arm in a strong and purposeful grasp.

"Let's get this Customs business out of the way quick," he said. "And then we'll go to Tiffany's and get you a ring. And then—" he turned swiftly to look into her face—"when can we get married?"

2

Joe's Plan

"BUT WE HAVE TO BE engaged a little while!" Betsy was explaining, an hour or so later, in front of the Pennsylvania Station.

Her trunk, her suitcases, and Tacy's doll had been checked and she had picked up her tickets. Mr. Ray had written Joe, asking him to make her reservations, and he had—on the latest train leaving New York that night which would make connections for Minneapolis in Chicago the following evening.

Betsy had given Joe his present, a British edition of Kipling's *Soldier Stories*. He had been pleased, but he had teased her about the Ray custom of bringing home presents. He and Betsy had met first in Joe's uncle's store in Butternut Center when she was buying home-presents after a visit to a farm.

"You Rays!" he scoffed. "Do you have a parchment scroll for recording these old family customs? Bringing home presents! Muffins for special occasions! Sunday night lunches!"

He stopped with a wide grin.

"That reminds me! Marriage is a fine old family custom. When are we going to get married?"

It was then Betsy had protested that they had to be engaged a little while.

A taxicab slued to a stop. "The Waldorf, skipper!" Joe said.

"The Waldorf!" Betsy's face was as bright as the corsage bouquet Joe had bought for her shoulder. She had heard all her life of the famous Waldorf-Astoria Hotel. They rolled in a great tide of motor cars and carriages to the corner of Fifth Avenue and Thirty-fourth Street, and Joe helped her out, her green taffeta petticoat swishing.

Inside the celebrated door, she was pleased to remember that her suit came from Paris, for the women strolling along the marble corridor known as Peacock Alley were extremely modish.

But I have the handsomest escort! Betsy thought. He was so poised, too, amid this sophisticated splendor. She walked proudly with his hand gripping her arm, and gazed up at the carved and frescoed ceiling and around at deep leather chairs, rich oriental rugs.

At the Rose Room door Joe checked his hat and cane. The violins seemed to be singing just for them. They were seated at a window table, and a deferential waiter spread Betsy's jacket over the back of her chair, and she transferred Joe's flowers to her blouse— snowy crêpe de Chine with pleated frills at neck and wrists.

While Joe ordered, she looked out at Fifth Avenue—or tried to. The broad windows held a procession of curious faces as passersby paused to look in.

"They look in to see the celebrities," Joe explained. "Celebrities like—oh, Betsy Ray! Author of 'Emma Middleton Cuts Cross Country.'"

"Joe, did you read that?"

"After your letter came, I hunted up an *Ainslee's*. Betsy!" His tone changed. "That was the happiest moment of my life—when your letter came."

"Was it?" Betsy asked tremulously.

"But now—this one is."

"It is for me, too."

Joe leaned closer, his blue eyes bright. "Today," he said, "I could do anything. I could swim seas, or topple mountains, or link the poles by tunnel. And that's why I believe I can persuade you to marry me soon."

Her cheeks turned to flames.

"Betsy," he said, "when your father wrote me, I thought at first that I wouldn't get those tickets. I thought, 'Why don't Betsy and I just get married and go to Boston?'"

"Joe!"

"I know. But I thought again. A Ray ought to be married in the bosom of her family. And I can wait a week!"

"A week!"

The waiter interrupted with eggs Benedict. Betsy asked hurriedly, "What are we going to do this afternoon?"

"That," answered Joe, accepting the change of subject, "is a problem. For dinner tonight we're going to a little French restaurant down in Greenwich Village and then, of course, you must see the Great White Way. But this afternoon—we have such a few hours, and this is such a marvelous mad city! Do you want the Metropolitan Museum? Or a *Thé Dansant*? (I can tango.) Or the Bowery because you're a writer, or Fraunces Tavern because Washington ate there . . . ? Betsy, you're not listening!"

"Yes, I am," she answered happily.

"Then what do you want to see most?"

You! Betsy thought. She couldn't keep her eyes away from him—from the strong, finely-modeled face. His eyes were dancing. His lower lip was thrust out in a reckless way she remembered. "I'll let you plan it," she said demurely, and he grinned at her.

"Then we'll go to Central Park and sit under a tree."

The waiter brought salad, and Betsy asked about the uncle and aunt with whom Joe had lived for a time.

"Uncle Alvin died last spring. I went back to Butternut Center for the funeral. Aunt Ruth is carrying on with the store. I think a lot of Aunt Ruth."

"I'm sorry about Uncle Alvin."

"What's new at 909?" Joe asked. That was his name for the Ray house. After Betsy finished high school, the family had moved from Deep Valley to 909 Hazel Street in Minneapolis.

She talked fast, telling him that her older sister, Julia, who was an opera singer, and Paige, her flutist husband, were in Minneapolis for a visit. Margaret was in high school now.

Joe had already heard Tacy's news.

"What about Tib?" he asked. Betsy, Tacy and Tib

had been a threesome ever since childhood when Betsy's short braids, Tacy's red ringlets, and Tib's fluffy yellow curls were always seen together on the Big Hill in Deep Valley.

"She was graduated in June from the art department at Browner. In Milwaukee, you know. She stayed with her grandparents there while she was going through college."

"This war will hit Tib hard," Joe reflected, "because of her German ancestry."

They talked about the war. Joe's heart, like Betsy's, was with the British and the French. His face grew grave when he said there was a great battle raging along a river called the Marne.

"I'm thankful you're home safe," he said.

"Joe," Betsy asked, "did you see me on the *Columbic*?"

"Yes. Don't mention it!" After a silence he added, "But sometime I want to hear all about your trip."

"And I want to hear all about your graduation. Oh, Joe!" Betsy said, and her voice trembled a little. "We have so much to catch up on!"

"We can do it," he answered consolingly, "sitting beside our own fire after we're married."

Feeling her cheeks grow hot again, Betsy looked away—at pink damask walls and glimmering crystal chandeliers.

"Won't it be long enough if we're engaged a week?"

Betsy looked back at him. "Why, we're not engaged yet!"

"But you said—"

"I meant that *after* we got engaged we'd have to wait a while. Joe Willard, you know very well that you haven't even proposed!"

His deep laugh rang out. "Well, I certainly won't do it here!" he said. "So hurry and finish your ice cream and we'll get up to Central Park. Then we must get that ring. Did I tell you I have seven hundred dollars in the bank? And no debts? And a job?"

"That," said Betsy, twinkling, "is the sort of thing you tell my father and not me."

"Gosh!" said Joe. "I'm thankful your father likes me. At least he used to. Do you think he still does?"

She finished her ice cream and coffee and Joe paid the waiter and left a lavish tip. He guided Betsy out of the room, gripping her arm as though she might vanish if he let go.

In another taxicab they rolled up Fifth Avenue, past the fine shops, and the Public Library, and the brownstone mansions in which millionaires lived.

"Many a heroine I have put in those mansions!" Betsy said.

They alighted where Central Park's hilly rectangle of grass and trees and rocks rolled northward, walled in by towering buildings. Near a fountain stood a row of horses hitched to ancient victorias with coachmen in tall hats.

"If I didn't have to propose," said Joe, "we could take a ride through the Park and I'd show you the Zoo and the Shakespeare Garden and the merry-go-round. We'd hire a rowboat and go riding on the lake. Sure you want me to propose?"

"Positive!" said Betsy.

So they found a bench under a tree which was dropping a few yellow leaves. Nursemaids were rolling carriages past, strollers were enjoying the sun, and a vendor was offering grapes and pomegranates and peaches while a hurdy-gurdy played "The Sidewalks of New York."

Joe took Betsy's hand and they smiled at each other.

"It's wonderful to be sitting here together," Betsy said.

"Together!" said Joe. "That's a beautiful word. So much nicer than 'apart.' Aren't you glad we're going to be married next week?"

"Now Joe!" said Betsy. "You know I've been gone from home almost a year. I can't leave Minneapolis right away. . . ."

"That's easy! We can live in Minneapolis."

"But I wouldn't for the world have you give up the *Transcript*!" Betsy cried, distressed. "I'll live in Boston or wherever is best for you, but . . ."

"What I want to do," said Joe, "is earn my living writing. And I'm going to do it sometime. But while I'm on a newspaper, I'd just as soon be in Minneapolis as Boston."

"Would you really?" Betsy cried joyfully. "Oh, Joe! And you have such a fine record back there! You wouldn't have a bit of trouble getting a job on the *Tribune* again."

"I could telegraph and get one," Joe said grandly. "The old man told me so when I left. I don't think, though," he added, "that I'll telegraph. I want a good salary. You know . . . I'll be a married man."

Betsy squeezed his hand.

"I'll go back to Boston," Joe planned. "I'll resign, pack my bags, and come out to Minneapolis. Wedding a week from today?" he questioned briskly, looking down.

Betsy burst into laughter. "You still haven't proposed!"

"Well, there isn't time now! Tiffany's will be closing." He jumped up but he sat down again.

"Wait a minute, Joe!" said Betsy, her voice serious. "Let's save our seven hundred dollars for your trip out, and renting an apartment, and buying furniture. I don't want an engagement ring. I don't care a thing about it."

"But I do. I want to buy you a ring and I want to buy it at Tiffany's."

A little smile crossed her face. "You might," she suggested innocently, "buy me a wedding ring?"

"By Golly!" cried Joe. "What a woman I'm marrying! That's exactly what I'll do!"

Hands swinging, they ran for a taxi, and in spite of late afternoon traffic, they were soon in spacious, haughty Tiffany's.

A clerk in a frock coat showed them trays of rings which Joe inspected critically. He acted, Betsy thought admiringly, as though he bought a wedding ring every day.

Wide bands, the regal clerk disclosed, were going out of fashion. Narrow bands were coming in. Platinum was much used.

"I like gold better," Betsy said timidly, and he measured her finger for a slender gold band. She put it on.

Joe took her hand. He turned it this way and that, judicially, as though the soft white hand weren't Betsy's and the ring their wedding ring.

"Do you like it, Betsy?"

"I love it."

The young man put it in a velvet-lined box which Joe dropped nonchalantly into his pocket. But back on Fifth Avenue he took it out and tore off the wrappings. He put the ring on Betsy's right hand, and lifted her hand swiftly, and kissed it.

"Oh, Betsy!" he said.

They boarded a double-decker bus—Betsy had loved them in London. They sat on a top front seat with Betsy's head on Joe's shoulder, and the hand with the ring on it spread out for both to admire. Ahead in the strip of sky between the city's buildings were thin banners of pink and great thick banners of mauve. It was an evening for banners.

At Washington Arch they put the ring back in its box and came down to terra firma. Skirting the north side of Washington Square, they turned into a maze of narrow twisting streets, of old houses and foreign-looking shops, and stables made over into studios. Betsy looked around delightedly. This, Joe said, was Greenwich Village where writers, artists, and musicians lived.

Chez Minette was in a basement. It was a place Joe came to often when he was in New York. Minette, short and stout in a tight black dress, sat at the cashier's desk. She greeted him with laughter.

"Ah, *m'sieu!* Tonight you make the *crêpes suzettes* again? It was droll, mademoiselle, when he came out to the kitchen! My husband attached to him an apron!" She dabbed at dewy eyes.

"Joe!" cried Betsy. "Can you really make *crêpes suzettes*?"

"Superb ones!" he grinned. "But not tonight. I'll toss some up when we're having company some night. Minette, permit me to present my fiancée."

"Ah, *la chère petite*!" cooed Minette, embracing Betsy. And when Joe and Betsy were seated, side by side, at a table with a red-checked cloth and a fat red candle in the center, he said triumphantly, "There! Our engagement is announced!"

They talked long and gaily over hors d'oeuvres, soup, roast chicken, and salad. Minette beamed on them but she did not interrupt even when a smiling waitress brought *crêpes suzettes* for dessert. Guests came and went. The candle burned low, and Joe's high spirits also flickered down.

"We'll have to leave," he said at last, looking at his watch. "I do want you to see Broadway at night— that glaring white light, and the crowd moving slow as molasses up and down. It's hard to let you go, though. But it's all decided; isn't it? We'll be married as soon as I get there?"

"As soon as I can manage it," Betsy amended. It wouldn't be easy, she knew, to persuade her family to such haste.

Joe held her hands closely in both of his, and he looked at her with an earnestness she had never seen before in his blue eyes.

"Betsy," he said, "I've been lonely for you these last three years. I was a pretty solitary kid, as you know, after my mother died. But I was never lonely. I was always self-sufficient. And after we fell in love I felt so warm and happy. But I should never have left you and gone away to Harvard . . ."

Betsy interrupted. "Why, Joe!" she cried. "What a thing to say! I was the one who failed, acting so silly and frivolous. But I never cared for anyone but you. Not for a moment!"

Joe did not answer that. He was silent for a long time.

"Betsy," he said at last, "I love you. I love you from that cloudy dark hair down to your slender feet. I love your eyes, and your soft hands, and your sweet voice, and the way your laugh chimes out. Everything about you is enchanting to me. But Betsy, it's lots more than that."

He seemed to be thinking out loud.

"I can always talk to you," he said. "I can make plans, or puzzle out ideas, or build castles in the air. I don't need to think what I'm saying or guard my words. You understand my high moods and my low ones. You understand *me*, I guess.

"I want to be married to you and have you around all the time. I want to come home to you after work and tell you about my day. I want to hear you humming around, doing housework. I want to support you. I want to do things for you. If we were married and I was coming home to you tonight, I wouldn't care if we had just bread and milk.

"You know, Betsy, we never quarrel when we're together. We never will, I really believe, when we are married. But if we aren't, something might come between us again.

"Betsy, you fit into my life as perfectly as a rose fits its stem. You and I match like the pieces of a broken coin." After a long pause, he said, "Love me always, Betsy! I have given my whole heart to you."

Betsy could not answer for a moment because her eyes and throat were full of tears. The restaurant was empty, except for Minette who was counting money busily into a long black bag. Betsy leaned close and put her wet cheek against Joe's.

"I love you, too. Just the way you love me. And we'll be married. I promise."

3
Objections

WHEN BETSY PUSHED UP the shade and looked out the window of her berth on the second morning after leaving Joe, the train was running alongside a mighty river. A wide sweep of cold living water surged between rocky cliffs to which pines and white birches were clinging in a pallid light.

It was the Mississippi!

"Minnesota, hail to thee!" Betsy whispered, staring out. Then she pulled her underwear out of the hammock swinging beside her berth. For since they were following the river they would soon be reaching St. Paul. And then came Minneapolis!

Her family would be waiting at the station. And 909 would be shining. Her father always joked that her mother scoured the coal scuttle when the children came home from a journey. There would be a fire in the grate if it were cool enough, and flowers everywhere, and delectable odors floating from the kitchen.

"Don't you dare eat breakfast!" Mrs. Ray would warn a traveler returning home in the morning. "Well, just a cup of coffee, maybe, if you want the fun of going to the diner! But breakfast will be waiting for you here."

Betsy could imagine the culinary splendor that would be waiting for her after a trip to Europe. Fried chicken, probably! Or sausages and scrambled eggs! Anna's muffins, and the choicest jams and jellies her mother had put up over the summer.

In kimono and boudoir cap, with toilet kit in hand, she went to the ladies' dressing room. Removing the cap, she frowned at a crop of curlers. "Whatever am I going to do about curlers after I'm married!"

But the problem was lost in the rapturous thought

of her engagement. She would not tell her family until evening, she planned. She did not want such glorious news lost in the hubbub of homecoming. Besides, it would take tact to reveal Joe's plans.

By the time she was clad in her Paris suit and hat, the train was in St. Paul. The wait there seemed interminable. Then they were on their way again. The porter brushed her and was tipped. He began to stack luggage out in the vestibule.

Betsy took up her handbag, camera, umbrella, and the mummylike package that held Tacy's doll. She was first in the line that started forming in the aisle. At last came the longed-for "Minneapolis!" The train slowed to a stop and, hidden behind a mountain of baggage, Betsy looked out to see a family portrait:

Her father, tall, portly, and erect, his straw hat in his hand, his hair thin and silvery above a face beaming with calm happiness.

Margaret, trim, dainty, and equally erect, beside him. She looked like a young lady, in skirts to her shoetops. She wore her hair, like Tacy's, in coronet braids.

Julia's smile poured out love and joy and eager welcome. Small but stately, with the carriage and manner of a singer, she clung to the arm of her tall young husband, Paige, and searched the train windows for Betsy's face.

Red-haired Mrs. Ray seemed to be shooting out sparks of excitement. In a smart green suit and jaunty hat with pheasant feathers, she looked like another girl.

They were all there, as Betsy had known they would be, except Anna, the hired girl, and she would be frying the chicken. The porter opened the door, and Betsy flew into their arms—home at last, out of the Great World and into this small, cozy, dear one!

The Rays kissed and hugged and wept. They talked and laughed and interrupted one another. Betsy's bags were collected and the party crowded into a taxicab. Paige sat with the driver but he kept looking around, quiet and smiling.

"Oh, how homesick I was!" Betsy wailed.

"Poor darling!" crooned Mrs. Ray.

"Darn fool girls!" grumbled Mr. Ray. "Getting married! Going to Europe! Only Margaret has sense enough to stay home."

"What's in that big bundle?"

"A doll for Tacy's baby."

"But how can you know it's going to be a girl?"

"Tacy couldn't have anything but a nice, quiet, little girl!"

"How's Joe?" Julia asked.

"Fine! Fine!" Betsy tried to sound offhand.

Mr. Ray wanted news of the war. "Teddy Roosevelt

and his Rough Riders could soon straighten things out."

Talk was still gushing when the cab stopped. Betsy gazed out at a gray stucco bungalow, gay with striped awnings and flowers still bright in window boxes around a glassed-in porch. The porch was covered with reddening vines which her father had transplanted from their home in Deep Valley.

"Stars in the sky!" cried Anna from the doorway, and Betsy flew up the steps. Anna had changed. The knob of hair atop her head was gray, and her broad, kind face looked thinner.

"We were lonesome for you, lovey!" She wept as they hugged.

"Well, she's home, Anna!" Mr. Ray said with satisfaction. "What's more, she's going to stay a while."

"She isn't going to stir from 909 for months and years!" Mrs. Ray cried gaily.

They swarmed into the wicker-and-cretonne-furnished porch. Betsy rushed for the chaise longue where she used to love to lounge and read. She flung herself down.

Jumping up, she spun through double doors into the living room, which had dark woodwork, leaded-glass panes, and a soft, green, oriental rug. At one end rose a small platform with a full-length mirror which reflected the stairway. At the other, the fireplace was flanked by bookcases, with niches above for photographs and the goldfish bowl. Her father's leather chair stood near. Betsy ran to hug it.

Margaret hurried from the kitchen lugging a huge fluffy cat. "This is Kismet. He jumps up on Papa's chair, and then up to the bookcase, and drinks from the goldfish bowl."

Julia dropped down at the piano and started to play, "You're Here, and I'm Here, so What Do We Care?" and Mr. Ray stood with his arm around Mrs. Ray, beaming. Anna pounded a brass gong.

"Remember, Julia," Betsy cried as they all pushed out to the dining room, "how Anna used to bang that gong for breakfast? But I never could get you up."

"Nobody else can either," Paige remarked.

The table was laid with place mats and the best china and silver. And there *was* fried chicken, and there *were* muffins!

"Did you have them, Margaret, on the first day of school?" Betsy asked. "Why aren't you in school today?"

"Because you came home from Europe."

"You notice," Mr. Ray said, "I'm not at the store."

"Paige and I," Julia remarked, "ought to be in New York this minute but we wouldn't leave until you got home."

"I should think not!" Mrs. Ray said, pouring coffee from the silver pot.

As soon as breakfast was over, Betsy brought out her presents.

"Lovey, it's puny!" Anna exclaimed, putting on a pink enameled pin. "Puny" was Anna's word for "beautiful."

The Rays admired, paraded, cried their thanks, while Kismet rattled tissue paper and darted fiercely at ribbons. It was like Christmas morning in the Ray living room when Tacy burst in.

"Where's that indefinable Paris air?" she shouted, as Betsy ran to hug her, but she was careful not to hug too hard for Tacy's usually graceful body looked large and cumbersome.

Julia, at the piano again, began the "Cat Duet."

"What's going on here?" Paige demanded as Betsy and Tacy howled and yowled in unison.

"They sang it all the way through school," Margaret explained with the soft amusement her sisters always roused in her.

Betsy tore herself away. "Here, my Titian-haired friend! See what I brought your child!"

Everyone watched expectantly as Tacy unwrapped the package. A pink plume showed, then flaxen curls, a pale blue dress, and pink gloves, shoes, and stockings.

"Wait till Harry sees this!" Tacy laughed. "He's

already bought his son a baseball mitt."

"We'll fool Harry!" Betsy cried.

But Mr. Ray shook his head in warning. "Harry Kerr almost always gets his own way."

Julia wanted to dress Betsy's hair in the new French roll. "The idea of your coming home from Europe wearing your hair the same way you wore it when you left!"

Betsy obligingly pulled out the pins, and Julia was brushing and twisting when a tall exuberant girl came in. During the last year Louisa Hilton had become Margaret's inseparable friend. She called Margaret Bogie and Margaret called her Boogie.

"I can't believe it!" Betsy whispered to Julia, for Margaret was the dignified one. Her sisters nicknamed her The Persian Princess.

Boogie stayed for lunch, and so did Tacy. Neighbors started dropping in. Betsy's trunk arrived. She settled her belongings in her blue and white bedroom, furnished with bird's-eye-maple furniture which she had inherited when Julia got married. Tacy helped her, while the others came in and out.

"Where's Tib?" Betsy asked.

"Back in Deep Valley. In the chocolate-colored house." That was their name for Tib's home which had seemed like a mansion to them when they were children. "She wants to work here in Minneapolis this winter," Tacy added.

"Oh, wouldn't that be scrumptious!"

"What did you do in New York?" Julia wanted to know, for Julia loved New York. And Betsy told them about lunch at the Waldorf and dinner in Greenwich Village, but she did not tell her secret.

She told it to Tacy, though, when Tacy left and Betsy walked with her down to the corner. She almost always told her secrets to Tacy.

"Joe and I," she announced abruptly, "are engaged."

"Betsy!" Tacy threw her arms around her. "Oh, I'm so glad! I was afraid it hadn't happened when you told us about New York. You acted so cool and collected."

"Cool and collected!" Betsy laughed, hiding a hot face in Tacy's shoulder. "I'm in a daze. I'm in a dither. I can't take it in."

"When are you going to be married?"

"Soon," Betsy answered. "Very soon."

She worried a little about that, walking back in the smoky September twilight. She had known all along that her father wouldn't like Joe's haste. And this talk about missing her so much, about her not leaving home . . . that made things hard.

But after dinner her father lighted a fire in the grate, and they all gathered in the dancing light—Paige and Julia on the couch, Betsy in a worn cherry-red bathrobe near her mother, and Margaret, with Kismet, on the floor beside her father, who was stretched out in his leather chair, his feet on a footstool, smoking. Betsy knew that the time had come.

"There's something I haven't told you folks," she began slowly, and stopped.

"It's about the war!" Mrs. Ray exclaimed.

"I hope you didn't run out of money," Mr. Ray said.

"Bettina!" cried Julia, her voice thrilling. "You're engaged!"

"Yes, I'm engaged to Joe." Betsy's smile broke through and everyone fell upon her with tender cries and kisses.

"You two were made for each other! Oh, Paige, isn't it wonderful?" sang Julia.

"I'm very happy for you, dear," her mother said. "But Betsy! You'll be living in Boston!" Mrs. Ray's voice took on a tragic note.

"You don't need to worry about that, Mamma," Betsy answered, radiant. "Joe is planning to come back to Minneapolis. He's going to get a job here."

"When will the wedding be?" asked Margaret, starry-eyed.

"Well," Betsy answered, "I want to talk that over." She smiled, but the smile looked anxious. "Joe wants to be married very soon."

"Why, that's all right! Isn't it, Bob?" said Mrs. Ray. "We can announce it as soon as you are rested from your trip. Would you like a bridge or a tea—for the announcement party, I mean?" Mrs. Ray looked businesslike as she always did when planning a party.

"There wouldn't be time for parties," Betsy replied. "When Joe says 'soon' he means 'soon.'"

"But you . . ." Her mother paused. "What do you think about that?"

"I wouldn't mind. I wouldn't mind at all."

"What about the job in Boston?" Mr. Ray asked, puffing.

"He's given that up." Betsy drew a deep breath. "He'll be here next week—to be married."

Mr. Ray put down his cigar. He looked displeased. "But he'll have to get a job first."

"Now, Papa!" Julia said soothingly. "You remember how long Joe worked on the *Tribune*? He won't have any trouble getting a job there."

"Probably not," Mr. Ray agreed, "though there's a new setup on the *Tribune*. New editor, I believe. But Joe does have to have a job. Marriage isn't all love and kisses, Betsy."

"Oh, we know that!" Betsy cried eagerly. "That's the reason I haven't an engagement ring. Joe wanted to go to Tiffany's and buy me a diamond as soon as I got off the boat. But we realized we needed our money to rent an apartment and buy furniture. So we only bought a wedding ring."

"A wedding ring!" His voice was shocked.

"Oh, dear!" said Mrs. Ray. "That does sound serious! And you're barely home, Betsy! You're hardly unpacked!"

"But Mamma!" Betsy cried pleadingly. "I'm going to be living right here in Minneapolis. I won't be going away."

"It won't be the same," said Mrs. Ray, and started to cry.

Mr. Ray spoke in the deliberate manner he always used for family pronouncements.

"I like Joe," he said. "He's a very fine young man. Of course it's three years since I saw him; and three years is a pretty long time. But I feel sure this can all be adjusted when he *asks* to marry you, Betsy." There was a faint but significant emphasis on "asks."

Betsy remembered in a panic the formal letter Paige had written, asking for Julia's hand.

"Oh, he's going to ask you, Papa!" she said hastily. "Don't think he doesn't realize he ought to do that! But he wants to be married so soon! Just the minute he gets here! That's why I thought I'd better explain. So we could be getting ready for the wedding. You know . . . some potted palms and things."

"Potted palms!" Mrs. Ray echoed, and Mr. Ray's

expression grew darker, almost forbidding.

"You mean," he said, "that Joe will ask me after he gets here and we've moved in some potted palms and the minister is standing up in front of the fireplace ready to marry you?"

That was exactly Joe's idea, and Betsy didn't know whether to laugh or to cry.

"Before," Mr. Ray went on accusingly, "he even has a job? He's given up the job in Boston, you say?"

"But I thought you'd be pleased about that!" Betsy cried, her voice shaking. "I thought you'd *like* to have us living here in Minneapolis."

"Oh, we do! We do!" Mrs. Ray exclaimed, wiping her eyes firmly. "We want that more than anything. Don't we, Bob?"

"Yes, I'll be pleased with the Minneapolis job— when he gets one."

"Papa!" Betsy's voice was almost angry. She had realized before from which of her parents she inherited her well-known stubbornness. "Can you imagine any newspaper in the whole wide world not giving a job to Joe?"

"Well," said Mr. Ray, irritably, "you're taking in a lot of territory. I'll admit, though, that Joe can probably get a job. And whenever he does I see no objection—after a proper interval—and if he has saved plenty of money—and when he and I have discussed the matter—to your having a beautiful wedding."

"But we don't want a beautiful wedding! That is, it will be beautiful to us, but we just want to stand up and be married."

She was near tears, and Julia came to the rescue again.

"Really, Papa," she said brightly, "it's providential! Paige and I have to go back to New York next week, and I couldn't bear not to be here for Betsy's wedding."

"Yes," said Mrs. Ray, now entirely on Betsy's side, in spite of losing a whole procession of parties. "Yes, we simply have to have Julia, Bob!"

"And Betsy simply has to eat!" said Mr. Ray, extremely nettled. Betsy now was wiping her eyes, and he relented a little. "We'll talk it all over when Joe comes," he added kindly and rose.

Everyone knew what would come next. For in every family crisis Mr. Ray always did the same thing.

"I'll put on the coffee pot," he said.

He moved majestically out to the kitchen. Kismet followed, mewing, and Margaret followed Kismet, but not without a pitying glance at Betsy. Julia and Paige and her mother gathered around her with comforting whispers. Betsy could not speak.

She felt sure Joe would find a way. He always did. But the trouble was—so did her father. Her father, with his inspired suggestions, which he called "snog-gestions," always made everything right. What happened, Betsy wondered forlornly, when he was on one side and Joe on the other?

"Bob," Mrs. Ray called, "bring some of those sugar cookies, the ones Anna made especially for Betsy."

4
Objections Overcome

IN A WEEK, LESS A DAY, Betsy was back in the cavernous railway station waiting for Joe.

At 909 the ritual of preparing for an expected arrival had been performed. The house was polished; there were flowers in the vases; Anna had remembered that Joe liked cocoanut cake and had made a towering beauty.

The dining room table was laid again with the best place mats, china and silver, and Betsy had asked for sausages and scrambled eggs—and muffins, of course. Joe was staying in a hotel, but Mrs. Ray had insisted upon his coming for breakfast. Betsy was to bring him back in double-quick time.

"No billing and cooing along the way!" Mr. Ray had joked. He must get to the store; Margaret had to go to school; and they didn't want to leave before they had welcomed Joe.

Everyone was talking cheerily about welcoming Joe for it was plain that Betsy was a little subdued. After her father's decision it had been impossible to set a wedding day, or buy a trousseau, or make any plans. Everyone spoke lovingly of her engagement, but no one mentioned her wedding, and Betsy kept remembering the urgency with which Joe had said he wanted that to be soon. She was troubled about Joe, and troubled too about her father, who went around whistling as he always did when he was worried.

But her spirits lifted, waiting beside the tall gates. Back in the city she loved, with the family she adored, she had still longed for Joe—morning, noon, and night.

I'm in love, all right, she thought, smiling.

She was wearing a green plaid skirt with a ruffled white waist, her hands thrust deep in the pockets of a short green coat. And although she looked so casual, she was waved, manicured, perfumed, and her green Gibraltar bracelets jingled as the train rushed in and she sped through the opening gates.

In seconds, Joe was swinging toward her, cane on one arm, a bag in either hand. In seconds, cane and bags were on the ground, and Betsy's new French roll was toppled. She pinned it up, blushing and laughing.

Joe surveyed her. "Wear that skirt on our honeymoon!" he commanded.

They hurried to the line of taxicabs; and one of the drivers, a large, harassed-looking man with gray hair, closed a door upon them.

"909 Hazel Street, skipper!" Joe said. He leaned back and put his arm around Betsy. "Well, I've given up my job! I'm a man of leisure. Nothing to do but get married."

He looked so shiningly happy that Betsy hated to tell her news, but it had to be told.

"Joe," she said, "I'm so sorry! But Papa doesn't like the idea of us hurrying things up. You know how proud Papa is, Joe. He just doesn't like it. Especially since—you haven't asked his consent to our marriage."

"By Jiminy!" Joe replied. He looked both chagrined and amused. "I ought to be ashamed of myself. But just you wait, honey! I'll ask him in style." Not at all perturbed, he leaned over and kissed her.

"But Joe!" Betsy persisted. "That isn't all. He doesn't like it that you haven't got a job."

"Haven't got a job!" echoed Joe. "Why I haven't had time to get one. I just got here."

"I know," Betsy gulped. "And he's awfully pleased, and so is Mamma, that you gave up the job in Boston. But what Papa says is—you ought to have a job before we talk about getting married. That's only good sense, he says. After you get a job, then he and Mamma will announce the engagement, and we can pick out our apartment and our furniture and have a lot of parties—"

Joe leaned forward abruptly. "Make it the *Tribune*, skipper," he said.

Betsy caught his hand and squeezed it joyfully. She had known Joe would straighten everything out!

"That's a wonderful idea!" she cried. "You can get a job there just by asking. There's a new editor, though."

"There is?" Joe turned abruptly.

"That's what Papa says."

Joe stared at Betsy but he did not seem to see her.

"Just watch Willard's smoke!" he muttered to himself.

The driver had turned his car, and they rode back down a morning-fresh Hennepin Avenue to Fourth

Street where the *Tribune* and the rival *Journal* offices stood. Joe did not speak; he was frowning; but the slant of his lower lip showed exhilaration in the nut he had to crack.

"Wait here, honey!" he said when the cab stopped. Before she could answer he was through the door of the *Tribune* building and halfway up the stairs.

The cab fare would be high, Betsy thought, but she wasn't worried. It was worth the money to go home with the announcement that Joe had a job. What concerned her was keeping breakfast waiting.

Oh, they'll think the train was late! she consoled herself, but she watched the door of the building eagerly, waiting for Joe to come bounding out with a triumphant smile.

When he emerged, however, he wasn't smiling. He came to the cab and spoke crisply—to the driver, rather than to her.

"Wait a little longer. I'm going into the *Journal*," he said. Cane on arm, he swung boldly up the street.

Betsy looked after him feeling half-scared but she was interested, too, in his single-minded drive. Was this the way he went about a newspaper assignment? Was this what he was like out in that world she did not know?

Well, whatever had happened at the *Tribune*—the new editor, of course!—he would soon have a job on the *Journal*. She still refused to think of the cab fare but a vision of her waiting family would not be banished.

She spoke with dignity to the large slumping back of the driver. "I'm going to telephone my mother."

He turned and glanced down at Joe's bags. "All right, miss," he answered gruffly and Betsy found a drug store telephone.

"What is it, darling? Was the train late?" her mother asked.

"Not that. We'll explain when we get there."

"Well, hurry! Anna has the muffins ready to pop in the oven, and Papa's getting hungry."

"We won't be long now."

Betsy reached the cab just as Joe did.

"I was 'phoning the family to tell them we'd be late," she began, but again she could see he wasn't listening.

"The *Courier*!" he said to the driver.

To her, during the short ride he said nothing at all. He did not look at her nor even seem to know that she was there, but Betsy understood. He had ruled out every thing, even her, in the strength of his determination.

He would soon run out of newspapers!

Waiting in front of the *Courier* building, she did give the cab fare a thought. But she tossed it away.

With Joe fighting like this, she had better things to think of—and to do.

"I'm going to telephone my mother again," she told the driver's back.

"Betsy!" Mrs. Ray wailed. "What's the matter?"

"I haven't time to explain. I just want to ask you please to go ahead with breakfast. Joe and I will put on the coffee pot whenever we get home."

"But Betsy! The table looks so lovely. I can't bear . . ."

"We can't help it," Betsy said. "Please, Mamma! Please!" and she put down the receiver.

This time she got back to the cab ahead of Joe, and he was gone so long that she began to grow hopeful, but when he came out she knew at once that the news was not good.

He strode forward with his usual vigor but it was like the vigor of a sleepwalker. He was not discouraged because he would not be discouraged. And if he was afraid, the fear was held deep down and not allowed to come up. He had closed his mind against any possibility of failure. He was going to get a job!

He jumped into the cab and said to the driver, "The Marsh Arcade."

The Marsh Arcade! Betsy thought to herself. Why was he going to that group of fashionable little shops? There were a few offices on the upper floors, she remembered, but could one of them hold a job for Joe?

It must! And she started praying. She prayed all the way up Nicollet Avenue to Tenth Street. There they reached the Arcade and Joe disappeared inside the swinging doors.

The driver turned around. "There's a foot doctor in that building," he said sourly. "But if your young man always uses taxicabs this way, he can't be looking for a foot doctor."

"Of course he isn't!" Betsy answered warmly. "He's looking for a job."

"A job, eh? Isn't this sort of an expensive way to do it?"

"We want to get married," she confided.

"Well, wait till he lands that job!" the driver advised.

Just like her father! Betsy thought.

"He'll get one," she said.

The seamy face softened a trifle. "I'll say this for him, miss. He isn't letting any grass grow under his feet."

The wait this time was the longest of all. It was very long. But at last Joe pushed through the swinging doors again, and his smile seemed to shed a glow on everything about him—the yellow hair, the dancing eyes, the now triumphant slant of his lower lip.

"Wait a sec!" he called and darted into a florist's shop on the main floor of the Arcade. He came out with an enormous paper-wrapped spray.

"For your mother," he said, climbing into the cab. "909 Hazel Street, skipper. You may now," he added to Betsy, "gather kith and kin for the wedding. I have a job."

The taxi driver heaved around. "That's getting a hit in the clutch, kid!"

"It's the Ty Cobb in me." Joe winked, and he toppled Betsy's French roll again.

"But what is the job?" she demanded, pink-cheeked, pinning up her hair. "There isn't any newspaper published in the Marsh Arcade."

"There's a publicity office," answered Joe. "A fine one."

"Begin at the beginning!" Betsy ordered.

"In the first place," Joe complied, "eight in the morning is no time to be looking for a job. It's almost the busiest spot in the day. I knew that, but I was desperate. My practically-father-in-law saying I was out of a job!

"At the *Trib* and *Journal* I couldn't even get to the city desk. I just filled out forms in the reception room. *The Deep Valley Sun,* the *Wells Courier News,* the *Minneapolis Tribune,* and the *Boston Transcript.*"

"And Harvard!" bounced Betsy. "You told them about Harvard, didn't you?"

"You bet I did! I almost told them about you. And

when my application blank reached Hawthorne, the city editor of the *Courier,* he must have sort of liked the looks of it, because he sent me to an office his wife runs. The Hawthorne Publicity Bureau. It's starting a big campaign to raise money for the Belgians."

"Joe, how wonderful!"

"And, Betsy, this Mrs. Hawthorne is a charmer!"

"A charmer?" asked Betsy doubtfully.

"An absolute charmer!" Joe replied. "She's tall and dark—a vibrant sort of woman."

"About how old?" Betsy sounded cautious.

"Gosh, I don't know! Ageless! And Betsy, we got to talking, and the first thing I knew, I'd told her all about you and—I hope you won't mind—I asked her to our wedding."

"Joe!"

"Yep, and she accepted. For herself and her husband and their little girl. I told her especially to bring the little girl."

"But you know, Joe, even with the job . . ."

"I know." Joe turned serious. "I think, Betsy, that your father will see things our way. But if you'd like to wait a while, have all those parties and things— why, honey, I'm yours on any terms." He smiled down at her. "Personally, I've waited long enough."

"So have I," said Betsy.

"And just on the chance," Joe went on, "I told

Mrs. Hawthorne that I'd rather not start work until Monday. That gives us three days for a honeymoon, if we're married tomorrow. . . ."

"Tomorrow!" cried Betsy.

"Tomorrow!" chortled the driver. "I told you, miss, that he didn't let any grass grow under his feet."

They were all laughing when they drove up to 909, and the fare the driver named wasn't so huge as Betsy had feared. Joe dug down for a magnificent tip.

"A wedding present in reverse, skipper," he said. He and Betsy ran up the steps and the family burst out the door in welcome. Any annoyance over the long wait melted away as Joe kissed Mrs. Ray and gave her the flowers, and kissed Julia, and was introduced to Paige. Margaret had had to leave, but Mr. Ray had stayed home, and his liking for Joe caused his face to brighten.

"You haven't changed," he said in a pleased tone as they shook hands.

"Anna is keeping some muffins hot," Mrs. Ray said.

"Anna," said Joe, "will you do something else for me?"

"Sure, I will."

"Keep those muffins hot just a little while longer," he begged with an irresistible smile. "I want to talk with Mr. Ray . . . if you have a few minutes, sir?"

"Why, of course, Joe!" But Mr. Ray's tone was stiff again. He led the way upstairs to a small back room which he called his study. It held a roll-top desk and a picture of the shoe store in Deep Valley and an even bigger picture of ex-President Theodore Roosevelt. He and Joe disappeared inside.

The others clustered around Betsy.

"Where under the sun were you?"

"It was pretty awful, waiting."

"Of course, we knew you had a good reason."

"Oh, we did!" Betsy laughed softly. "Joe was looking for a job. And he got it!"

"The *Tribune* took him on!" Mrs. Ray sighed with satisfaction and relief.

"No, the Hawthorne Publicity Bureau. It's run by the wife of the city editor of the *Courier*. She needed a very good man to raise money for the Belgian refugees, and of course she snapped Joe up. And Mamma! He asked her to the wedding."

"The *wedding*!" Mrs. Ray looked alarmed. "But Betsy, even though Joe has a job, you know how Papa feels. . . ."

"I know," Betsy answered soberly. Everything would depend, she thought, on how that interview in the study was progressing.

Everyone had the same thought, and they sat in silence, listening. They heard a steady flow of voices.

Joe and Mr. Ray. Joe and Mr. Ray. Joe for a long time, and then Mr. Ray for a long, long time, sounding excited and positive.

Once an intelligible phrase floated out. "Leave it to Teddy!" Mr. Ray was saying.

The group downstairs looked at each other in complete mystification. What, their raised brows seemed to ask, did Teddy Roosevelt have to do with Betsy's wedding?

"Politics!" Mrs. Ray said scornfully.

Anna brought Betsy a cup of coffee. She brought her a muffin. Mrs. Ray and Julia wanted coffee, too, and Paige started pacing the floor. At long last the door of the study opened.

"T.R. is as right as rain," Betsy heard her father declare as he and Joe came down the stairs.

Mr. Ray beamed at the huddled group. "What are you women wasting time for?" he asked jovially. "There's plenty to be done around here, if we're having a wedding tomorrow."

"Tomorrow!" everyone cried out as Betsy and the taxi driver had done.

"Why, didn't Betsy tell you that Monday Joe starts his new job, helping those wonderful Belgians? He and Betsy are entitled to a little honeymoon, aren't they?"

Betsy fled to Joe's arms.

"I told him, Jule," her father continued, "that I felt I could speak for you. I told him we both realized that he and Betsy had known each other for years and ought to know their own minds. They've waited long enough! Especially with this war business on. We may be in that ourselves, if it hangs on. Jule!" His voice warmed with interest. "Joe interviewed Teddy just a short time ago. He's been giving me all Teddy's views. Teddy thinks just as I do, and just as Joe does, that this is an assault on civilization. . . ."

Mrs. Ray was gasping. "But tomorrow! Couldn't it be next week? One day—for a wedding dress and cake and decorations . . ."

Mr. Ray gave Joe a tolerant glance which said: "These women!"

"You only need to organize things," he replied indulgently. "I'll go over to the florist and get him to work on some decorations. How about a wedding bell over the fireplace?" Mr. Ray smiled. "We were married under a wedding bell; weren't we, Jule? And it took pretty well."

"You and I, Mamma," said Julia, "can take Betsy downtown and help her buy a dress. Maybe we could pick Margaret up at school? She ought to be in on this. Anna can do everything that needs to be done here. You'll have a caterer make the wedding cake, won't you?"

"She *will* not," came Anna's voice from the door-way. "I may be getting old, but I can still bake cakes, and decorate them, too. I made the cake when the McCloskey girl was married!"

The McCloskeys were an almost mythical family for whom Anna had worked in the distant past. Any mention of them always served to quell the Rays.

"I'll take Joe to call on Dr. Atherton," said Paige. Dr. Atherton was the Episcopal clergyman who had married him and Julia. "We have to get a license, too, boy!"

Joe did not reply. Betsy's head was on his shoulder. His cheek was on her hair.

"Hey!" Mr. Ray called. "Hey, you kids! Do you want to get married, or don't you?"

Joe and Betsy came back from some deep dream. They smiled at each other, and out at the smiling faces.

"Yes, sir. Certainly. Sure," Joe said hazily.

"Yes, Papa!" chimed Betsy.

5
The Wedding

ON THE MORNING OF her wedding day, Betsy woke early. She lay snugly under the blankets looking around the dim, familiar room and out through a misty filigree of branches at a world still indistinct.

Everything was ready for the great event. This had not been accomplished easily. After Joe and Betsy came out of their daze, the preceding morning, and began to plan, they had promptly run into difficulties.

Paige would be best man and Julia matron-of-honor. That was understood. But when Betsy started blithely naming bridesmaids, her mother had protested.

"Darling, you can't have bridesmaids at a small wedding like this!"

"But Mamma! Tacy couldn't have Tib and me for bridesmaids! The three of us ought to be together in *one* wedding," Betsy had argued.

"Then Tib will have to have a big wedding. You wouldn't! Remember? Besides, Tacy couldn't do it just now."

"That's right! But I'd like Margaret to be something."

"Margaret," said Mrs. Ray, "will be my right-hand man, as usual. And there will be plenty to do, even though it *is* just a family wedding."

"Of course," Betsy hinted, "Tacy and Tib are family."

"Well, practically!"

"And Katie and Leo." Katie was Tacy's sister.

"They've moved to Duluth."

"And Carney and Sam are family," Betsy pleaded, for Carney was almost as old a friend as Tacy or Tib, "Besides, we'll need Carney to play the wedding march."

"That's true," Mrs. Ray admitted.

"And Cab! Cab's certainly family. Remember how

he used to stop in for breakfast on the way to high school, Papa?"

Mr. Ray chuckled. "I certainly do."

Betsy had kept on talking rapidly. "Alice is family, Mamma. I've known her all my life. And Winona, and Dennie, and Irma . . ."

"Betsy! Betsy!" Mrs. Ray broke in. "We'll stop with Cab or there'll be no stopping at all."

Joe looked sheepish. "I've invited the Hawthornes, Mrs. Ray."

"They're very welcome," Mrs. Ray said warmly. "And now we must do our 'phoning, for we have to get downtown.

Betsy smiled, lying in bed, to remember that wild telephoning. After her mother had invited the uncles, aunts, and cousins, Betsy began. With Joe at her elbow, she had called Tacy first, then Carney. Sam, her husband, had been transferred to Minneapolis, and they lived with a baby daughter just a few blocks away.

"What do you want me to play?"

"Why, *Lohengrin*."

Joe pushed Betsy aside. "Dum, dee, dee, dum," he hummed.

"Would you like 'Song Without Words,'" Carney asked, "for that fateful moment when you're waiting to come downstairs?"

They telephoned Butternut Center, but Aunt Ruth could not come. Homer, her helper in the store, was ill.

"I'll come down to see you soon. Bring my wife," Joe told her grandly.

They telephoned Deep Valley. Tib's light, excited voice floated through the room like Tib herself.

Cab had a surprise for them. "Sorry! I'd love to come to your wedding, Betsy, but I have to go to my own."

"Cab! Do I know her?"

"No. She's a North Dakota girl. You'll love her, though."

"Oh, I'm so glad!" Betsy said. It seemed beautifully fitting that she and Cab, friends of so many years, should have the same wedding day.

Betsy had telephoned Mrs. Hawthorne. It wasn't easy, but she summoned her poise for Joe's sake, and the rich joyous voice at the other end of the line reassured her.

"Do you really want us? We'd love to come. I don't know why it is, but I feel already as though I knew your Joe."

Then Mr. Ray had departed for the florist. But before Joe and Paige left to see Dr. Atherton, Joe had called Betsy aside.

"Where shall we go on our honeymoon?" he asked. "We haven't time to go far. Shall I make reservations at a hotel right here in Minneapolis?"

"How about Lake Minnetonka?" Betsy whispered. "I'd like the country better. Wouldn't you?"

"Of course. And there are hotels at Minnetonka. What a woman I'm marrying!" He kissed her.

"Enough of that!" called Paige. "Find out what flowers she wants for her bouquet."

"Anything, and forget-me-nots," said Betsy.

"I'm never going to forget you, honey."

"I just want to be sure."

"Forget-me-nots," said Paige, "may be hard to find at this season."

"If Betsy wants them, I'll find them," Joe replied. He was in his sea-swimming, mountain-toppling mood.

"We'll have Bachelors' Dinner at Shiek's," Paige said. "I'll round up Harry and Sam. That will keep us out from underfoot."

For Anna had poked her head out of the kitchen to say meaningly, "Everyone ate out, the day before the McCloskey girl's wedding!"

Mrs. Ray, Julia, and Betsy were whisked downtown by taxicab. This was no day for trolleys! And they found a lovely dress—almost as fine as a dressmaker could have made, Mrs. Ray remarked. The sweeping white silk was frothy with tulle. It even had long tulle sleeves. And Betsy planned to wear the tulle cap and veil, edged with orange blossoms, that Julia had worn for her wedding.

"You'll wear it next, Margaret," Betsy said, for Margaret had joined them. Julia had 'phoned the principal in her most impressive voice. After lunch they had all helped Betsy buy silken slips, chemises, night gowns, a pleated pink chiffon negligee, and a boudoir cap, trimmed with tiny rosebuds.

When they reached home, Mr. Ray was making a fire in the grate. They had picnicked around it.

"Just the five of you! You look like Deep Valley!" Anna had said fondly, looking in.

Everything had been attended to. Everything was planned, or ready. After so many years of loving him, Betsy was going to marry Joe.

She stared out the window where the sky behind the elm trees was streaked now with crimson and gold. She was going to be married tonight, and she wanted her marriage to be perfect.

"Just perfect!" she said softly, aloud.

She wanted her home to be happy and full of love, as the Ray house was. She wanted to be all Joe expected her to be. He knew her well; Betsy was glad of that. She wouldn't have wanted to go through life pretending to be someone she wasn't. He idealized her, though.

Jumping up, she closed the window and found a pencil and paper, and getting back into bed, she made a list. Betsy was always making lists. She had done it for years, resolving at various times to brush her hair faithfully, or to manicure her nails, or to study French, or to read through the Bible.

But I never made a list as important as this one, she thought, writing at the top,

RULES FOR MARRIED LIFE.

1. *Handle Joe's money well.* That, she knew, was important. She had noticed that married people had more trouble about money than almost anything else. She would keep accounts, she resolved, and never be extravagant—unless Joe wanted to be.

2. *Keep yourself looking nice when Joe's around. Don't plaster on sticky creams at night, or wear your hair in curlers.* She would put up her hair after he went to work, she planned.

3. *Wear pretty house dresses, like Mamma does, and see that they're always clean.* Some organdy aprons would be nice, too.

4. *Learn to cook.* Betsy frowned over that one. *You're fairly bright. You can learn if you try.*

5. *Always, always, be gentle and loving. No matter if you're tired or feeling cross.* Papa and Mamma don't quarrel, she thought. You and Joe don't need to, either.

She read the list over several times, looking sober. Then she tore it up and, getting out of bed again, she knelt down and pressed her head against the blankets.

Back in bed, she heard her father going downstairs. He would be opening the furnace, for September mornings were cool.

But her wedding day was going to be fair. The sky was already radiantly blue.

Margaret came in, her long black braids hanging over her night gown. She snuggled into bed beside Betsy.

"I've been thinking!" she said. "When it's time for you to be married, I'm going to put Kismet in the basement. You know how he hops up to that niche above the fireplace to drink out of the goldfish bowl? What if he should do it in the middle of the wedding?"

"Margaret," said Betsy, "you think of everything!"

Julia came in. This was unexpected for, with Julia, getting up was a major undertaking. She came in, blinking sleepily, her curly hair in wild disorder, and climbed in on the other side of Betsy. She closed her eyes.

"Breakfast in bed," she murmured, "would be nice. Golly, it would be nice!"

Betsy and Margaret giggled.

Mrs. Ray came in, crisply dressed. She looked like

a general planning a campaign.

"You three get up!" she ordered.

"Mamma," murmured Julia, still with closed eyes, "do I smell coffee, or do I just imagine it?"

"You just imagine it. Get up!"

"It's Betsy's wedding day, you know."

"That's why you have to get up. There's lots . . ."

"I think I hear Papa!" Julia opened her eyes. She cocked her head. She sprang to a sitting position. "Papa!" she cried. "You're an angel!"

"An absolute angel!" Betsy echoed.

"Why do you go and get married then?" asked Mr. Ray, beaming, as he passed a loaded tray. "You stick by us, Margaret!"

Mrs. Ray sat down with a cup of coffee and a slice of buttered toast. "Your father," she observed, "is a man in a million. Don't expect Joe to do this for you, Betsy."

"Joe!" said Betsy with a lilt in her voice. "I wonder how soon he'll be coming."

"Why, not until evening, of course!"

"You won't see him until you meet at the altar."

"Oh, no!" Betsy wailed.

"Someone's coming in now," Margaret observed, trying not to laugh, and Joe halloed from the foot of the stairs in a loud and happy voice.

"Joe Willard!" Julia called. "You're not allowed to

see Betsy until the wedding."

"Bosh!" shouted Joe. "May I come up?"

"No!" cried Betsy, for her hair was still in curlers. She bounced out of bed; and Mr. and Mrs. Ray went downstairs, laughing.

"Maybe Joe could use a cup of coffee," Mr. Ray said.

Joe was drinking coffee when Betsy joined him on the small back porch. He put down the cup to take her hands.

"I have wonderful news! The Minnetonka hotels are closed for the season, but Harry and Tacy have a cottage out there. They'll loan it to us, Harry says."

"Joe!"

"Doesn't it sound like a dream?"

The day passed like a dream. Betsy and Joe sat on the little back porch which was covered with morning glories, still in bluish-pink bloom. They wandered, hand in hand, around the leaf-strewn lawn. They weren't allowed indoors.

Anna was barricaded in the kitchen, beating and stirring and grumbling. The cake was to be a surprise.

The florist carried in potted plants and long cardboard boxes which exuded a wet flowery smell. But the transformed fireplace was to be a surprise, too.

Julia was pressing, for Betsy. Margaret was polishing silver. They kept running out with telephoned messages. Tib had arrived at Tacy's. Carney warned that Sam was buying rice and collecting tin cans.

Joe and Betsy smiled at each other. They had a wonderful getaway plan.

Joe left after lunch. He would not see her now until he saw her coming down the stairs to marry him. He put his arms around her.

"I love you. I could set those words to music," he said, very low.

Betsy was sent upstairs to rest. She went—so she would not see the fireplace—by way of a short flight of stairs that ascended from the kitchen to a landing where it met the flight that came up from the living room platform.

She lay down but she could not rest. It was a good thing, she thought, that she had made her resolutions earlier, for now her head was whirling. She looked around the blue and white room that she would leave so soon.

"I'll be back often. But, as Mamma says, it won't be the same." She could not feel anything but happy, though.

Julia came in to help her pack. She lined a suitcase with tissue paper and folded clothing with exquisite care, slipping in satin sachet bags. Betsy added a worn limp leather copy of Shakespeare's *As You Like It*.

After supper and the early autumn nightfall, she

429

bathed and put on the new silk undergarments, and Julia dressed her hair.

"How many thousands of times you've fixed it for me!" Betsy said.

"You'll be an old married woman when I do it again, Bettina," Julia answered. She and Paige were leaving the next day.

Margaret slipped in, flawlessly dainty in her best blue silk. Beneath the crown of braids, her eyes were sparkling. She held out a box.

"Your bouquet!" she cried. "And there's one for Mamma, and one for Julia, and even one for me!"

Betsy opened it quickly, and he *had* found forget-me-nots! Blue and reassuring, they were scattered among pink roses above a shower of white satin ribbons.

Mrs. Ray swept in, gleaming in satin, filling the air with Extreme Violet perfume. While Margaret looked on, she and Julia lifted the snowy wedding dress over Betsy's head. It rustled to the floor, and Julia's deft fingers put the bridal cap in place and spread out the flowing veil.

"Betsy," said her mother, stepping back to gaze, "you look lovely! Go and dress now, Julia! Hurry! And Margaret, get downstairs and turn on all the lights."

She kissed Betsy, and went out, and closed the door. Betsy stood in the middle of the room. She didn't want to crush her veil by sitting down. The doorbell began to ring. She heard doors opening and shutting, and gay voices, and steps on the stairs.

Margaret would be guiding the ladies to her mother's bedroom and the gentlemen to her father's study. Julia would still be dressing, humming to herself, and surveying effects with a hand mirror. Julia was always late.

A knock sounded. Tacy came in, smiling, and behind her appeared a swirl of golden curls, a doll-like face! Tib flew forward with arms outstretched—but she stopped.

"Betsy! You look so pretty! Much prettier than you are!"

Betsy and Tacy twinkled at each other. "Just like Tib!" their glances said.

"Of course I look pretty!" Betsy cried, shaking Tib and kissing her. "I'm supposed to! I'm a bride!"

"*Liebchen*," Tib said, "I'm so glad you're back! And about you and Joe! He's exactly right."

Dear little Tib! Betsy thought, when they went out. She must find the right one, too. And then she will have that big wedding. And Tacy and I can be bridesmaids....

It was good to plan someone else's wedding, for, facing her own, her heart was beginning to thump.

Betsy turned to the mirror. She did, indeed, look

prettier than she was! The veil was a white cloud around her dark slenderness, her flaming cheeks, and shining hazel eyes.

"I look too happy. Brides are supposed to look shy." But she couldn't manage to look anything but happy.

Margaret, coming up to hurry Julia, darted in. "Kismet's in the basement. I've put paper in the telephone and stopped the chime clock."

Mrs. Ray came up to hurry Julia. "Everyone's here. Papa's pacing the floor, and Joe is almost crazy."

"I'm ready," Julia's voice came sweetly. "Tell Carney she can start." And Betsy heard her mother go downstairs, and the tender melody of "Song Without Words" began to drift upward.

Julia came in, dressed in pale green and carrying violets. She studied Betsy with unhurried attention.

"Carry your bouquet this way, darling. See? You look divine! And go slowly! Remember, they can't start without you." She winked. Then, going to the top of the stairs, she assumed a grave, heavenly expression, and just at that moment came the stirring and familiar strains of the wedding march!

Julia started slowly down the stairs. She turned left at the landing, and disappeared.

Betsy started after her, holding Joe's flowers, the white veil floating behind. She too went slowly, but lightly, on the tips of her toes. She turned at the landing, and descending toward the platform mirror, she glimpsed a gauzy phantom.

She turned again, and faced the crowded room. Her father was waiting, proudly erect, wearing his white vest, and a white carnation on darkly gleaming broadcloth.

Carney sat at the piano. A salmon-pink sash fell over her spreading white skirts. Sam was turning her music.

Dr. Atherton had his back to the fireplace which was quite concealed by fragrant greenery, and golden chrysanthemums, and lighted golden tapers. On one side of a flowery golden bell stood Julia, holding her violets; on the other, Joe and Paige, spruce and pressed, also with lapel carnations.

Joe's blond hair shone. His eyes shone. His lower lip thrust out, of course. Betsy moved forward slowly on her father's arm.

"Dearly beloved . . ." The words of the service came through faintly at first. "We are gathered together here in the sight of God and in the face of this company, to join together this Man and this Woman in Holy Matrimony. . . ."

Joe and Betsy smiled at each other.

"If any man can show just cause why they may not lawfully be joined together, let him speak now, or else hereafter forever hold his peace."

No one spoke.

Betsy heard a long "Wilt thou . . ." and Joe's deep voice answering, "I will." The solemn question came to her. "Wilt thou have this Man to thy wedded husband. . . . Wilt thou love him, comfort him, honor and keep him, in sickness, and in health; and forsaking all others, keep thee only unto him, so long as ye both shall live?"

She heard her voice answering, "I will."

"Who giveth this woman to be married to this man?" She found her hand in Joe's. Then Joe spoke again; then she, herself.

"I, Elizabeth, take thee, Joseph, to my wedded husband, to have and to hold, from this day forward, for better, for worse, for richer, for poorer, in sickness and in health, to love and to cherish, till death us do part . . . and thereto I give thee my troth."

The ring she and Joe had bought in New York was placed on her finger, and in a few moments Joe was kissing her, and everyone was kissing her.

"Mrs. Joseph Willard!" they were saying. How beautiful it sounded!

"I want to meet Mrs. Joseph Willard," came the rich voice she had heard on the telephone, and Betsy found herself greeting a queenly woman with reddish-brown hair, and brown eyes that looked into her own with such warmth Betsy could hardly believe they were meeting for the first time.

Bradford Hawthorne was a small, alert man, with eyeglasses on a humorous face. Little Sally Day—red ringlets and a white lace dress—had the same puckish expression.

Except for the Hawthornes, all the guests were relatives or old, old friends. There was something heartwarming, Betsy thought, about a small wedding like this where everyone knew you and loved you.

Tacy's Irish eyes were smiling around Anna, who was wearing black silk and the pink enamel pin. Tib was laughing delightedly at everyone's jokes. Sam's eyes were crinkled with mischief, and Carney's dimple flashed as she whispered, "He's tied cans to your uncle's car by mistake."

Harry murmured, "Your bags are locked in the Buick."

Joe was gripping Betsy's arm. He did not let go until Margaret called them all to the dining room which swam in the light of more golden tapers. Golden baskets were tied with tulle and filled with yellow roses.

The tables were laden with trembling salads; plates of sandwiches; hand-painted dishes of candies and nuts. Mrs. Ray sat behind the silver coffee pot at one end, and at the other stood Anna's masterpiece—a great gleaming cake trimmed with flowers, ribbons, and a dove!

"Anna! It's too beautiful to cut!" cried Betsy as the crowd gathered around and she poised a silver-handled knife.

"I think the dove is puny," Anna answered, trying to sound modest. "But cut it, lovey! I made it for folks to eat."

Other people ate. Betsy couldn't eat a crumb.

Tib sat on the step coming down from the platform, sketching. "I'm drawing a picture of you, Betsy, so Joe can remember always just how you looked tonight."

"I'll remember," Joe said, but when Tib had finished, he folded the paper and put it in his pocket.

Mrs. Ray spoke casually, loud enough for everyone to hear. "Time to change, Betsy, if you're going to make that train! Why don't you help her, Tacy? And Joe, go get us all more coffee, please."

So Tacy went upstairs, and Betsy followed.

She paused above the platform. Tib, Margaret, little Sally Day, and some girl cousins gathered expectantly below. Betsy took a forget-me-not out of her bouquet and tucked it into her dress. Then the bouquet sailed down, ribbons streaming, and Sally Day caught it and jumped up and down with joy.

Betsy fled up the stairs, but only as far as the landing.

With her wedding veil still floating behind, she went down the back stairs to the kitchen. Tacy, in a warm coat, was waiting there. Anna held Betsy's velvet wrap.

Joe came in, followed by Harry, who took Tacy's arm without speaking and sped out the back door. Joe caught Betsy's arm and Anna threw the wrap over her shoulders, but Betsy stopped long enough to give Anna a kiss that belonged—not just to her, but to Betsy's father, and her mother, and her sisters, and the happy Ray house.

The crisp dark had the smell of autumn in it. Chilly stars were looking through the branches. Lights were streaming out of all the windows, and music streamed out, too.

Julia—to help the plot—had gone to the piano. She had begun her father's favorite song:

"Believe me, if all those endearing young charms . . ."

Everyone was singing.

Tacy was seated beside Harry, at the wheel. He had started the engine of the Buick.

"We can make Minnetonka in an hour," he was saying as Betsy gathered her white veil together beneath the velvet wrap and climbed into the back seat. Joe followed.

But before they rolled away, a shower of rice flew over their heads. They looked out to see Anna, weeping joyfully and waving.

"They threw rice," she shouted, "at the McCloskey girl's wedding. It's for good luck, loveys!"

6
The Golden World

"YOU'RE A VERY NICE wife," Joe announced. "Shouldn't be surprised if I stayed in love with you for a considerable length of time. Say—I want to be reasonable about this—say, a lifetime."

Betsy frowned in thought. "Well," she answered, "since you're being so conservative, I will be, too. I'll stay in love with you for a lifetime, too."

And they went, laughing, into each other's arms,

and caught hands, and ran out of their cottage—a rough, unplastered, lakey-smelling cottage, perched on stilts, and painted green. They ran across the lawn which was sprinkled with fallen leaves, and down a steep flight of steps to a dock, stretching out into Lake Minnetonka.

It was the third and last day of their honeymoon. Tonight they would take a streetcar boat to Excelsior where they would catch a streetcar for Minneapolis and the Ray house. Tomorrow Joe would start work at the Hawthorne Publicity Bureau and Betsy would go hunting an apartment.

Last chance for a swim, Joe had said, but Betsy had declared it was too cold. She settled herself in the sunshine on the dock and Joe dropped his towels, flexed his arms, walked to the end, and plunged.

Betsy shivered. "But Joe likes it," she remarked to a gull, posing on a bark-covered post. "My husband likes to swim in icy water."

The gull looked unimpressed.

At the side of the dock was a small wire enclosure used for bait. "But he doesn't like to fish. My husband doesn't like to fish," Betsy told the gull.

He looked scornful.

"My husband," Betsy informed him, "is the handsomest, dearest, cleverest, most wonderful person in the world."

At that, the gull flew away, and Betsy laughed, and hugged her knees into her arms. She was wearing the green plaid skirt Joe liked, and a middy blouse, with a narrow green ribbon tied around her hair which was dressed in the old way, low and soft around her face. Of course, she had not been able to curl it. But, blessing of blessings, Joe liked it straight!

The water looked like polished green glass—but mobile glass. It came moving toward her, slantwise. The whole great body of the lake came moving toward her, speaking softly, plashing against a rowboat which was moored among the rushes.

The neighboring docks and diving boards were all deserted. So were many of the cottages. The bank here was high and wild, crowded with bronzy undergrowth and trees leaning over the water.

Across the bay, the shore was flat, and there was a boathouse with a little peaked tower. It had an oriental air, Betsy had observed to Joe.

"We must have come to Japan on our honeymoon!"

"I never did trust that Kerr!" Joe replied, and they had laughed as though at scintillating wit.

Betsy turned around and watched him shooting out into the lake. She wished he'd come back.

It was warm, sitting in the sunshine. The weather had warmed up gloriously every day, but the evenings and the mornings had been cold. Joe had sprung up early, while the lake still slept under an eiderdown of mist, to start a fire in the plump air-tight stove. Betsy loved that stove, roaring importantly, gleaming in comic threat through the front damper.

Joe had cooked breakfast—coffee, bacon and eggs, French toast—even sour-milk pancakes. Betsy had breakfasted elegantly in the pink chiffon negligee and the boudoir cap trimmed with rosebuds. But after breakfast she had put on a sailor suit, and one of Tacy's starched aprons, and had washed the dishes, and made the bed, and swept, and brought in bouquets—goldenrod and starry asters, or a spray of thorn-apple berries.

Each morning they had walked to the store, along a road where the trees met overhead, comparing progress on their red and yellow leaves. The roadsides were gaudy with fall growth.

"Those bursting milkweed pods," Joe said, "make me think of grade school. I always expect to be asked to draw them."

"I'll bet your drawings were pinned up on the blackboard."

"They were used to scare the children."

Trying to act like an old married couple, they had bought melons and doughnuts and tomatoes and frankfurters and syrup and milk and crusty bread. The storekeeper, an old Scandinavian woman with bright observant eyes, treated them with great respect.

When they returned, Betsy had tied on the apron again, but Joe did most of the cooking. The kerosene stove was a mystery to her; and, of course, her talents at any stove were meager. Tacy had left a chocolate cake, with fudge frosting half an inch thick, and it proved a boon.

They always lunched on the porch, and sometimes a flicker knocked against the wall.

"You can't come in," Joe would call. "Don't you know this is a honeymoon?"

A little white-tailed rabbit would run across the lawn.

"Don't you know," Joe would ask, "that we're supposed to be left alone?"

The squirrels paid no attention to them. They were busy burying nuts.

In the afternoons Joe and Betsy had sat on their lofty lawn, looking out at the lake which was sometimes cloth of silver and sometimes a carpet of diamonds. They had read aloud—poetry.

"Nothing but poetry is allowed on this honeymoon," Joe had announced on the first day, bringing out a volume of Keats, and one of Shelley, and one of Tagore, and one of Alfred Noyes.

"Shakespeare was a poet," Betsy had replied,

producing *As You Like It*. Joe had given it to her one Christmas when they were in high school. He had written on the flyleaf: "We'll fleet the time carelessly as they did in the golden world."

They had read Alfred Noyes the most. Joe had read aloud about the forty singing seamen, and the highwayman who came riding, riding, riding, and "Come back to Kew in Lilac Time," which Betsy had loved in London, but, especially, "Silk O' The Kine."

Betsy quoted it softly now.

". . . her hand lay warm in his clasping hand:
Two young lovers were they . . ."

She thought of those young lovers swimming to their death.

"Out, far out, through the golden glory
that dazzled the green of the bay:
Two strong swimmers were they. . . ."

Joe was a strong swimmer but Betsy was glad, looking around again, to see that he was headed toward her.

He came up, dripping.

"Colder than blazes!" he said, blowing and snorting and rubbing vigorously. He sat down beside her.

"Do you know what I was thinking out there? It would be fun to live in a place like this."

"It would be perfect!" Betsy cried. "Just perfect for two writers! Let's buy that place with the Japanese boathouse."

"All right," said Joe. "Of course, first, I have to earn the money."

"And I have to learn to write things that will sell to the good magazines. Some of my stuff," Betsy admitted, "is pretty awful."

"I'll tell you all old Copey taught us." Professor Copeland had been Joe's favorite teacher at Harvard. "Betsy, maybe you'd do better with a novel. Why don't you try one?"

"Maybe I will," said Betsy, "when we're living out here."

And they began to plan.

"I'll get on a paper when Mrs. Hawthorne's campaign is over," Joe said. "I'll enjoy a stretch of newspaper work. And after a year or so, we'll move out of the apartment and buy a little house—not at the lake yet . . ."

"And have a baby," Betsy put in.

"A boy or a girl?"

"Both. The boy first, so he can take her to parties."

"Let's name the girl Bettina," Joe said. He liked Julia's nickname for Betsy. "And before we settle down, we might travel a bit. New Orleans, California. Have a fling at New York. Would you like that?"

"I'd love it," Betsy answered. "But we won't stay."

"No, we'll come back here to Lake Minnetonka, and write."

It was beautiful sitting on the dock in the sunshine, planning out their lives, but they had to go in. They had to have an early supper, and pack, and row over to the streetcar boat. Harry had said he would pick up the rowboat at the landing there.

They rose reluctantly, and Joe dropped an arm around Betsy's shoulders. They looked up at the wild bronzy bank, the yellowing trees, the little cottage standing sturdily on stilts.

"I hate to leave it," Joe said. "I hate to leave our golden world."

"But our own apartment will be nice," said Betsy. And they climbed the steep stairs, stopping to pick some wild grapes from the flaming vines that loaded the trees.

"I'll get supper," said Joe, when he was dressed.

"All right," answered Betsy. "And I'll pack. But Joe, I'm going to learn to cook. It's the very first thing I'm going to do."

"All I ask," he answered, getting out the bacon, "is for you to learn to make two things: rice pudding and lemon pie."

"Rice pudding and lemon pie," Betsy repeated obediently. "I promise."

Her wedding dress was hanging in the rough damp closet. It looked remote, ethereal, draped in its white veil.

"I'm never going to put it on again," Betsy said dreamily. "Not once! Except, perhaps, for our golden wedding anniversary. Of course, Bettina can wear it for her wedding if she wants to."

"Sentimental!" Joe scoffed. But he looked pleased, and left the bacon to help her fold the dress carefully into a big box which Tacy had remembered to put in the car.

Betsy opened her suitcase and took down the pink negligee. Joe left the bacon again and came over to rub his cheek against hers.

"My pink silk wife!" he said. He liked to say that. After a while he went back to the bacon.

"Shall I pack my husband's things, too?" Betsy asked.

"Certainly. Don't you know your duties as a wife?" he replied, chopping cold boiled potatoes with the top of a baking powder can. He was very proud of this accomplishment. "I ought to make a sour-cream cake," he remarked. "Leave it for the Kerrs."

But there wasn't time. Supper was hurried. And Betsy washed the dishes while Joe mopped the floor.

They wanted to leave the cottage as neat as they had found it.

When they had finished, they put on their wraps, and locked the door, and went down the steps to the rowboat where Joe stowed away the bags. He got the oars and slipped them into the oarlocks.

"I haven't taken one of those streetcar boats for years," he said as they pushed off.

"They're yellow like the streetcars. They're fun. And the streetcars going in from Minnetonka are fun too. They go like lightning, and there's one motorman—or used to be—who puts his hands behind his head and doesn't touch the wheel."

"He's probably been fired by now."

They talked fast and did not look back at the cottage.

The sun had disappeared, and the lake was dull. It was slate-colored, under a slate-covered sky, flecked with pale gray clouds.

A motorboat approached, its prow lifted, throwing out spray. A hunter hailed them, and his boat went on, leaving a widening avenue behind. Waves set the rowboat rocking.

Neither Joe nor Betsy spoke.

When it was quiet again, Joe folded the oars across each other. Moving carefully, he came and sat down beside Betsy. He put his arm around her.

About that time the pink of the afterglow stole into the west. It spread over the sky. It spread over the lake, growing rosier and rosier, and even seemed to tint the gulls who swept back and forth as though reveling in this bath of beauty. The gray clouds became gossamer pink. Joe pointed to one.

"That cloud," he said, "makes me think of you in your pink silk negligee. You're my pink silk wife. You're my wife made out of flowers."

No matter what Joe said, Betsy knew she was just Betsy. But she loved to hear him say these beautiful things. He kept on saying them so long that they almost missed the streetcar boat which took them to the streetcar where they sat on the back seat and held each other's hands.

The motorman drove with his hands behind his head, but Joe and Betsy didn't even notice.

7
Three Rings of a Bell

It was Margaret who found Joe and Betsy their first home.

They had been living for a week at the Ray house—Joe working with great satisfaction at the Hawthorne Publicity Bureau, Betsy dashing all over Minneapolis to look at apartments. She went alone, with her mother, in Carney's automobile. Tib was now living in town;

she had found a job in art-advertising with one of the department stores. But she was too busy to help, and Tacy wasn't feeling well.

"I'll be glad when that baby gets here," Betsy confided to Carney as they drove up and down the autumn-tinted streets. "I'll be glad for Tacy, and, besides, I want to see the little redhead. I know she'll be adorable."

"Of course," Carney chuckled, "she could be a 'he.'"

"Tacy isn't the type for a boy," Betsy answered loftily.

Tacy, too, expected a girl, and the doll Betsy had brought from Germany flaunted her pink plume and yellow curls among the couch cushions in Tacy's living room. Betsy and Carney dropped in there often after the day's hunt was ended.

Day after day, it was a fruitless hunt. Betsy had budgeted Joe's salary of $155 a month—the budget was her department, he had said—and she would not pay more than thirty dollars for rent.

"Not more than thirty," she insisted, "if we have to sleep in the park!"

The search for an apartment at that figure took them all over Minneapolis, and Betsy thought often how beautiful it was—set on the storied Mississippi, glimmering with lakes. A chain of lakes ran actually through the city. Their shores were lined with homes, and even closer to the water lay the public boulevards, scattered with picnickers, fishermen, children with buckets, adventurous masters of sailboats and canoes. Betsy had taken all this for granted once, but not now, remembering the war-stricken cities of Europe.

"How lucky we are to live here!" she exclaimed.

"Nice place to bring up Judy," commented Carney, glancing at a cozy bundle in a basket on the back seat.

When not apartment-hunting, Betsy sat with her mother on the bright glassed-in porch, hemming dish towels. (Mrs. Ray hemmed six to Betsy's one.) After school Margaret and Louisa blew in, the green-and-white ribbons of their high school streaming from their coats.

Blooming, wide-eyed Louisa was always bursting with talk.

"There's nobody, absolutely nobody, left on the football team, Mrs. Ray! And Mrs. Willard, too, of course. That is, if I call you Mrs. Willard. I suppose I do. It seems funny, though. Last year we were champions but everybody graduated. Absolutely everybody! It's simply awful! It makes me feel as though Bogie and I ought to play. I stopped the coach in the hall and asked him why girls couldn't help out in an emergency like this. He seemed surprised, but I mean it! I'm awfully husky, and Bogie is perfectly healthy. Isn't she, Mrs. Ray?"

Louisa paused for breath and gazed at them beseechingly.

Next day it was something else.

"There's a tall skinny boy works in the lunch room. He's crazy about Bogie, Mrs. Ray, and Mrs. Willard. If I call you Mrs. Willard?"

"Oh, please say Betsy!"

"All right, but it doesn't seem respectful. You *are* married, you know. But he just piles gravy on Bogie's roast beef sandwich. Honestly, he does! Mashed potatoes, too. The rest of us don't get a bite, hardly."

"Boogie!" Margaret choked.

"It's true, Bogie. You can't deny it. And I *like* mashed potatoes. Especially with gravy. I get *hungry*. . . ."

"How about some cookies and milk while you're doing your homework?" Mrs. Ray suggested.

Mr. Ray and Joe came home from work, and dinners were jolly. Betsy's father was already Dad to Joe, but Joe and Mrs. Ray had animated discussions about what he should call her: Mother, Mamma, Ma . . .

His preference was for Jule, Mr. Ray's name for his wife, and at last Mr. Ray gave him written permission to use it, sending Margaret for pen and ink while Betsy contributed green sealing wax to make the paper official.

"Stars in the sky!" Bringing in peach cobbler, Anna shook with laughter.

Evenings, they talked around the fire. Her husband and Joe talked war too much, Mrs. Ray declared. The German advance had been stopped at the Marne by a heart-stirring effort of all the French people. Even the Paris taxicabs had rattled up to the front with troops. But the Rheims Cathedral was bombed. A church! An art treasure! It seemed impossible.

That night none of them could talk of anything but war.

Mrs. Ray recalled that her father had fought in the Civil War. And Betsy told a story her grandmother had told her.

"They were living in Indiana, in a log cabin. Grandpa was teaching country school. Lincoln had called for volunteers, but Grandma didn't want Grandpa to enlist. Uncle Keith was only a baby. You weren't born yet, Mamma. One afternoon she saw him coming through their cornfield—tall and thin and redheaded, she said. And he was carrying all the school books in a pile, with the school bell sitting on top. The minute Grandma saw it, she knew what had happened, and she began to cry."

Everyone was silent.

"But she was proud of him, she said," Betsy added.

"And I have the letters they wrote to each other

while he was away. Regular love letters!" Mrs. Ray made her tone light for Margaret had jumped up, blowing her nose, and gone to find the cat.

Oftener they didn't talk about war. Betsy told them about Europe, and Joe told them about Harvard, and Mr. Ray told them funny things that had happened at the store. And every evening there were wedding presents to unwrap. Betsy never opened them until Joe came home.

Her parents had given them a set of plated silver. There was a bird in the pattern; Joe and Betsy had picked it out themselves. And they had selected their china, English china, with pink and blue and lilac-colored flowers. Paige and Julia had started them on that. Margaret gave them a statuette of three little monkeys. One was covering its ears, and one its eyes, and one its mouth, and the legend read: *Hear no evil, see no evil, speak no evil.*

"Boogie helped me pick it out. We thought it was funny. And instructive, too," Margaret said.

Tacy and Harry gave them framed prints of two Maxfield Parrish pictures, "Homekeeping Hearts are Happiest" and "The Hanging of the Crane."

Tib sent a cookie jar. "Now learn how to fill it!" she wrote.

The Hawthornes sent a mantel clock. Joe's aunt sent a carving set. Betsy tried to imagine Joe carving at the head of his own table! There were candlesticks from Sam and Carney, a tray from Katie and Leo. There were books and bonbon dishes, vases and jelly spoons, a tea wagon.

"Fine! Fine!" Joe exclaimed. "But where are we going to put all this? Maybe we ought to go up just a little on the rent. Thirty-five, say?"

"Not more than thirty," answered Betsy, "if we look forever."

And it seemed as though they might, indeed, look forever, but on the second Sunday Margaret, who had gone off with Louisa, came into the house with star-bright eyes.

"You know, don't you, that Boogie lives in an apartment? Well, her mother owns the building! And she has an apartment for rent. The people just moved out."

"How—how much?" asked Betsy from the couch where she and Joe sat poring over real estate advertisements.

"Twenty-seven dollars and fifty cents!"

"What a sister-in-law!" Joe shouted, whirling Margaret who was trying to act calm. Betsy ran for a hat and jacket.

"And it's just around the corner on Bow Street!" Mrs. Ray cried joyously as Margaret, Joe, and Betsy hurried out.

Louisa was waiting at the foot of the Ray porch. She exploded into speech.

"I thought it was more tactful not to come in. But if you rent it, Betsy, Bogie and I can come in to see you every day after school. We can keep you from getting lonesome. That is, I *imagine* you'll get lonesome. Going away from home all alone with just a husband! Oh, excuse me, Mr. Willard!" she added in confusion as Joe grinned at her.

Bow Street was an old street. The elms were old and had turned yellow and were spattering the lawns with leaves. The houses were old, with spacious porches; and few of the barns had been made into garages. In front of one house, a horse and buggy was hitched.

"It's like Deep Valley," Betsy said, clinging to Joe's arm for he was striding along so fast she could hardly keep up with him.

The apartment building was set on a large elmy lawn. It had an entrance porch with fat fluted pillars, and looked like a large, stone, private house except for sets of triple windows, bulging out.

Oh, I hope we get one of those bays! Betsy thought.

She waited in a rapturous daze while the girls ran to call Mrs. Hilton and Joe walked briskly around the building.

"Looks fine! Looks all right!" he said, returning. His golden eyebrows bristled with excitement.

Bogie and Boogie emerged with Boogie's serene, white-haired mother. They all followed her inside, up a flight of carpeted stairs, to the left-hand back apartment. Betsy calculated quickly. "It will face south and east!"

They entered a small foyer, shiningly empty, but she envisaged a slim table with a silver tray for cards. They turned left into the empty living room, and Betsy ran forward, for at the end was one of those three-winged bay windows. And it looked straight into a yellowing elm tree! Right into the branches!

"Oh, what luck!" she thought. "What luck!"

Joe turned right, into the small kitchen. He returned in a flash to the living room and turned right again, through an archway, into the bedroom. He peeked into the bathroom, and came up to Betsy who was still looking out blissfully into the elm.

She smiled at him. He smiled at her.

"We'll take it," he said to Boogie's mother. "May I write you a check?"

And Betsy kissed Margaret, and hugged Louisa, and said to Mrs. Hilton in a housewifely tone, "We'll eat our meals in front of this window sometimes."

The home Margaret had found for them was perfect, family and friends agreed—near a streetcar line so Joe could get to work conveniently, near the Ray house so Betsy could get back often, not too expensive, and not too big. That last was a factor for it must now be furnished.

They had discovered, in the Rays' basement, an old drop-leaf table. Mrs. Ray's father, when he came to Minnesota after the Civil War, had made it himself out of a black walnut tree. Mrs. Ray, who didn't like old-fashioned furniture, used it to hold the laundry basket. Joe and Betsy dragged it out in triumph.

In a secondhand store, Betsy and her mother found two small walnut chairs. They were just the period of the table and upholstered in rose damask. They found a big armchair for Joe, upholstered in blue.

In a new furniture store, they bought a handsome bookcase, and a blue and rose rug, and blue and rose draperies to hang at the sides of the triple-winged bay. "No lace curtains! Nothing to hide my elm tree," Betsy insisted.

They bought a white-painted bedroom set, stenciled in blue and rose, and white ruffled bedroom curtains, and blue checked kitchen ones. All these treasures, along with a broom, dustpan, carpet sweeper, and shiny pots and pans! Betsy's desk came over from 909. And Mrs. Hawthorne gave Joe Saturday off, to settle.

"By afternoon," Betsy said at breakfast, "we'll be

459

ready for callers. Why don't you be our first caller, Margaret, since you found us the apartment?"

"May I bring Boogie?" she asked eagerly.

"Of course."

"But don't come too early," Joe warned. "For after we get settled, we'll have to go out and stock up with groceries. And I mean stock up!"

"I've allowed ten dollars," Betsy said firmly.

Laden down with bags, and boxes full of wedding gifts, and a picnic lunch from Anna, Betsy and Joe went over to their apartment. Mrs. Hilton gave them the key. They went in, and closed the door, and hugged each other. Then Betsy tied an immaculate apron over an immaculate house dress, and Joe rolled up his sleeves.

They started by laying the blue and rose rug on the gleaming varnished floor. Next, they placed the bookcase against the right-hand wall, and settled their books. They wound the Hawthornes' clock and put it on top, in the center.

"Listen to it tick!" Betsy cried, as though no clock had ever ticked before.

On one side of the clock they put a dark blue vase that Joe's mother had treasured because Joe had bought it for her with money he had earned selling papers. On the other side they put a tall cup, striped in pink and blue and gold. It had been given to Betsy by a young baroness in Munich, and the poet Goethe was said to have drunk from it.

Opposite the bookcase, they placed the old-fashioned table, one leaf raised to lean against the wall. Betsy put more books on this, between book blocks, and a small pottery angel which had been made and given to her by the Christus of the Passion Play in Oberammergau.

She arranged the chairs, and Joe brought out a tape measure and a hammer which Mr. Ray had thoughtfully loaned, and hung the pictures where Betsy wanted them hung.

"Homekeeping Hearts are Happiest" and "The Hanging of the Crane" were spaced precisely to the left and the right of the clock, above the bookcase. Over the old walnut table went Lenbach's "Shepherd Boy." Margaret's three monkeys fitted into a niche beside the bay, and Joe's Harvard etchings hung in the foyer. They would make a dignified impression, Betsy said.

Van Dyke's "Flight Into Egypt" went into the bedroom, and a Japanese print of a long-legged bird in a marsh was hung above Betsy's desk. It had always hung there. For some mysterious reason, Betsy claimed, it made her feel like writing.

Everywhere were framed and unframed photographs of Betsy's family, Joe's father and mother, his uncle and aunt, their friends from high school and college. On the bureau stood Betsy in her high school graduating dress, and a snapshot of Joe which she had steamed out of a kodak book and carried through Europe.

The more they settled the apartment, the more beautiful it looked. They beamed upon it, eating Anna's lunch in the bay window, and as soon as they had finished, they started working again.

"This is the last big job," Joe said, tackling the curtains. "As soon as I finish this, we'll go out and buy our groceries. I hope ten dollars buys a lot, Mrs. Hetty Green." He dropped a curtain rod to come over and kiss her. There was a ring at the back doorbell.

"That will be Margaret and Louisa. The idea," Betsy exclaimed as she ran, "of our first callers using the back door!"

Joe, returning to the curtain rod, did not follow until he heard a shriek.

Betsy was sitting on the kitchen floor beside a huge box overflowing with groceries. A smiling delivery boy was just closing the door.

"Who sent them?"

"He wouldn't say. But they're for us."

Joe dropped down beside her. He lifted out a dozen eggs, a half dozen tomatoes, a cucumber, some onions—two bottles of milk, a pound of butter, bacon, a slab of strong cheese—a loaf of bread, a coffee cake, doughnuts.

"Pretty good," he said, devouring one.

Betsy was pulling out coffee, cocoa and tea, vinegar and oil, salt and pepper, oatmeal, tapioca, molasses, raisins.

"And cocoanut!" she cried. "I can make you a cocoanut cake as soon as I learn how!"

Next came flour and sugar, baking powder, soda and vanilla. Beside a box of graham crackers stood a jar of jelly and one of pickles. Potatoes and apples spilled from their sacks.

"See here!" said Joe, presenting a large moist package on which someone had scrawled: "Joe is to broil this. Don't trust Betsy."

"It's Papa's writing."

"You have some father!"

"*We* have, you mean! Oh, I wish the 'phone was connected so we could call and thank . . ."

A doorbell was ringing again, the front one this time. And this time it was Margaret and Louisa.

They wore their new fall suits. They wore their hats, white gloves. Betsy wiped her hand on her skirt before she offered it in welcome. But they ignored her disheveled appearance. Their manners were as flawless as their attire.

Boogie presented a bouquet of chrysanthemums.

"My mother sent them. She hopes you will be very happy here, and so do Bogie and I." Then she closed her lips, plainly resolved not to babble. Her rosy face took on an artificial smile.

"The apartment looks charming," said Margaret.

While Betsy ducked into the bathroom to wash, Joe hung their jackets in the closet off the foyer.

"We'll get calling cards when we graduate," Margaret remarked, glancing at the empty silver tray.

He showed them around the apartment with his best Harvard air, and they made small admiring sounds. When they reached the kitchen, with its dazzling display of groceries all over the floor, Louisa did give one squeal, but she put her hand over her mouth. Betsy passed her a doughnut.

"Isn't this just like Papa!" Margaret said in a fond superior tone.

Shortly she glanced at the watch Betsy had brought her from Europe. She glanced at Louisa. A first call, her look warned, only lasted fifteen minutes.

Louisa gulped her second doughnut. She sprang up and put on the artificial smile. She and Margaret shook hands with their hosts again and, with unimpaired dignity, departed.

Joe and Betsy leaned on the closed door, shaking with laughter.

Twilight was falling. Beyond their bay window, the gold of the elm tree was growing dim.

"I'm hungry as a curly wolf," said Joe. "And it takes you longer to dress than it does me. You may have the shower while I put away the groceries. And I'll broil the steak."

"I'll set the table," Betsy said. She wanted to make it beautiful for their first dinner.

Fresh from her bath, dressed in dark maroon silk and her sheerest apron, she opened the leaves of her Grandfather Warrington's table. She set it with a snowy cloth and napkins, and the silver with birds on the handles, and the china with pink and blue and lilac-colored flowers. She put white candles in the Hutchinsons' candlesticks, and Boogie's flowers in a vase.

Joe, resplendent now in white shirt and tie, was whistling as he broiled the steak. He shouted so many comments on his remarkable skill that Betsy came out to admire. He had set potatoes boiling, and she sliced a tomato and cucumber, and put bread and butter and jelly on the table. She made the coffee.

The steak was lifted to a hot platter, hissing. Betsy lit the candles, took off her apron, and sat down. Joe came in, holding the platter high, and at that moment a door bell rang a third time. They looked at each other in dismay.

"Oh, dear!" said Betsy. "Who could come calling at this hour?"

"On our first evening alone!" grumbled Joe. But he put down the platter and went to the door. Betsy followed.

It was Margaret, and she looked very different now. The hat was gone. So were the gloves. Her coronet braids had come loose, and one hung over her shoulder.

"Betsy!" she cried, but had to stop for breath. Her eyes were enormous. "They 'phoned us because your 'phone isn't connected."

"Who did?" Betsy asked. "What is it?"

"Easy now!" said Joe.

Margaret steadied herself against the door.

"Harry Kerr! About Tacy! She has a baby!"

"Oh! Oh!" Betsy fell upon Margaret with ecstatic hugs. "And Tacy's all right? And the baby? Does she have red hair?

Margaret's laughter was a soft, amused fountain.

"Betsy! Keep still, and let me finish telling you! You brought that doll from Germany for nothing! It's a boy!"

8

Of a Meat Pie and Other Things

"MRS. JOSEPH WILLARD," read the new calling cards.
Betsy looked at them with delight. She was very proud
of being a wife, of Joe, of his extravagant devotion.
She was radiantly happy in her new life.

It wasn't easy, though, to become a housekeeper.

Betsy had always joked about her lack of domestic
skills. She couldn't thread a needle, she was wont to

announce blithely at sewing bees, and usually read aloud.

"Here, let me do that!" Joe or Cab or almost any boy in the Crowd would offer when Betsy started to make cocoa or scramble eggs.

"*Liebchen,*" Tib used to say, preparing a snack, "you sit down and watch. What you don't know about cooking would fill one of those books you plan to write."

It had been funny, but it wasn't funny now, with Joe coming home from work, smiling and hungry. He wanted something more for dinner than place mats and candlesticks. After kissing her fondly, he would go, sniffing, out into the kitchen.

"What's to eat?" he would ask.

That was a terrible moment!

Keeping the small apartment charming was not hard. It was a pleasure to wash the new dishes, to make the white bed with care, to dust the wedding presents and run the carpet sweeper up and down the living room, looking out into the elm and watching its leaves—as the days rolled by—turn from gold to brown, and fall, revealing a pattern of boughs which became, at last, narrow shelves for snow.

She did not do the heavy work. Joe had insisted on a weekly cleaning woman. Betsy had scoffed at the idea, quoting their split-penny budget.

So much for rent, so much for food and clothing, so much for telephone, gas and electricity, for the wet wash (she would do the ironing herself) and their personal allowances. A casual sum called incidentals was to cover the doctor, dentist, and amusements. Joe's insurance premiums must be paid. And they had resolved that ten dollars would go into their savings account every month if they had to live on corn meal mush.

"No!" Betsy had insisted. "No cleaning woman at two dollars a day!" And really, she explained earnestly, a child could keep their tiny apartment clean!

Joe, however, was adamant. And when Joe was adamant, Betsy soon discovered, he was even more adamant than she could be herself, although Betsy was famous for a will of iron. If her will was of iron, she thought now, there must be some undiscovered metal, even stronger, to describe Joe's will.

"I observed you, Mrs. Willard, on your honeymoon, and I feel sure you have never scrubbed a floor."

"I'm not too old to learn."

"I concede that it would be foolish for the average wife not to save two dollars weekly out of one hundred and fifty-five a month, by dispensing with outside help. But you're not the average wife."

"That's what every husband thinks."

"You want to be a writer. You want that more than anything else in the world."

"No," Betsy interrupted. Her voice was sober, "There's one thing I want more, Joe. I want to be a good wife to you—and a good mother to our children."

Joe patted her cheek. "We'll put it this way," he said. "You *are* a writer. You've always been writing stories, and the last few years you've been selling them."

"But except for that beautiful surprise when I got a hundred dollars from *Ainslee's,* I've never sold one for more than ten or twelve."

"Ten dollars," Joe replied triumphantly, "would pay your woman for five weeks."

She was stubbornly silent.

"It will be hard enough for you, honey," he ended, "just to learn to cook. You've promised to learn to make lemon pie and rice pudding. Remember?"

So Betsy juggled the budget and engaged a stout Marta to come every Friday, and soon she was very glad that Joe had overruled her. Learning to cook gave her plenty to do. Cooking was harder even than algebra had been.

She was thankful for her high school Domestic Science training, distant as that was. She still had the Dom. Sci. cookbook, but it was regrettably full of things like English monkey, banana and nut salad, and cream puffs.

She yearned to produce some of Anna's masterpieces, but when she asked about fried chicken:

"Why, lovey, you just put it into a skillet and fry it."

And about Lady Baltimore cake:

"I'll send one over to you tonight. Margaret can bring it."

Mrs. Ray's recipes called for too many eggs and too much butter and whipping cream for the Willard budget. And she, also, was vague. Of her divine pie crust, she would say, twinkling her fingers, "You just put in lard till it feels right."

Betsy tried hard—with the pie crust and everything else. She did not forget the resolution she made on her wedding morning: *Learn to cook*. She did not forget the other resolutions, and was curled, powdered, perfumed, and wearing a pretty dress when Joe burst in after work. His face when he saw her was more than worth the trouble. But then would come that terrible question.

"What's to eat?"

One night when he went out to the kitchen, sniffing expectantly, the odor was acrid and smoky.

"What's wrong?" he asked.

"Nothing much," Betsy answered lightly. "I've

made a meat pie and a little spilled and burned on the bottom of the oven."

"I love meat pie," said Joe, and went, whistling, to wash.

Betsy approached the oven dubiously. The accident had been a little more than "nothing much." She had thought she remembered just how Anna made meat pie—cutting leftover meat into chunks, and dropping it into gravy along with potatoes and onions and carrots, spreading biscuit dough on top. But something had gone wrong. The dough had overflowed and stuck to the floor of the oven, and burned. She had scraped it off, and scraped and scraped, but it kept on overflowing and sticking and burning and she had run frantically to fling up all the windows and run back to scrape some more. Eventually she had decided that the oven wasn't hot enough and had turned it up as high as it would go. Then the top of the depleted crust had burned.

Her meat pie didn't look like Anna's but she carried it bravely out to the dainty table.

Joe served it, and there was nothing else to serve, except sliced cucumbers. The value of a meat pie, she had been told, was that everything necessary to a nutritious meal could be included in it.

Joe took a bite. So did Betsy. Where the crust wasn't burned, it was soggy, and the vegetables tasted very queer. Joe took a second bite.

"A mighty good idea," he said briskly, "using up that pot roast in a meat pie. It's tasty, too."

Betsy put down her fork and tears came into her eyes.

"Why, honey!" Joe exclaimed. "What's the matter?"

Betsy began to cry. She pushed back her chair and ran out of the living room and threw herself across the white bed.

Joe followed. "What is it?" he asked anxiously. "Didn't I say your meat pie was good?"

"That's just the trouble!" Betsy sobbed. "It's so awful— and you were so—so—nice about it!"

At this Joe laughed his ringing laugh and kissed her tears away. "Next time I'll beat you."

"Next time," said Betsy, wiping her eyes fiercely, "it's going to be good! At least it's going to be fit to eat."

The following afternoon she went to see Tacy and the baby. She had seen the baby first in the hospital, and had been disappointed again. Kelly Kerr not only wasn't a girl—the next one would be, Tacy promised—but he wasn't at all pretty. He was red and had hardly a spear of hair. When Betsy started the soft admiring coos that people make over babies, Tacy had stopped her. She looked beautiful, sitting up in bed, her long red braids against the white pillow, but her eyes were a little anxious.

"Don't say he's handsome," she had said, "for I know better. He's going to develop a wonderful personality, though. That's what people do when they're not good looking, Harry says." And she cuddled the mite protectively.

The joke of it was that now he was getting pretty. He wasn't so red any more; light curls were sprouting; and he had Tacy's Irish eyes.

"I never saw such a change in a child!" Betsy cried, and Tacy let her hold him while she went out to the kitchen.

Over coffee and gingerbread, Betsy poured out the tale of the meat pie. Tacy was comforting, as always.

"Meat pie is hard," she said. "I still can't make a good one. I think, Betsy, you'd better stick to easier things for a while. Pork chops and baked potatoes. Meat loaf. Macaroni. Joe will like them just as well." She passed the gingerbread. "Learn to make this, before you try a Lady Baltimore cake."

It was good advice and was backed up shortly by a gift from Tib.

"This cookbook," she declared, presenting a businesslike-looking volume, "tells all about everything. It practically says, 'take an egg and break it.' It's just right for people like you, Betsy, who otherwise might think the egg went in, shell and all."

Betsy burst into laughter. The practical gift was so in contrast to the appearance of the giver! Tiny, delicately formed, with a shower of golden curls, Tib seemed to have strayed out of a fairy tale. But cookbooks, Betsy well knew, were more in her line. She was highly proficient in all the domestic arts. When she came out to the Willards', she would find Betsy's mending basket and empty it while they talked. Or if it were near mealtime, she would tie on an apron.

She did that now, after taking off a feathered hat and the jacket of a pale green velvet suit. The skirt was draped to show a pleated underskirt.

"Pretty. *Nicht wahr?*" she asked. Tib often threw in German words, and her English had a little foreign twist. "I made it myself. It may not be just the thing for the office, but I dress as I please."

"It's simply darling! So original! But Tib, what heels! You need a husband to look after you!" said Betsy. "When are you going to settle down?"

"Settle down?" Tib gave an airy shrug. "Why should I settle down? I'm good at my job. Saving money. Like my boardinghouse. And one young man takes me to the dancing teas—all the hotels have them now—and another one takes me to everything good that comes to the Met."

"Like either of them?" asked Betsy cannily.

Tib got down a crockery bowl and the flour. She

proposed to make dumplings for a lamb stew Betsy had on the fire. "They're *Lausbub'n!*" she replied. "That's what Grosspapa Hornik used to call the silly boys who kept 'phoning me in Milwaukee. Wanting to spend their money! Falling in love! And all because I have a few yellow hairs."

Betsy chuckled appreciatively.

"What does *Lausbub'n* mean?"

"Oh, good-for-nothing scalawags! It's slang. But they were all nice boys. Grossmama had to approve of them or I couldn't accept their invitations."

"How are your grandparents?" Betsy asked. She had visited Tib in Milwaukee and knew her relatives there. On the Muller side they were German, and rich. The Horniks, with whom Tib lived during her college years, were Bohemians from Austria. Grosspapa Hornik was a tailor.

"They're fine," Tib replied. "Of course they're upset about this dreadful war. So am I."

"Of course!" Betsy's voice was sympathetic. The war must be hard on German-Americans like Tib who naturally would favor the Germans.

"The President asks us to be neutral," Tib went on.

"You try to be, I know."

Tib looked up in surprise. "*Lieber Gott,* I'm not neutral!"

"You're not?"

"Not by a jugful! And neither are my brothers!" She stirred vigorously. "Germany ought to get rid of that Kaiser. *Lausbube!*" she added scornfully.

Betsy burst into laughter again.

"I thought," she explained, "that you meant you weren't neutral because you favored the Germans."

"Ach, Betsy!" Tib replied. "Of course I love the German people. But you must remember that Grosspapa Hornik was a Forty-eighter."

"I know," answered Betsy. "He told me all about it. He came to this country in 1848 when he was a little boy. There had been a revolution in Austria, and his parents were in it, and they had to get out fast."

"Well," said Tib, "why do you think they objected to the old country? Too many uniforms! Too many wars! 'Kaisers are *nicht gut*!' Grosspapa is always saying. He mixes up German and English. But nobody loves America more than Grosspapa Hornik."

With a practised hand she dropped spoonfuls of batter on top of the bubbling stew.

Betsy studied the cookbook Tib had brought. She studied it with a concentration worthy of a profound scientific work. And following Tacy's suggestion, she mastered meat loaf. She learned to fry pork chops so they did not end up dry as chips, and to boil vegetables so they did not emerge waterlogged and soggy.

Doggedly she pushed on to lemon pie and rice

pudding. The rice pudding his mother had made, Joe explained seriously, was a custard rice pudding, rich and yellow, with plenty of raisins in it.

"Betsy!" he exclaimed in delight as he ate. "You got it right!"

Tacy gave her a recipe for Never Fail pie crust. The filling was easy, and it was almost fun, Betsy admitted, to make a meringue. Certainly it was fun, when Joe came home, to escort him proudly to a golden brown pie.

He stared admiringly and cut a huge wedge.

"Joseph Willard! That's for dessert!"

He tasted it, rolled his eyes, kissed her solemnly on the brow.

"We are now," he declared, "officially man and wife."

"I'll call Dr. Atherton. He'll be so pleased!" said Betsy.

There were still plenty of failures, and on those nights Joe helped with the dishes. They were always in a hurry to get dishes done, for evenings were beautifully cozy. With shades drawn against the wintry night, Joe settled himself in the secondhand blue armchair, to read aloud. He was reading *Sentimental Tommy*. Sometimes Betsy tried to darn, but darning, for her, was a major undertaking, and when she grew interested in the story she made mistakes.

Sometimes Joe would say, "Just be beautiful tonight!" And she would put on the pink negligee and let down her hair.

He talked about his work. The campaign had gone well. Minneapolis was digging deep for the Belgians, and Betsy was sure it was because of Joe's stories. He was another Richard Harding Davis, she said.

He had a problem, though. He was not sure he wanted to stay on with the Bureau. Mrs. Hawthorne's office, he told Betsy, was no place for him or any other man.

Mrs. Hawthorne brewed afternoon tea over a spirit lamp, sending one of the girl workers out for cakes. She took a great interest in their personal lives and was kept up to date on their beaus, their parties, their worries, and their clothes. Her warm rich laughter floated out over the office.

"She's brilliant. She's a whiz at her job. But I'll get soft if I stay."

"You'll be going on to the *Courier*," Betsy prophesied.

And that was exactly what happened.

"I can't afford to pay you what you're worth," Mrs. Hawthorne told him when the campaign ended. "But my husband has a place for you now."

To discuss this change, the Willards were invited to the Hawthornes' for dinner. Betsy wore the dark maroon silk, dressed her hair with care, manicured her nails, added bracelets and perfume. Joe changed his tie twice, and they went out on the streetcar through a frigid December night.

The Hawthorne house stood on a corner. An arc light gleamed over the snowy lawn showing tall oak trees and a tall house with so many narrow gables that it seemed to rush up into points. Lights were pouring through the windows and a ringletted head peeked out of one.

Sally Day answered the door, wearing a reddish-brown velvet dress that matched her curls and eyes. Smiling elfishly, she drew them in and offered to play her new piano piece.

"Sally Day! Take their wraps!" Mrs. Hawthorne clapped reproving hands but the warm loving laugh Joe had described floated out over the hall.

Dinner was served by a maid in cap and apron. The atmosphere, however, was anything but formal. Mr. Hawthorne kept taking scraps of paper from his pockets, and reading aloud things he had liked and clipped or copied down. When he finished he would look around, eyes bright and eager behind his glasses.

He and Joe kept telling each other of books they ought to read, and Mr. Hawthorne kept jumping up to fetch books from the living room. At last he had a great stack beside his plate. He read aloud from

Don Marquis, about archy and mehitabel, all through dessert.

Sally Day kept asking permission to play the new piece, and at last she, too, dashed into the living room, and played it. Returning to the table, she suggested that she dance.

"After a while, dear! Maybe Joe wants to walk on the ceiling."

Sally Day turned to Joe. "You can't!" she challenged.

After dinner, when Joe's transfer to the *Courier* was being discussed, Mrs. Hawthorne turned to Betsy.

"It will be hard for me to fill Joe's place," she said. "Would you like to try? I know you write. You might enjoy working in a publicity office."

Betsy was very pleased but her answer came promptly. "Oh, Mrs. Hawthorne, I know I'd love it! Joe has told me how delightful your office is. But, Mrs. Hawthorne, I already have a job."

"You have?" She sounded surprised.

"Yes. And it's important, and very hard. It's learning how to keep house."

Mrs. Hawthorne swept her arms around Betsy with laughter. "That's the girl!" she said.

9
A Plot Is Hatched

BEFORE JOE BEGAN THE new job, he and Betsy went to
see Aunt Ruth. Betsy found it exciting to be a married
woman visiting her husband's family—and Aunt
Ruth was all the family Joe had. They were not re-
lated, really; her husband had been Joe's father's
brother. But Joe had lived with them for several years
after his mother's death when he was twelve.

Snow was packed along the flat streets of little Butternut Center. It was only a handful of houses, a church, and the general store, Willard's Emporium. Betsy had met Joe there, the summer before they started high school.

"You were eating an apple and reading a book the first time I saw you," she said. "Jinks, you were handsome!"

She had come again when they were eighteen and beginning to fall in love.

"That was when I met Uncle Alvin and Aunt Ruth and Homer." He was the clerk who now was helping Aunt Ruth run the store.

She lived above the store among fat chairs and sofas, all hung with old-fashioned tidies. The rooms were stuffily hot from a glowing pot-bellied stove. She was thin, gray-haired, with a kind, sad face. Betsy did not get very well acquainted with her, for Aunt Ruth and Joe were busy talking about people Betsy did not know.

Aunt Ruth cooked Joe's favorite dishes, and she wiped her eyes while he ate, saying how proud Uncle Alvin had been of him. "Your going through college and all!" She depended on him, too; asked his advice about the store. Joe listened thoughtfully.

"It sounds to me as though the store's pretty hard on you, Aunt Ruth. Homer wants to buy, you say.

Why don't you sell?"

"Maybe I will," she answered. "I might go to California and get away from these cold winters. I have a niece out there."

But she always changed her mind.

"No," she would say, after a while. "I've lived in Butternut Center all my life. I was born here. And I think I'll stay on."

Christmas approached. The Willard apartment had a wreath in the snowy bay window. Mistletoe, tied to a small Santa Claus, swung in the doorway. There were hospitable dishes of candy and nuts about. There was even a small Christmas tree. But the heart of the holiday remained in the Ray house to which Joe and Betsy, laden with packages, tramped through a spectral Christmas Eve.

Joe had never seen a Ray Christmas before but he joined in with enthusiasm. After carols and reading beside a tree that glittered to the ceiling, Mr. Ray turned out the lights and everyone scrambled about, filling the socks and stockings that hung around the fire. In the morning, between grabs at a buffet breakfast, they pulled out their presents in uproarious gaiety.

Joe gave Betsy a cameo brooch. She pinned it ecstatically into the cherry-red bathrobe while Kismet lunged through tissue paper after catnip and Mr. Ray paraded with a cane his wife had given him.

"Now swing it like Joe does!" she commanded, and Mr. Ray marched up and down, eating a sausage and imitating Joe's swagger way with a cane.

Canes were not so common in Minneapolis as they had been in Boston. Only Jimmy Cliff, among Joe's fellow workers on the *Courier,* carried one. Joe described this young man delightedly. A reporter, he was also a poet—hugely stout, wearing loose easy clothes, a slouch hat, and a Windsor tie.

"A wonderful kid who'll never grow up. He's married, and wants us to come out to their house and talk writing."

Meeting Jimmy Cliff was one of the few pleasant experiences Joe had had since returning to the *Courier.* He had been assigned to the courthouse—not a bad run, he said—but he had found trouble there.

Joe told Betsy about it cheerfully at first. The two rival reporters were older, and cronies. They made the rounds of the courthouse offices together, and had not suggested that he join them.

"In fact, they froze me out."

Joe had not minded making the rounds alone, but he had found news sources equally difficult, especially one bearded official who was the political bell-wether of the building.

"I don't know what the old fellow has against me."

"What *could* he have against you?" It was inconceivable to Betsy that anyone should dislike Joe.

"Plenty, evidently! He never gives me any news that isn't already public property."

In a few days an important courthouse story appeared on the front page of the two other newspapers. It was missing from the *Courier*. Joe was humiliated and ashamed.

"Hawthorne chewed me up," he said.

"That nice Mr. Hawthorne?" Betsy cried in indignant astonishment.

"Friendship doesn't hold him back when the paper is scooped, and it darn well shouldn't!"

After this incident, Joe stopped talking about his work, and he cut Betsy short if she brought up the subject. She started to read all three newspapers, and one day she found that the *Courier* had missed another big courthouse story. It happened a third time.

Joe started coming home late, looking grim. He was almost always in the mood of intense concentration he had shown the day he was hunting for a job. Betsy knew he was trying desperately to solve his problem. She tiptoed about, trying not to disturb him.

One evening, in spite of herself, she chuckled out loud. She was reading a feature story on the front page of the *Courier*. It was only a paragraph long, but very funny—about a will that concerned seven Siamese cats. Joe looked up darkly, and she hastily grew sober.

But the next night she chuckled again, over a similar brief story about a suit filed by a party-goer who had been brought low by a two-inch *femme fatale*—his host's daughter's dolly.

"Who's writing these?" She looked at Joe suspiciously. "They sound like you."

"I'm writing 'em," Joe said, but so glumly that she did not say more. She kept looking for the little features, though, and they kept on appearing, and a night came when Joe burst into the apartment, grinning from ear to ear. He handed her the *Courier*, and the biggest story on page one was a courthouse story signed by Joseph Willard.

"Darling!" Betsy hugged him, and he hugged her until she pulled away to sit down and read. "But how did you get it?"

He began to talk excitedly. "I was sunk. I couldn't get any news, and Hawthorne kept chewing me up. So, trying to make up for the stories I was missing, I started spending hours in the document room. The other boys never go in there. It's just a morgue for papers."

"What kind of papers?"

"Oh, papers filed by citizens having court troubles—complaints, countercomplaints, bills of particulars, suits for damages. You have to dig to find one with a story in it. And even when you've found one"—Joe looked mischievous—"you have to know how to put in the twist that makes it funny, or tragic, or heart-warming."

"You have to write like Joe Willard!" said Betsy. "But you found those features there!"

"Yes, and Hawthorne played them up. And today came the pay-off. The other boys approached me, sweet as pie. The reason I hadn't been getting all the news, they said, was that the old bellwether didn't like me. He felt the paper had insulted his dignity by sending a kid to the courthouse. He didn't like my way with words. He didn't like my cane.

"'But he isn't a bad sort,' the boys said. 'You start making the rounds with us. When he sees you're one of the gang, he'll come around.' And he did." Joe thumped the paper. "He not only gave me this story—he started kidding me about my cane!"

"But those miserable reporters!" cried Betsy. "What brought about their change of heart?"

"Why, their city editors were chewing *them* up because they were missing the stories I'd dug out of the document room. Those boys are swell, really, Betsy. They just hadn't seen any reason why they should drop in my lap news sources they'd spent years developing. But they see now, and they've smoothed things out for me, and naturally they've suggested that when I find a good story I might just tell them which document to look at."

"And will you?"

"Of course."

Betsy bounced. "A lot of good it will do them! *They* can't write like Joe Willard! Oh, Joe, I'm so happy!"

She was very happy—because of his triumph, and because his low mood was gone. But although things went smoothly on the *Courier* after that, Joe's low moods came back sometimes.

Betsy had known, of course, that he had low moods, just as he had high ones, but she had not known the low ones reached such subterranean depths. For a time they made her deeply anxious. Was she to blame? Did he regret his marriage? Not love her any more? But she knew that wasn't true.

Joe, she came to realize, had a complex temperament, quite different from her own which was simple and easily understood. He had boundless courage. In a bad situation he always fought back. But he worried to a degree incomprehensible to Betsy.

He had told her he worried about money. That was why he wanted her to manage the budget. She found out now that he worried about his work, about his contacts with people.

It's astonishing, when he's so wonderful, she thought, trying with might and main to understand.

Perhaps his imagination was too vivid? He could invent too many possible bad happenings. Or perhaps being orphaned so young—those years of loneliness—had been harder on him than he knew?

When he was feeling gloomy he did not want to be praised or encouraged. He wanted to be let alone. All she could do, she decided, was what she did instinctively—show him always that she loved him and admired him and was proud of him.

And so she adjusted herself to Joe's low moods. "He's probably adjusting himself to plenty of things about me. My cooking, for example."

That was improving, and so was her ironing. At first, she felt sure, Joe had not dared to take off his coat in the office. But now she could manage those awkward collars and cuffs. She had almost stopped scorching. And as housework grew less demanding, she had more time for other things, especially—being Betsy—her writing.

It was good for her writing to be alone all day in the quiet apartment. Sometimes there were frost patterns on the windows, strange scenes that had never been created before and would never be created again. Sometimes a fierce, brilliant bluejay perched on their elm. After a snowfall blankets of white covered the boughs, the lawns, the rooftops. It was all clarity and purity, up and down Bow Street.

Betsy would stand looking out the window. Then she would get a tablet and some pencils and start a story.

In the evenings Joe read her stories and made suggestions for improving them. "Silver Hat" paid Marta for a month. Joe made up a plot, and Betsy wrote the story, and he rewrote it. "Mr. Forrester Leaves for Tibet," signed by both of them, paid Marta for six weeks more. Joe started another. Betsy couldn't help with that one; it was about a prize fight and she couldn't understand it. But "The Uppercut" paid Marta twelve weeks into the future.

Joe and Betsy began to dream great dreams.

The dreams filled many evenings, which was well. If the budget was to operate—and it did, with the help of corn meal mush now and then—they could not go, as the Hutchinsons did, to the Symphony Orchestra concerts or, like Tib and her beaus, to the plays that came to the Metropolitan. They went to the stock company, sometimes, on passes picked up at the *Courier,* and to the movies to see long-curled Mary Pickford and that funny, sad man, Charlie Chaplin. But for the most part their lives were quiet, and Betsy was pleased when Tib called one morning and asked her downtown for lunch.

"There's a cute new place. You telephone your order from the table."

Betsy enjoyed dressing up in her Paris suit and hat, her high pearl-buttoned shoes and heavy coat. She took the streetcar downtown, and Nicollet Avenue was crowded, shop windows were exciting, and the new restaurant was gay.

Betsy arrived first, and heads turned when Tib came in, walking haughtily on her high heels. Perhaps because she was so diminutive, Tib affected a disdainful air. It was confusing, like so many things about her, for she was the soul of good nature.

Her dark coat sprang out below her tiny waist in fur-edged tiers. A fur cap sat on her sunrise hair.

"Mrs. Vernon Castle in person!" Betsy cried, for that goddess of the dance affected caps.

Tib gave her tickled little laugh. "Well," she answered factually, "I'm going dancing after the store closes."

"One of the *Lausbub'n*?"

"No, Fred."

Her brother Fred was studying architecture at the University. A slender, fair-haired young man, he danced as beautifully as his sister did and often took her to his fraternity parties or a *Thé Dansant*.

When Tib had efficiently telephoned their order, Betsy asked, "What happened to the *Lausbub'n*?"

Tib gave her airy shrug. "Oh, they always find out that I'm not what they think I am. I could tell them in the first place. In fact, I try to. I'm not a flirt. The trouble is they never believe me."

Betsy began to laugh, but Tib spoke seriously. "Every man has a secret notion that he's going to marry a blonde. And when he sees me, he thinks I'm it. But I'm not!"

"You're a blonde."

"But not the kind of blonde I look like. For example, they think I live on rose petals." And she raised delicate eyebrows at the corned beef and cabbage the waitress had just placed before her.

"Oh, Tib! Tib!" laughed Betsy.

"They think I'm frivolous," Tib went on, "because I have so many pretty clothes. But you know I make most of them myself. Often I rip a dress up at night and it comes to the store a different one next day."

"I know."

"But that's not the worst of it." She put down her fork. "Just because I'm small, men think I'm a clinging vine. They think I need to be protected. Imagine that! Why, I like to paddle my own canoe! I like adventure. I want to see the world."

She was so much in earnest that Betsy stopped

laughing. "Don't be so hard on them, honey! You *are* deceiving! Take the war—"

Most people didn't think much about that any more. Since the opposing armies had settled down for the winter in so-called trenches, the war wasn't so interesting as it had been at first. Betsy grieved about it sometimes. But she was so happy that she tried to put it out of her mind. Tib was different.

"You're so much more concerned about the war than anyone would expect you to be," Betsy tried to explain.

"*Ja*, that's another thing! I'm serious. I read the newspapers. But these men think I'm a *Dummkopf*. Don't bother your little yellow head about the war, they say! Think about me, instead! *Lausbub'n!*"

Tib turned to apple pie à la mode. "I'm saving my money to buy an automobile," she remarked in her usual cheerful tone.

"An automobile!" Betsy did not know an unmarried girl who owned an automobile. They were still not common. Old Mag, the Ray horse, had not liked Minneapolis and had long since been sent to the peaceful countryside. But Mr. Ray had not bought an automobile.

"No one in our family even knows how to drive," Betsy said.

"Well, I do!" answered Tib. "I used to drive my

Uncle Rudy's auto. When I've bought my own, I'm going to go traveling."

"In the *auto*?"

"In the auto."

"But the roads! You'd get stuck! And who'd change your tires?"

"I would."

"Or some man who thinks he's going to marry a blonde."

Betsy burst into laughter again, and this time Tib joined her. Tib was sometimes a little slow to see a joke. But when she understood, she responded with delight. Her appreciation of other people's wit was one of her most endearing traits.

"*Ja*, that's good! Let them change my tires, the *Lausbub'n*! I'm going to drive my auto all over the United States."

If she keeps on talking like that, Betsy thought, Tacy and I will never be bridesmaids. And the next day she telephoned Tacy and asked her to bring the baby and come over, to discuss something important.

Tacy came in, her color even richer than usual from the cold. Kelly's cheeks were like winter roses. Tacy took off his bonnet and proudly fluffed up his light hair. It was perceptibly thick and curly now.

"What a chunk of sweetness!" Betsy cried, hugging him.

"Isn't he a cherub?"

When Betsy had brought in coffee and muffins—muffins were her latest accomplishment—she reported Tib's plans.

"She isn't even thinking about getting married!" Betsy cried. "She goes out all the time but she doesn't give a snap for the men."

"When girls don't marry young," Tacy said profoundly, "they get fussier all the time."

"That's right. You know the old saying about a girl going through the forest and throwing away all the straight sticks only to pick up a crooked one in the end." Betsy looked wise as befitted an old married woman.

"There's a lot of truth in that."

"And Tib will soon be earning so much money that she won't meet many men who earn as much money as she does."

"That would be bad."

"And then she'll start driving around in her car, and getting more and more independent, and she won't marry at all, maybe! And then what will she do when she's old?"

Betsy and Tacy looked at each other in alarm.

"She can come and play with my children," said tender Tacy. Although Kelly was sleeping, she picked him up and hugged him.

"Of course," volunteered Betsy, "she can have a share in Bettina. Whenever I *get* Bettina! But the best thing, Tacy, is for you and me to get busy and find the right one for her. Ask Harry to think about it. Joe's friends are all newspaper men, and they're very interesting, but they're *not* rich, and you know Tib! She's so practical. She'd be more apt to marry someone with money."

"Harry can find someone," Tacy said confidently.

Tacy thought Harry could do anything. Betsy thought Joe could do anything. But with the perfect accord which had always characterized their friendship, they agreed that both husbands were supermen and never made comparisons.

Kelly had been wakened by the hug, and Tacy discovered that it was time to go. But while Betsy made macaroni and cheese—a good winter meal, and cheap, too—she kept thinking about their plan.

She told Joe about it at dinner, but he didn't take it seriously.

"You women! I should think anyone as pretty as Tib could do her own matchmaking!"

Before Betsy had time to reply, the telephone rang, and it was Tacy, her voice quivering with excitement.

"Betsy!"

"Yes."

"You know what we were planning—about Tib?"

"Yes, yes!"

"Well, Harry has just the one. He's a New York millionaire!"

"A millionaire!"

"Well, practically!"

Betsy squealed until the small apartment echoed. Joe came rushing to share the receiver.

"Can you and Joe come to dinner Saturday night? If I can get Tib, that is! Harry has already called this Mr. Bagshaw."

"Yes, yes, we'll come! Oh, Joe! Isn't it thrilling?"

But Joe, after discovering the nature of the news, had gone back to his macaroni. It was good.

10

A Millionaire for Tib

"BAGSHAW!" SAID JOE. "Bags of money—p'shaw!" And he was so pleased with his joke that he took Betsy for a running slide along the frozen sidewalk. "Wait till I tell that to Harry and Sam!"

"Joe Willard!" Betsy panted, "Don't you dare!"

"Lady, I dare anything!" Chuckling wickedly, he hurried her along under the icy stars and into the sizzling lobby of the Kerrs' apartment building.

Harry greeted them, holding a sturdy angel in a white flannel night gown, embroidered in blue, who inspected them brightly while scraping a rattle across his father's well-brushed hair.

"Here! Stop that!" Harry said. "I'm putting him to bed, Joe. Want to help? I'm sure our Little Aids to Cupid need to talk over their big enterprise."

Joe threw an arm around his friend's shoulders. He hissed, "Bags of money—p'shaw!"

"You two behave yourselves!" Betsy ordered as they whooped, and she ran into the bedroom to drop her wraps, pat her hair, and smooth down the dark maroon silk.

The roomy apartment was even more immaculate than usual—and Tacy was always a meticulous house-keeper; Betsy never ceased to marvel at it. There were daffodils and pussywillows on the living room table. The dining room waited in formal splendor.

"Hello!" Tacy called from the kitchen. She was kneeling at the oven, gingerly drawing out a roasting pan. She lifted it to the top of the stove, and trans-ferred a plump, savory bird to a hot platter.

"Roast chicken," she remarked, covering it snugly, "and chocolate meringue pie are my company din-ner. It's a great help, Betsy, to have one company dinner that you know how to make really well."

With the assurance born of practise, she set about compounding giblet gravy.

"When I can make gravy for a millionaire," Betsy said, "I'll think I have arrived." She perched on a kitchen stool. "Tell me about our hero."

Tacy laughed and stirred. "Well, he's a widower! Older than Harry! Out here for an eastern bank. He's trying to get the bank's money out of a bankrupt wholesale dry goods house. He'll be in town several months, Harry says."

"How marvelous!"

"He's a friend of Harry's boss. Mr. Goodrich is in Florida and asked Harry to meet Mr. Bagshaw's train and help him get settled. He's staying at the Club."

"The Club! It sounds like an English novel."

"He plays bridge with a group there. He knows all the Minnesota bigwigs, including Sam's father. And he's taken a great liking to Harry. He *hinted* that he'd like to come out here. He hinted it the very day you and I were talking about Tib."

"It's Fate!" Betsy cried, jumping up, and the doorbell rang and Tacy stripped off her apron, revealing dark green elegance, but she put the apron on again, for the new arrivals were only Carney and Sam.

Sam joined the men in Kelly's room and Carney, looking as pretty as a pink, came out to the kitchen, borrowed an apron, and started to mash the potatoes.

Tacy was stirring up baking powder biscuits now. Betsy was allowed to make ice water.

"But don't fill the glasses yet. Tib will be a little late."

"We planned it that way," Betsy explained.

"Does she know about this scheme?" asked Carney.

"Heavens, no! We're acting very casual."

"She asked if she shouldn't bring a man."

Carney snorted. "You two always did dream up fantastic things!"

"I don't see what's fantastic about Tib marrying a millionaire!" said Betsy, righteously indignant.

"Tib won't be a bit flustered by a million dollars," Tacy said.

"She'll be as cool as a cucumber in a Fifth Avenue mansion," said Betsy. "Brownstone fronts! I've seen 'em!"

"But it's so ridiculous! You marry someone you fall in love with."

"Well, how can Tib fall in love with this Mr. Bagshaw until she meets him?"

Carney was stumped by that. The doorbell rang again and this time Tacy and Carney both pulled off their aprons, and Tacy joined Harry at the door.

Mr. Bagshaw was tallish, thin, with a small dark mustache and dark hair carefully arranged to hide a bald spot! He wore convex eyeglasses which gave him an inscrutable look. He seemed able to see them better than they saw each other. And he was, Betsy admitted with a shock, definitely older even than Harry, who topped the rest by a few years.

"He must be nearly forty."

But he had the fascination of this great maturity. Suave, leisurely, he passed a leather cigarette case, selected a cigarette, and poised it in long, slender fingers, inquiring about Sam's father. Betsy followed Tacy to the kitchen.

"Isn't he perfect?" she whispered.

Tacy's eyes sparkled. "Speaking of English novels! He'll expect the men to stay behind after dinner with port and cigars."

"If he were spending the night, he'd put out his boots!"

Tacy popped the biscuits into the oven and she and Betsy dashed back to the living room, for the bell was ringing again.

Betsy heard Tib's light, gay voice saying good-by to a male voice on the threshold. Then she came in, waving her muff.

"*Wie gehts?*" she cried and ran to kiss Betsy and Carney, and threw elfin kisses to Joe, Harry, and Sam. When Mr. Bagshaw was presented, however, the affectionate little Tib vanished.

"How do you do?" she asked, putting on her disdainful air.

When she acts like that, Betsy thought, she's like a little girl playing lady.

Tib drew Betsy to the bedroom where she doffed her fur cap and fur-trimmed coat. Betsy expected a question about Mr. Bagshaw, but Tib only wanted to show off her dress—lavender messaline with a short tunic wired out above a slinky skirt.

"I finished it after work tonight," she said, pirouetting.

She took down her yellow hair and dressed it again in the feathery swirl which was Tib's version of the French roll. She liked this style because it made her look taller, and put in a shell pin which added another inch.

Back in the living room, the boys began to tease her while Mr. Bagshaw took off his glasses, polished them with a snowy handkerchief and put them back, looking at Tib all the while.

"How's the big business woman?"

"What dance have you learned today?"

"And what dance did you learn yesterday?"

"The lulu-fado. And if you weren't such clodhoppers, I'd show you how to do it."

Mr. Bagshaw spoke softly. "They were dancing the lulu-fado when I left New York."

Tib raised her eyebrows. "Do you dance it?"

"I attempt it," he replied in polite deprecation.

"After dinner," she said loftily, "if we can find the right record, I'll see how you do it." She turned to Tacy. "May I make the gravy, darling?"

"All made. Everything's ready." Tacy acted calm, but her cheeks were like flames.

At dinner the talk continued to be youthfully lively. Mr. Bagshaw did more listening than talking, and more looking than either. He looked at Tib. Now and then polishing his glasses, now and then poising a cigarette in long, nervous fingers, he watched her intently. Tib had forgotten him and was laughing and chattering, enjoying the ease of being with old friends.

The company dinner was perfection.

I must learn a company dinner, Betsy thought as Harry carved second portions and the gravy, steaming hot, was passed again.

Mr. Bagshaw, although he ate sparingly, accepted a second biscuit with high praise.

"See what I mean, Rick?" asked Harry. He always found it easy to get on a first-name basis.

Carney decided to help out the plot. "You ought to taste Tib's cooking," she observed.

Mr. Bagshaw smiled at Tib. "What does she specialize in? Rose petals?" he asked, and Tib gave Betsy a look.

Oh, dear! How unfortunate! Betsy thought.

But when they finished the chocolate meringue pie and coffee, and gathered in the living room again, Mr. Bagshaw redeemed himself. He not only talked, he took command of the conversation and was most interesting.

He had been present at the sensational New York opening, two or three weeks before, of a motion picture called *The Birth of a Nation*.

"It was stupendous!" he said.

He spoke of *The Ziegfeld Follies* and *The Passing Show*—of Rector's, where one dined and danced in a grove of palms.

"I plan to go to New York some day," said Tib in a patronizing tone.

He had seen Mr. and Mrs. Vernon Castle and discussed their effect on the dance craze. They had not returned, he said, to the old forms; they used the new rhythms, but with grace and elegance.

"They've brought us out of the turkey-trot–bunny-hug vulgarity. The maxixe and the tango are quite lovely."

"That's true," Tib said, looking at him with respect.

Sam, returning from a trip outside to warm up the engine of his car, suggested bridge, but Harry demurred.

"Rick wouldn't like our bridge, woman bridge and no stakes."

"I'm sure it would be delightful," Mr. Bagshaw

said. "But how about that lulu-fado Miss Muller was kind enough to suggest?"

"Yes," said Tib. "What records do you have, Tacy?" And she and Mr. Bagshaw strolled out to the glassed-in porch where the phonograph stood. Betsy and Tacy exchanged meaningful glances.

Evidently the Kerrs did not have the proper record for a lulu-fado.

"We'll have to go to the Radisson and dance it," Betsy heard Mr. Bagshaw say.

They began a maxixe.

Tib's dancing was lighter than foam, lighter than a hummingbird, lighter than a flower in a breeze. And Mr. Bagshaw was dexterous in the turns and dips and tricky skating steps. He danced very well, despite his age, Betsy noted with relief. The plot would have collapsed if he hadn't.

They put on a fox-trot, and everyone started dancing.

"By the sea, by the sea,
By the beautiful sea . . ."

Betsy whirled in Joe's arms.

"You're the prettiest girl at the party," he whispered.

They put on "Tipperary," but then in the midst of all the gaiety something pressed on Betsy's heart. For she had seen the British Territorials march off to war to that tune, just boys most of them, and many had not come back. Crossing battle lines, she thought of her dear German servant, Hanni, who had so wished to come to America, and of the Baroness Helena who had given her the cup that Goethe drank from!

Betsy was glad when "Tipperary" ended. (The next record was "I Didn't Raise My Boy To Be a Soldier.") Soon everyone stopped dancing except Tib and Mr. Bagshaw, who executed a tango. As they finished that, his voice floated into the living room.

"You don't look like Mrs. Castle. She looks like a boy, and you look like a sprite. But you dance with the same impersonal grace."

Betsy leaned toward Tacy. "Even Tib can't resist that!" she whispered.

When the party broke up, Sam called out that he would drive everyone home. Joe and Betsy accepted with thankful shivers, but Tib refused carelessly.

"Thanks a lot. Rick's taking me," she said.

Rick! Betsy and Tacy telegraphed that to Carney.

"Boy!" said Sam. "I didn't know you had a car here, or I'd have warned you. You have to go out and warm up the engine once in a while, in this Minnesota weather."

"Oh, my chauffeur is picking me up!" Mr. Bagshaw glanced surprisingly at his wrist. He was the first man Betsy had ever seen wear a watch on his wrist.

"He's out there now."

Tib did not flick an eyelash.

They all heaped Tacy with compliments, and Mr. Bagshaw took her hand.

"The Club chef could not duplicate that dinner, Mrs. Kerr. But may I duplicate the guests? Can't you all dine with me a week from tonight?"

He turned to Tib, but she reverted in a flash to her disdainful air.

"Really, Rick!" she protested. "I can't make an engagement without my book. I do know, though, that I'm busy for the next two Saturday nights."

Mr. Bagshaw seemed amused, but respectfully so. He restrained a smile. "Then we'll make plans after Miss Tib has consulted that overstuffed engagement book. I do hope we can find an evening when all of you are free."

Next morning early Betsy and Tacy were on the telephone. Mr. Bagshaw, they agreed triumphantly, had fallen. Now the vital issue was Tib's reaction. Had she liked him, and how well?

"She seemed impressed."

"But did you notice how she crushed him when he tried to make a date?"

"Oh, that was just technique! No girl gives a man the first date he asks for."

"I hope you're right." Tacy was a little doubtful.

"Well, we can talk it over tonight. Harry and I are going to 909 for Sunday night lunch."

"Oh, good!" Betsy exclaimed, for she was longing to turn the subject inside out, and Joe was already bored with it.

"Tib will never marry that grand-daddy!" he said.

"Joe, he's only a little older than Harry, and perfectly fascinating!"

"So are you—fascinating, that is."

"Don't you like him?"

Joe grinned. "Well, it was entertaining to see the colonel unbend to the privates for the sake of a pretty girl."

He was more interested in the pancakes he was tossing than he was in getting Tib married. "Did you ever see more beautiful pancakes? Butter this stack, Betsy, while I fry some more."

He and Betsy both loved Sunday, when they were together all day long. One thing troubled her a little. She had almost stopped going to church. Joe had gone very seldom since leaving Butternut Center, and now although he went with Betsy when she asked him to, he seemed to feel that the proper Sunday routine was to sleep late and make pancakes for breakfast. Betsy ate them in pink negligee and cap. Then she had an extra good dinner to get, and Joe liked to read the Sunday papers, and they fed the squirrels that came to their snowy window ledge. This morning a robin appeared in the elm—fat, bright, and undismayed by the still arctic cold.

"After all, it *is* March!" Betsy pointed out that afternoon when she and Joe walked down to the lake to watch the skaters. "Tacy and I could find crocuses up on the Big Hill, if we were back in Deep Valley."

They ended the walk at the Ray house where Sunday night lunches were a family tradition. Mr. Ray always made sandwiches. There was a crackling fire, and friends of all ages dropped in. It made Betsy feel very much married to see Margaret playing the piano while her high school friends sang.

Margaret had not acquired a real Crowd such as Betsy had had in high school. But Louisa was always there, and sometimes a boy or two. Betsy asked her mother how Margaret got on with boys.

"They admire her," Mrs. Ray said thoughtfully. "They take her to school parties. But they're a little scared of her, I think. You know how dignified she is, and she does nothing to encourage them."

"How about Louisa?"

"She and Margaret help each other. Margaret helps to tone her down, and she draws Margaret out of her shell."

After the Kerrs arrived, they talked about last night's party. Mrs. Ray was in on the plot.

"Three Little Aids to Cupid!" Harry chortled, and the men withdrew to discuss the Great War, as it was beginning to be called. Spring, everyone believed, would bring a big British offensive which might end the conflict.

Mrs. Ray, Betsy, and Tacy aired their great topic like a blanket suspected of moths.

"Have you heard from Tib today?" Mrs. Ray asked.

"No, and whenever we do, we must be sure to act casual."

"If we didn't, we'd antagonize her, Mrs. Ray."

"You should have heard her, Mamma, when he tried to make a date for next Saturday night!"

"I wish she'd 'phone," Mrs. Ray said.

"She won't. She won't think he's important enough. You know Tib!"

But the telephone shrilled through this prophecy, and the war, and Margaret's friends' singing. And it was Tib!

"I knew where to find you, *Liebchen*," she laughed. "I'm sorry to interrupt those onion sandwiches, but Rick has telephoned twice. He does want to get that party at the Club arranged. I told him I'd check with you and Tacy."

Betsy stiffened in her effort to keep calm.

"Tacy's here," she said offhandedly.

"Then how about a week from Friday night?"

"Hold the line!"

Betsy and Tacy conferred in hushed jubilation.

"All right with everyone," Betsy reported brightly. "What do you think? I saw a robin today."

Tib lowered her voice. "Betsy," she said, "I have something else to tell you."

"What is it, dear?" Betsy's voice was gentle, but she signaled wildly to Tacy who rushed up on tiptoe, Mrs. Ray following.

"*So soon?*" she whispered. Betsy put a finger to her lips.

"Something perfectly marvelous," Tib went on. "It's the most marvelous thing that ever happened to me."

Betsy rounded her eyes at Tacy and shook an elated hand in the air. "Tell me about it, honey."

"Well, you know Rick took me home!"

"Yes." Still rounder eyes, a more elated hand.

"Well, that car—it's just one he's been renting! He's having his own car sent from New York. And, Betsy, what do you think?"

"About what?"

"About the car, of course!" Tib sounded impatient, for Betsy's tone was suddenly flat. "He's going to let me drive it. Think of that! I'm going to practically have my own car, all summer long."

11

No Troubles to Pack

"Pack up your troubles in your old kit bag,
And smile, smile, smile ..."

THE CROWD OF OLD FRIENDS, and Mr. Bagshaw, had
no troubles to pack, but to that tune they danced
away the summer.

Of course, "Pack Up Your Troubles" was a war
song, but a new one, and the war was a fire burning

very far away. Twice in the spring its glare reached them briefly. When a strange new horror called poison gas was used by the Germans, Americans saw that glare. They were shocked because Canadian troops were stricken; Canada was close to home. And when a U-boat sank the British liner, *Lusitania,* one hundred and fourteen Americans were drowned.

That night Joe came home late, looking tired and sober, but excited, too. He took Betsy slowly into his arms.

"We'll be in it now," he said and she felt cold fingers on her heart. But President Wilson announced there was such a thing as being "too proud to fight," and although Joe and Mr. Ray and many others, including Colonel Roosevelt, objected to that view, it seemed to cool the country's wrathful fever. No big offensive came. Everything quieted down. And through that carefree summer of 1915, young and old continued to dance.

Certainly the Crowd danced—in smart hotels as Mr. Bagshaw's guests, in their homes entertaining Mr. Bagshaw, and, when the weather turned hot, at country clubs and leafy lakeside places Mr. Bagshaw was aware of. They danced the merry one-step and the swaying, gliding tango and the maxixe and the hesitation.

Mr. Bagshaw delighted in leading Tib out to the

dance floor, a blond sprite in a gossamer dancing cap and filmy dress, the jeweled ribbons of tango slippers tied about her dainty ankles.

Ankles could be seen, for skirts were getting shorter. Girls were standing straighter. The debutante slouch was gone. Minneapolis quoted, chuckling, from its popular columnist, "Q":

> *"The joyful news is with us,*
> *Let paeans now be sung.*
> *The girls again have vertebrae*
> *On which their forms are strung.*
> *No longer does a figure S*
> *Come slouching down the street,*
> *The girls have got their backbones back,*
> *Instead of in their feet."*

"I'd like to meet that 'Q,'" Betsy said. "Why don't you ask him out some night?"

"Him!" laughed Joe. "It's a girl. A very nice, demure one. She and Jimmy Cliff are always swapping rhymes."

There were Expositions going on in California. Mr. Ray took Mrs. Ray and Margaret to see them. They would visit Mrs. Ray's mother, too. Anna took Kismet and the goldfish bowl to the country. Betsy missed them all, but being so entirely on her own made her feel even more married than usual, and that feeling was sweet.

Louisa, lonely for Margaret, dropped in with bouquets from the garden. The elm tree now was thickly, darkly green. But all the secrets of its branches were revealed to the Willard bay window. Running her carpet sweeper blithely up and down, Betsy watched a robin's nest, the eggs, the fledglings.

"I think I'll write a story about a little girl going to live with the birds!"

It was hot and she did her housework early, then closed the windows and drew the shades as she had seen her mother do. When Joe came in from work, he remarked with satisfaction that their apartment was the coolest spot in town.

Usually they were off for a swim or a sail or a picnic. Mr. Bagshaw dodged the picnics. But the Willards and the Kerrs met often at Lake Harriet's picnic grounds, adjoining the pavilion where band concerts were played.

"A Betsy-Tacy picnic!" Betsy and Tacy would say, spreading the table.

It wasn't exactly a Betsy-Tacy picnic. There was much more food than they had ever carried up the Big Hill. With husbands to feed, they brought salads, cold meats, pots of beans, layer cakes, and thermos bottles full of coffee. Kelly would be put down to crawl. He crawled very young, Harry and Tacy pointed out, watching the curly head progress in determined jerks across the grass.

Clearing the table, Betsy and Tacy would discuss Tib and Mr. Bagshaw. He wanted them to call him Rick and they managed to when he was around, but when he wasn't they still used the respectful "Mr. Bagshaw."

Tacy was able to report on him because Harry saw him every day. On Tib, Betsy was better informed. She and Joe were frequent companions of the romantic couple on weekends when the Kerrs were at the lake.

"Mr. Bagshaw is really smitten," Tacy announced.

"Well," Betsy answered jubilantly, "she says he isn't a *Lausbube*!"

The news grew even better. "Mr. Bagshaw had to go to New York but he hurried back here like mad."

"Tib likes him. She says he appreciates . . . listen to this . . . ! he *appreciates* her giving him so much of her time."

"Flowers, dances, a Rolls-Royce, and *he* appreciates!"

"Isn't that just like Tib?"

And later: "This almost settles it! She thinks he looks like John Drew!"

He really did, Betsy thought, resemble that aging matinee idol. He had the same thinning hair, perfect tie and spats, an urbane yet weary air. She reflected on this again later in the evening.

Usually they listened to the concert from a blanket spread on the grass. The real seats were in the pavilion, but there were listeners in carriages and automobiles all around and in canoes on the lake. Tonight the Kerrs left early and Joe and Betsy rented a canoe.

Floating under the stars with her head on Joe's shoulder, the music coming dreamily over the dark water, Betsy was thinking how wonderful it was to be married, when she gave a dismayed start. Could Tib float in this haze of joy with anyone so old and worldly as Mr. John Drew Bagshaw?

"Why, he doesn't even like canoes!"

He liked sailboats, though. Sam kept a sailboat on Lake Calhoun and all of them, including the New Yorker, found it very pleasant about sunset to be out on the gilded, bouncing water. The Crowd scrambled over the boat, dove again and again, and swam around and around, calling insults and challenges. Mr. Bagshaw did not swim. He polished his glasses and smilingly watched Tib.

In a shepherd's-check bathing suit, like no other on the lake, Tib was worth watching. She wore silk stockings instead of the usual cotton ones. Her pretty legs gleamed as she balanced gaily before her birdlike dive. (When modestly under water she peeled off the stockings, hanging them neatly on the boat, but she always put them on again, under water, before climbing back.)

Although Mr. Bagshaw never swam, he was an excellent sailor and looked trimly nautical in immaculate blue coat and white duck trousers. When he took the tiller, Sam's boat showed its heels to every other boat of its class. He held his own with the younger men at tennis, too.

"His forehand is classic," Joe said. "His backhand is murder. If only he weren't always so anxious to win!" For Joe and Sam, although they battled furiously, never really cared who won.

"Probably he wants to impress Tib," said Betsy.

"No! It's the same ruthless drive that made him a millionaire."

"You like him, don't you?" she urged, a little anxiously.

"Sure! Sure!" Joe said.

They all did, in spite of his handicap of wealth and position. He tried so hard to be one of the Crowd that they were almost sorry for him. He did not know how to join in their crazy banter. At first he did not even understand the wild rush for a popcorn wagon.

These inviting vehicles paraded the summer streets, whistling shrilly, trailing savory smells. After he understood, Mr. Bagshaw made a point of stopping every one. With a great affectation of boyishness he brought dozens of buttery bags back to the Rolls-Royce.

He liked to be out in his big automobile, perhaps because Tib was so delighted to be driving it. Yellow hair bare, she settled herself behind the wheel with an amusing air of efficiency. Mr. Bagshaw sat sidewise, smiling at her.

The Crowd took him to see all the sights.

Fort Snelling, high on a bluff above the meeting of the Mississippi and Minnesota Rivers! The old fort had seen almost a hundred years of history, the Crowd announced.

Minnehaha Falls! They were as well known in Europe as Teddy Roosevelt, Betsy said. Because of Longfellow, of course. She started to name the many people to whom she had promised post card pictures of the Falls but she did not finish. Too many of them were in trenches or war-blackened cities.

Lake Minnetonka! One Sunday afternoon they called on the Kerrs. Joe and Betsy reached for each other's hands at the first sight of the little green cottage on stilts.

Harry and Tacy hospitably brought coffee and cake out to the lawn but, as soon as she could, Tacy took Betsy aside. Her news was sobering.

"Mr. Bagshaw's business here is finished, Harry

says. He could go back to New York if he wanted to. He just doesn't want to . . . without Tib."

"Without Tib?"

"Without Tib!"

New York seemed suddenly very far away.

"He'll propose before he goes back, as sure as shooting," Tacy said.

"Hmm!" said Betsy. Pushing her hands deep into the pockets of a green cardigan sweater, she looked across at the Japanese boathouse.

"Hmm!" said Tacy.

That very evening Mr. Bagshaw invited them all to a farewell dinner dance at the Inn on Christmas Lake. This sophisticated inn, which pretended to be rustic because it was in the country, was one of his favorite places.

It was to be a gala party, merrily jangling telephones reported over the next few days. Orchids for the ladies, and souvenirs . . . would they prefer gold mesh bags or vanity boxes? Tib asked seriously.

Joe insisted that Betsy must have a new dress. He had proposed that before, but Betsy always said she had plenty of dresses. As a matter of fact, the clothes fund had leaked mysteriously into the grocery fund . . . or off to the dentist.

"The budget just won't allow a new dress," she admitted at last.

Joe swung his shoulders. "The budget," he said, "isn't buying you this dress."

"Then how . . ."

"My bonuses," he answered.

The *Courier* gave a bonus for the best news story every week. A five dollar bonus, and Joe had been winning and had kept all his prize money out of both budget and savings account.

"For a new dress," he explained now. So he and Betsy went downtown and picked out a white chiffon with a blue velvet bodice. The flounces were edged with blue velvet, and blue velvet ribbons tied a malines ruff around her neck.

"I never felt so married as I did when I paid the clerk for that dress," Joe remarked as he watched Betsy prinking on the night of the dance. He also was pleased with everything that made him feel married.

"Do I look nice?"

"Like a dream!"

He was putting on the white coat he wore with blue trousers to summer parties when the doorbell rang and Betsy went to answer it. On the threshold stood a tall, handsome, smartly dressed girl with a mischievous expression. Peering over her shoulder were lively green eyes.

"Cab!" Betsy shouted joyfully. "And this is Jean!"

"My Missus!" he answered proudly, and Joe ran

out and they all pumped one another's hands. Cab had been an important member of the old Deep Valley Crowd. His solid dependability was engagingly wrapped in rollicking high spirits.

He looked just the same, Betsy thought as they went inside—slim, springy, and neat as a bandbox. But when he took off his shining straw hat . . . ! Where was his thick black hair?

Cab followed her gaze. "I admit it," he said. "But I'm not as bald as I was the first time Jean saw me."

Jean laughed, a throaty contagious laugh. "Tell them about it, Cab," she said. Everyone sat down.

"Well, I was losing my hair. And someone told me that the way to make your hair grow was to shave your head. I was making a business trip way out to North Dakota, and it seemed a good time to try this cure, so I had my head shaved."

"There wasn't a spear left!" cried Jean. "Not a spear!"

"The first night there, I was out with the fellow I'd come to see, a nice chap from Georgia. Reb and I ran into Jean and another girl. Reb knew them and introduced me. Of course I started to take off my hat, but then I noticed what a wow Jean was, and I kept it on."

"I wondered why," said Jean, her throaty chuckle tumbling out again.

"Reb had an auto, and we all went for a ride. That was fine. I could keep my hat on. But when we stopped at an ice cream parlor I simply had to take it off."

"And I thought . . ." Jean's voice sank to a calamitous whisper. "I thought, 'The guy's bald-headed!'"

She and Cab both burst into laughter.

"He was cute," Jean insisted. "Bald head and all. And when he went back to Minnesota he sent me one of those boxes of chocolates a yard long."

"I had to work fast," Cab explained. "She was going off to Boston to study elocution."

"He liked my family," Jean said, winking.

"You bet I did!" Cab grew solemn. "Especially her mother. And my mother used to say to me, 'Caleb, when you go to pick out a wife, look at her mother!'"

"And did you?" Betsy asked breathlessly.

Cab rubbed his head. "Well, I didn't have much time to look at her very hard. I was too busy looking at Jean."

And they went off into laughter again.

She's just the one for him! Betsy thought.

"Say, Betsy," Cab said, "wasn't it swell that we got married the same day? Let's celebrate our anniversary together some time. You two come down to our little house in Deep Valley. Jean likes Deep Valley, and of course I love it, but I wish there were more of the old Crowd around."

At the word Crowd, Betsy dashed to the telephone. And when Tib learned who was sitting in the Willard living room, she said just what Betsy had hoped she would say.

"Oh, bring them to the dance! Please do! Rick would want them."

So Betsy went back to report a Crowd party that night.

"It's your chance, Cab, to introduce Jean to everyone."

"Who's giving it?" Cab asked.

"Oh, a New York millionaire who's in love with Tib."

Jean hooked her arm in Cab's. "I hope," she said, "he's as nice as my struggling young business man."

"Not struggling to get away from you, angel!"

For some reason this light-hearted exchange made Betsy feel blue.

She felt blue driving out to Christmas Lake, although the Hutchinsons had picked them up and there was more joyful excitement over Cab and Jean. These welcome visitors enlivened the party, too, but Betsy felt bluer and bluer through the whole superlative affair.

As usual, in a smart restaurant Mr. Bagshaw was at his gleaming best. As usual, he had secured a table next to the dance floor, the waiters were hypnotized by his regal air, and the orchestra leader hurried over to pay his respects. There were boutonnieres for the men, as well as orchids for the ladies. There was a mesh bag even for the unexpected Jean.

Betsy was glad of the new chiffon, for everyone wore something special. Tacy's black and white striped taffeta, with white blouse and black bolero jacket, brought out her autumn coloring. Carney's cool marquisette had the simplicity she loved. Tib had thrown together a yellow silk marvel. Below a tight vestee, dozens of tiny ruffles raced down to her ankles.

"I painted the slippers to match," she confided, extending a tiny foot.

Although Mr. Bagshaw was usually so polite, he did not dance with anyone but Tib. When she danced with someone else, he watched. He pulled out the leather cigarette case, passed it absently, and selected a cigarette, hardly removing his eyes from those whirling yellow ruffles.

"He'll propose tonight. I feel it in my bones," Tacy whispered glumly.

And sure enough, when the orchestra rested and the Crowd moved out to the broad piazza, he asked Tib to walk down to the lake. He very pointedly did not suggest that anyone else come along, although the lake shimmered under a full August moon. He and Tib strolled off through a warm darkness filled with the flashings of fireflies. They disappeared down rustic stairs leading to the water.

Betsy and Tacy sat close together for comfort. Tacy burst out: "I had the fun of marrying for love!"

"So did I!" said Betsy. "I should say I did!"

"So did Jean."

Jean joined them. She asked in a mirthful whisper, "Who is he? He freezes my bones."

The orchestra began to play "Araby" and the Crowd went back to the dance floor . . . except for the two who had gone down to the lake.

The orchestra played "You're Here, and I'm Here, so What Do We Care?" But Tib wasn't there, and Betsy and Tacy found that they cared terribly. Why had it seemed such a fine idea for Tib to marry a New York millionaire?

The orchestra played "Pack Up Your Troubles," and for the first time that summer Betsy and Tacy felt they really had a trouble to pack. Tib and Mr. Bagshaw returned. His face was inscrutable, as always. Tib had been crying. She had powdered; she was smiling; but she had been crying. Betsy and Tacy looked at each other with stricken eyes.

Why had she been crying? Because she had turned him down? Tib was very tender-hearted. Or because she was going to New York to live in lonely grandeur? The evening ended without any chance for intimate conversation. The dressing room was crowded with chattering women.

Mr. Bagshaw bent over their hands with his customary urbanity. Tib's farewells were a little subdued, and they drove off in the big impressive car.

The Kerrs followed. Sam and Carney delivered Cab and Jean to their hotel, then dropped the Willards off at their apartment. And when Joe and Betsy went in, they found a special delivery letter in their mailbox.

12

A Letter from Aunt Ruth

THE LETTER WAS FROM Aunt Ruth. Joe tore it open as they went upstairs, and inside the apartment Betsy dropped into a rocker and waited. Her cheeks, above the chiffon dress, were still flushed from the party.

Joe sat down in his blue chair and read aloud. The letter was short but its impact was powerful. Aunt Ruth had sold Willard's Emporium to Homer. He had been married, and he and his wife were going to live in the rooms above the store. He had bought the furniture.

"I feel all upset," Aunt Ruth wrote. "Selling out was hard on me, and I don't know what to do next. I wish I could come and stay with you folks."

That was all, except "Your loving Aunt."

Joe put the letter down and looked at Betsy, his eyes troubled.

"We'll have to let her come," he said.

"Why—why—how can we?" Betsy faltered. He couldn't know what he was saying. Let her come? Let anyone invade their Paradise? "We—haven't room for her," she added lamely, choosing the least important of the many objections hammering at her heart.

"We'll have to find room," Joe said. "That isn't what bothers me. It's asking so much of you, Betsy, that makes me feel bad. But I can't say no. It isn't as though she wanted to live with us indefinitely. She probably just wants a chance to make some plans. And I'm the only relative she has—around here, I mean."

"You're not exactly a relative," Betsy said in a choked voice. "You were Uncle Alvin's nephew."

"She didn't think about that when they let me come to live with them."

But Joe, Betsy thought rebelliously, had paid his own way. He had worked in the store, and after he was ready for high school, he had moved to Deep Valley and supported himself.

Joe read her thoughts. "I know I always helped around the place. But just the way their own son would have done. In Deep Valley I worked, of course, but I spent Sundays and holidays out at Butternut Center. And Aunt Ruth never let me go back without a basket full of apples, or cookies, or a fruit cake. I sent my mending to her—laundry, too, sometimes. And often when she wrote to me she'd stick in a dollar bill. Now she's feeling lost and wants to be with family for a while. I can't refuse her, Betsy."

Betsy gazed around the little honeymoon apartment. It looked sweeter than it had ever looked before. The glow of lamplight rested on the old chairs, the books, her grandfather's table. The elm tree beyond the bay window was swallowed up in the night, but she could feel it out there.

"Our lease is up next month. That's a good thing. We can rent a place with more room. Betsy!" Joe looked up, and his voice took on a new note. "We've saved some money. Maybe we could make a down payment on a house? Pay for it like rent?"

Betsy heard the lift in his voice. She wanted to reply with warmth, with enthusiasm, but she couldn't seem to do it. She couldn't bring herself to speak at all.

Joe pushed both hands over a worried forehead. "Oh, we can't afford it, I guess! I wish I'd get another raise," he said in a discouraged tone.

Betsy couldn't stand that. She got up and crossed the room and kissed him. But she kissed him quickly and went to hang up her coat.

"You're earning plenty," she said. "And I think we have enough for a down payment. We have over five hundred dollars. If we have to pay more by the month than we're paying Mrs. Hilton, we can add what we're putting in the savings now. I can juggle the budget."

But Joe knew that her brisk cheerfulness was false. He followed her out to the foyer and put his arms around her.

"Thank you, Betsy," he said. He sounded humble.

They did not talk any more but got ready for bed quickly. Usually, after a party, Betsy hated to undress. It was as sad as dismantling a Christmas tree, she would say, admiring herself in the mirror from all angles, and when she had taken off her dress, she would pull the pins out of her hair slowly, and shake it around her shoulders and pose until Joe came, laughing, to stop her.

Tonight she took off the new dress promptly and was soon in bed.

She lay in Joe's arms a few minutes and then he went to sleep, but Betsy could not sleep. She felt overwhelmed. It wasn't that she minded buying a house, living more cheaply, giving up luxuries . . . none of that mattered at all. Besides, she was confident Joe's salary would rise to any need. What she minded was giving up their delicious privacy, the fun of it being just the two of them, keeping house all alone. She wouldn't mind giving it up for a baby, but for anything else she would.

"Why couldn't it have been a baby?" she asked, and a few tears dripped into her pillow.

But she remembered the eagerness in Joe's voice when he had mentioned buying a house, and how she had quenched it. She remembered his humble, "Thank you, Betsy." He had thanked her just for accepting his decision; he knew as well as she did that she had done it grudgingly.

It was the best I could manage, Betsy thought, still crying a little. But next morning at breakfast she tried harder.

"I'll tell Mrs. Hilton today that we won't be renewing," she said, brightly casual. "Will you write Aunt Ruth, or shall I?"

"I'll write from the office," Joe replied. "And maybe you'll have time to call some real estate men?"

"As soon as I get the family officially welcomed."

The Rays were arriving from California. "I'm taking them a cake."

"It will be fine to see them."

Joe was brightly casual, too. But he was unhappy. Betsy could see it in his eyes and in the way—after he had kissed her good-by—he squared his shoulders, and ran downstairs, and went swinging out into the street.

She washed and wiped the dishes and hung the tea towels to dry. She made the cake and it turned out well, and she ran the carpet sweeper up and down, pausing, as usual, to look out into the elm. She looked for a long time.

I love that tree, Betsy thought. Last night's tears came back and ran slowly down her cheeks. She went to the bathroom and washed them off, and powdered.

The telephone rang, and it was Joe.

"You all right, Betsy?"

"Why, of course! Almost ready to start for the train."

"I just thought I'd like to talk with you," he said. There was a pause. "I've written to Aunt Ruth."

"That's good. And don't worry, dear." She tried to put the proper reassurance into her voice but she knew she hadn't succeeded.

"I love you, Betsy," Joe said softly.

"I love you, too."

After she put down the receiver, she cried some more.

Tacy telephoned, wanting to know whether Betsy had heard from Tib. Betsy didn't tell the news about Aunt Ruth. Tacy would have been a good one to tell. She was unfailingly tactful. But she would be sorry, and Betsy didn't want to be pitied.

She didn't tell her family, although it was comforting to see them. Mr. Ray's smiling face was tanned by the California sun.

"And look at my freckles!" Mrs. Ray cried. Her red hair curled beneath a broad-brimmed hat. "I bought this hat, and wore gloves, and carried an umbrella all summer. But look at me!"

"And look at me!" laughed Margaret. Margaret did, indeed, have a new sprinkle on her nose. And that wasn't the only way she had changed. She had a new shy sparkle.

"Boy cousins!" Mrs. Ray whispered, walking toward the taxi. "Two of them, just her age. They teased her and flirted with her and tore her dignity to tatters."

Louisa was waiting on the Ray front steps.

"Bogie!" she shouted and catapulted into Margaret's hug. They rushed to find Anna, who had returned the day before—and Kismet. The goldfish were back above the bookcase and Kismet stood with a paw on either side of the bowl looking contentedly downward.

Margaret and Louisa disappeared, but Betsy and her parents sat on the back porch and drank coffee and ate Betsy's cake. She had felt a little foolish, bringing it, because of Anna, but it seemed the sort of gesture a married daughter should make. They talked and talked and Betsy almost forgot Aunt Ruth in the news of her grandmother, and the two Expositions.

When she said that she had to go home and start dinner, Mrs. Ray telephoned Joe.

"Anna has peaches for a short-cake."

"Lady, I'll be there!"

He came in, smiling broadly, although he gave Betsy an anxious look when he kissed her. And after the short-cake, presents were brought out. The Willards were given a pottery hanging basket.

"For flowers and vines," Mrs. Ray explained. "I thought it would be pretty in your bay window."

"It would be lovely anywhere," Betsy said.

Joe reached for her hand. "I guess Betsy hasn't told you. We're thinking of buying a house."

"You're giving up that darling apartment?" Mrs. Ray exclaimed.

"We need more room. No . . ." He grinned. "It's not a baby! My Aunt Ruth wants to come and stay with us a while."

"She's sold the store and feels lonesome," Betsy explained, striving for a natural tone.

She knew, without looking at her parents, what their reactions to the news would be. Mrs. Ray would think it was too bad, although she would not say so, and she would agree that Betsy should do whatever her husband thought best. Mr. Ray would approve. Sure enough, he spoke heartily.

"That's a mighty kind thing for you kids to do."

Walking home, Joe said, "Your father took me out on the porch, while you were telling your mother about Bagshaw's party. He wanted to loan us money enough for our down payment. It was grand of him, but I'd rather not borrow. How about you?"

"I wouldn't like to either," Betsy said. "Saving out a couple of hundred dollars for the extra furniture we'll need, we could still pay down three hundred dollars."

But when they started house hunting, they found that three hundred dollars was considered very meager. They met discouragement everywhere, but at least Tib's news was good.

"Why, of course, I turned him down!" she said. It was on the telephone. "Did you think for a moment that I wouldn't? He's very nice, and I liked him, and I adored his car, but *marry* him! *Lieber Gott!*"

"Better luck next time," Betsy joked to Tacy, passing on the news of their failure. They were immeasurably relieved.

Joe was amused, and he and Betsy discussed Mr. Bagshaw's exit at some length. Any fresh topic seemed welcome these days. There was a strange new feeling in the Willard apartment.

Betsy couldn't quite understand it. They were loving to each other, as always. Both of them made an unusual effort to be entertaining. Perhaps that was what made the strangeness? Or perhaps it was just because they weren't happy? But the feeling grew like a thickening fog.

Betsy went house hunting every day, alone and with real estate agents. But she had no success. On any house that pleased her, the owner wanted more than three hundred dollars down.

"Maybe we'll have to rent after all," Joe said.

He never suggested holding Aunt Ruth off, and Betsy did not even hint at such a solution, but in her reveries the prospect of Aunt Ruth grew darker and darker.

She would have to be included in all their parties, and she wouldn't fit in at all. She wouldn't have any interest in their friends, or they in her. She would sit around and listen to Joe and Betsy talk. What about their little private jokes, the tender intimacies they were in the habit of exchanging as they cooked or washed dishes or sat together in the evenings? Even the reading aloud would not have the same flavor, with Aunt Ruth listening, too.

The grimmer her thoughts were, the harder Betsy tried to find a house. Getting tired over that search eased her conscience a little. And her conscience hurt sharply. It was almost terrible that it should be so hard to reconcile herself to Joe's wishes.

I wouldn't have believed it! she thought.

She said her prayers fiercely, and Saturday night she decided that church would help, so next morning she slipped out of bed early. Joe roused up but she whispered, "Go back to sleep. I'm going to church."

He murmured, "Say a prayer for me, honey."

"I will. I always do."

It had turned cold in the night. Flowers were frozen, there was hoarfrost on the lawns. Betsy had always loved this early service, partly because it took her out into such a fresh and empty world. But this morning she only wanted to get to church.

She wanted to wrench out, if she could, her hateful resentment about Aunt Ruth.

I agreed to let her come, yes. But "the gift without the giver is bare," she told herself angrily, hurrying along.

She could hear her father's voice. "That's mighty kind of you kids." But she didn't feel kind. She wished she did; but she didn't.

Inside St. Paul's, she flung herself down on her

knees. The church was almost empty. Morning light came through green-and-yellow windows and made a pattern on the clean white walls. It was a plain church—plain brown choir stalls, a plain cross on the altar. The service began.

"Almighty God, unto whom all hearts are open. . . ."

Betsy dug her head into her arms. "Help me, God! Please help me!" she prayed.

This was the first real problem of their marriage. Up to now, everything had been perfect. Her struggles with cooking, Joe's low moods hadn't mattered, really. This was different. It was a real disagreement.

Joe had decided it. "But I wanted him to. One person in a family has to have the final word. I want it to be Joe, always."

If only he could have decided that they didn't have room for Aunt Ruth . . . that it was too bad, but she would have to manage some other way. . . .

That thought brought Betsy's head up, sharply.

Would she really have liked that, she asked herself? Why—why—it wouldn't have been Joe! How would she like Joe not being Joe? If she needed him, or someone in her own family needed him, how would she like Joe not being Joe? What would it be like, not to be sure, always, that Joe would do whatever he thought was right?

All of a sudden everything came clear.

The beautiful ritual unfolded, and Betsy began to make the responses, a little absently, but with a heart so full of love and thankfulness, she knew God wouldn't mind. She felt all right. She felt like herself. When the service ended, she went home on flying feet.

Joe, in his dressing gown, was sitting in the blue easy chair, with the Real Estate section of the paper. His face looked worried, but it changed when he saw Betsy's face. He stood up, and she came over and slipped her arms underneath his so she could hug him tightly. She put her head down on his chest.

"Joe," she said, "I feel all right about Aunt Ruth. I mean—I think it's the right thing to do. I don't mind, any more."

"Oh, Betsy!" Joe said. He sounded as though he'd like to cry. They hugged each other until Betsy broke away.

"See here!" she said. "I don't smell coffee. What kind of a husband are you, anyway?" She shook him. "I'll make some. And you get dressed. And we'll go find us a house."

"If there's anything I don't like, it's a bossy woman," Joe said, and pulled her back into his arms.

After breakfast Betsy put on her green cardigan over the ruffled blouse and green plaid skirt Joe liked. Swinging hands, they started out.

Previously they had decided that the Bow Street neighborhood was too expensive for them. They had been searching farther out. All Joe's clippings from the paper today were for more distant places. But now, instead of taking the streetcar, they headed for the lakes.

"We're at home in this part of town. Let's give it a try," Joe said.

The hoarfrost was gone. Sunshine gleamed on lawns and sidewalks. They crossed Hennepin Avenue at a small business district and were walking toward Lake of the Isles when Betsy stopped. She waved toward a short street that cut off a pie-shaped section of more important avenues.

"I think that Canoe Place is cute," she said, "because it's only a block long."

Then she squealed, and Joe said, "Well, for crying out loud!" For on a lawn halfway down Canoe Place was a For Sale sign. They started to run.

The brown-and-yellow cottage was set on a very small lot. It didn't have a barn or a garage. At the back rose the back of a tall apartment building, but there were only houses on Canoe Place itself. There were maple trees along it, and the cottage had a neat lawn, cut in two by a walk leading to the porch.

The porch was big; it was screened. "We could eat out there," Betsy said, "all summer long."

The porch door was locked and the house was plainly empty. They walked around to the left side and saw lofty leaded windows.

"They'll be over a built-in buffet. That must be the dining room. The kitchen's behind, probably," Betsy decided.

On the right side were two large windows and one small leaded one. They peeked in on what was certainly a living room. The leaded window rose above a turn of the stairs.

They squinted at the upstairs windows.

"Must be three bedrooms," Joe said.

They walked around in back and Betsy clutched Joe's arm. "Darling! An apple tree!"

The apples were red, and there was a birdhouse in the branches.

The For Sale sign directed Joe and Betsy to a Mr. Munson on nearby Hennepin Avenue. They rushed off to find him.

Mr. Munson reminded them both of Mr. Ray.

"Yes, young folks, that's a good little house."

"What does it sell for?" Joe asked.

"Four thousand, five hundred."

"We could stand good monthly payments," Joe said. "And we're responsible people. I'm on the *Courier*. But we can't pay much down."

"Just three hundred dollars," Betsy put in.

Mr. Munson tapped his teeth thoughtfully with a pencil. "I don't believe," he said, "that the size of the down payment matters much in this case. The owners are old people; well fixed; going to California. I think it could be arranged."

Joe looked at Betsy, blue eyes snapping. Her hazel eyes were snapping too, and color was dancing in her cheeks.

"Did you bring the check book, honey?"

"Yes, dear." She drew it out of her bag.

"Whoa!" said Mr. Munson. "I can't show you that house today. I can't get a key until tomorrow."

"We looked in the windows," Betsy explained politely.

"They might as well have our three hundred dollars, sir," said Joe, taking out his pen.

"I won't cash that check," said Mr. Munson, "until you can look through the house. Of course, it's all right. It really is. A good hot water furnace. Hardwood floors."

He stopped for they weren't listening.

Joe was proudly waving the check to dry it, and Betsy looked off with dreamy eyes. She was thinking about the apple tree, and the apples. And the birdhouse, too, of course.

13
Night Life for the Willards

"NEXT SPRING," SAID Mr. Ray, "I'll make a cutting of that vine I brought from Deep Valley. I'll plant it beside your front porch."

He surveyed the new Willard home with a smiling satisfaction which was shared by all the Rays.

The Crowd inspected 7 Canoe Place with eager interest; Joe and Betsy were the first ones to buy a house. Everyone went upstairs and down through the shiny, empty rooms and even into the basement—all but Tib, who lingered in the kitchen.

"You could really cook here, Betsy," she said. "I'll come sometime and roast you a duck with apple dressing."

Anna, too, when she came to help Betsy paper the shelves, smiled on the big, sunny room. "This is a good kitchen to have a cup of coffee in, lovey," she said. And coffee they had often through September, sitting happily on packing boxes, for Joe and Betsy moved by degrees from the apartment to the new house.

They came over every day with linen for the linen closet, or clothes for the clothes closets, or just to walk proudly around their new domain.

"This," Betsy said, standing in the smallest bedroom, "will be the study—until we need it for a nursery, that is. We'll hang the Harvard etchings here."

"And the long-legged bird," said Joe.

"No, I'm going to write in our bedroom, beside the window that looks down on our apple tree."

He nodded, munching one of the apples. "Wonderful flavor!" he remarked in an aside.

It was delightful, planning the rooms, but troubling, too. For the apartment furniture would make only a spatter in this mansion. And there were so many,

many windows! White, ruffled curtains all over the house would be both charming and inexpensive, but rugs were a more serious matter. Betsy and her mother scoured the secondhand stores, ending triumphantly with two ancient orientals. In living room and dining room, their faded colors glowed.

The blue rug from the apartment would go into their bedroom, Joe and Betsy planned. And their white bedroom furniture would look very well there. But what would they put in the third bedroom, equally large, assigned to Aunt Ruth? Their savings were sinking like water in a sand hole. They had bought a dining room set on monthly payments.

"And there mustn't be any more of *that*!" Betsy said.

The problem was still unsolved when their wedding anniversary came around.

Joe brought home a box of red roses and Betsy put one radiantly into her hair, but after dinner they went over to Canoe Place to settle their books in the built-in bookcases. They were busy with this blissful task when they heard a motor car. It was the Hawthornes.

"We just stopped by to tell you we remembered," Mrs. Hawthorne said, in a mirthfully affectionate tone. "It's paper, isn't it, for the first anniversary?" She extended Donn Byrne's *Messer Marco Polo*.

"Oh, thank you!" cried Betsy. "I haven't read it."

"I have. And I'm certainly glad to own it."

"Well, where shall we put it?" Brad Hawthorne dropped down beside the pile of books. He and Joe began to browse, and Betsy showed Mrs. Hawthorne over the house. In Aunt Ruth's room she explained:

"We're still shopping for this one. We do want it to please her, but we can't spend much. Joe and I just won't go into debt."

Mrs. Hawthorne looked around. "Does Aunt Ruth like old-fashioned things?"

"Oh, yes! She's very old-fashioned."

"Then we have just the set! It's been gathering dust in our attic for years. Come on! We'll go look at it."

And, running downstairs, she and Betsy pulled the men into the motor car. At the tall peaked house among the oaks, they ran up two flights of stairs, joined by Sally Day in yellow pajamas.

The lofty headboard of the old black walnut bed was covered with ornate carving, and so were the bureau, the chest, and the washstand, which had a marble top.

"Of course, we'll pay you for it," Joe said.

"Nonsense!" Mrs. Hawthorne answered. "We've no use for it. I've just had a sentiment about giving it away. But you two seem like our own children."

"Do me a favor! Take it!" her husband hissed.

"If you take it," Sally Day chimed, "I'll have more

room for the circus I'm giving up here. I'm going to do tricks. Want to see some?"

"It's all decided, and now we'll celebrate with waffles." Mrs. Hawthorne led the way to the kitchen.

She stirred up batter—Joe advised the addition of a sprinkle of nutmeg. He made coffee while Mr. Hawthorne read aloud from *Penrod*, and Betsy set the dining room table with green glass dishes trimmed in silver. Sally Day was sent to bed and came bouncing back, was sent to bed again and again came bouncing back, and at last was allowed one waffle—butter and syrup unlimited!

On the day the movers brought the furniture from the Willard apartment they went to the Hawthornes' and picked up the old bedroom set.

It was thrilling to see the furniture put into place in the new house. Numerous bare spots remained, but Joe and Betsy filled them mentally with things which would come later—a piano here, a phonograph there, a couch . . ! The porch was still empty but it would be ridiculous, Betsy said, to furnish an open porch in the fall. Next spring they would buy a swing, and wicker chairs and tables.

Joe, who had taken the day off, rushed about with a tack hammer. Betsy rushed about with Goethe's cup, Joe's mother's vase, the angel from Oberammergau, and other treasures she was afraid to put down.

Coal was delivered. It rattled into the basement bin and Joe ran down to watch while Betsy listened, smiling, to the cozy sound!

She was sweeping colored maple leaves off their front walk, when Joe came out briskly.

"I started a fire. We don't really need it. But I thought I'd better get acquainted with that furnace."

"It's a fine idea," Betsy said.

Eating baked beans and pumpkin pie that Anna had sent for their supper, they listened proudly to the sizzle of heat in their radiators. And before going to bed they went out on the porch and looked up at a misty moon.

"Joe!" said Betsy. "Isn't it wonderful to have our own house?"

"Now that we've taken the plunge," he confided, "I'm scared."

"Now that we've taken the plunge, we'll swim."

"It may be hard swimming. Gol darn newspaper salaries!"

"You wouldn't be anything but a newspaper man. And I wouldn't have you be, until you can be an author."

"I could use a raise," Joe said dourly.

The next night when he came home for the first time to 7 Canoe Place, to candles on the dining room table and Betsy in a hastily-tied-on frothy apron, he was grinning, but the grin was dour.

"Well, the Lord and Brad Hawthorne helped us out! I have a raise."

"Joe Willard!" Betsy hugged and shook him. "What's the matter? Why aren't you pleased?"

"I am pleased. But it's night work. Six to two."

"Why, we won't mind that! I'll keep the same hours you do. It will be sort of interesting, working and living at night. Sit down and tell me about it."

Joe sat down, frowning. "What I don't like, really, is that I won't be writing."

"You won't be writing!"

"I'll be on the copy desk. I worked there while I was going to the U, you remember. I'm good at editing copy, writing heads."

"But you're good at writing stories, too. You're wonderful! It isn't worth the extra money," Betsy cried indignantly.

"We can use ten dollars more a week. It will settle all our worries." He reached out for her hand. "Don't think I'm blue. This raise makes me think somehow that we're doing the right thing."

Betsy didn't answer. It was strange, she thought, how things worked out. Something was given to you but something was taken away. An apple tree for an elm tree. A raise, but you lost the chance to do what you really wanted to do. Joe was a *writer*.

He was stroking her hand. "Maybe," he said, "this new setup will give me more time for fiction."

Betsy looked up. Her hazel eyes, which had been close to tears, grew luminous.

"Of course!" she said. "Of course! I was just trying to think it through. Good things come, but they're never perfect; are they? You have to twist them into something perfect."

Joe laughed. "You have to wrestle with them," he said. "Like Jacob with the angel." Joe hadn't gone to church very much but he knew the Bible better than Betsy did.

"What about Jacob and the angel?"

"Why, Jacob took a grip on him and said, 'I will not let thee go, except thou bless me.'"

"Well, we won't let this job go until it blesses you!" Betsy cried. "And I don't mean any old ten dollars a week. You can sleep until noon and then go into that little study and shut the door and pound your type-writer . . ." She stopped, sniffed, and shrieked.

"My pork chops! Burning on!"

She dashed for the kitchen and Joe followed, chortling. "Well, at least it isn't a meat pie!"

He was to begin his new work Sunday, and that afternoon Aunt Ruth arrived. She was welcomed according to Ray tradition—Willard tradition now—with a shining house, a gala dinner.

Following Tacy's example, Betsy had long since learned a company dinner. Scalloped potatoes cooked with ham, canned peas, a moulded salad, muffins, and a lemon meringue pie. Everything but the muffins could be prepared ahead of time. She baked them after the return from the depot while Aunt Ruth rested.

Aunt Ruth seemed tired when Joe put her bulging bags down in her bedroom. She pushed back wisps of hair and looked around, almost bewildered, at the big soft bed under a snowy comforter, the old bureau with its bouquet of petunias, the washstand turned into a bedside table for magazines and a shaded lamp.

But she came down to dinner wearing a black silk dress with a handmade lace collar, her grayish hair smoothly brushed. She looked nice.

"The minute I touched that bed, I went to sleep," she said. She was carrying presents for Joe and Betsy; a jar of watermelon pickles, pillow cases with crocheted lace edges, a big silver coffee pot.

"Alvin gave me that for our silver wedding, and I want you children to have it," she said, smiling at their pleasure.

She didn't eat much, but her eyes were bright as she looked around the pretty table.

Joe left for work—it was twilight and other husbands were coming home. Aunt Ruth went to bed early. The house seemed strange that night. But Betsy knew that she and Joe would adjust more easily to a third member in the household because their routine had changed so drastically.

As soon as Aunt Ruth seemed at home, Betsy began to keep Joe's hours. They all shared an early dinner, and after the dishes were washed, Aunt Ruth crocheted. Betsy brought out her mending basket, but Aunt Ruth took possession of it.

"I'm used to mending," she said.

Crocheting or mending, she wore a shawl, for no matter how warm the house was kept, Aunt Ruth was always cold. And through the long evenings, she talked and Betsy listened.

Betsy had loved her grandmother's stories and she loved Aunt Ruth's now. Stories about Joe's father, about his beautiful mother, even about Joe when he was a baby. Stories about Uncle Alvin's wooing, about the death—stillborn—of their only child, about the elopement of Aunt Ruth's sister.

There's a plot in every one, Betsy thought, and started taking notes.

Fires, blizzards, grasshopper plagues went into that notebook. Aunt Ruth loved disasters. But she was far from gloomy even though her usual expression was sad. She laughed and laughed when she told of barn raisings and bobsled parties. She laughed until she cried over Betsy's meat pie.

Always, after the stories, they made tea. Astonishingly Aunt Ruth preferred tea to coffee. They took this snack in the kitchen where sometimes bread was baking.

Copying country-bred Mr. Ray, who always "put down" staple foods for the winter, Joe and Betsy had stored in their basement a barrel of apples, and baskets of potatoes, turnips, and onions. But it was Aunt Ruth's idea to lay in a big sack of flour.

"In Butternut Center they used to say, 'Uneeda loaf of Ruth Willard's bread,'" she told them roguishly.

Betsy watched with interest the kneading down and rising up of the dough. It was cut and shaped into loaves which were greased and put in the oven. While they baked, the kitchen filled with a mouth-watering smell. The golden brown loaves were put on a clean cloth and buttered.

"I remember Tacy's mother doing that," Betsy said. "When the bread cooled, she'd give me a piece."

So did Aunt Ruth, a thick one, with butter and honey.

After Aunt Ruth went to bed, Betsy changed to a house dress and put her hair in curlers. She got out the dust mop and carpet sweeper. And when all was neat, she sat down at her desk. The apple tree was lost in shadows, but she saw the lighted windows of the tall apartment building behind the cottage. She watched the windows darken, one by one. A single one, like her own, stayed bright all night. How friendly!

Betsy's forefingers pounced on the typewriter keys.

Before Joe came home she powdered and perfumed and did her hair. She made cocoa and sandwiches and set a table for two. Sometimes she put on a coat and went out to the porch to watch for him. The stars were sharp and bright above a sleeping world.

Joe would come in, stamping his feet, his face cold when he kissed her. As he ate he told her what good heads he had written, news of the Great War. And Betsy passed along Aunt Ruth's tales. Sometimes one of these had provided a plot for the story she was writing. Sometimes one of them flashed into a plot for Joe. They sat and talked while the darkness outside paled. Often the sky was on fire before they went to bed.

After a noon breakfast (luncheon for Aunt Ruth), Joe shoveled snow or he and Betsy put out bread for the birds. Then he did what Betsy had prophesied. He went into his study, shut the door, and wrote. Afterwards he had a few free hours but other men were working, so the Willards did not see much of the Crowd.

Carney and Sam were busy, for Judy had a baby brother. And Tacy was going to have a second child in the summer. She came to tell Betsy the news.

"It will be so nice for Kelly," she said.

Kelly could talk now. Not just his parents understood him; seventeen words were plain to anyone. He staggered around on plump legs.

"Luscious as he is," Betsy cried, snatching him, "the next one must be a girl!"

"I have that doll packed away, waiting," Tacy laughed.

Often Joe, Betsy, and Aunt Ruth strolled over to the Rays'. They read letters from Julia and Paige, dizzy with the brilliance of New York's musical season. They heard Margaret's news.

She and Louisa, juniors this year, were going out with two good-looking boys who were also inseparable friends. The four went out interchangeably. One time it would be Bill and Bogie, Bub and Boogie. Next time it would be Bill and Boogie, Bub and Bogie. Betsy found the situation most confusing.

"Don't any of them mind?" she asked her mother.

"Not that I can see."

"When I was their age, I got crushes."

"Margaret doesn't seem to have any preference. And neither does Louisa, and neither do the boys. It's beyond me," Mrs. Ray said.

Soon Joe and Betsy were hanging a holly wreath on their front door. They were tying the small Santa

Claus to mistletoe on their chandelier, and trimming a Christmas tree in that corner of the living room where after Christmas—this was Joe's secret—a phonograph would stand. Aunt Ruth was baking Christmas cookies of every shape and kind.

At the Ray Christmas, Aunt Ruth listened, tender-eyed, to the reading of the Bible story. She joined in the carol singing and attacked her bulging stocking with excited eagerness.

"I'd been dreading Christmas, but I was happy all day long," she told Betsy when they said good night.

Henry Ford had sent a Peace Ship to get the boys out of the trenches by Christmas. But he hadn't succeeded. And no Allied offensive had been able to break the German line. U-boats were still sinking neutral shipping. Americans grew less neutral all the time. Then some German plotting in the United States was exposed, and there was a rising suspicion of all German-Americans.

This was on Tib's mind when she came out to the Willards' late one Sunday afternoon. She had been skating with her brother Fred.

"We had such fun!" she exclaimed, shaking out of her wraps and pinning up her loosened hair. Tib was as expert on the ice as she was on the dance floor. "Fred and I could be exhibition skaters! Maybe we will be!" she boasted gaily. But at supper, with a sobering face, she brought up the German-American talk.

"I don't mind. You know I'm always philosophical. *Nicht wahr*, Betsy? But it's hard on my brothers, especially Hobbie."

Hobbie, born during the Spanish-American War, had been named for its naval hero, Hobson, but he was seldom called by that dignified moniker, being short and dimpled and full of mischief. He went to high school in Deep Valley where the Mullers lived.

"Hobbie says he's going up to Canada and enlist."

"Oh, I hope he won't do that!" cried Betsy.

"Well, Mamma's doing plenty of worrying! And so am I."

Next day Betsy telephoned Tacy.

"I know," she said, "our idea about Mr. Bagshaw was crazy. But Tib has this German-American business on her mind. And she doesn't give a snap for any of her beaus. Maybe we ought to try again."

Tacy chuckled. "Well, Harry and I did our best! Now it's up to you and Joe."

Betsy agreed. But she and Joe had little time for scouting. He had only one free evening weekly, and oftenest they gave it to a newspaper group that met at the Jimmy Cliffs' . . . to talk writing, read aloud, argue, and drink coffee while Jimmy Junior dashed up and down on his kiddy car.

In Minneapolis there was a sedate and ladylike group called the Violet Study Club. One night when the Willards and their friends were gathered at the Cliffs, and the kiddy car collided with hot coffee and an even hotter argument about Sherwood Anderson's work, the girl columnist "Q" remarked, "We ought to call this the *Violent* Study Club."

The name stuck.

If I find a husband for Tib, Betsy thought, it will be at the Violent Study Club.

14
At the Violent Study Club

"FIRST MEMBER TO GET BOTH hands up reads first!" boomed President Jimmy Cliff.

Up and down the firelit living room, books, note-books, and pencils clattered to the floor as members hastened to obey the unexpected order for two hands. One plump, dimpled pair rose with suspicious ease and the President nodded at the plump, dimpled owner.

"You win, Patty. No doubt because I warned you. However, this club is all for cheating, so you may read. And how nice that you have brought one of my favorite books!"

Tib's bewildered voice came through the hubbub of protest. "But I never saw a club run like this! Don't you have any rules of order?"

"Miss Muller," answered the President, "this club is very anti rules of order."

"That two-hands stuff, though, was really underhand!" Joe's pun brought jeers and groans.

"Mr. Willard! Do you deny your President the gratification of a momentary whim? Or to be plainer, do you want your fair share of the Cliff coffee and doughnuts? Read, Patty!"

But before she could begin, Jimmy Junior roared out on his kiddy car, yelling, "Pop! Bang! Pop!" His tall, slender mother rushed to carry him off to bed. His large, stout father, wedged into an oversized armchair, shook with laughter.

The Violent Study Club, which met whenever the spirit moved its members, was in session.

Tib was laughing now. "Why, I love this club!" she cried. "It's wonderful! It reminds me of that Okto Delta we had in high school. Doesn't it you, Betsy?"

Tib, Betsy thought admiringly, fitted into any group. She was never ill at ease, and so good-natured—

falling in with other people's ways, laughing at their jokes, looking out for chances to be useful! She jumped up now to put away the kiddy car, but hurried back to her sofa, not to miss a word of the hilarious proceedings.

A black velvet dress swathed her from neck to ankles. She meant it, probably, to make her look like a vamp—a word brought into the language by the moving picture actress, Theda Bara. Tib's flowerlike face, flushed with fun, was not at all like Bara's, but she looked pretty enough to fascinate anyone.

Who was there, tonight, to fascinate? From her chair beside the fire, Betsy appraised the room. MacTavish, the bony Scot, whom everyone looked up to because he sold verse to magazines of quality (although for very little money), did not seem Tib's type. The pleasant, serious reporter was a bachelor, long confirmed. The magazine editor was very good-looking, but he had come with "Q."

Betsy had been surprised, when she first met "Q," to find her young, with shining hair and very pretty legs—although she was always pulling down her skirts. Only vivid blue eyes gave a hint of her wit.

Sigrid, the vivacious, nut-brown girl reporter, waved a left hand on which a diamond shone.

"If Jimmy likes Patty's book, we all smell Dickens!"

she cried above the uproar.

Patty and Jimmy both loved Dickens; and Dickens would have loved them, Betsy thought. Jimmy's face, above his flowing Windsor tie, was one of the kindest she had ever seen. Patty was making futile dabs at her soft hair. It was forever falling down, and her very clean petticoats were forever peeping below her skirt, and her shoelaces were forever trailing. Patty did not care. She lived for books . . . and for friends, and collected both in large numbers.

"It's *Martin Chuzzlewit,*" she said in her breathless voice. "I'm trying to turn the book into a play and I want to ask you all whether this incident I've selected could be worked up for the second act."

Members of the Violent Study Club not only read aloud from books they liked; they used fellow members to test plot ideas, completed stories, and writing styles. The members took their responsibility as guinea pigs seriously, and the room became quiet at once.

"Please go on talking!" pleaded Patty. "I want to wait for Marbeth." Modest Marbeth Cliff was the most valued critic in the club.

"While we're waiting," said the President, "let's hear what the rest of you have brought."

Sigrid shouted, "Stephen Leacock! Funniest man alive!"

"A beautiful book called *The Song of the Lark*, by Willa Cather," said "Q."

"I know you all think Lowell is old-fashioned," Betsy said. "But I want to read, 'The snow had begun in the gloaming.' Because it *did* begin in the gloaming, and it's so lovely, and it's all over the trees and bushes, and goodness only knows how we're going to get home!"

"That's my wife!" said Joe. "I've brought Leonard Merrick's short stories. Grand technique!"

The magazine editor smiled meaningfully at the frail MacTavish. "We might hear a poem that one of our colleagues has just sold to my magazine. It's a war poem. A hum . . ." But the "dinger" was lost in a burst of unforced joy.

"The Naughty Chair! The Naughty Chair!" everyone cried at once . . . everyone except Tib who asked wildly, "*Was ist los?* Who's been naughty?"

No one answered. All the members were pulling the blushing MacTavish to his feet. They were pushing him toward a chair at one side of the fireplace—a tall, straight chair, carved of dark Indian mahogany with a yellow velvet seat.

Marbeth tried to explain. "We call it the Naughty Chair because Jimmy Junior has to sit there when he's naughty."

"But Jimmy Junior has gone to bed!"

"Yes, but when any member makes a sale he has to sit in the Naughty Chair."

"*Lieber Gott!* What's naughty about a sale?" Tib laughed until she almost choked. She swung her small feet off the floor to the sofa. "I'd better watch out. I'll be trampled to death in this *verruckt* club!"

MacTavish was pushed jubilantly into the place of honor. The President, beaming as though he had sold a poem himself, rapped noisily for order.

"You will all settle down—and sharpen your wits! I'm pleased that we have someone in the Naughty Chair tonight, for a most important visitor is coming—provided he's not stopped by Lowell's snowfall, or, more likely, ten beautiful girls."

"Jimmy!" Sigrid clapped. "Did you really get him?"

"I certainly did," President Cliff said proudly. "Rocky in person!"

Sigrid inspected her diamond. "Oh, if it weren't for this!" she murmured dreamily.

"He certainly is a charmer," smiled "Q."

"He's a genius," declared the serious man reporter.

"*Ja, ja!*" said Tib, in the soothing tone of one humoring infants. "Tell us about him, Mr. Cliff, please."

Jimmy settled back in his big chair.

"Rocky," he began, "is one of the last of a fast-vanishing breed, the tramp newspaperman. He never stays on any job long. But he's so good that every city editor welcomes him back. At twenty-seven he's been a star reporter in San Francisco, St. Louis, Kansas City, New Orleans, Minneapolis—some of you remember when he was here before."

Betsy looked inquiringly at Joe, but he shook his head. "While I was in the East," he said.

"He landed in town yesterday," Jimmy went on. "Brad put him on the payroll as soon as he walked in and the city room has been buzzing ever since. The men all stop work and listen when he talks; the girls all look when he walks by. He never went to college, but he's read everything. He came in yesterday with Ouspensky's *Tertium Organum* under his arm."

Tib threw up her hands. "Who's Ouspensky? What's Organum?"

"Joe's got a college degree," Jimmy said. "Ask him!"

"If I had a month free, I might try to answer." Joe grinned. But before he had time to make any attempt, firm, strong feet stamped themselves free of snow on the Cliff's front porch.

"Here he is, folks! The Great Rocky!" Jimmy said.

The young man whom Marbeth admitted was hatless. His hair was a tangled shock of rusty-brown curls and he combed them back with both hands, but they sprang up again with an electric vigor. He was only medium tall and would have seemed fat if he had not been so solidly muscled. His forehead was broad, his eyes were keen, and a firm chin was slashed by an enormous dimple. His lips were full, and the smile he turned on the roomful of young women and men was—yes, Betsy decided—sweet.

"Let's see!" said Jimmy. "You know all the newspaper folks . . . except Joe Willard."

Introductions began, and MacTavish rose from the Naughty Chair, but no one explained why he had been sitting there.

Rocky seemed to be casually measuring everyone in the room. He shook hands silently, smiling, and still smiling turned to the sofa, swung Tib's tiny feet to the floor, and settled himself alongside her, sitting cheerfully on his backbone.

"There aren't two smaller feet in the world," he drawled. "But they do take up a mite of room." And hauling out a worn bulldog pipe, he looked at Marbeth for permission.

Betsy looked at Tib, expecting the disdainful air, but Tib was regarding the newcomer with amused astonishment.

"Why do they call you just Rocky?" she asked. "Don't you have any other name?"

"I was Rocky in the cradle. I was Rocky when I took to my pipe at the age of four."

"*Four?*" cried Tib, round-eyed.

"The terrible Rocky is what folks usually say." He smiled at her, and after a moment Tib began to laugh. But the laughter gave way to an almost awed inspection.

Hooray! Betsy exulted inwardly. She and Tacy had failed with Mr. Bagshaw, but this looked very promising.

She turned to Joe, wanting to share her triumph. He, however, was looking at Rocky. And soon he and all the others were listening to Rocky, as well. They were listening willingly and with absorbed attention.

Patty did not read from *Martin Chuzzlewit.*

"No! No!" she whispered in an agony of shyness when Marbeth remembered to suggest it. Rocky discussed the Dickensian trace in G. K. Chesterton.

MacTavish's poem was mentioned, but it was not read. Rocky plunged into a discussion of the *Spoon River Anthology*. Willa Cather, strangely enough, sent him into a yarn about Jack London, whom he had known in San Francisco. He called the great London "Jack."

Rocky talked on and on, magnetically piloting the Violent Study Club into uncharted seas. Tib looked dazed when she jumped up at last to help Marbeth with coffee and doughnuts.

Talk became general, and someone referred to

President Wilson's Preparedness tour. Colonel Roosevelt had long been urging preparedness, and now the President had fallen into line.

Rocky drew on his pipe. "I don't know what's got into the Professor," he drawled. He called the President, "Professor." "But I know one thing. We're going to be in this war if he doesn't keep his head."

Tib put down the coffee pot from which she was refilling cups.

"Don't you mean," she asked, "that we're going to be in it if the Kaiser doesn't stop sinking our ships?"

Rocky looked as surprised as though a canary had pecked him.

"See here!" he said. "What kind of talk is that from a girl named Muller?"

Tib's eyes darkened. "It's American talk," she answered, and Rocky's sweet smile broke across his face. He put his hand for a moment on her black velvet arm.

"Spoken like a pint-sized patriot!" he said.

Betsy waited anxiously. Tib smiled.

The Violent Study Club had never run to such a late hour before.

"My public will say I'm slipping if I try to be bright on this little sleep," said "Q," putting on her wraps. Marbeth flashed on the pillar porch lights, and everyone was exchanging good nights when Rocky came up to Tib. He looked at her with brightly quizzical eyes.

"Where can I find you?" he asked, and this time Betsy held her breath.

"Why do you want to know?" asked Tib.

"I'm going to take you to lunch."

And to Betsy's joyful amazement Tib named the store where she worked in the art department. She told him she lunched between one and two. She sounded almost docile.

The Willards, Tib, and "Q" left in the magazine editor's car, after pushing a cushion of snow from its top. Betsy could not bring up the subject most on her mind, but as soon as she and Joe were inside 7 Canoe Place, she burst out:

"Isn't it glorious? Did you notice how taken Rocky was with Tib? And she really liked him! Even after that spat about preparedness, she said she'd have lunch."

"Um-hum," murmured Joe, hanging up his coat and hat.

"I think they're very well suited," Betsy said. "You know, Tib understands writers because of you and me."

"Um-hum," said Joe. He was halfway up the stairs.

Oh, dear! Betsy thought. Aren't men unsatisfactory! But it was too late to telephone Tacy, who would have shared her excitement. She followed Joe to their bedroom and kept on talking.

"I don't suppose he earns much, but you know Tib! Makes all her own clothes, and can get up a simply delicious meal out of nothing. Why, Tib was just meant to starve in a garret!"

Joe undressed and scrambled into bed. Betsy, in a pink cashmere robe, started to brush her hair. She brushed and brushed until it spread over her shoulders, dark and shining. Usually Joe liked to watch her do this but tonight he lay with his hands under his head, looking up at the ceiling.

Betsy began to worry. Maybe he wasn't just unsociable? Maybe he disapproved? She turned around, brush in hand.

"Darling," she said, "do you think I'm wrong? Don't you like this Rocky?"

Joe sat up in bed, and Betsy told herself that she must never allow him to wear any pajamas but blue ones.

"Look, Betsy!" he said. "Rocky's a good enough guy. But he lives in a different world from Tib's. He—has different ideas. He's—been around. I'm worried about Tib."

Betsy put down her brush, and sighed in relief.

"Is *that* all!" she said. "Well, you don't need to worry about Tib! Men eat out of Tib's hand. He'll be

following Tib around like a little puppy dog. Why—"
Betsy began to giggle. "Tib will be tying a pink ribbon into that bushy hair of his."

"That," said Joe, "I'd like to see!"
But he chuckled, and went to sleep.

15
Rocky

As soon as she woke up, Betsy telephoned Tacy.

"What shall we wear?" Tacy cried. "Yellow or blue?"

"Oh, the bride picks the bridesmaids' colors!"

"Well, it can't be pink, on account of my red hair!"

They were almost as jubilant when Betsy telephoned after the next meeting of the Violent Study

Club. Tib had come with Rocky. She had left with Rocky.

"He calls her Tiny Tib."

"How cute!"

"She isn't haughty with him," Betsy said, a little puzzled. "She doesn't order him around."

"Maybe a masterful man is just what she needs?"

"I think you're right," Betsy replied.

But her enthusiasm began to wane. The Violent Study Club wasn't so much fun with Rocky there.

He dominated the once carefree meetings—sitting on his backbone, puffing at his pipe, being brilliant in his drawling voice. He had an engaging playfulness, sometimes, but it couldn't be trusted.

When others spoke, he listened with what seemed to be flattering attention, but then he tore their arguments to humiliating tatters. He discussed the books they brought with such scornful irony that no one felt free any more to bring just whatever he was enjoying.

"Irvin S. Cobb's *Speaking of Operations* is simply rich. But you have to bring Dreiser or Shaw to the club now," Sigrid grumbled.

As for reading their own work—the members were soon reluctant to expose themselves to his attacks, so unlike the friendly, helpful criticisms of pre-Rocky meetings. He followed his scathing remarks with an apologetic smile, but this no longer seemed charming. One night there was an indignation meeting in the kitchen.

"I wouldn't bring a story to the club any more for a farm."

"What magazines has he sold to? What books has he written? He's older than any of us!"

"Jimmy says he's a genius. But Jimmy finds excuses for everyone."

"Don't worry! We always break up in the spring, and he'll be gone before fall." "Q"'s words were consoling to everyone but Betsy. She was disturbed about Tib, who had sat looking at Rocky with an awe close to reverence.

Betsy understood. Tib's great capacity for admiration, in which she and Tacy had often sunned themselves, was called into full glow by Rocky's magnetism.

Betsy was as worried now as Joe, and Tacy started worrying harder than either of them.

"What do they have in common?" she asked anxiously. "Are they congenial? Do they like to do the same things?"

"I'll try to find out," Betsy said.

She made a date for lunch with Tib on a cold bright day and remarked casually over the restaurant table:

"Fine skating weather! You and Rocky doing a lot of skating?"

Tib laughed fondly. "Rocky's too fat for skating."

"Do you go dancing then?"

"Rocky thinks dancing is effete." Tib laughed again. "I asked him, as a favor, to come to the Radisson and watch Fred and me do a tango."

"Your tango is a poem."

"Rocky said he couldn't help believing that the human mind—any human mind—deserved a better problem than figuring how many steps to take and when to sway and glide."

Tib seemed to think this showed a superior intelligence and Betsy smothered her indignation.

"He doesn't like the theatre, either," Tib volunteered. "He thinks it's silly for people to memorize somebody else's words and stand up in front of other people and spout them."

"What *does* he like to do?" Betsy asked.

After profound thought Tib said, "He likes to talk. And eat. We go a lot to that new restaurant—you know, where a chef in a white cap makes pancakes in the window? Rocky talks, and eats stacks of pancakes.

"That reminds me!" Tib added. "He likes *Sauerbraten* and you can't get it fit to eat anywhere, outside of a home. May I come out to your house some Sunday and fix *Sauerbraten* and ask him to dinner?"

"Of course, dear," said Betsy. "We'll ask the Kerrs and make it a party." She tried to sound enthusiastic but she was so perturbed that she went straight from the restaurant to the streetcar and out to see Tacy.

"She's feeling domestic about him!" Betsy groaned.

Tacy agreed that this was very bad. "But at least," she said, "the dinner will give us a chance to meet him. Harry is worried, too."

"He and Joe aren't joking us this time about being Little Aids to Cupid."

Tacy made coffee, and they cheered themselves with Kelly, who was shouting on the sun porch over a toy duck that was losing its stuffing.

"Won't it be nice," Tacy said, "for him to have a baby brother? Sister, I mean."

"I forgive you. What new words has he learned?"

"He learns some every day. And Betsy, he can understand even when we *spell*. Harry says, 'It's time for Kelly to go to b-e-d.' And Kelly shouts, 'Don' wanna b-e-d.'"

"That's the smartest thing I ever heard," Betsy said.

"Harry always makes a game of putting him to bed. After Kelly's undressed, Harry carries him around to look out the windows. He's made up a rhyme."

Tacy chanted:

"We go around and turn out the light
And we go to the windows and say good night
To the moon and the stars that shine so bright
And we go to bed, and everything's right."

Kelly threw down his duck. He looked up at his mother with deep blue eyes, like hers.

"B-e-d!" he spelled. And Betsy and Tacy whooped with delight.

Betsy was pleased to have the joke to tell Joe. He was feeling a little blue these days. He didn't like it that his stories were still selling only to the same small magazines. He and Betsy tried each new story on the big magazines, especially on *The Thursday Magazine,* the biggest one of all. *The Thursday Magazine,* however, kept sending them back.

And the war news was grim. In France, big guns were thundering again. But the Germans, not the British, had launched the great offensive at Verdun.

And spring was slow in coming.

At first the snow which melted in the daytime froze at night. But at last water babbled in the gutters all night long. Watching for Joe, Betsy walked along

Canoe Place to the corner. She waited among the sleeping houses, the dark apartment buildings.

"'Behold the height of the stars, how high they are!'" she whispered sometimes, staring upward.

At last the glittering streetcar rattled into view, and Joe came swinging toward her.

If they talked long over their cocoa, they were interrupted by bird voices. While the world was still dark, there would be a drowsy chirp or two, then a small burst of song, then another, and finally a jumbled chorus. Joe and Betsy would go out on the porch. Blackness had now paled into gray, and the stars had faded—except for a big bright one in the faintly flushing East.

"Venus!" Joe would say. "In the spring, the morning star is Venus."

"It's the first time I ever watched spring come at night," Betsy observed.

Daytime spring was a more familiar joy, and yet there was a new ecstatic excitement in watching leaves bud on their own lilacs, in poking around their own walls among matted leaves to see what was coming up.

"Iris and lilies of the valley," Aunt Ruth told them, examining the first green spears.

It was hard for Joe to get in any writing, but he almost always did, and when that was behind him . . . what raking and burning! What painting and digging!

Mr. Ray planted the cutting of that vine from Deep Valley. He and Joe planted hydrangea and bridal wreath bushes around the big porch.

Joe and Betsy bought their porch furniture. (He was head of the night copy desk now and had had another raise.) Just as planned, they bought a swing, wicker chairs and tables, and rattan curtains for when it rained. They started eating out.

"It's divine! We smell lilacs while we eat. Why don't you run over from school for lunch sometimes?" Betsy asked Margaret and Louisa, when they dropped in.

Louisa's eyes grew wide. "Oh, we couldn't, Betsy! He'd collapse! He'd die! He just lives for the noon hour."

Betsy thought, A clue at last! For Margaret and Louisa still alternated between Bill and Bub with mysterious unconcern. Betsy asked casually, "Who'd collapse? Bill or Bub?"

"Why, neither of *them*!" exclaimed Louisa. "I mean that Long-legs who works in the cafeteria."

Betsy was bewildered. She remembered vaguely hearing of such a boy, but a very long time ago.

Margaret interrupted with a sparkle in her long-lashed eyes. "Boogie! Don't be silly! I wouldn't even know his name if he didn't play basketball or something."

"Basketball or something! Betsy, he's a star! At everything long-legged. Basketball, track, tennis! You should see him at tennis. He jumps like a grasshopper when Bogie's at the matches."

"Even if she's with Bill or Bub?"

"All the higher then."

Margaret's slim foot put the swing into motion. She changed the subject with her Persian Princess air.

"You know, Betsy, that Julia and Paige are coming for their vacation. Well, what do you think Papa's going to do to celebrate? He's going to buy a car!"

"A car!" This news was so sensational that Margaret and Louisa had gone before Betsy remembered the long-legged tennis star.

Was *he* the reason Margaret had no choice between Bill and Bub? Margaret always kept her own counsel.

"And I didn't even get his name!" Betsy mourned.

In front of the house the maple trees were hung with lacy tassels. In the small back yard the apple tree seemed to be spreading arms to display its rosy bloom.

"Remember Mr. Gaston?" Betsy asked Joe. "How he scolded me in high school English because I said apple blossoms were rosy? And you defended me."

"He was speaking to the future Mrs. Willard," Joe replied.

Sparrows settled in the birdhouse. This was intended for wrens, Aunt Ruth said, but sparrows were just as absorbing. The father perched on the roof, when he wasn't replacing the mother on four speckled eggs.

Sally Day came to see the spectacle. With a piece of Aunt Ruth's coffee cake, she sat on the kitchen steps announcing that she was going to sit there till the eggs hatched.

Brad Hawthorne dipped into a pocket for one of his little folded papers. "John Burroughs!" he said, and read aloud:

"As the bird feathers her nest with down plucked
from her own breast, so one's spirit must shed
itself upon its environment before it can brood
and be at all content."

He looked at them keenly through his glasses. "You kids don't realize that yet, but it's true," he said.

Like Mr. Ray, he always called Joe and Betsy "kids"; Mrs. Hawthorne said lovingly, "you children." But they were Brad and Eleanor now to the

Willards. Neither Joe nor Betsy was conscious of any difference in age between the Hawthornes and themselves—except when, as now, the Hawthornes shared their wisdom.

"Yes," Eleanor Hawthorne nodded. "You have to live in a house before it's home. Not just be happy in it, but work in it, suffer in it, build up memories."

"I'll remember Sally Day settling down with coffee cake to watch the sparrows hatch," said Joe.

"I'll remember Aunt Ruth telling me stories while the bread baked," Betsy said. She loved these nightly sessions, but in a few days she learned that they would end in the autumn.

She and Joe and Aunt Ruth were eating lunch-breakfast on the porch.

"I might as well tell you," Aunt Ruth said abruptly. "I've written my niece that I'll come to California in the fall."

"Why, Aunt Ruth!" Betsy cried.

"When did this happen, Auntie?"

"Oh," said Aunt Ruth, "we've been writing back and forth! Bertha says that together we can afford to buy a bungalow. And I can keep house while she teaches school. She's my own sister's daughter, and we've always gotten along. But I couldn't have gotten along with anyone better than I have with you and Betsy, Joe."

"You'd get along with anyone!" Betsy said.

"I have only one bone to pick," said Joe. "That homemade bread is making me fat."

Aunt Ruth wiped her eyes. "Well, I'm going to keep on making it till I leave. And I want to put up some things for you, Betsy. Strawberries, peaches, watermelon pickles, tomato preserves."

Betsy jumped up and kissed her. "We'll miss you, Aunt Ruth," she said, and knew she really meant it. "You've been so good to us!"

Aunt Ruth wiped her eyes again. "Well, I certainly did appreciate you two taking me in! I was so upset about Alvin—and selling the store. But you know I've always wanted to go to California. I do hate the cold. I even tried to make Alvin move out there."

"We'll just have to have a good time till you leave," said Joe.

"We'll go riding in Papa's automobile!" Betsy jumped up. "Joe! I forgot! It's been delivered. It's out in front of 909 right now."

The new car was a fine black Overland and Mr. Ray displayed it proudly.

"What will Paige and Julia think of this, hey? It's got all the newest wrinkles. Get in, Joe! Take us for a ride!"

"Don't you want to drive, Dad?"

"I don't know how. And to tell you the truth,"

admitted Mr. Ray, "I don't want to learn. But Jule's going to learn. Aren't you, Jule?" he asked his wife coaxingly.

"I'm starting lessons tomorrow," she replied.

Joe took the wheel. Mr. and Mrs. Ray, Aunt Ruth, Margaret, and Betsy piled in and went whirling out into the country, past blooming orchards, brimming lakes, hillsides where wild plum was white.

"Oh, the picnics we'll have!" cried Mrs. Ray. And next day she did start driving lessons. But after two of them, she stopped.

"I got on better with Old Mag," she said. "Margaret's seventeen. Let Margaret drive."

So Margaret started lessons. But she didn't like driving, either.

"If you don't mind, Papa," she said politely but firmly, "I'm not going to do it."

Betsy wouldn't even try to learn. "I'm not the type," she shuddered. "I'd be making up a poem when I ought to be honking, or stopping, or something."

"I'm certainly glad you came into the family, Joe," chuckled Mr. Ray.

So with Joe at the wheel of an always overflowing car, they went riding almost every afternoon. There were snow drifts of bridal wreath now along Minneapolis streets. They called on Carney, and on Tacy, who always asked, "When is Tib going to cook that dinner?"

And at last Tib 'phoned to ask whether next Sunday would be a good day. She came out on Wednesday and put an enormous chunk of rump beef to soak in vinegar and water and bay leaf.

"It has to soak for four days," she said with delighted importance. "I'll be out early Sunday to set it stewing. I'm going to make potato dumplings, and we'll have new peas, and a little wilted lettuce."

"I could make an apple cake for dessert," said Aunt Ruth.

"*Wunderschön!* I'll serve it with whipped cream."

Betsy urged Tib to stay, but she couldn't. "I'm meeting Rocky for a movie. He doesn't like many movies, but he does like Charlie Chaplin."

"It doesn't matter to Rocky," grumbled Betsy later, "that *Tib* does like movies, and the theatre, too." But as Sunday approached she cleaned and polished, wanting the house to be a credit to Tib. She picked iris for the vases, and Aunt Ruth's apple cake looked luscious but she would not let Joe cut so much as a sliver.

Tib came out straight from church, wearing a taffeta suit of Copenhagen blue, a tilted hat made from the same material, and a snowy feather boa. She divested herself of boa, hat, and jacket briskly and tied on a scrap of apron. She was excited and happy, chattering to Aunt Ruth, and while the beef simmered in a covered iron pot, she began to grate potatoes for the dumplings.

Betsy's heart softened toward Rocky a little.

Maybe he *is* the one for her, she thought, setting the table with fastidious care. You can't choose a husband for another woman. Maybe she likes him bossy and selfish. She certainly likes to cook for him.

He walked in shortly, in the spruce golfing knickers he liked to wear—although he scorned golf. Running his hands through his unruly hair, smiling his charming smile, he shouted, "Where's Tiny Tib?" He sniffed and tasted and Tib's laughter trilled.

Betsy's heart softened more and more.

The Kerrs arrived and joined the rest in the kitchen. Tib fluttered efficiently about. The tiny apron was quite inadequate even for her tiny person, but Tib never spilled or spattered. She was as dainty at cooking as at dancing.

They all sat down to the shining table.

"Some groceries!" Rocky kept saying. And he'd blow a kiss. "Here's to you, Tiny Tib!" Tib smiled with delight, and Tacy gave Betsy reassuring glances. He was nicer, she signaled, than she had expected him to be.

They lingered over apple cake, heaped with whipped

cream, and second or third cups of coffee. Rocky was eloquent on a subject that was stirring the city. Mexican raiders under Villa had attacked a New Mexican town, and President Wilson had ordered Brigadier General John J. Pershing into old Mexico to catch the bandit. National Guard units had been called out—four regiments from Minnesota.

"It's almost the last straw for Hobbie," Tib said. "He's so wild to get into a uniform! I suppose it's being named for Hobson's-choice–Hobson that makes him so warlike." She repeated this family joke with her little tickled laugh, and the Kerrs and the Willards laughed too, but Rocky grimaced.

Rocky, Betsy remembered, was never very good humored when he wasn't doing the talking himself. Tib, too, seemed to remember and fell silent. But Tacy asked about Fred, and Tib brightened. He was graduating this month.

"With honors in architecture," she said proudly.

Rocky looked around as though appealing for sympathy. "I've heard of nothing but Brother Fred for a week now," he said. "Tib wants to drag me over to the Commencement exercises. As though no other male had ever got a sheepskin! Frankly, I'm a bit bored with the Muller family."

Betsy spoke quickly, resolved not to show her rising anger.

"The big news in the Ray family," she said brightly, "is the new automobile which no Ray will drive. Just Joe, who's only a Ray by marriage. Papa insisted on leaving it here tonight, on the chance we'd like a spin. Or we have some new records—'Nola.' 'Poor Butterfly.'"

"What would you like to do, Tib?" Joe asked, turning toward her with emphasized courtesy. Joe was angry, too.

Tib laughed a little nervously. She said what she almost always said in answer to such a question. "Oh, whatever the rest of you want to do!"

Rocky clapped his hands to the table.

"I wish, Tiny Tib," he said, "that just once you would express a preference. Do you really not like anything better than anything else? What shall we call her, folks? Miss Rubber Stamp? Miss Jelly Fish?"

Tib blushed to the roots of her yellow hair.

Betsy did not dare to speak. And neither Joe nor Harry—she could see by their furious faces—could be trusted either. She was thankful when Tacy took charge. The once shy Tacy had acquired poise since her marriage. Relief flooded into Tib's face as Tacy spoke with calm decisive graciousness.

"Let's drive around the lakes," she said. "I love to see the street lamps making exclamation points in the water. Tib, that *Sauerbraten* was perfect."

She smiled. But alone with Betsy, when they went upstairs for wraps, her eyes flashed.

"I wish this tramp newspaper man would tramp on to Timbuctoo and leave our precious little Tib alone."

"The trouble is," said Betsy slowly, "I don't believe she wants him to. Oh, Tacy!"

16
"Everything's Almost Right"

ONE HOT JULY DAY JOE did not write for just two hours as usual, but all afternoon. The study door did not open. The typewriter clacked on, and on, and on.

"We won't disturb him," Betsy said. "Not for anything." And she broke an engagement they had with the Rays. She and Aunt Ruth went softly around the house which was closed and darkened against the soaring heat.

"I wonder why he's writing so long," Aunt Ruth whispered.

"Oh," answered Betsy, "something just hit him!"

Pondering what it might be, she recalled a conversation early that morning. It had stayed hot all night and she and Joe had sat a long while on the porch where there was a little freshness. She had told him one of Aunt Ruth's stories of harvesting around Butternut Center.

"I remember that," Joe had said abruptly. "I was visiting there with Mother. It was before she died, and I was a very little boy. Someone let me take water to the men working in the fields."

"Maybe that set him off," Betsy thought.

She and Aunt Ruth were in the kitchen, preparing a cold supper, when they heard the study door open. Joe came downstairs looking fagged, and handed Betsy a sheaf of papers.

"Tell me what you think of this, will you?" he asked, and went outside, and began to water the lawn.

Betsy was making a salad, but she put it aside, washed her hands, and took the story up to her bedroom.

It *was* laid in the harvest fields. It was named, "Wheat."

When she finished reading it, she ran down to the yard. Joe dropped the hose and she threw her arms around him.

"I think it's perfectly wonderful!" she said.

"Any criticism?"

"No!" Her voice was puzzled. "It's rough. If it were my own, I'd polish it, probably."

"Then why shouldn't I?"

"Because it seems meant to be like that. It has a vigor, a power—you might polish that away. I think you'd better just copy it and send it off. Let me copy it for you."

"I wish you would," Joe said, "I don't want to look at it again."

That night after Aunt Ruth went to bed, Betsy typed the story in her best style, and the next day she and Joe mailed it to *The Thursday Magazine*.

Usually after they sent off a story, they discussed it endlessly. Would it sell? And for how much? And what would they do with the money? But about "Wheat" they did not say a word. It seemed to go off into a void. It was lost like a stone thrown in a lake.

Julia and Paige arrived, and the Willards were caught into a whirlwind. Julia always created an aura of excitement and gaiety. She was telling stories of the opera in New York, practising for a summer opera engagement near Chicago, trying out people's voices. She scolded Tacy lovingly for neglecting her music.

"The more babies, the better you should sing. Look at Schumann-Heink!"

Julia played for everyone to sing.

"There's a long long trail a-winding . . ."

"Sing it in parts!" she commanded, and Bill and Bub produced magnificent tenor and bass. Paige whipped out his flute and invented an obbligato.

He liked best to play his flute and go for automobile rides. Minnesota was so wonderful after New York, he kept exclaiming, although he and Julia loved New York; they wouldn't live anywhere else. Joe took them for countless rides. Wind rushed past their faces and they left the heat behind. There were thunder showers and ear-splitting crashes, and jagged arrows of lightning, and pouring rain.

"Sounds like the fourth movement of Beethoven's *Sixth Symphony*," Paige remarked.

After the rains, the leaves and roadways glistened. The birds sang and the wet lawns smelled of clover.

They took a picnic to Fort Snelling. Betsy loved the old army post—the round tower with its ancient musket slits, the commandant's house looking proudly down on the meeting of the waters. They went to Lake Harriet for band concerts and to Cedar Lake to swim.

Julia's skirts, Tib observed, came only to her shoe tops, and Tib turned up her own. She brought Rocky to meet Julia, who observed him closely for she knew all Betsy's qualms.

"He's wrong for Tib," Julia agreed. "I don't like it at all."

Julia wore her hair in deep soft waves—marcel waves, she said they were called. She took Betsy to a hairdresser for "a marcel." It was vastly becoming but the heat soon flattened it out.

"Never mind!" said Julia. "They're perfecting a machine that will put waves in *permanently*."

"Isn't science wonderful?" cried Betsy.

They talked war—and politics. The British had opened an offensive on the Somme. And in the United States a presidential contest was raging. It was Wilson against Hughes. Mr. Ray groaned at Wilson's campaign slogan, "He kept us out of war."

"He doesn't dare let them say, 'He'll *keep us* out of war.' He knows as well as Teddy does that war is coming."

"Papa! You must admit he's made the Germans restrict submarine warfare!" Julia had turned Democrat. Mr. Ray could hardly believe it. But the arguments were exhilarating, especially when Joe was around to bolster his father-in-law. Mr. Ray always hinted that Joe had inside information, straight from Colonel Teddy.

One Saturday afternoon Joe and Betsy stayed late at the Ray house, arguing.

"I won't have time to eat supper," Joe said, as they hurried home. "I'll just grab a sandwich."

Aunt Ruth was waiting on the porch.

"Any mail?" Joe called, as he always did.

"There's a letter for you," she answered, and he took the steps, two at a time.

The letter, lying on the old-fashioned table, was from *The Thursday Magazine*. "Wheat" was accepted. The editor hoped four hundred dollars would be satisfactory. He would like to see more of Mr. Willard's work.

Betsy flung herself into Joe's arms, crying and laughing. He was laughing, and almost crying, too. They caught Aunt Ruth into their hug.

"Oh, I'm so proud!" she cried.

"You helped!" Joe said. "Something you told Betsy about harvesting in Butternut Center started me off."

"Aren't you glad, Aunt Ruth," Betsy sang, "that we kept quiet while he was writing?"

"Oh, I'm so proud!" Aunt Ruth kept repeating.

"Won't I have something to tell my niece, and her friends in California!"

Betsy rushed to 'phone the Rays. Their wild joy reverberated over the wire.

"Promise me you'll tell Brad," Betsy said when Joe had to leave, "and I'll 'phone Eleanor."

"All right," said Joe. "But don't tell the whole town."

So Betsy only telephoned Mrs. Hawthorne, who was rapturous, and the Cliffs, who cried out that they would dust the Naughty Chair at once, and the Kerrs, whose cheers woke Kelly, and Tib. Betsy did not expect to find Tib at her boardinghouse on a Saturday evening, but for a wonder she was!

"I'm so tickled!" she cried. "I'm coming right over. Could you put me up tonight?"

"Could we! On that couch in Joe's study. Aunt Ruth and I are simply bursting to talk."

Tib came as fast as the trolley would bring her, and Betsy showed her the wonderful letter and the check. Aunt Ruth stirred up some cup cakes and they had a powwow over the evening tea. When Aunt Ruth went to bed, Betsy and Tib washed up the cups, chatting more quietly.

"Why aren't you with Rocky tonight?" Betsy asked.

"I wouldn't see him," Tib replied. She dropped her

head forlornly on Betsy's shoulder.

"*Liebchen,*" she said, "you're lucky to have a husband like Joe."

"I know it," Betsy answered soberly. "He really loves me."

"*Ja,* and he *respects* you. He confides in you, listens to your opinions, asks your advice. He thinks your work is important. He thinks you are important—as a human being, not just as a girl."

Betsy hugged her, wanting to cry.

"Rocky and I," Tib said, "could never be partners like that. He loves me but he's always so contemptuous. He thinks I'm silly and prudish. Maybe I am prudish, but that's the way I intend to stay." After a moment she said, "I ought to go away."

"Tib, darling," Betsy began, but she was interrupted by a pounding on the porch door.

"Anyone home? Betsy—it's Rocky. Is Tiny Tib here?"

"*Ja,* I'm here," called Tib, and they went out to the shadowy porch, and Tib sat down in a corner of the swing as Betsy opened the door.

Rocky was coatless, and his hair stood on end.

"Whew!" he said, pushing it back. He stood looking down at Tib. "You led me a chase, little one! No message at your boardinghouse. I've been kicking my heels for hours."

"I told you I was busy tonight."

"I can't get along without you. You've gotten to be a habit. You're my opium."

Betsy started to go inside but Tib said, "Wait, Betsy! Please!"

"At least," Rocky said, "I can walk you home."

"I'm staying here all night," Tib replied.

"Then how about walking down to the lake a few minutes?"

"I'm sorry, no. But would you like me to make you some coffee?"

"No, thanks," he answered, almost gently. He sat down and stared at the floor.

"How about tomorrow?" he asked at last.

"Call me," said Tib.

"Couldn't I pick you up at church?"

"Just call me," Tib replied.

He went over and took her small face between his hands. "See you tomorrow," he said, and hurried out.

Tib was quiet in her dim corner. Betsy locked the porch door.

I wish I could lock him out of Tib's life! she thought.

She did not speak, and neither did Tib. Fireflies flickered under the shadowy maples. Down the street a phonograph was playing.

Tib stood up. "I'm going to call home," she said.

"It's late, but Mamma won't mind."

They went inside and after Tib had given the Long Distance operator the number, she said in a shaky voice, "Mamma's worried about Hobbie. And Hobbie and I are good pals. I have quite a little influence with him. I think I'll be more useful there this summer than I would be in Minneapolis." She turned back to the phone. "Is that you, *liebes* Mamma?"

Betsy went out to the kitchen. She buried her head in her arms but she could hear Tib's voice. It sounded cheerful and natural. But when Betsy went back Tib was sitting in Joe's chair and tears were running down her cheeks. She didn't try to speak, but looked up at Betsy with a wordless appeal. Betsy hugged her closely and cried, too.

"Darling, if it's any comfort, I think you're doing the right thing."

"I know I am," Tib said in a small voice through her tears. "That's how I can do it."

She wiped her eyes, blew her nose, and spoke firmly. "I told Mamma I'd be down on the early train. So I won't stay here, after all. I'll go back now to my place and pack."

"I'll go with you," Betsy said. "I'll 'phone Joe to pick me up there."

"I'd like to have you."

"Well, you have me! You have both of us."

She had them, as a matter of fact, until her train left. Joe waited on the boardinghouse porch until she was packed. And then it was too near morning to go to bed. They went to the depot, and drank coffee, and Joe joked, and Betsy hung on to Tib's hand.

Rocky went down to Deep Valley, Joe reported, on Monday. But he came back the same day.

"He seemed dazed. He couldn't believe any girl would turn down the Great Rocky. He resigned, and is off to Chicago."

Tib's letters did not mention this visit. Fred, she wrote, was going into their father's office; they'd be architects together. Her boss wanted her back. He didn't want to lose her. Nice, *nicht wahr*? But she was going to stay home until the start of Hobbie's senior year—and the football season. He was sure to be the quarterback. And he'd be all right then.

Julia and Paige were gone, and Aunt Ruth had bought her ticket, when Joe telephoned one August night to tell Betsy that he had some news. He wouldn't say what it was, but as soon as he stepped off the streetcar, it came tumbling out.

"Brad is putting me back on the day side. To write. Features, mostly. He said I had what a feature writer needed—wit, a light style, an eye for the angles, and a gift for getting on with all sorts of people, from stage stars to truck drivers."

"Good!" exclaimed Betsy. "Every word true!"

"He said," Joe went on, "that he'd put me on the night side last fall for two reasons. First, he'd had a hunch I could use more money, and that was the only spot in which he could give it to me. But second, because a young man who showed promise ought to be shifted around.

"'But now,' he said, 'it's time for you to get back to writing. We can use a writer who sells to *The Thursday Magazine.*'"

"Joe! Joe! Joe!" Betsy cried, unable to express her prideful joy.

They sat on the porch swing, talking.

"Joe," said Betsy, "how beautifully this year has turned out! I was a little blue when you first went on night work, and Aunt Ruth was coming. But now—I almost hate to see her go."

"And I got the plot for 'Wheat' from her, in a way."

"And the night side gave us so much time for writing, and thinking, and talking. It certainly pays to wrestle with an angel."

"Let's get out the Bible and read the story of Jacob," Joe said.

"I'm going to do more than that," said Betsy with sudden vigor. "It's shabby the way I just go to church when I'm worried. I ought to go when I'm thankful and happy, too. I'm going to start going every Sunday."

"I've been thinking the same thing," said Joe.

Before that eventful August ended, Tacy's second boy was born. And after she returned from the hospital, Betsy went out to the Kerr apartment. She went in the early evening, for Joe was still working at night. Tacy was in bed, the baby beside her, a brown-haired, brown-eyed elf.

"I just can't be sorry he isn't a girl," Tacy said.

"Neither can I. He's so sweet! And it *is* nice for Kelly to have a baby brother."

Tacy laughed. "That's funny," she said. "Before he came Harry and I talked about him always just in relation to Kelly. But now he's come, he isn't just Kelly's brother. He's himself. And we adore him."

"No wonder!" Betsy said, touching the soft cheek.

Harry was getting Kelly ready for bed. Splashes and shouts of laughter emerged from the bathroom, and at last, Kelly—curly-haired, flaming-cheeked, in snowy fresh pajamas, upright in his father's arms. They made the round of the windows and came to the bedroom. Kelly yanked down the shade, trying to join in his father's chant.

> "We go around and turn out the light
> And we go to the window and say good night
> To the moon and the stars that shine so bright
> And we go to bed, and everything's right."

Harry held Kelly down to kiss his mother, and his brother, and Aunt Betsy.

"Everything's right!" When they were gone, Tacy put out a slim freckled hand, and took Betsy's, and squeezed it. "Everything *is* right; isn't it? Joe's story selling, the new job, and Harry and I with our new son. Of course it's not completely right," she added, "until things get right for little Tib."

"Everything's *almost* right," said Betsy.

Things couldn't be perfect, for herself or Tacy either, unless Tib was happy too.

17

Just Like Tib

TIB SEEMED ALMOST LIKE Tib that winter, although Betsy
and Tacy, who knew her so well, were aware that she
was unhappy. Toward men who thought all blondes
were frivolous she perfected a crushing disdain. With
people who expected all German-Americans to be un-
patriotic, she relied on the adage that actions speak
louder than words. Her small skillful fingers made

better bandages faster than any other ten in the Red Cross workroom. They were swift, too, on her drawing board, back at the store, and at making her own lovely fragile dresses. She had her accustomed good-natured cheerfulness.

She did not return to the Violent Study Club although that was its merry self again. Betsy knew it made Tib's heart ache to go to the places or do the things she associated with Rocky. She loved to go out to the Kerrs' and play with the babies, and she rejoiced wholeheartedly in the Willards' good fortune.

Joe had sold a second story to *The Thursday Magazine*. Betsy was able to save only a part of the magnificent checks. For their second wedding anniversary, he had bought her a wrist watch, and he insisted on buying her clothes—a blue, smartly belted coat and a furry blue felt hat. Bedecked with a chrysanthemum, she wore these to the Homecoming Football Game at the U. He bought her a swooping black velvet hat.

"It makes me look like a vamp," Betsy protested.

"Well, who vamped me?" Joe asked.

A coral silk dress trimmed with silver lace was fine for the nights they went with Sam and Carney to hear Dr. Oberhoffer conduct the Minneapolis Symphony Orchestra, and for plays at the Metropolitan. With

Joe working days again, they were able to entertain. Betsy had learned a second company dinner. Chicken fricasseed in cream, and a marshmallow pudding!

She tried it out on Margaret and Louisa, who were charmed to be dinner guests. Margaret was soft-voiced and formal but Louisa exploded into excitement.

"This food is scrumptious!" she declared. "Isn't it, Bogie? And I heard you say, Betsy, that you didn't know how to cook when you got married. I suppose that after you get married you just sort of know how, automatically. Is that it? You're married, and so you're keeping house and so naturally you know how to cook. Is that the way it is?" And Louisa opened wide, inquiring eyes.

"Well, sort of!" Betsy said. "What's new at school?"

"A new drinking fountain!" Louisa cried. "No germs anymore! I don't know how we survived with that old cup on a chain. Really, I don't! But I'm certainly glad I did survive, because it's so nice to be a senior." She stopped. "You know, don't you, about the Senior Sleigh Ride? Bogie, have you told them?"

"How could I?" answered Margaret. "We only voted for it today."

"That's just it!" said Louisa. "It didn't take that Clay Dawson two minutes to get over to Margaret. Of course, he's got awfully long legs. That's why he's so good at jumping. He jumped over to her, absolutely jumped, and asked her for the sleigh ride."

"He's the boy from the cafeteria?" Betsy asked.

"That's right."

"Going with him, Margaret?"

"Oh, yes!" Margaret lifted pointedly indifferent brows. "This pudding is delicious, Betsy. You ought to give the recipe to Anna."

"What," Joe could not resist inquiring, "are Bill and Bub going to do?"

"Both of them," replied Louisa, "are taking me! One on either side in the sleigh! Won't that be jolly? Oh, I hope we'll have lots of snow! Do you suppose we will, Joe?"

At Christmas time Anna fell ill of the grippe, and Betsy entertained the family. Joe stuffed the turkey and her mother brought the pies.

Christmas at 7 Canoe Place this year wasn't just a reflection of 909. The Ray traditions were all observed—stockings, joke presents, the readings, and the carols—but new Willard traditions were forming—the red Santa holding up mistletoe, window-candles to light the Christ Child on his way.

There was a doll under the Christmas tree. It was for Sally Day, who busily undressed it and draped it in a napkin to represent a fairy.

"I'm Queen of the Fairies, so naturally I have to have some fairies," she explained, rolling her eyes.

"I have an idea," Betsy said to Joe after everyone was gone, "that when Bettina comes, she'll be quite a bit like Sally Day."

"I think so, too," said Joe.

In one department, the Willards behaved parentally toward the senior Hawthornes, who always spent lavishly and then were rueful about their extravagances. On a mirthful New Year's Eve, budget-wise Joe and Betsy reckoned up what their prodigal elders should spend weekly, and what they might save.

"Why, we'll be millionaires!" Eleanor Hawthorne cried with mellow laughter.

"We can take a trip to Japan," Brad announced.

Joe and Betsy made personal resolutions. They were going to write and write and let nothing interfere. Betsy, in all her years of trying, had never made a sale comparable to Joe's sales to *The Thursday Magazine*. She didn't mind, but Joe did. He tried to put his finger on what was wrong.

"Your stories don't express you, Betsy. I think you need the meadowlike space of a novel. I'm going to make you start one in 1917."

But as February blew in, chill and bitter, 1917 began to reveal its own menacing purpose. The Germans resumed unrestricted submarine warfare, and President Wilson broke diplomatic relations with the Kaiser's government.

"It means war, Betsy," Joe said.

"Maybe not. Our troops are coming home from Mexico. That turned out all right."

She could not look war in the face, although she felt it staring at her. She treasured, more and more, the cozy, lamplit evenings at home.

"You were eating an apple and reading a book, the first time I saw you," she reminded Joe one night, when he put down Charnwood's *Abraham Lincoln* to go to the kitchen for an apple.

The porch creaked and the doorbell rang. Joe turned back to answer it. Stamping snow from their feet on the threshold, were Tib and a tall young man.

"We've been skating," said Tib, which was obvious from her dress. She had long since made herself a skating suit, trimmed with white fur at the neck and around the closely-fitted jacket and the flaring skirt. The little peaked cap had a knob of fur. She was slapping her cold cheeks, laughing, and there was a look about her, Betsy thought quickly, that had not been there since. . . .

The tall young man had wavy dark hair, and bright dark eyes.

"Betsy and Joe Willard, Jack Dunhill! He's just back from Mexico," said Tib, as they came in, "and feeling gay."

"I'm feeling gay," he admitted, "but it has nothing

to do with getting back from the Border. I just don't pick up a girl like this every day."

"It's a joke!" Tib explained. "He means he picked me up from the ice."

"That," said Joe, "I refuse to believe. Tib fall on the ice? Never!"

Tib and Jack Dunhill went off into gales of laughter.

"Well, she did tonight!" he said. "I was watching her perform, the conceited little monkey, and wondering who she was. Everyone was wondering and watching. I skated close, willing her to fall."

"And I fell!" trilled Tib. "And was I furious! Especially when he started picking me up, for he said he'd been watching me."

"And she said," Jack Dunhill put in, "'I am *not* the blonde you've been looking for.'"

"And he said . . ." Tib bubbled with laughter, "'How do you know you're not?'"

"The logical answer, wasn't it? And I suggested that we go somewhere for a cup of coffee and talk the whole thing over."

Tib sat down, pulling off the peaked cap. "And I said *Ja*, I'd go to have coffee, if he'd let me pick the place. And he said, of course he would. And so, here we are! He thought it was a restaurant until Joe opened the door." She laughed and laughed. "But we can have some coffee, can't we, Betsy, honey?"

"You certainly can," Betsy said. It was the first word either she or Joe had been able to get in since Joe's remark about Tib falling.

Joe took Jack Dunhill's leather jacket, and Tib ran upstairs. She came back with her curls pinned into place, and she and Betsy went to the kitchen.

Jack was an advertising man, Tib said as they made the coffee. "And you know, Betsy, I'm in advertising, in a way. I do art-advertising at the store. Jack wrote copy in a big advertising office. He went there right after he graduated from the U. And he gave up a good job when he left with the Guard for Mexico."

"It seems to me," said Betsy, "that you learned quite a lot about him, just walking up from the lake."

"Ach!" said Tib. "I walked him all around Robin Hood's barn, looking for that restaurant which didn't exist." And she and Betsy were still laughing when they wheeled a loaded tea wagon into the living room.

The men were briskly discussing the war.

"If we get into it," Jack was saying, "I'd like to be an aviator. Golly, how Pershing needed airplanes in Mexico! They could have sailed over those mountains where Villa was hiding, and we could have gotten somewhere. I've put in my application for aviation training."

"What's your rank in the Guard?"

"Lieutenant. I'm staying in for the time being."

"How do you like him?" Betsy asked Joe as soon as Tib and Jack were out of the door. "I like him," said Joe. "I like him a lot."

"I almost think it's the real thing."

"So do I."

"Do you? Oh, Joe, I'm so happy! I won't even tell Tacy. I'll just pray."

Tib 'phoned the third day. She was driving Jack's car. "It isn't a Rolls-Royce but it's a perfectly beautiful Ford."

The next time, they had gone dancing. "He loves to dance. He's as good as my brother Fred. He's a marvelous skater, too, and he's going to teach me to play golf. I'll be good at it, he says."

And the time after that: "I wish Jack would hang on to his money. He has two thousand dollars in the bank. What do you think of that? But it won't last long with roses for me all the time and big boxes of candy. I'm taking him down to Deep Valley over Sunday."

Betsy broke down and told Tacy then. "I didn't call sooner for fear of jinxing it."

"I wondered," Tacy cried, "why she hasn't been coming out to see the baby! Well, 'phone me the minute she gets back! I can't bear this suspense."

"Neither can I."

"My folks are crazy about him," Tib reported on Monday. "He loaded Mamma with flowers. He and my dad talked golf, golf, golf, and he told Fred and Hobbie about the army. Hobbie brought half the boys in Deep Valley to meet him." Her tone grew serious. "Betsy, when can I see you and Tacy? I'd like to see you together. Can you come down to lunch with me soon?"

"We can!" Betsy cried. "Tomorrow!"

Tacy called for Betsy in the Buick around noon.

"Now don't get your hopes up!" Betsy warned, climbing into the auto. It was April weather, although the calendar still said March. The air was balmy, snow and ice were melting, and children were sailing boats along the gutters.

"Fine romantic day, though," Tacy said. "We could almost have made it a picnic. I wonder why she wants us at the *Radisson*?"

"Don't wonder! Don't jinx it!"

"If you could know the trouble I had finding a woman to stay with the babies! But I'd have come if I'd had to bring them both."

Tib was waiting outside the swinging doors of the hotel.

"Come on in! Jack has reserved a table for us. He isn't rich like Mr. Bagshaw," she commented, "but he certainly knows how to do things."

He certainly did! The table bore three corsages of violets and roses.

"Tib, what *is* this?" Tacy asked, and Betsy's frown warned, Don't jinx it!

"I love a corsage!" she remarked in a careless tone.

As soon as they were seated, Tib stripped off her gloves. Brimming with smiles, she extended her hand to show a diamond.

"It's set in platinum," she said.

"Radisson or no Radisson!" Tacy cried and jumped up and kissed her. So did Betsy. Tib kissed and hugged them both.

"When did it happen?" Betsy asked.

"I guess it began when he picked me up off the ice. I never felt before the way I felt when I looked at him. He just—thrilled me. He still does."

"And when are you going to be married?" Tacy asked.

"That's what I want to talk with you about. Soon, because Jack thinks we're going to be in this war."

"That's what Harry thinks," said Tacy.

"Well, Harry probably won't have to go, on account of the children. But Jack will go. And I want him to, if he wants to. But of course we must be married first!"

"Of course!"

The waiter served their soup, but Tib did not touch it. She sat straight and spoke in a businesslike tone.

"I've been thinking," she said. "I don't want a hurried-up wedding. Both of you had that kind and mine ought to be different. I told Mamma so when we were talking it over. I told her I wanted a big beautiful wedding. She liked the idea.

"I want it to be in church, in our little St. John's Episcopal Church in Deep Valley. I want the church to be decorated with flowers, and I want everyone there, all the old Crowd.

"I want a white dress," Tib went on, shining faced. "I won't have a train. I'm too short. And do you know what else I want?" She looked up brightly.

"This is one reason I planned the big wedding. Did you ever stop to think that we'd never been bridesmaids for each other? It isn't right; we've been friends so many years. I'll have two or three more, of course. But I'm asking you two first. Will you be my bridesmaids?"

Would they! Betsy and Tacy braved the crowded dining room again to fall upon her with kisses. They pulled away to look at each other with laughing eyes. They said together:

"Isn't that just like Tib?"

"Why—why—what did I say?" cried Tib. "I just

asked you to be my bridesmaids! There's nothing wrong with that, is there?"

"No, darling!" cried Betsy. "There's nothing wrong at all. Everything is beautifully, wonderfully, magically all right!"

18
The Nest Is Feathered

"THE WORLD MUST BE made safe for Democracy," said President Woodrow Wilson on the second day of April, and he asked the Congress to declare war on Germany. It did so. On April sixth he announced that a state of war existed.

"Betsy," said Joe, "you know without my saying so that I'm going to get in—and soon."

"I do know, darling!" Out in the purple spring twilight a robin's song went up and down, up and down.

A few days later he said, "There's talk of opening a camp for training officers. Out at Fort Snelling. I'd like that, if I can make the grade."

"It would be wonderful. You wouldn't be going too far away for a while."

The Officers' Training Camp was soon officially announced. It would open early in May and would commission successful students after three months of study. Jokes came thick and fast about Ninety-day Wonders.

"What if West Point does take four years to make a lieutenant!" Betsy cried indignantly. "We haven't got four years."

"If only I'm accepted," Joe grinned, "they can call me anything." With hordes of other young men, he submitted a summary of his college and employment record and the three required letters of recommendation.

"Imagine!" Betsy cried to her mother. "He's been back less than three years but a Federal Court judge and a big banker wrote two of his recommendations." His managing editor had written the third.

"Even those good letters," Joe said, "may not be enough. The camp can take only twenty-five hundred men. Lots more than that are applying. Sons of millionaires! Fellows backed by United States senators! Football stars! The competition is something fierce."

"You'll be accepted," Betsy said.

It wouldn't do any good if he wasn't, she thought. He'd just enlist and be gone all the sooner.

Betsy did not feel very patriotic, although she tried to. Patriotism had burst out all over, faster than spring. Flags like tricolored trees rose above factories, offices, and homes. Flags like tiny flowers bloomed in buttonholes. Tib wore one when she left for Deep Valley to get ready for her wedding. Carney and Betsy wore them when they went down to Nicollet Avenue to watch the Loyalty Parade.

Sam had applied for Officers' Training, too.

"He's warning me," said Carney, "that if he gets out from under my thumb he's going to grow a mustache and *wax* it."

"Joe," said Betsy, "will probably grow a beard."

The parade rang with martial music, as sunshine glittered on horns and trumpets, tubas, clarinets, and the jubilant sliding trombones. Drums beat and a field artillery regiment was shouting:

> *"Over hill, over dale,*
> *As we hit the dusty trail,*
> *Oh, the caissons go rolling along. . . ."*

You heard "The Star Spangled Banner" at the movies, at the theater, wherever you went. Up and down Canoe Place phonographs were spinning out "Tipperary," "There's a Long, Long Trail," and "Keep the Home Fires Burning."

"I don't want you to keep the home fires burning here," Joe told Betsy. "I don't want you to be alone."

"I'll go back to 909," said Betsy. "The folks are urging me to."

"I'd want you to pay board."

"Yes, of course."

"Let's get this place rented then," he said.

"Furnished!" said Betsy firmly, and they put an advertisement into the *Courier*. The cottage was snapped up in no time. The renters had a little girl. She would like it, Betsy thought, that wrens were nesting in the birdhouse.

Betsy went briskly about the business of packing away dishes and silver and the most precious wedding gifts. She took down the box that held her wedding dress, and opened it, and put her face into the soft white silk. But tears came and she put the cover on again for she was sternly resolved not to cry. She added the box to the pile they would be taking to 909.

They made the last trip on a warm soft Sunday. Neighbors were uncovering flower beds, raking and burning, and birds were scouting through the budding trees. The shrubs had greened over. The bridal wreath Mr. Ray and Joe had planted would soon be in bloom. Betsy tried not to think about it.

If it takes something more than joy, and love, and happy memories to feather a nest, this one's feathered, she thought, but she acted busy and cheerful. She did not want to weaken her courage—or Joe's.

Not that there was much danger of weakening Joe's. Exhilaration was mixed with his sadness at renting the house and leaving Betsy, although he worried about her and she knew it. Shifting a dozen parcels, he found her arm and squeezed it as they walked away.

They settled themselves in Betsy's old blue and white bedroom, with their favorite books and other dear belongings—the long-legged bird, Joe's mother's vase, and the Goethe cup—in spite of the fact that it came from Germany and Joe would be fighting the Germans. The curtains had been freshly washed, and there was a big bouquet of daffodils. The whole house was flower-filled in welcome.

We're awfully lucky, Betsy reminded herself as they fell into the pleasant home routine. Joe was still working at the *Courier,* and watching for the post card which would tell him he had been accepted at the Officers' Training Camp.

Cocoanut cake, Mr. Ray complained, was coming out of his ears, and Anna switched to strawberry short-cake. Mrs. Ray mentioned the government's request for meatless and wheatless days.

"Meatless and *wheatless*, Anna," she emphasized.

Anna snorted. "Meatless, yes, if the President says so. But he's eating well in the White House. Joe, poor lovey, is going off to fight the Kaiser." (Single-handed, she implied.) "And Joe was always one for dessert." She whisked a batch of cookies into the oven.

Mrs. Ray was almost as indulgent. She was being careful, Betsy could see, not to express unnerving sympathy, but her every word and glance was tender. Mr. Ray, like Joe, was excited about the war. He thought the United States had done right in entering. But his eyes were anxious when he looked at Betsy.

Margaret was the easiest one to be with. Shyly delighted to have her sister at home, she came to Betsy's room or followed her about, sometimes with Louisa.

"Betsy," said Louisa breathlessly, "tell me something important! When Joe is through at Fort Snelling, and an officer, will soldiers salute him?"

"I suppose so."

"And will he salute back?"

"Why, yes!"

Louisa heaved an enormous sigh. "Then when Bill

and Bub are officers, *they'll* be saluted. I'll certainly feel proud."

"Are Bill and Bub going after commissions?" Betsy asked.

"They'll be training at the U next fall."

All the high school seniors who wanted to enlist were being given their diplomas, Margaret said, and one day she came home with a luminous face. Clay had enlisted! With all the Commencement glories right around the corner! He had come to school in his uniform, she said.

Next day he came to the Ray house, tall, gangling, and sheepish in olive drab. Margaret made lemonade for him. She brought out cookies. She walked with him proudly up and down the block and introduced him to the neighbors.

"How do you like Clay?" she asked Betsy.

"Oh, I like him!"

"I'm wearing his class pin," said Margaret. "Nothing serious. I'm just sort of taking care of it while he's over there fighting. He's going to send me a silk handkerchief from Paris, and some German shells and things."

One Friday morning when Margaret was in school, and Mrs. Ray had gone shopping and Betsy was alone in the house except for Anna who was making a rhubarb pie, the mail brought the post card Joe had been waiting for. He was to report at Fort Snelling the following Monday.

Betsy went straight to the telephone. He was excited, overjoyed, triumphant.

"I made it!" he cried. "By Gosh, I made it! I was more worried than I let you know, honey. Sam's in; he just called me. What day do I report, do you say?"

"Monday."

"Then I'll tell Brad and clear out my desk. Golly, I'm relieved!" He checked his enthusiasm. "You all right, dear?"

"Oh yes, sweetheart!"

"You know I'll be practically at home all summer."

"You bet I do. I'm going downtown right now and buy some pretty summer dresses, and a big floppy hat with flowers on it to wear when I come to the Fort."

"Planning to vamp me, eh?"

Betsy went slowly upstairs. She put on her suit and hat and threw a fur around her neck. She tucked the little flag into her buttonhole and went out of 909 where a bigger flag was waving in a sweet May morning. Mr. Ray had the biggest flag in the block.

Joe had said he would clear out his desk. He would come home tonight bringing his dictionary, and the tennis shoes and racquet he always kept in his locker for tennis with Sam after work. Sam would be doing the same sort of housecleaning.

Like Grandpa Warrington, Betsy thought, coming across the cornfield with his school books and the big bell sitting on top! *"And the minute Grandma saw it she began to cry."*

War! Betsy thought, holding back her own tears with all the force of her stubborn will. War! Women never invented it.

She did not buy any new dresses, nor the big floppy hat, but went straight to the Marsh Arcade, and up the stairs to the second floor and the Hawthorne Publicity Bureau.

This was the happy office of which Joe had told her so often. One of the girls whose romances Mrs. Hawthorne had watched with such interest sat behind a desk. Mrs. Hawthorne's reddish-brown head was bent over another typewriter. At the sound of the opening door, she looked up with her queenly air but, seeing Betsy, she rose quickly, affectionate concern flowing into her face.

"Joe's card has come. He goes to the Fort Monday."

"That's hard."

Betsy nodded.

Mrs. Hawthorne kissed her, but she turned quickly and brightly. "I want you to meet my secretary, Celia. She knows Joe."

The small merry-faced girl smiled without speaking.

Betsy smiled and sat down.

"Eleanor, I came for advice. I want to work while Joe's gone, but I want to do something that's helping in the war."

Mrs. Hawthorne's low laugh rang in welcome. "Just hang up your hat!"

"You mean . . . ?"

"We're up to our ears in war work; aren't we, Celia? Half our clients are launching campaigns. Recreational centers at army camps, for example. There's a big project for such a social center at Fort Snelling. How would you like to be sent out there for some assignments during the summer?"

"Oh, Eleanor!" Betsy winked away tears. Mrs. Hawthorne ignored them.

"When do you want to start?"

"Next Monday. The same day Joe does."

"Be here early! We need you desperately. And about salary?"

"Can we talk that over Monday?" Betsy murmured, and fled.

That was a stirring weekend at the Rays'. Everyone was pleased about Betsy's job. And Joe brought home not only the dictionary, the tennis shoes and racquet, but a poem Jimmy Cliff had written about the boys from the office who were going into the service. There was a verse about Joe:

*"No matter what happens to Willard
Where demons of Shrecklichkeit stalk
There'll still be a trace of a swagger
A don't-give-a-damn in his walk. . . ."*

"I never knew how to describe your walk before!" Betsy cried, and Joe winked at her.

"That's just Jimmy talking!"

On Saturday Mr. Ray brought home a service flag, with a big red star for Joe.

"We won't hang it until Monday," he announced with great conservatism.

"We'll soon have to exchange it for a flag with two stars," Mrs. Ray said. Paige was going in too, Julia had written.

Sunday night lunch was crowded with guests, come to say good-by to Joe.

"Going all the way to the Mississippi River. Must be five miles," he joked to Tacy and Harry.

Sam was picking him up at five the next morning. They wanted to be at the Fort by daybreak. So the party broke up early, and Joe and Betsy went to their room.

Joe began to put things into the one small bag he was taking, talking about the next day. He'd present the post card, he planned, and then he'd be given a physical examination, probably, and be assigned to a company, a squad, his barracks, and pick up his olive drab.

"I'll send my civies back here. Then we'll be given rifles and start drilling."

"And Saturday noon you'll come home."

"I'll come on the double. And we'll go dancing. Or canoeing on Lake Harriet, maybe."

"And I'll be coming to the Fort, on assignments. Wearing that big new hat I'm going to get."

"And I'll say to the fellows, 'That's my girl.'" He broke off. "Where's your picture, Betsy? The one you had taken in your new coral silk dress?"

She found it for him.

"Write on it," he said. And she wrote across it, "Betsy."

Joe took the pen and added, "who is the loveliest lady in the world."

All of a sudden, in spite of herself, Betsy began to cry.

Joe took her into his arms. "Honey, honey, don't do that! Just when we're making such nice plans!"

"But the summer . . . won't last forever. You . . . you'll be going overseas."

Joe's arms tightened. "Listen, Betsy! Listen hard! I'm coming back. Do you hear? I'm coming back. And I'll love you even more than I do now, if that could possibly be. I'll miss you so."

Betsy wept softly.

"Nothing in the whole world could come between you and me, Betsy. We're . . . woven together. You know that. And darling, when I come back we'll have our little home again. We'll have Bettina."

"How do you know all these things?" Betsy asked through her tears.

"I know," he said. "I feel it in my bones." And he held her closer and let her cry as long as she felt like crying.

19
Bridesmaids at Last

WHEN THE BRIDESMAIDS arrived at the small, stone, ivy-covered church, organ music floated out to meet them. They hurried up the steps—fanciful figures in lilac and yellow organdy with large organdy hats—drawing "Ohs!" and "Ahs!" from neighborhood children crowded along the canopy. Tacy's eyes sparkled toward Betsy.

"At last!" she said.

"At last!"

Tib had designed their costumes. Tacy, Carney, Alice, and Winona wore yellow with lilac sashes and hats. Betsy, as matron-of-honor, wore lilac with a yellow sash and hat. In the vestibule they were given flags to carry.

"What a grand idea it was," Tacy whispered, "to make it a military wedding!" Betsy nodded and they tiptoed to peek into the nave.

Flags along the wall melted into the ruddy hues of the stained glass windows. Candles beamed on the altar. Roses and delphinium made a garden of the chancel, and bouquets were tied to the front pews.

The church was almost filled, although the grooms-men, trim and erect in newly tailored uniforms, were still seating a few late comers. Looking around the church, Betsy thought, was like taking a long happy look back over her own life, and Tacy's—as well as Tib's.

Her eyes picked out Tib's Aunt Dolly from Milwaukee, whose beauty had so enchanted them as children when she came to visit in Tib's chocolate-colored house. The hotel owner's actress-wife who had taught Tib to dance. Their curly-haired algebra teacher, and almost all the old high-school Crowd.

Tacy's sister Katie and her husband, come from Duluth. All three Rays.

A groomsman, one of Jack's brother officers, was escorting Jack's mother to a pew on the right side, and whispers in the vestibule caused Betsy and Tacy to turn.

"Is it time to take Mrs. Muller down?"

"No one can be seated after the bride's mother, you know."

"Well, Tib's getting out of the car!"

Another officer groomsman gave his arm to Mrs. Muller. Short, plump, and calm in a gray, crystal-trimmed dress and turban, diamonds in her ears, she was escorted to the pew of the bride's family, on the left.

And back in the vestibule, Tib came in, a snowy cloud on the arm of her father who was almost bursting out of his cutaway with solemn emotion. Smiling, serene, she revolved for the bridesmaids. Her dress was made of chiffon, in bouffant style. The point-lace veil which framed her flowerlike face and cascaded all around her had been Aunt Dolly's wedding veil.

"Aunt Dolly never looked lovelier," Betsy thought.

The wedding party lined up for the procession and whispers died into silence. The brooding organ music ceased, and the church was charged with electric excitement by the strains of the wedding march.

The rector in his sober robes came out of the vestry room, followed by Jack Dunhill and Tib's tall, fair brother Fred, both in uniform. They walked out to the chancel and stood waiting.

With a click of heels the groomsmen came down the aisle. They walked two and two. Jack's brother officers first, then Joe and Sam, sternly military of stride and bearing, determined that Ninety-day Wonders, in training, should acquit themselves no less well than National Guardsmen, even though the latter wore officers' bars and sabers. Sam's waxed mustaches ended in gleaming needles.

Behind them, slowly, to the music's stately beat, came the bridesmaids. Tacy and Carney, followed by Alice and Winona, and then Betsy, alone—trying to remember to stand straight and not to smile. They might smile to Mendelssohn, coming back, they had been told at rehearsal.

Now it was Wagner:

"Here comes the bride,
Here comes the bride . . . ."

Betsy could not see the bride, just eight beats behind, but all along the aisle she heard breath caught in delight, and she saw the look in Jack's dark eyes as he stepped forward.

The groomsmen had divided and taken their places; the bridesmaids divided, and Betsy stationed herself on the left opposite Fred. She was worrying about receiving Tib's bouquet. Fred, no doubt, had the ring on his mind.

Tib arrived. Her father gave "this Woman to be married to this Man," and joined his wife. Jack and Tib, with Fred and Betsy, moved up toward the altar and Betsy took the bouquet without mishap, and Fred produced the ring.

The vows were echoes in Betsy's ears of the vows she and Joe had taken:

> "... for better, for worse, for richer, for poorer,
> in sickness and in health, to love and to cherish
> till death us do part...."

The ring went on Tib's finger; she received her bouquet safely; Jack kissed her and they turned radiant faces as the Mendelssohn Wedding March sounded its great peal of joy.

At the chancel steps, they paused. Tib waited with complete composure, smiling. One of the two brother officers spoke in a low voice, and, as the wedding guests gasped, two sabers flashed out and clanged together to make an arch. When Jack and Tib, laughing, had passed through, the sabers flashed back into their scabbards again.

Each groomsman joined a bridesmaid for a gay race up the aisle and out to the vestibule where now a second garden bloomed. As soon as she had kissed Tib and Jack, Betsy ran to Joe. He looked so wonderful in his olive drab, she thought! He was tanned from drilling in the sun, and above his brown cheeks his hair looked almost silvery.

The Fort Snelling contingent had arrived just a few hours earlier, for they had only a two-day leave. Betsy, Tacy, and Carney had come to Deep Valley the day before, and Betsy had many gaieties to describe as the Rays and the Willards drove to the Muller house through the late afternoon sunshine.

Jean had given a shower for Tib. It was strictly for ladies, but Cab had attended, beaming, in a uniform.

"Spickest, spannest private in the U.S. Army!" Jean had declared, patting his arm.

"Jean's going back to North Dakota to stay with her parents," Betsy reported. "And she says the baby will come before Cab gets back, if the Kaiser doesn't hurry and give in."

Betsy and Tacy had stayed with Cab and Jean, for the Muller house was overflowing with relatives.

"And this morning," Betsy said, "Tacy and I went

off by ourselves. We went up to Hill Street and saw where we used to live."

Hand in hand, they had stared at the two houses, now so surprisingly small, which faced each other at the foot of the green billowy hills. They had drunk at Tacy's old pump. At the cottage which once had belonged to the Rays, they had looked up fondly into the backyard maple, where Betsy used to write her stories and keep them in a cigar box.

Hand in hand, they had climbed the Big Hill which rose behind Betsy's old house. How many times they had climbed it—with Tib along, of course—taking picnics or exploring or just picking flowers! Today they had picked wild roses, pink and very fragrant, which were growing everywhere.

Reaching the top, they had sat down in the grass, just as they always used to do, to survey the town in its broad valley. They had particularly liked to look down on their own rooftops and the tower of Tib's chocolate-colored house.

"We thought that was the most wonderful house in the whole wide world," said Tacy.

"Because it had front and back stairs, and a tower room, and colored glass in the front door."

Joe was stopping the Overland in front of it now. As the Rays and the Willards went up the walk they saw a service flag in the tower-room window. It bore two stars, one for Fred and one for Hobbie who dashed up to take charge of Margaret.

If Cab was the army's spickest and spannest soldier, Hobbie was its proudest recruit. He somehow managed, although he was short, with embarrassing dimples, and a uniform which fitted nowhere, to look hard and military.

"The day that boy lands in France," said Joe, "the Kaiser had better start ducking."

The door with the ruby glass in it was open, and again music sang a welcome. A three-piece orchestra was playing in the hall where Mr. Muller, stout and jovial, and tranquil Mrs. Muller, greeted them.

Betsy hurried her parents and Joe into the study to see the wedding presents. Jack had given Tib an electric sewing machine.

"It was all she wanted," Betsy said. "And she's just ecstatic about it."

The study glittered with china and crystal, silver bowls and platters, embroidered linens from relatives of Jack in England. But Betsy was called away to join the receiving line in the flower-filled, round, front parlor.

Tib's hand was tucked into the crook of Jack's olive drab arm. Tall and straight, he smiled down at her and she smiled back, when she wasn't being kissed. Beneath the point-lace veil and her golden cloud of hair she was rosy from being kissed.

The bridesmaids were busy greeting the visiting relatives. Betsy was pleased to see Tib's Milwaukee relatives again. Grosspapa and Grossmama Hornik, uncles, aunts, and cousins. Aunt Dolly was fortyish now, but still very fair.

There were old friends to talk with, too. Dennie, engaged to Winona. The siren Irma and her young doctor husband. Katie and Leo, who were teasing Sam about the mustache.

"Doesn't he look elegant?" Carney crowed. "But I have to be darned careful when I kiss him, not to stab myself."

At supper, most of the old Crowd squeezed in at the Bride's table. There were plenty of tables—in the spacious back parlor and all around the porch, which had a view of the sunset. Waiters hurried hospitably everywhere with cold turkey and ham and potato salad and hot, scalloped dishes and fresh rolls and pickled herring and anchovies and olives. But at the Bride's table, when it was time for toasts to be offered, Jack's brother officers jumped to their feet.

"Draw, SABER!" And the sabers flashed and crossed above Tib's head while Fred gave an Army toast to the bride.

"Do it again!" she cried, with happy laughter, and they did.

Using Jack's sword, and with Jack's strong hand guiding hers, Tib cut the wedding cake. There were favors inside!

Dancing began in the parlors and out on the porch, where the sunset had faded now. The evening sky looked like the inside of a shell. Jack and Tib led off, and then Tib turned to her father while Jack sought smiling Mrs. Muller. Soon everyone was dancing. Mr. and Mrs. Ray danced, he like a stately ambassador, she like a leaf in a breeze.

The older guests began to go home, except for the Muller relatives who gathered in the dining room. They were laughing and talking with Tib's father and mother over steins of beer. Betsy and Joe, dancing past, paused to look in.

The speech in the dining room was German because Grosspapa and Grossmama could not understand English very well. But in that enemy tongue. . . .

"To the Herr Doktor Wilson!" cried Grosspapa Hornik, raising a foaming mug.

"*Und* Teddy!" put in Grossmama.

"*Ja*, to the Herr Teddy!"

"Teddy!" and the steins banged.

"It does something to my heart," Betsy whispered to Joe who answered soberly, "What a wonderful country we have!"

They started dancing again. Jack was dancing only

with Tib now, and Joe only with Betsy, and Harry with Tacy, and Sam with Carney, and Cab with Jean, and so on down the line. They sang as they danced. "Poor Butterfly!" "Pretty Baby." "The Sunshine of Your Smile!"

> "K-K-K-Katie
> Beautiful Katie"

How Hobbie—that hard, dimpled, military man—roared to that one, swinging Margaret!

They sang and danced to the war tunes—to "Tipperary," and "Pack up Your Troubles," and "Good Morning, Mr. Zip, Zip, Zip!" They were dancing to "The Long Long Trail" when Joe danced Betsy out to the porch, into the starlight and the warm June darkness, scented with honeysuckle.

> *"There's a long long trail a-winding*
> *Into the land of my dreams...."*

She was in the land of dreams now, Betsy thought. The future and the past seemed to melt together.

She could feel the Big Hill looking down as the Crowd danced at Tib's wedding in the chocolate-colored house.

Maud Hart Lovelace and Her World

(Adapted from *The Betsy-Tacy Companion: A Biography of Maud Hart Lovelace* by Sharla Scannell Whalen)

Maud Palmer Hart circa 1906

Estate of Merian Kirchner

*Maud Hart Lovelace

MAUD HART LOVELACE was born on April 25, 1892, in Mankato, Minnesota. Like Betsy, Maud followed her mother around the house at age five asking such questions as "How do you spell 'going down the street'?" for the stories she had already begun to write. Soon she was writing poems and plays. When Maud was ten, a booklet of her poems was printed; and by age eighteen, she had sold her first short story.

The Hart family left Mankato shortly after Maud's high school graduation in 1910 and settled in Minneapolis, where Maud attended the University of Minnesota. In 1917, she married Delos W. Lovelace, a newspaper reporter who later became a popular writer of short stories.

The Lovelaces' daughter, Merian, was born in 1931. Maud would tell her daughter bedtime stories about her childhood in Minnesota, and it was these stories that gave her the idea of writing the Betsy-Tacy books. Maud did not intend to write an entire series when *Betsy-Tacy*, the first book, was published in 1940, but readers asked for more stories. So Maud took Betsy through high school and beyond college to the "great world" and marriage. The final book in the series, *Betsy's Wedding*, was published in 1955.

Maud Hart Lovelace died on March 11, 1980. But her legacy lives on in the beloved series she created and in her legions of fans, many of whom are members of the Betsy-Tacy Society and the Maud Hart Lovelace Society. For more information, write to:

The Betsy-Tacy Society
P.O. Box 94
Mankato, MN 56002-0094
www.betsy-tacysociety.org

The Maud Hart Lovelace Society
277 Hamline Avenue South
St. Paul, MN 55105
www.maudhartlovelacesociety.com

IN THE FICTIONAL WORLD of Betsy-Tacy, there is a long gap between the eighth and ninth books in the series. At the end of *Betsy and Joe*, Betsy Ray and Joe Willard have just graduated from high school and are looking forward to facing "the Great World," together. But *Betsy and the Great World* opens with the twenty-one-year-old Betsy embarking on a tour of Europe by herself. On her first night aboard the S.S. *Columbic*, Betsy recalls the events of the past several years—and her fictional life during that period closely matches Maud's real-life experiences.

The years between Maud's high school graduation in 1910 and her trip abroad in 1914 were eventful ones, filled with change. Maud enrolled in the University of Minnesota in the fall of 1910, but she withdrew shortly after beginning her freshman year, on November 22. As Maud explained in a letter to a friend: "I didn't adjust to college very well. I was just recovering from an appendix operation. . . . When I went home for Thanksgiving my family saw that I wasn't well and they kept me at home until after

Christmas when I went to California, and that was a very happy experience." It was in California that Maud sold her first story, for ten dollars. It was called "Number Eight," and it appeared in a magazine-style Sunday supplement to the *Los Angeles Times* on June 4, 1911.

While Maud was recuperating in California, her family moved to Minneapolis. The March 29, 1911, edition of the *Mankato Free Press* reported, "Mr. Hart has been a resident of Mankato for twenty-eight years and Mrs. Hart for a longer period. They are highly respected and have many friends who will regret their going away. Mr. and Mrs. Hart did not want to move, but the fact that their daughter Maud is attending the university and Miss Kathleen is interested in matters musical in Minneapolis, and the further fact that Mr. Hart is on the road for Foote-Schultze & Co. determined the question of their removal." Luckily, Bick's (Tacy's) family moved to Minneapolis shortly thereafter, so Maud still had her best friend nearby.

Maud returned to the "U" in the fall of 1911. Like Betsy, she joined her sister's sorority, Gamma Phi Beta. But sorority life was only one of Maud's interests. She was the Society Editor/Woman's Editor of the college newspaper, the *Minnesota Daily*. And though she hadn't met Delos, her future husband,

This photo of Maud and Bick was taken on a picnic along the Mississippi River.

yet, Maud led a very active social life. The character Bob Barhydt is based on Maud's sweetheart, Russell McCord, to whom she was engaged. Maud wrote in her unpublished memoir, *Living with Writing*, "My fiancé and I were always getting engaged, [but] we never got married."

Maud also continued to write. One of her stories, entitled "Her Story," appeared in *Minnesota Magazine* in May 1912, and was praised by the famous professor Dr. Maria Sanford. The college paper described it

Estate of Merian Kirchner

Maud was once engaged to Russell McCord, who inspired the character Bob Barhydt.

as "the strongest piece of fiction in the number and . . . unusual in college work. In simplicity, in directness, emotional power, and skill in the structure, it is superior to the average story found in our best magazines." Maud finished the academic year on this high note, but attended only one more semester, and left college for good on December 14, 1912.

Mr. Hart was inspired with the idea of sending Maud to Europe. She recalled, "My father [decided] I would be helped in my writing by a year abroad, which was quite true." So Maud set sail from Boston on Saturday, January 31, 1914, on the S.S. *Canopic*. And as she wrote in a letter to a friend in 1973, "I wrote that book [*Betsy and the Great World*] from my letters home, of which Mother had saved every one." When Maud quotes one of Betsy's letters home, she is quoting from one of her own letters (or from one of Kathleen's)—much as she quoted actual diary entries in the high school books. So it is not surprising that Betsy's experiences during the trip—from the people she meets to the places she stayed—parallel Maud's in so many ways.

In Munich, Maud stayed at the Pension Schweiz, which was very much like the fictional Pension Geiger. There she became friends with a Swiss girl named Else as well as a young baroness named Hertha von Einem. And just like Betsy, Maud had to sneak into a

Maud sailed for Europe on the S.S. Canopic.

WHITE STAR LINE.

S.S. "CANOPIC"

Maud wrote many letters home on this stationery.

Maud on board the Canopic

suite occupied by two German officers, with servants as "bodyguards," in order to take a bath. In a letter home, she lamented: "Oh, those officers seem to be of most domestic habits! Night after night they stayed at home with watchful eyes upon the bathroom. They guarded their treasure with dog-like fidelity, but I was biding my time. . . ." It was also in Munich that Maud learned that "Emma Middleton Cuts Cross Country," had been sold to *Ainslee's* magazine. Maud was paid seventy-five dollars for the story, which was published in June 1915.

After brief trips to Sonneberg, Nuremberg, and Oberammergau, Maud arrived in Venice, where she stayed at the pension of the Conte family and became good friends with their son, Paolo. Maud wrote to her family, "Of course, I rather like him or I wouldn't have started curling my hair again." But like Betsy, tenderhearted Maud burst into tears when she turned down his proposal. In a letter to her family marked "Personal" (meaning that it was not to be circulated to family and friends, as her other letters were), Maud described her relationship with Paolo—and the description mirrors Betsy's experience with Marco in chapter eighteen of the book almost exactly.

After leaving Venice, Maud visited Switzerland and Paris. But she didn't count either as a place in which she had really lived. In a letter written to a friend in

Maud's Swiss friend, Else, who inspired the character Tilda

Hertha von Einem, aka "Helena von Wandersee"

Maud feeding pigeons at St. Mark's

1962, Maud described her pension in Paris as "crowded and unsatisfactory, full of American tourists. I saw [Paris] very well, didn't miss anything, and I've always been thankful for that . . . but I didn't really live there." It is interesting to note that Maud's daughter, Merian, actually wrote chapter nineteen of the book, which describes Betsy's visit to Paris. In a 1952 interview with the *Minneapolis Daily Tribune*,

Maud remarked that Merian "can pitch in and write a chapter beautifully. In fact, she can out–Betsy-Tacy Betsy-Tacy."

Maud spent the final months of her trip in London, at Mrs. Brumwell's boarding house at 5 Taviton Street, where she felt very much at home. Maud later wrote: "I didn't see the British Museum (it was closed on account of the suffragettes). . . . I loved the galleries, Westminster, the changing of the guard at

Betsy and Marco at St. Mark's

Paolo Conte inspired the character Marco Regali

Maud wearing her new hat on Fusina

Buckingham Palace, Windsor Castle and Hampstead Heath. We went boating on the Thames. (Taking tea along.). . . . Even in the movies, they serve tea!"

For Maud as for Betsy, the beginning of World War I meant that the journey had to end. Maud returned home on the American ship the S.S. *St. Louis*, which left Liverpool on September 4, 1914, and arrived in New York on September 12. Having experienced the great world, it was time for both Maud and Betsy to learn about a whole new one—marriage.

The Crew at Mrs. Brumwell's boarding house in London. Maud is in the center row, fourth from the left.

About Betsy's Wedding

THE BETSY-TACY BOOKS are so very autobiographical
that it is sometimes hard to believe that one very important plotline—Betsy and Joe's relationship from
their first meeting in *Heaven to Betsy* to the day they
get married in *Betsy's Wedding*—was entirely made
up. In real life, Maud did not meet her future husband, Delos Wheeler Lovelace, until 1917, well after
her high school days. As Maud said: "Delos came
into my life much later than Joe Willard came into
Betsy's, and yet he is Joe Willard to the life." Maud
made sure of this—she asked her husband to give her
a description of his boyhood before she began work
on the high school books, and then gave his history
to Joe. Their daughter, Merian, wrote: "I have no
trouble accepting the plot of *Betsy and Joe* as pure
fiction. . . . Because it's a story Maud made up about
how she and Delos might have met, it's especially precious." But readers may be interested to know the
real story behind their courtship and marriage.

Delos Wheeler Lovelace was born in Brainerd,
Minnesota, in 1894. Like Joe's parents, Delos' father
was a lumberjack and his mother, Josephine Wheeler

Lovelace, was a dressmaker. She didn't die when Delos was a young boy, though, as Joe's mother did. According to Merian: "Maud was very fond of her mother-in-law, and Aunt Ruth's personality is probably modeled on Josephine's at least to some extent."

After attending high school in Detroit, Delos worked for the *Courier News* in Fargo, North Dakota, and the *Daily News* in Minneapolis. Then, in 1915, Delos began to work for his friend Harry B. Wakefield, city editor of the *Minneapolis Tribune*. He also freelanced at the Wakefield Publicity Bureau, which was run by Harry Wakefield's wife, Lillian Hammons Wakefield.

At this time, World War I was raging in Europe, and in 1917, the United States entered the war. Delos left the publicity bureau to join the First Officers Training Camp at Fort Snelling. Maud was hired to fill his position. She recalled that Mrs. Wakefield "told me to look through the collection of articles and materials to see the kind of thing they were doing. I remember coming across Delos' name and saying, 'Why, what name is this? It sounds like a valentine.' Then I went on to read some of the things he had written and I said, 'My, he certainly writes well.'" In April, perhaps sensing a good match, Mrs. Wakefield invited Maud, her little sister, Helen, and Delos to dinner. Maud remembered: "Delos and I were

This photograph of Maud and Delos was taken on the porch of the Hart family home in Minneapolis.

As a model of a happy marriage Maud had the example of her parents, Stella and Tom Hart.

Delos in uniform.

*Maud and Delos'
first apartment,
2400 Aldrich
Avenue South,
also known as
the Bow Street
Apartment.*

*Maud and Delos'
first home, 1109
West 25th Street,
also known as
the Canoe Place
House.*

seated across from each other and we kept eyeing each other. I remember Helen walked home and then Delos and I walked and walked, around the lakes, and talked and talked—it was practically dawn before we reached my home." Seven months later, Maud and Delos were married at the Hart family home, on Thanksgiving Day, November 29, 1917.

After a three-day honeymoon, Delos had to report to Camp Dodge near Des Moines, Iowa. Soon afterward, he was sent overseas to France, where he served as a second lieutenant in the 339th machine gun battalion. The war ended on November 11, 1918, and after a four-month-long wait for space on a troopship home, Delos was able to return home to Maud—and the two began their long and happy life together.

Although the beginning of their relationship was very different from Betsy and Joe's, many of the events in *Betsy's Wedding* were based on Maud and Delos' early life together. Maud commented that "all the early housekeeping experiences are actual." Maud was in charge of the household budget—it was her task to keep "the Budget Book" (now in the collection of the Minnesota Valley Regional Library). In addition to payments for groceries and other expenses, the book also contains Maud's housekeeping plan:

Monday:	cleaning, icebox, breakbox, mending.
Tuesday:	cleaning, kitchen, white enamel, wood work, silver.
Wednesday:	[no entry]
Thursday:	[alternately] cleaning, kitchen floor, drawers and closets, [or] shampoo.
Friday:	cleaning, plate rail, wainscotting, shelves, white furniture, [and] ironing.
Saturday:	cleaning, bathroom floor, baking.

Apparently, Maud was just as determined as Betsy is to be a good housekeeper.

Portraying Delos as Joe in this book gave Maud great pleasure—for the first time, she was writing about a period during which she knew him. Maud commented, "It was so pleasant for me to have Delos really and honestly in the picture. I had always tried, in the earlier books, to have Joe walk and talk and behave like Delos, but as one of my friends said to me about *Betsy's Wedding*, Delos walks right off the pages."

After the publication of *Betsy's Wedding* in 1955, Maud was urged by her readers to write another Betsy-Tacy book. She remarked: "In *Betsy's Wedding*, Betsy's husband went off to the First World War and many letters have begged me to bring him safely home. The letters even offer me titles for another

This photo was taken in late 1924, during Maud's first pregnancy. Sadly, the baby died soon after birth.

Merian, the Lovelaces' second child, was born in 1931. She shows a remarkable resemblance to Delos in this photo.

*Maud and Delos spent their last
happy years together in this house
in Claremont, California.*

book, obviously in the friendly assumption that
when a writer has found a title he is over the hump.
Welcome Home, Joe! was suggested by one. Many
have asked for *Betsy's Baby*. And some have even hit
upon the title I have selected myself, *Betsy's Bettina*."
Although Maud did start to do some research, she
never got around to writing *Betsy's Bettina*. Perhaps
this is because, as she wrote, "I have always felt that
the last lines in *Betsy's Wedding* were a perfect ending
for the series."

Whatever Happened To . . .

BICK KENNEY (Tacy) married Charley Kirch (Harry Kerr) in 1920. The couple had two sons. Bick and Maud remained lifelong friends—in 1968 they traveled to Europe together, and even visited Madrid, home of the King of Spain.

MIDGE GERLACH (Tib) married Charles Harris (Jack Dunhill) in 1918. She was reunited with Maud and Bick for Mankato's Betsy-Tacy Day celebration in 1961.

KATHLEEN HART (Julia), Maud's older sister, was married twice—first to Eugene Bibb (the couple later divorced), then to Frohman Foster (Paige). Kathleen became an opera singer and later taught music.

HELEN HART (Margaret), Maud's younger sister, married Frank Fowler (Clay Dawson), whom she met in her high school cafeteria, in 1924. Although they had no children of their own, they took in several foster children and adopted one. Helen worked as a librarian in Minneapolis.

MARION WILLARD (Carney) married Bill Everett (Sam Hutchinson) in 1919. They had three children and lived in Minneapolis. After the publication of *Heaven to Betsy* in

Like his fictional counterpart, Cab, Jab Lloyd got married on the same day as Maud.

This photo of Helen Hart was probably taken in the spring of 1917, the year she graduated from high school.

1945, Marion commented: "I felt rather foolish at first, having been made a character in the book, but then excited high school girls began to approach me and ask, 'Are you really Carney?' Then I naturally became very proud."

JAB LLOYD (Cab) really was married on the same day as Maud. He and his wife had two sons and a daughter. After living in different parts of the Midwest, the Lloyds returned to Mankato, where Jab started his own lumber business.

ELEANOR JOHNSON (Winona II) married PAUL FORD (Dennie). They lived in Minnesota and had two sons.

TOM FOX (Tom Slade) attended West Point and pursued a career in the military.

RUPERT B. ANDREWS (Larry Humphreys) and HELMUS W. ANDREWS (Herbert Humphreys) both graduated from Stanford University in 1914. Rupert became an engineer, married, and had two children. Helmus earned a law degree but then decided he did not want to be an attorney. Instead, he set up business as a produce broker in San Diego. He married and had one daughter.

THE COMPLETE BETSY-TACY SERIES

THE BETSY-TACY TREASURY
The First Four Betsy-Tacy Books
ISBN 978-0-06-209587-9 (paperback)

THE BETSY-TACY HIGH SCHOOL YEARS AND BEYOND

HEAVEN TO BETSY AND BETSY IN SPITE OF HERSELF
Foreword by Laura Lippman
ISBN 978-0-06-179469-8 (paperback)

BETSY WAS A JUNIOR AND BETSY AND JOE
Foreword by Meg Cabot
ISBN 978-0-06-179472-8 (paperback)

BETSY AND THE GREAT WORLD AND BETSY'S WEDDING
Foreword by Anna Quindlen
ISBN 978-0-06-179513-8 (paperback)

THE DEEP VALLEY BOOKS

EMILY OF DEEP VALLEY
Foreword by Mitali Perkins
ISBN 978-0-06-200330-0 (paperback)

CARNEY'S HOUSE PARTY AND WINONA'S PONY CART
Foreword by Melissa Wiley
ISBN 978-0-06-200329-4 (paperback)